CASABLACK

CASABLACK

BY CHRISTOPHER LEOPOLD

DOUBLEDAY & COMPANY, INC.
GARDEN CITY, NEW YORK
1979

Casablack was originally published in England by Hamish Hamilton Limited in a slightly different version.

ISBN: 0-385-14388-5
Library of Congress Catalog Card Number 78-20238
Copyright © 1978 by Christopher Leopold; Copyright © 1979 by Doubleday & Company, Inc.
All Rights Reserved
Printed in the United States of America
First Edition in the United States of America

Library of Congress Cataloging in Publication Data

Leopold, Christopher.
  Casablack.

  1. World War, 1939–1945—Fiction.   I. Title.
PZ4.L58537Cas   1979   [PR6062.E727]   823'.9'14

Excerpts from the lyrics of "White Christmas" by Irving Berlin at pages 216 and 217, © Copyright 1940, 1942 by Irving Berlin, © Copyright renewed 1968, 1969 by Irving Berlin, are reprinted by permission of Irving Berlin Music Corporation.

This book is dedicated to

Humphrey Bogart
Ingrid Bergman
Claude Rains
Paul Henreid
Conrad Veidt
Sydney Greenstreet
Peter Lorre
"Cuddles" Sakall
Max Steiner
Hal B. Wallis
Michael Curtiz

and all those inspired people at
Warner Bros. who first put Casablanca on the map

CONTENTS

NOTE

After Independence the names of many Casablanca streets and locations were changed. This book uses the names and designations of the 1940s, when France was still the protecting power.

CASABLACK

Preview:

LOUIS: Well, Rick, you're not only a sentimentalist, but you've become a patriot.

RICK: Maybe, but it seemed like a good time to start.

LOUIS: I think perhaps you're right. . . . It might be a good idea for you to disappear from Casablanca for a while. There's a Free French garrison over at Brazzaville. I could be induced to arrange your passage.

RICK: My letter of transit? I could use a trip, but it doesn't make any difference about our bet. You still owe me ten thousand francs.

LOUIS: And that ten thousand francs should pay our expenses.

RICK: *Our* expenses?

LOUIS: Uh-uh.

RICK: Louis, I think this is the beginning of a beautiful friendship.

(*Couple walk off into fog of Casablanca airport. Fade. Cut. End of film, end of story. Wrap.*)

The lights went up in the Fifth Avenue preview theater. They revealed a grinning motion picture executive dressed in a snazzy loose-fitting pinstripe that was emphatically fashion in the early autumn of 1942.

"Well, folks," he said, "I guess you can see now why all of us at Warner Brothers are over the moon about *Casablanca*. Bogart, the all-time toughie, meets Bergman, the coolest of ice-cool cuties. I mean has there ever been teaming like it? And that tune, how about that tune . . . ?"

He didn't need to go on. The hand-picked audience of bankers, media people, and opinion formers had burst into spontaneous applause.

"All I can say, gentlemen"—the Warner Bros. executive beamed (authentically this time)—"is, I just wish Mike Curtiz, the director, and Hal Wallis, the producer, could be here this morning to see your reaction. It says one thing to me and it says it in six-foot caps.

THIS MOVIE IS BOX OFFICE

"Just for once, Vincent," said Lurleen Marx of *Time-Life*, "you could be right."

"We're releasing the movie seven weeks from now on November 27. So you newspaper people should be able to make your deadlines! In between times we'll be previewing the movie to selected audiences of US servicemen scheduled for active service overseas. It won't have missed you good folk that there's an effective fighting message at the heart of this great motion picture!"

There was a murmur of approval.

The New York *Herald Tribune* exclaimed, "I love that Sam character! Who the hell is he, anyway?"

The editor of *Variety* said, "You could pick up a best-supporting-actor nomination for 'Cuddles' Sakall, too."

A man from CBS asked, "Who wrote that tune? I seem to remember it from way back."

Look magazine said, "You guys must be feeling like a million dollars."

The *Saturday Evening Post* said, "'We'll always have Paris'—I like it, it works."

A voice at the back of the little preview theater said, "Crap!", and then said it again. "Unholy, untruthful, unmitigated crap!"

The interruption could have had more impact if it hadn't emanated from the semirecumbent person of Nad Klaf, of the Sodersheim Syndicate. It was only eleven-thirty in the morning, but it was like Nad to be already half stoned.

"I knew the guy," he muttered. "Met him in Casablanca last year. You've got it all wrong. He didn't work in a place like that. He didn't act in a way like that. He didn't even volunteer for Brazzaville. He was goddamn kicked there. What the hell have you done with my story?"

Nobody answered. Not even the pinstripe executive from Warner Bros. After all, it was only old Nad, canned again before they had even handed out the free highballs.

SECTION I

THE TRAVELER'S RETURN

On the sultry afternoon of 28 October 1942, at 5:20 PM to be precise, a converted Heinkel bomber circled over the airport at Rabat. It flew in low from the south, just skirting the final pinnacles of the Atlas Mountains, dipped its wings in friendly salute to the sinking sun, then with a squeal of tires ripped a few more chunks of mud-red matting off Rabat's main runway and gently subsided to a halt.

A stout gentleman, whose sheer force of *avoir du poids* made the flimsy disembarkation stairs wobble, stepped down onto Moroccan soil. In full field dress of a Wehrmacht general, he halted for a second at the bottom of the gangplank, whilst the viciously torrid desert wind cut across his purpling features. A full six foot three in height, and straight as a ramrod, with much excess flab but also an impressive degree of muscle, General Joachim Kellerman was one of the finest-looking examples of that Spartan breed, the Junker officer type. He also happened to be intellectually one of the least subtle. And, in the opinion of Field Marshal von Manstein, whose armies were at this moment swinging in a wide arc to encircle Stalingrad, he was also the most easily expendable. Another thing was true of Kellerman: simple good nature shone through him. That quality didn't necessarily make him a wow with Manstein, but it would certainly help to put a bit of much needed gloss on German-Vichy relations.

But the clincher finally accounting for General Kellerman's withdrawal from the line at this critical moment in Marshal von Manstein's enfilading movement concerned a curious *drôle de guerre* called the LVF. The LVF was a quirky collection of trigger-happy French fascists, *cagoulards*, and suchlike, who carried their enthusiasm for Adolf Hitler to the extent of volunteering to fight alongside the German Wehrmacht on the Russian front. Some took the business of Hitler's United Free Europe movement even further than that and were committing acts of outrageous gallantry against the Bolshevist bear. It had been Joachim Kellerman's lot to command these Rolands in battle. So, on his tour of Morocco, he would be able, in set speeches and suchlike, to make direct reference to the gallantry of French contingents fighting Hitler's war. And even encourage some of *les autres*, the beefy stay-at-homes of the PPF and SOL, to join their brethren on the eastern front.

In front of him at this moment stood a different kind of *homo sapiens*. Blinking into the sun, and dying to unbutton the clasp at the neck of his general's field-gray tunic, Kellerman found himself confronted by a pair of worldly-wise, hooded gray eyes, smiling up at him. General Auguste Nogues, with his yellow, wizened visage, had the look of a rather old monkey. The Resident-General of Morocco, total dictator of one of the biggest provinces in the Vichy empire, was at his most patronizingly charming.

"Welcome to Morocco," he said, "on behalf of the Sultan and myself."

But this necessary civility, which Nogues emitted in his blandest and most bored tones, did not produce its expected soporific effect. General Joachim Kellerman's red face was beginning to twitch and then to convulse, whilst a kind of hiccup was only just suppressed behind his tightly clamped-down mouth. Meanwhile beads of sweat broke out all over his face and his limpid blue eyes danced wildly. General Nogues was intrigued. Maybe his visitor was about to have a stroke . . . A man of his age and his weight, the humidity of the afternoon . . . The Resident-General put a gentle hand on the German's sleeve. And then it exploded, a great guffaw of laughter that had Nogues's hand hastily retreating.

"Who the hell are those puppies?" panted General Kellerman. "Those chocolate soldiers in pantomime kit. My, we could have done with a division or two of those at Rostov."

He was referring, of course, to one of the picturesque glories of Morocco. The intrepid spahis, glittering symbols of French colonial rule, with their white capes, blue hoods, white turbans, and red blouses. Now a full regiment of them, mounted on pure white Arab steeds that cavorted and whinnied in the desert breeze, was stationed just twenty yards from Kellerman's Heinkel.

"They are a useful frippery," concurred Nogues. "The Sultan, whom you will meet, is childishly attached to them. A bit of show? Why not? one asks. But they are there in your honor, *mon Général*. Would you do them the honor of inspecting them?"

"Inspect them? The insolent puppies, the poppycocks," said Kellerman, still purple with mirth. "Certainly I will inspect them. But how Reichsmarschall Goering would envy their dress."

So General Kellerman and General Nogues stood on the saluting base as the spahis galloped past.

"Good horsemen," commented the German. "Good uniforms, good moustaches, and good horses. They are prettier than panzers."

"Your trip will be short," Nogues was telling him as the spahis formed up at the far end of the airport for a ceremonial charge. "A few days' hunting round Rabat. Meet the Sultan. Meet his son, a mere boy of fourteen. And, of course, the Grand Vizier. Then your itinerary will take in Safi, Fez, and Meknès before arriving at Casablanca on the morning of November 2. A week in Casablanca—rest assured you will be comfortably quartered at your base at the Hotel Miramar, Fedala, with the traditional reviews and ceremonies. Believe you me, *mon Général*, we will endeavor to make your tour informative and enjoyable."

"Can you find me a girl?" inquired Kellerman. "She needn't be in the full bloom of youth, but she needs fine breasts and a spanking-big bottom. And she must know her business. An old chap like me needs a bit of assistance, don't you know?"

"For a man who has commanded the flower of French soldiers in battle," replied Nogues, courteously ushering the General into his Delage, "anything will be possible."

Then they drove off in a cloud of red dust, surrounded by a posse of twentieth-century police motorcyclists. The instructions to treat this one as Top Security had come from the very top. Much as he disliked that little upstart, Pierre Laval, manipulator in chief of the Vichy Mafia, Nogues was taking his warning seriously. Not a single gray hair of General Joachim Kellerman was going to be touched.

There was another kind of reception committee awaiting General Kellerman on that humid afternoon, though it could not boast the picturesque gaudiness of the Spahi Guard. No one, not the German General, nor his simian-faced host, nor the vigilant Inspector Roth of the Vichy Sécurité noticed them, but then anonymity was useful. A short prematurely balding young man of about thirty, who blinked at the sunlight through large horn-rimmed glasses, and a couple of equally unnoticeable friends stood chatting by the airport car park —you might put them down as teachers, or maybe junior *fonction-neurs* in some remote ministry.

Claude Lupin, like his idol Robespierre, was physically stunted, fastidious, and unprepossessing. But his amiable shortsighted looks gave no evidence of a brain to put beside that of André Malraux— nor of the dandy either. His glasses had a bit of plaster stuck round the side, and his linen suit stood in need of a pressing.

Lupin was one of those Marxists, young, totally ruthless, dedi- cated, who had decided to back de Gaulle. The reasons were very clear. De Gaulle's short-term aim was to kick in that vainglorious fabric for the protection of the French bourgeoisie called Vichy and then put its ringleaders up against a wall and shoot them. Lupin concurred. That was why Claude Lupin had accepted the position of chief African representative of an underground organization called BCRAM: short for Bureau Central de Renseignements de l'Action Militaire. What was worrying BCRAM was a special Allied project that went under the code name TORCH. Despite the many attempts at camouflage, it hadn't taken men like Colonel Passy (Lupin's chief in London and head of the Gaullist Secret Service) long to realize what it meant. The nub of the problem was summed up in a confidential document that now lay on Claude Lupin's humble desk back in the rue Pierre Loti, in Brazzaville.

Diagnosis:

An Allied fleet is at this moment assembling at Gibraltar. Large detachments of American and British troops are also being de- canted into it. What purpose does this expedition have? The target must be French North Africa. So Algeria, Tunisia, and Morocco will be freed from Vichy, and be thrown into the balance to fight the forces of fascism. Is this not good news? Then why the secrecy? Why has Churchill on many occasions snubbed our leader in London and declined to give him details, when our help alone could ensure the success of this mission? Why does Roosevelt refuse to see our representatives in Washington? *The diagnosis is clear.* The Allied plan called TORCH is aimed less against Vichy or Nazism than against the Free French cause. Its purpose is an entente with the Vichy powers in French North Africa to ensure that the government of Pétain, Laval, and Darlan remains in effective control after North Africa has joined the Allies. This all amounts to an Anglo-Saxon conspiracy against the Free French cause.

Solution:

In fact there are two. The first, and best, would be to get there first, to preempt TORCH by persuading North Africa to declare for us before so much as an Allied soldier landed on its shore. The second is to wrest Africa from the Vichy-Allied hands after the successful outcome of TORCH. That is, by activating the committees in the best Lenin-type manner to take over by stealth in the places of power. Of these two plans the first must be tried without fail. We have Free French caucuses in Algiers, Oran, Casablanca, Rabat, etc. We also have leaders who might be persuaded to declare for de Gaulle. Of these the most interesting is General Nogues, Resident Governor of Morocco. Nogues's line has always been one of delicate ambiguity governed by the demands of self-interest. If he could be persuaded to declare for us, there is enough Free French zeal in the army to give us control there. Imagine a Free French bloodless revolution throughout North Africa in the style of Chad, Gabon, and the Congo. The Allied forces of TORCH welcomed to Free French shores by our leader in person!

The only other written evidence of the thoughts of Claude Lupin were a few notes, written in tiny handwriting in a lined school exercise book entitled, *Lycée Français, Deuxième Classe.* The notes are terse, even peremptory, but they have their value.

"Need to maintain pressure on N. Unrelenting. The carrot and the stick. We need a great crime, a *cause célèbre.* A *coup-de-main* the Nazis will not forgive. Something sensational. Something to turn German touchiness to hysteria.

"October 23. Projected visit of General Joachim Kellerman SS to

Casablanca as guest of German Armistice Commission. The sacrificial lamb."

And now the sacrificial lamb had arrived, but Claude Lupin's reception committee was missing two vital members—two professionals from the prewar Marseilles underworld, specially sent over from France, who could be relied upon to carry out a job of assassination with minimum fuss.

For the past week or so the Gaullist cell had been aware of the garlic-ridden breath of Inspector Roth's *flics* breathing hot down their necks. Contacts had been taken in for questioning and had not since been seen outside the Sécurité buildings. It was a matter for conjecture if they had found the opportunity to bite on their cyanide capsules.

But the real blow had fallen that morning. Lupin had called on a seamy little apartment in the Medina of Casablanca and found his two assassins still in bed at ten in the morning. The other unusual thing was that the sheets had changed color to red. The toughs had been stabbed and then left—presumably *pour encourager les autres.*

Which left the problem of who was going to bump off the sacrificial lamb very much in the air.

The urgency was that replacements had to be found and brought to the scene of action within three days. Lupin's brain, as tidy and precise as any filing system, had been playing with the problem now for five hours. But now if you got close enough to the horn-rimmed glasses you could see he was almost smiling, as if in possession of a secret joke.

The logical brain of Claude Lupin had traveled thousands of miles south, back to the seamier side of unsophisticated Brazzaville. Wagner, a prototype American expatriate, i.e., a rootless drifter and drunk, who stumbled in and out of other people's causes with all the passion of the self-deluding romantic gangster. The evidence: a crumpled piece of yellow cardboard with the haunted staring eyes and the sunken, unshaven cheeks of a man who hadn't eaten well recently. A temporary document (*une pièce d'identité*) that officially marked the triumphant entry of one Stephen S. Wagner into the French Republic on 23 March 1938, issued and stamped at Bayonne.

Other documents were in the tatty file back in Claude Lupin's office in the rue Pierre Loti. They punctuated key points of

Wagner's progress round the prewar world. A sojourn in Shanghai, with an extradition order alleging that Wagner had attempted to run dope. A foray into Abyssinia, followed by a trek across the bush into Somaliland, because it was hinted he didn't exactly hit it off with Mussolini's occupying legions. A short but belated session with the International Brigade in Spain (with another document signed by Steve's political Commissar to the effect that he was "politically unreliable"). More recently it seemed Wagner had been on the run again—this time from the advancing Germans in 1940 (it might have been here that he shed his temporary entry permit into France, now in Lupin's slim, elegant hands). That led Lupin through to the most recent documents in the dossier, relating to Wagner's supposed conversion to Gaullism. What was verifiable was that he had become involved, as manager, in a gambling scandal at a place called Ritzi's Bar in Casablanca, having cheated the undoubtedly crooked owner of the place of several thousand francs of his ill-gotten gains. This event had no doubt hastened the American's touching conversion to militant Gaullism. And led him to team up with another interesting individual and to make a dash for it to the Gaullist stronghold of Central Africa.

Which led him to question mark No. 2. In this case a police identity card with the pale face, sunken, world-weary eyes, snappy little moustache, and short-cut sandy hair, balding a little on top, of one Auguste Berthier, formerly head of the Department of Fraud in Casablanca. Claude Lupin had put the two disparate photos together and subjected them to fierce scrutiny: the romantic hoodlum and the crooked cop. They were thousands of miles south and hardly the best advertisements for the Cross of Lorraine. But they knew Casablanca like few others, and although they might not admit it, hadn't much to lose. Would anything better come to hand?

The mosquitoes loved the café Chat Brûlé.

Even though the joint frankly lacked the class of Ritzi's place in Casablanca, it was packed with enough sweating humanity to satisfy any bloodsucking insect winging its way around Brazzaville, capital of General Charles de Gaulle's equatorial empire. But you had to say this about the old Chat: it was positively the hottest thing of its kind for miles around. Between Jo'burg in the south and Alexandria in the north there was no bed of vice quite to compare with it.

At least, this was what Steve Wagner was paid to tell the clientèle, at approximately half the money he had earned as croupier back at Ritzi's in Casablanca. You could say it was a pitiful waste of a talent. Why hadn't someone back in Casablanca said he could make a fortune in the movies with that slight Bogart look he had about the eyes and that square jaw he had which this Nat Clap, Nad Klaf (what was the bum's name?), had assured him was the spitting image of John Garfield's. Sure he could have made a fortune in the movies, married Henry Ford's daughter, and won the world series for the New York Yankees. It was just that things had turned out a little differently, as they usually did in Steve Wagner's life. Whoever it was who dealt the cards had dealt a stinking little *boîte* (with a flickering neon sign) just off the rue Pierre Loti in what passed for Brazzaville's red light district.

Did you know it was cabaret night at the Chat Brûlé? Up to now your kicks have been strictly orthodox: some overpriced hooch; some interesting girls; an American in a yellowing tuxedo trying to lend the whole thing tone. Hold on: the night of 21 October 1942, at the Chat Brûlé is still young. By order of the *patron*, Monsieur Bimbo Heureux, a curious new attraction is under way.

One kid has two legs and two arms, except that the arms stick out at right angles from the elbows. His younger brother (now almost eleven) has normal arms and one leg at least is sound. The other has been doubled back at the joint so that it stretches out parallel to the ground. A third kid, like the statue of a Siamese goddess, is totally symmetrical. That is, she has both legs and both arms set at right angles. But her voice is OK. She shrieks out, not in fear but delight, as the truck plunges straight from black starlit bush into the shantytown that fringes Brazzaville. It was nothing new to French Equatorial Africa that October of '42. Anyone who had chanced his arm fifty or so miles beyond the pale into that primeval lurking thing called the African bush had seen it at every crappy little market village: kids surgically deformed from birth to make a queasy-conscienced Westerner part easily with a few coins. The indigenous population might yawn with boredom, but then this kind of customer didn't exactly abound at Bimbo Heureux's Chat Brûlé club. Another thing: these mutilated juveniles were mighty hot stuff on a whole collection of primitive African instruments. Even now, as they sped towards the center of Brazzaville in an open truck, they were jangling their cymbals, pounding with hand, foot, or chin hard down on their tightly stretched oxhide drums. Making music, you might say. The truck itself had permission to travel—normally reserved only for ambulances or police cars. It had an appointment to keep, a consignment to deliver, and the fact that it had one smashed front headlight, another dangling from a wire, clanking against the bumper, a ripped-off silencer, and nonevent brakes meant that nobody was going to impede its passage. This was important, because for the kids this starry night was going to be one they'd remember. They'd never seen the big city lights before.

"Hi, Steve." . . . "Allo, Monsieur Wagner." . . . *"Bon soir, mon ami."* . . . "Allo, Steve." . . . He had to worm his way through the throng as though he were the prize candidate at some national convention. And the girls put their hands on his ass as he passed and touched him, and some fat sweaty French planter from way up state kissed him, and it was called turning a no-go joint into the big box-office spinner of Brazzaville from sweet nowhere.

Somehow Steve Wagner just had to breathe on the place and suddenly it was filled up to the rafters with wide-hipped nigger ladies in tangerine and ultraviolet skirts who thrust their deep-cleft asses at you as they squeezed past; with rancid-breathed, puffing planters, pools of moisture already welling outwards from their armpits, and whiny little *fonctionnaires* who got so tight up against you in the crush you could almost feel their dentures wobble. It was Steve's magic touch, and suddenly a tumbledown barn was swooning and shaking to the rhythm of Alexandra M'ba's band. And to make the thing perfect, wherever he craned his neck there was the grinning gargoyle visage of Bimbo Heureux at the end of the vista with that warm buddy smile that said, "You made me, Steve, and I'm gonna break you, and then mebbe we'll be quits."

Except that tonight Bimbo's face has been cleaned up nicely, as if for a big occasion. Why? You could say he looked like a big beautiful pink baboon. Not that there was anything wrong with pink baboons. Steve Wagner was one himself. In fact, he was founder member, president, and bankrupt treasurer and nonentertainments secretary of the Society of Pink Baboons. The essential qualification for membership? Any sucker who can sink to a dump like this.

Consider how it is: you're in a corner being chatted up by the Chat Brûlé's resident weasel. A minor civil servant—except that two years ago he had been a senior civil servant. But then de Gaulle's crowd had staged their sensational *coup d'état,* and this little *fonctionnaire,* whose name happened to be Pinchon, hadn't been able to adjust to the fact that the senile old collaborator, Marshal Pétain, was no longer his boss.

"As an American, Monsieur Steve," the little man was hissing, "you must have heard what your President Roosevelt is saying about de Gaulle. He says he is a *poseur,* an adventurer, an insignificant officer who should concern himself with the battlefield—not politics. It is no secret that his special envoy to Vichy, Admiral

Leahy, is on the most intimate terms with the Marshal, and has established cordial contacts with Pierre Laval."

"I'm not interested in politics," you said.

"De Gaulle is the creature of Churchill," Pinchon insisted under his breath, "a puppet of English Zionism. Did you know he was backed by the Rothschilds?"

"I'm not interested in politics," you repeated, "but I'll give you a piece of free advice. I'd be careful what you say about de Gaulle. For a lot of strictly non-Aryan folk around here who are scared of the Third Reich, he's a hero."

"I assure you his regime is doomed," Pinchon persisted with sozzled single-mindedness. "I have it on the best authority there is to be an arrangement between America and the Marshal. As a result these colonies will be returned to France, the real France—and ffttt!—de Gaulle will be nowhere!"

It was the same whenever a couple of white men got down to talk about anything in this fetid center of Gaullist Black African power. The conversation got round into politics and hovered there. Got stuck in politics, and politics was one of those things that had never quite taken a hold on Steve Wagner. As a Pink Baboon he didn't give a heck for it, and that was only one reason why Brazzaville stank in his eyes (as well as his nose). Even when he'd served in the International Brigade in Spain he had never quite got round to working out what a commissar was, or what Hitler's Condor squadron of Heinkels and Dorniers was exactly up to, flattening peaceable places like Guernica. He had been there by virtue of some kind of hunch. Not from bravery, still less from idealism, but because he felt it was a possible place to be. Étretat in 1942 had been the same because at that moment, under the June sun with the panzers racing down the Normandy coast towards the town, there might be something called living to do there.

Here it was different. You had to keep on reminding yourself of your Pink Baboon oath—"Never give a damn, or even one half a damn." It's just that craning your neck around to get away from Pinchon's evil molars and twitchy yellowing irises your eyes plow down another vista and go smack into Bimbo again, positively shining out malevolence, seemingly at you. Which is worth a moment's thought—if you can think beneath Alexandra M'ba's wall-shaking pulsations. OK, in true obedience to the shimmering ideals of the

Pink Baboon brotherhood Steve had gone to work for the most sadistic crumb in Brazzaville, on the general philosophical grounds of who gave a damn, anyway? A vast, shambling, charmless, ugly-minded mulatto, slumbering behind the glass pane of his office, a tumbler of the little remaining Courvoisier cognac never far from his outstretched grasp, and the books and money box firmly locked in the top drawer of the Empire bureau, which had now withstood for years the onslaught of Bimbo's eighteen and a half stone.

Of these assets Steve enjoyed sometimes five, sometimes fifteen, sometimes nought percent, depending on Bimbo Heureux's generosity at the moment. For the rest he was paid (sometimes) a kind of salary, a pittance, it is true, but money was scarce in Free French Equatorial Africa, and Steve's needs were small.

"That would be ironical for you, Monsieur Steve," the jumped-down little civil servant was saying, "an *entente* between your country and Vichy? You would find you had backed the wrong horse, *n'est-ce pas?* You would discover you should have stayed in loyal Casablanca? But perhaps that was not possible for you."

Steve didn't like politics. He didn't like this little water rat Pinchon either. Nor his breath. Nor his soft line in racialism. Least of all did he like the insinuations he was beginning to make.

"Listen, buddy . . ."

A vein twitched on Steve's clenched fist. In the next second Pinchon would have been talking politics through a smashed pair of dentures. But Bimbo Heureux, even in his cups, had a sixth sense about his customers' welfare. As it happened, he was a de Gaulle supporter, but this little Vichyite spent a lot of money running down de Gaulle in the Chat Brûlé. Bimbo's normally watery eyes shot Steve a sharp gleam of warning.

And you started to ease your way through the crowd towards him, partly to lose the creep Pinchon but mainly because there was something about Monsieur Bimbo Heureux tonight that you fancied even a shade less than usual. And you felt an urge to tell him where he could put his little glances of warning, and for that matter his valued customers, whom a wandering genius impresario called Steve Wagner had somehow beckoned into the dive. Except that in a place like the Chat Brûlé there is many a slip between Intention and Fulfillment, which is another way of saying it can take one heckuva long time to cover a few yards of ground.

Undeterred by Georgette's delicate fingers pushing their way past your trouser buttons, you press on. But when you're within hugging distance of King Kong somebody throws the light switches and Bimbo had leaped onto the stage and he's waving his arms about and telling his clients what a swell night they're going to have, how the Chat Brûlé's always looking for the cute openings, and how he'd gone two hundred miles to bring some new talent into town. And it's coming onto the stage, or rather it's crawling onto the stage, and five of them at least are belly-wobbling onto the stage, and the scene's a whole lot crazier than Javanese shadow puppets.

The eldest is about ten, and Daddy gave her a great present at birth. By doing a reset job on her arms he's fixed it like she'd never have to work again in her life, like she was Rockefeller or something. Her dad was really on to a sure thing. The money just has to leap from your pocket, not an earthly chance it can stay put when these kids are around. But Daddy's gone and double-fixed it, handed round a whole collection of crazy drums, a tom-tom, and things that look like tambourines, only the sound is more hollow. And they're swinging their limbs to the music, which is creepy because the arms and legs are never where you'd expect them to be. And even so the kids are doing great and you're keeping your fingers crossed for them because if anyone were to laugh . . .

Steve Wagner didn't see his face, he didn't have to. He heard the foulness, much more he smelled it in him. But the first bit was the hearing, and he realized that the place had got very quiet, because Bimbo Heureux's Deformity Paradise Band was in its way a hit; that is, it had stunned the audience, as Bimbo must have known it would. Things that Steve had seen on the odd trip into the backwoods were unknown to most of the bourgeois audience here tonight. So behind the soft drumming and glassy shimmering of the children's band, who were somehow by foot, arm, mouth, or chin managing to manipulate their musical instruments, you couldn't have heard a colon fart.

Instead you got the preliminaries of what you might have thought was an incipient earthquake; or maybe a maniac was having an attack. It was a low, guttural, half-suppressed heaving that came deep down from around the belly and started to spiral upward. The fat neck in front was beginning to wobble, the whole giant sixteen stone beginning to shake. And then Bimbo bent double, like a man beginning to retch, to vomit out laughter.

And that was when Steve Wagner took him. There were no histrionics. He just edged his way to a situation directly behind the heaving giant and when he got there quietly delivered a vicious rabbit punch to Bimbo's bulging neck. There wasn't much room to spin round, but the force of Steve's blow did have the general effect of making the proprietor revolve. And when he did, Steve Wagner was there waiting for him, and the blow that slammed into his lower guts did no good to his recently digested dish of roasted yams.

Of course it was the end of Steve's association with the Chat Brûlé, but his exit was dignified. Whilst the muscle men worried over the body of their fallen boss, Steve walked slowly back to the bar and told the barman to hand him a bottle of scotch.

"That was ill advised you know, Steve," cut in a cool voice behind him as he yanked off the stopper of the hooch and tilted the bottle upwards to his mouth. "I thought we agreed you don't play games with our dear Gaullist friend and ally, Monsieur Bimbo Heureux."

"Hi, Pink Baboon," said Steve Wagner, eyeing the seamy remains of his once immaculate friend and enemy, Auguste Berthier, late Inspector of Fraud of the Casablanca police force. "Whatdoyadoin' hiding back here?" He was frowning at the dimly lit foyer of the Chat Brûlé, with its touch of shantytown and nickelodeon. "I offered you a grandstand view."

"Steve, we must go. It is foolish to linger here," came ex-Inspector Berthier's quietly solicitous voice.

And then they walked home to their lodgings among the evil-smelling warehouses bordering the black expanse of the River Congo, thinking of another place and another time.

The owner of Brazzaville's smartest night spot was down on the floor like a heavyweight out for the count, and like many a bruiser before him, showing an extreme reluctance to beat the bell.

Not that he had any special reason to hurry. He was total dictator of everything and everyone he surveyed. The Chat Brûlé was his, and the cashbox, and the waiters in their sleazy white dinner jackets, not to mention little Georgette, so young and yet so syphilitic. He could indulge himself. Lie there, all eighteen and a half stone of him, moan, and swear.

"When you find him, remember one thing," he croaked at his ringside posse. "Do not forget. This *cochon* bastard is my baby. I'm going to tidy him up real good, this Monsieur Steve Wagner. You will see, my friends, how Bimbo tidies him up."

It was no idle threat. Bimbo Heureux had more to his credit than the sleaziest haunt in Brazzaville. His eighteen and a half stone might have gone to fat, but it still boasted an impressive proportion of genuine muscle power. His left jabs might signal themselves from afar with massive obviousness, but there were plenty of helpmates around to trip up an adversary whilst Bimbo Heureux delivered his 16-inch shells. If that didn't work, Bimbo had other, subtler weapons to hand. For example, Felix Eboue, Governor and supreme boss of the Gaullist enclave in Equatorial Africa, as powerful as any banana state Caligula, if more pleasantly presented.

That was Bimbo Heureux, a dangerous man to cross in these perspiring latitudes, and Steve Wagner, American expatriate, had done precisely that. Delivered plumb into the solar plexus with sinew and with malice.

Fortunately it was a combat that must prove unequal. On Bimbo's side the underworld and demiworld of Brazzaville with its crooked policemen and accommodating *fonctionnaires*. On Steve Wagner's just a seedy ex-Inspector from Casablanca, who was cautiously going through the available womanhood of the town. Even so, life was never quite that easy, even for a man like Bimbo Heureux. There were still formalities to consider, in particular the exigencies of the Code Napoléon that France had inflicted on the place for the past seventy or eighty years. Propped up in his chair behind his desk, in his patron's private retreat, Bimbo's keen, mean mind pondered revenge whilst a waiter wiped the sicked-up yams off his huge chocolate face.

And that was where Nad Klaf found him half an hour later,

fanned by Georgette whilst he farted into his huge fake Empire mahogany chair.

The accent didn't do him much favor to Bimbo's sharp ears. And the cut of his white linen suit with the huge necktie bespattered with Hawaiian sunsets. But at least, unlike that *merde* Steve Wagner, this American smiled at you and shook your hand, and even knew your name.

"Monsieur Heureux, I presume," he emitted in pleasant parody, "gee, it's been a long time meeting . . ."

"Who is this?" asked Bimbo of his staff. "Who admitted this *cochon?*"

"Course you won't know me," continued the American. "Fact is, I've only just hit town. But I guess we might have friends in common."

"What does he want, this *pissoir?*" asked Bimbo Heureux in his deep chocolate voice as he surveyed the newcomer through blood-shot eyes.

One of the waiters, who also happened to be handy with a flick knife and acted as Bimbo's "heavy," started to move towards the visitor.

"This time is bad, monsieur. Tomorrow maybe, Monsieur Heureux would be delighted."

"But I can't wait that long. I've got business to do with a lousy bum, who I gather is quite a force around here these days. A fellow American; you'll know him if you see him. An ugly guy who happens to look the spitting image of John Garfield. That is if anyone around here happens to know what John Garfield looks like."

"Tell me about your friend," Bimbo inquired softly.

"Well, there's not much to say. He bums around places for a bit, and then he flips it. Either the cops get him or he runs out of loot, or some ladylove kicks him out of bed. And then—Abracadabra—Steve Wagner's on his travels again."

"Steve Wagner? This monsieur, he is a friend of yours?" asked Bimbo Heureux in a voice so quiet it was almost a whisper.

"OK, he's not Ronald Colman or even Charles Boyer, but he does the kind of things that's just about becoming a craze. You know the kind. The sentimental hood, in the style of Georgie Raft or Humphrey Bogart. The inarticulate natural guy who acts mean but has a heart like melting butter. Only difference is, Steve isn't acting. He's a genuine thickhead."

"How long you know this Steve Wagner?" came Bimbo Heureux's voice with a voice like a pianissimo cello.

"Met him up at Casablanca. Come to think of it, the guy owes me something. He's a vital piece of evidence in a little Philo Vance cliff-hanger about copyright. I'm here to try and personally subpoena him back into the law courts of Uncle Sam. The bastard owes me that much, for old times' sake."

With a loud belch that rumbled its way out of his voluminous blue and white striped trousers Bimbo rose to his feet and waded towards the amiable American. Bimbo was in a mood for polishing. And if he couldn't have one American, fate had presented a handy substitute in the person of this oversmiling friend.

"You are a *cochon*. Bimbo polish you," the club owner purred as he waded towards him.

"Hey, you've got it wrong. Steve Wagner's a sonofabitch. I've just come to put forget-me-nots on his grave, that's how much I fancy the guy."

It had been done better even in the Warner Bros. B films that Nad Klaf tried to bring about. Wrongfooting the opposition, then the quick skedaddle for the doorway. And certainly the Hollywood scout was niftier on his feet than the owner of the Chat Brûlé. But as Nad turned to dodge away, the door clearly in view, his legs buckled under a trip from behind and he was making close acquaintance with Bimbo Heureux's rush matting.

"See how I shine up this *cochon*," roared Bimbo Heureux as his huge black boots began to rough up Nad Klaf's linen suit.

Dear Vincent,

Long time no see, but the fact is I've hitched myself a ride into General de Gaulle's colonial empire, a kind of mix between Quai des Brumes and Sanders of the River. And believe you me, Vincent, the whole place is absolutely humming with *donnés*. I mean, when Crosby and Lamour have got tired of the usual places, you could send them on the Road to Brazzaville. Punks, mutilated kids, four-teen-year-old whores, roast yam stews, and quite a lot of fancy gun play—you name it, this country's got it, and when I get back to L.A. I'll be glad to show you a few scenarios.

But life isn't all good, Vincent; you have to believe me. OK, I've got a room in a hotel, thanks to the pulling power of the mighty dollar, and I only clouted twenty-two bedbugs last night. And, OK, there is a fancy bit of fifteen-year-old screw called Georgette, who can't speak a word of English but has a nice way of smoothing down the troubled mind. But this place is hell, Vincent, and I'm here really, if you care to judge it, because of you. That is, to spell it out, I've crossed the Atlantic in a junk ship, got pestered by a U-boat, and seasick and landed in King Kong's private cabin, where a nig-nog who's a kind of colored version of William Bendix virtually booted my soul out of my body. And why, Vincent? OK, I'll tell you, and you may not like it, but believe you me when you get to a place like this the ordinary decencies of life do tend to appear a shade phony.

Look, I'm on the track of a bum called Steve Wagner, who as it happened was the prototype of a guy called Rick, as played by Bogart, who looks like making you the biggest killing since GWTW. You see, *Casablanca*—well, it's Steve's life story, along with a corrupt randy cop (the Claude Rains role) and a fancy dame, played by Ingrid You-know-who.

Problem is, Vincent, I wrote the whole lot out for you in a four-teen-page scenario which your people seem to have lost, except that you bring out this film with all my bits in it.

Well, I was figuring if I could get this guy Steve Wagner back to L.A. you could meet him, and being the guy you are . . . well, heck, I'm only asking for a slice of the action. Come to that, you might think you owe Wagner something, I mean for using bits of his real life story.

Anyway, in the immortal words of Tom Jefferson (I think), the bird has flown. Wagner crapped out of a club just as I came in, and typically Brazzaville now is too hot to hold him. But I'm asking you to believe that someday I'll find him, and it might be best to put in those credits on the film before it gets general release. For old times' sake, I mean.

Your old friend,
NAD KLAF

The converted Potez 631 three-seater fighter bomber cruised lazily over the wastes of that still Vichyiste equatorial sand dump they called Niger. Beneath, in the endless dried-up mud bath which constituted the southernmost limits of the Sahara desert, terra-cotta gave way to tawny brown, finally transfusing into straw yellow.

The Free French pilot, dispatched by Lupin from a remote airfield deep inside French Morocco, was of the taciturn type. Hunched over the controls, he let out thin sibilant whistles as the Potez's Gnome-Rhone engines choked and hiccupped (apparently the gasoline was not quite of the quality required by the Potez's specification).

In the two rear seats Steve Wagner and Auguste Berthier nudged and jolted together, one of the Potez's 75-mm machine guns sticking into Steve's back.

There wasn't much cause for conversation. It was an old case of the *fait accompli*. Hiding away in a whorehouse in downtown shanty Brazzaville for a couple of nights hadn't quite proved to be an African safari, with the imminent prospect of being lynched by grinning *gendarmes*.

Then one day Auguste Berthier had done some scouting and finally come with a one-way ticket out of trouble. Somebody up there wanted them both back in Casablanca. Auguste had urged and Steve had agreed. You don't, at Steve's age, get that many breaks in life. Just the odd favor. Like the bottle of punk brandy that he and Berthier slugged back together, and sticking into his rear the other side of the machine gun was its identical twin.

Prize jerk! Here he was in the land of the Pink Baboon, getting fired for picking fights with gone-headed niggers like Bimbo Heureux and looking less like John Garfield with every glass of hooch he sank, in the stifling heat of this foul-smelling frog crate. Let's have another one, heh? Not for the road. Not for the dames, because for you there's only one dame, and she left you standing at the door of the Golf Hotel in Étretat all of two summers ago. But another one for another one's sake. If you couldn't die, if you couldn't kill or be killed, maybe you could try to murder the image of her face that would float into your mind any time of the night or day, even on the equator.

"Here's killing you, kid!" he giggled, raising his glass to the struts on the ceiling. He winked at the naked bulb dangling inconsequentially on its umbilical cord of twisted flex and the bulb winked back.

"Didn't you hear me?" he addressed it. "Get lost, I said, get lost." The bulb grinned back and then did a polite loop-the-loop as the Potez ran into an air pocket.

Prize jerk, prize bum. But then so what? From the Gulf of Finland to the Burma Road people were doing immaculate bull's-eyes on other people's intestines. There was room in the world for just one Pink Baboon or two.

Auguste Berthier's delicate nostrils snorted beside him as he recovered from a booze-drenched reverie, and his slightly waxed sandy moustache did an insouciant twirl.

"Hi, Pink Baboon," slurred Steve. The rules were simple. There were fraternities back in the States where men got together in predatory packs and gently, lovingly, took the town apart, just for kicks. The Pink Baboon club was dedicated to the contrary. You didn't nudge so much as a finger into the Great Beyond. You lay on your bed and got slowly stewed. If you wanted to vomit, or pee or crap, you lay on your bed and went right ahead and did it. If a mosquito landed on your nose, you made friends and let it suck your blood. If somebody came through the door and started to beat hell out of you, you let him. If the whole goddamn joint went up in smoke, you complimented yourself on your ringside view. That was what being a Pink Baboon meant; it meant doing fuck-all. It also meant thinking fuck-all, the phrase having strictly nothing to do with that lousy pursuit called fucking.

So you lay back in this screwy kite, nobody at home, just a roommate and fellow exile. Monsieur Auguste Berthier, formerly of the Casablanca police (Department of Fraud). And you slurped down tooth-mugfuls of raw African brandy, the stuff they called jungle juice, and pondered screwy things like life and love and war and glory. And Auguste quotes some creep French writer and you who'd said words to the effect that all's for the best in the best of possible worlds. Or the worst, you offered, now how about the worst? Until, having worked that one to the bone, you both reckoned there wasn't a dime in it between best or worst or something dead center between the two.

So you just sit here with the machine gun poking one buttock and the bottle of hooch the other and say boo to all those goddamn boy scouts who spent their life saluting pieces of colored cloth. Crap your Pétains, Stalins, Churchills, Roosevelts, Wallaces, and Hulls. Screw your filthy war because I'm gonna just lie here with fellow Pink Baboon crime squad specialist Berthier. Juz lie here and count the buzzards wheeling over the sick-hued desert. Or the blowfly now twitching on friend Berthier's moustache.

And wonder who or what or why now required the presence of Steve Wagner back in Casablanca.

Sure Auguste Berthier had muttered something about a "Lupin," but who the hell was Lupin? To which Auguste Berthier gave him a little twiddle of sandy moustache and a kind of blink in the eyes which was too insidious to be a wink. One thing was straight, although Steve Wagner had not exactly heard of him or met him in the elevated milieux in which he moved, he communicated something to Auguste Berthier. He also had the oomph to transport two Gaullist bums from the African swamps three thousand miles in a fancy aircraft with French Vichy markings.

"What does he want us to do?" slurped Steve Wagner. "Blow up the Sultan? . . . Or General Nogues?"

Again that warning glint of Berthier's eyes.

"But that kind of thing could get us killed too."

Then Berthier took a swig of the hooch and gave his old friend what was almost a wintry smile.

"You know, Steve, that thought's beginning to worry me too. They didn't give us much choice, though," he added.

It didn't take Nad Klaf long to decide the Hotel Suchet wasn't quite in the same class as the Beverly Hills in L.A., where he had spent many an idle hour waiting for Vincent from Warner Bros. to join him in a white lady, or hanging around the bar on the off chance of ogling Carmen Miranda.

It was a dump that did more for its insect than its human guests.

But Nad Klaf was in no way able at this moment coolly to appraise the missing amenities.

His temperature was touching about 104 as a result of the beating he'd taken from Bimbo Heureux, or the later consolations he'd exacted from the nubile fifteen-year-old Georgette. Or maybe an ill-advised dish of *dindon roti congolese* with black-eyed beans had been the culprit. Problem was that the more Nad showed signs of wanting to quit the place, the less cooperative the possessive Georgette was becoming. She had determined in her mind that she would marry the Hollywood scout and set up house here in Brazzaville, and she held all the key cards because Nad Klaf's slick Hollywood jokey American could not penetrate her barrier of pidgin French. All of which meant that he was forced to sweat it out here on the fetid bed, staring up at the yellowing fan revolving like the wheel of fate above him whilst Georgette gently tickled his toes. What Nad, normally a master of communication, was trying to tell her was that he'd bribed his way onto a contraband boat which the captain assured him was bound to touch in at Dakar—a port halfway up the African coast. From where he could fly to Casablanca, where every gut instinct Nad had told him his quarry had fled to. But Georgette wouldn't listen. All she wanted was to keep him here, spend his money, and tickle his toes.

"It's become obsessive, Georgette," he moaned, mopping his brow with a flashy spotted silk handkerchief. "It's this guy and me, and when I get him—boy-o. I'll sue Warner's for everything they've got—I'll prove they pinched my story."

"You want whiskey?" asked Georgette. "You want sleep? You want good fuck?"

"Sure, oh God, NO! Look, Georgette, I'm running a temperature and maybe I'm not making too much sense. Look, fucking's great. When I've tracked down Wagner we fuck plenty. We fuck all day. We fuck all night."

"Who this Wagner?" she asked.

28

"A sonofabitch who gives me the break of my life and then vamooses on me just when I'm going to collect."

"Look, Vincent, you've got to believe me . . . please, Vincent . . ."

For leaning over his feverish bed now and framed before the revolving fan was the Warner Bros. man himself with that probing stare and wire-framed glasses and that little pearl stud he always plonked sock in the middle of his necktie.

"Look, Vincent, you've got to believe me . . . I saw the film, Vincent, that Bogart character he was my guy. Picked him up eighteen months back at a flea pit in Casablanca with a creep owner who could have been mistaken for Sydney Greenstreet, and OK, it wasn't Rick's Place—but Ritzi's—now, isn't that a coincidence, Vincent?"

"Go on, Nad, I'm listening," lisped Vincent's deceitfully receptive voice.

"It all fits, there was a crooked cop; heck, I wrote it. Like Claude Rains, no he *was* Claude Rains. And then there was a million-dollar Queen Bee with a gushing soul and great big lips. The Scandinavian iceberg herself!"

"Know something, Klaf?" came Vincent's voice again. "You're the fifth bum who's come to me in a week and tried to pull that story!"

"No, Vincent, it was ME. ME. ME!"

Georgette looked down at her beautiful white prisoner and smiled secretly. He had the fever. He looked bad. But he would get better. She knew just the place where they were going to buy—a little white bungalow with a bath and a veranda, just out of town.

SECTION II

CITY BY TORCHLIGHT

Casablanca was a lot of different places all in one place. A part of it, the Medina, was an old Arab town. Another part was an ultramodern French city, complete with boulevards almost as broad as the Champs Élysées. Yet another part of it was a dusty industrial town. Casablanca was also a major port for shipments to France of phosphates and manganese ore. In fact this was the reason why the French had come in the first place, officially as protectors of the Sultan.

Casablanca was a mixture of races just as it was a jumble of architecture. Consequently the population could be said to have mixed feelings towards the Vichy regime of Marshal Pétain and Pierre Laval. There were Arabs who were a hundred-percent loyal to the Marshal; there were others who actually preferred Hitler. There were twenty thousand Jews crowded around the Porte Negve who went in fear of their lives from both of them, because the Vichy regime had imposed anti-Semitic laws almost as tough as the Nazi model. The richer French residents were right behind Vichy. The less well off tended to have a sneaking regard for the unfashionable General de Gaulle, but they kept quiet about it.

You could say Casablanca was the most cosmopolitan city on the coast of Africa. If you had money in your pocket and the correct right-wing affiliations, it could be a wonderful town. There was rationing of course; but champagne was still in good supply, and the girls were plentiful, willing, and multicolored.

With the right credentials you could be cock of the walk in Casablanca. Alternatively you could be a corpse floating in the inky waters of the harbor, just like this corpse which this evening was being hauled like an outsize fish onto the Grande Jetée.

A *gendarme* flashed his torch onto a bloated face, as white as the underside of a mullet. Then he moved it down to the neck, where pink air bubbles were glistening in an incision which looked as broad as a smile.

Another *gendarme* stooped down and took a wallet from the body's sodden white jacket, and carried it over to a tall man wearing a civilian raincoat.

"This is not a murder case. There will be no investigation," said the tall man, whose name was Chief Inspector Lucien Roth. "The individual was a Jew."

At least the room was an improvement on Brazzaville, not to mention their luxury berths in the Potez fighter bomber. They had two beds as comfortably sprung as you had a right to expect from a hideout in one of Casablanca's leading whorehouses. There was also an electric fan, a luxury they hadn't run into in Brazzaville, and if the smell of cheap scent and old orgies seemed to cling to the faded flower-patterned wallpaper, you could lean out of the window and catch the homely whiff of the bazaar, blended with the scent of gasoline and Gauloises that together constituted the unique smell of Casablanca. For two men without a mission it would have been a pleasant enough hideaway. As it was, they had a mission calculated to make a man like Auguste vomit with fear. Also Madame Carpentier, who knew them of old, was already becoming suspicious, owing to the fact that they hadn't yet sent for any of her girls. For example, Auguste hadn't even made a grab for the mascara-eyed seventeen-year-old who'd brought their breakfast of croissants and coffee. Girls were strictly against Lupin's orders, not that Auguste meant to be fastidious about obeying Lupin's orders; it was simply that at the pit of his stomach, like a bad oyster, he was gripped by the sickening terror of their mission, which was to kill Wehrmacht General Joachim Kellerman, now visiting Morocco as Resident-General Nogues's guest. A mission like that was enough to put anyone off sex.

Steve was opening the tarpaulin package which Lupin, with a flimsy little smile, had described as "your hunting equipment—*l'appareil de la chasse.*"

"What do you know, the rifle that lost the Battle of France!"

He was examining a French MAS 36, glossy with oil to protect it on its journey.

"Claude Lupin must be an even crazier patriot than I thought," he pondered, looking through the specially fitted telescopic sight. "Why the hell couldn't he have got us a Russian Moisin-Nagant? It isn't French, but it can kill at long range. I worked with one in Spain. If he couldn't buy Russian, he could have borrowed a Lee Enfield off the British; it's heavier than this bb gun, but it shoots straight. The French MAS 36!" He grimaced savagely, working the rifle's bolt. "You'll notice it hasn't even got a safety catch."

"Are you suggesting we cannot carry through with our mission?" It was said with a smile, but there was a trace of eagerness in Auguste's tone.

"I'm suggesting," Steve said bleakly, "that if we're going to kill this fascist bastard we'll have to go in close. I guess it's just as well I packed my Walther P38."

"I'm sure you realize that will be suicide. The Casablanca police force may have its off moments, but allow me to insist we were never complete fools."

"You've been saying we're committing suicide ever since we boarded that Free French bathtub," Steve told him laconically, picking out of the package a French pineapple grenade as if it were a piece of rotten fruit.

"And you don't deny it. You've never attempted to deny it. You actually seem to revel in the hopelessness of this absurd mission. Anyone would think you had volunteered for it. You of all people, Steve, the founder member of the Pink Baboon club!"

Steve let the grenade bounce in and out of the palm of his hand, perhaps because he knew it was making Auguste nervous. He said, "Did no one tell you there was a war on? I know you'd never have guessed it in Brazzaville, but a lot of guys are killing Germans and getting killed by Germans. You could say we're privileged, we've got a genuine kraut general to kill. Don't you know Pink Baboons can kill if they're kicked hard enough?"

"Steve, mon ami, there are thousands of German generals, but there are only two of us."

Steve put the grenade away and lit a cigarette. As with the MAS 36, he could see no useful purpose for the grenades that Lupin had stuffed into their kit, except perhaps if they had to make a getaway. He said, "Auguste, you ought to get off that bed and start renewing your contacts with the Casablanca police. If Kellerman's due in town next week we'll need a detailed itinerary."

Auguste sat up on his bed; he didn't put on the pince-nez which he had chosen as his disguise. He said, "I'd really like to know what good it's going to do Lupin, or Brigadier General de Gaulle if by some hundred-to-one chance we succeed in killing this salle Boche. No, please, Steve, don't give me a sermon about Brigadier de Gaulle's honor and integrity; I am well aware he's absolutely sincere and quite heroic. But between ourselves Free France hasn't been a tremendous success, has it? Oh, I know they've got French Equatorial Africa, but speaking from bitter experience, one might ask who wants French Equatorial Africa? They certainly didn't want de Gaulle in Dakar; nor, I gather, in Damascus. I don't think it made him any more popular that he had to sneak in behind English tanks. Believe me, I appreciate his problems, but is it really going to help his cause to have a German general shot while he is the guest of the Protectorate of Morocco? You realize they're bound to do more than put you and me up against a wall, Steve; they're going to shoot every Gaullist sympathizer in Casablanca they can lay hands on."

It was unusual for Auguste to raise his voice or to swear, but now he did both.

"*Merde*, by the time we've finished with this little mission there won't be one Gaullist sympathizer left in Casablanca."

Steve picked up the stubby MAS 36 rifle and pointed it, for emphasis, at Auguste's stomach.

"Listen, you dumb little Frenchman. You made a decision here in Casablanca a year ago. Maybe it was a bad decision. Maybe you didn't quite appreciate what you were letting yourself in for. But you made a decision—the kind you can't go back on! So let's get back to the business of killing Germans. Pink Baboons can if they're pressed."

"It was your decision," Auguste Berthier shouted. "You pretend it was a mutual arrangement. I'm telling you it was blackmail. You misused the indiscretions I was insane enough to make to you. You gave me no other choice but to escape with you to that sewer Brazzaville. I tell you Steve . . ."

He didn't finish because the door opened and their hostess, Madeleine Carpentier, put her curling-pinned head into the room to see what the noise was about. She saw the rifle in Steve's hand, and she screamed.

"You told me you were not here for politics. You must go at once."

In fact they had told their old friend Madeleine Carpentier a lot of things that weren't exactly true. For example, that their journey was strictly sentimental. Or rather that they had found Brazzaville so little to their taste they were prepared to run any risk to get back to the cosmopolitan delights of Casablanca. They had even hinted that arrangements were being made through unofficial channels to fix a pardon from General Nogues. And they had produced a wad of counterfeit Vichy notes, as if to make the point. They had told Madeleine Carpentier a lot of half-truths which in normal times two gentlemen wouldn't tell a lady, particularly an adaptable lady like Madeleine Carpentier.

Steve put down the rifle.

"Just a little self-protection, Madeleine. We didn't want to get arrested before we've fixed up our reprieve," he grinned. He could still grin disarmingly when he wanted to.

Madeleine looked at the glinting weapon, which in spite of the things Steve had said about it could still drop a man at two thousand yards.

"No, that is for killing. You are here for politics."

"You know I've always hated politics, honey."

She said, "Listen, for us the war is over. We are neutral in Casablanca. We do not want to know about de Gaulle or Churchill. They are warmongers. We are at peace. You know something else? We have a new Chief of Police who will do everything to keep it that way. I mean everything."

She didn't add that she had a Jewish mother living in Toulouse, but if she had it would have been relevant to her argument.

Steve suddenly got up and took Madeleine in his arms and kissed her tenderly. Auguste couldn't remember when he'd last seen Steve take a woman in his arms. He knew only that his friend had been shamefully underplaying a tremendous natural asset. Tieless and unshaven, there was still no one who could take a woman in his arms like Steve. You could see Madeleine was itching to take her curling pins out.

"Tell you what, Madeleine," Steve purred, "before you throw us out why don't we send down for a couple of bottles of Veuve Cliquot and let's have a talk about old times? Hey, and I guess Auguste would love to meet one of your new mademoiselles. He's been starved of female company down there on the equator."

"Steve, you are very sweet, but you are very dangerous. You don't know how dangerous you are."

"OK, if it'll make you happier, babe, I'll lay down my arms." Steve grinned like a Norman Rockwell kid caught stealing apples in Iowa. He took the rifle and presented it to her with a mock humble bow.

"Honest. You can hang it over your fireplace as a souvenir, or give it to the police if you want. I'm in your hands. 'I surrender, dear.'"

"Congratulations," Auguste said when Madeleine had left to fetch the champagne and her most luscious new recruit. "Your charm still seems to work miracles." He added tentatively, "I take it you've decided our hiding place is more important than *l'appareil de la chasse*. Can I assume our 'mission' is temporarily postponed?"

Steve was leaning out of the window. His face had hardened again in the glare of the morning sun.

He said, "Maybe she'll forget the offer. Maybe she won't. I told you I don't need that lousy MAS 36 anyway. I'm going in close with the Walther. Incidentally," he asked tonelessly, "did you remember you can see Ritzi's from here?"

It was a crazy mixed-up thing to do, like putting your *papier-mâché* jaw up on the line and asking Joe Louis to do you a favor and knock it into kingdom come. Besides, it was *absolument défendu,* that is if you had the guts and the discipline to keep your nose clean and obey orders.

"And no doubt, *mon ami,* you'll be steering clear of the old familiar haunts," Lupin had told him. "No sentimental pilgrimage back to Ritzi's. Apart from placing your whole mission in jeopardy it would be a sad homecoming, my dear Steve. They tell me it has changed beyond recognition. The new clientèle is really not your class."

But then if he had been that wise he wouldn't be sitting here in Madame Carpentier's pastel-shaded brothel, knocking back bad cognac out of a tooth mug and counting the holes and crevices in his face, and figuring what kind of bum had thought of comparing him to John Garfield. And if he'd been that smart he wouldn't have left the window wide open, so that on a still night you could just catch Bobbi's tinkling piano reverberating at you through the jasmine-scented night; or craned his neck out and given himself a blow in the guts from the sight of that new neon winking CHEZ MAURICE at you.

Sorry, Mister Loopy Lupin, you might have got it all figured out in that tidy little plot of gray matter of yours, but if you insist on using a couple of prize jerks in your grand stratagem things could just go off course. Except you *did* have it all figured out, Loopy, didn't you? A couple of dumb clucks who knew the local scene to do your dirty work for you, whilst you slunk in higher up the game to pull the real cards. (Slurp down the dregs of the cognac.) "Sorry, Loopy," Steve muttered to himself as he slid on his jacket and adjusted the Walther nice and snugly in his hip pocket, just in case. "But didn't someone warn you about that crazy mechanism called the human heart?"

"Hi, pavement," said Steve's best pair of patent leather shoes as they felt out the contours of that familiar street that led you up to and under the old MGM-style neon sign that now blinked out its lying message of bare-assed effrontery—CHEZ MAURICE. "Hi, crazy-paving. Hi, elephantine mosaics. Didn't Ritzi pick you up in the bazaar at a buck a hundred pieces? Hi, rush mats. Hi, mausoleum of dead hopes and memories. Hi, old rat hole, glad to remake your acquaintance!

The clientèle was a whole new scene, and there wasn't a big-time gambler or a damsel in distress among them. It wasn't so much a collection of beautiful mugs, clubbing together for sheer warmth and camaraderie. It was a Nuremberg Rally, a Falangist parade in Franco's Madrid, a bonzo among the "Itey" bullfrogs in Musso's Eternal City. It was crap, collectivized crap on a grand regimental scale. This clientèle wasn't clad in the old regulation sweaty white jacket and crumpled bow tie, nicked out of some down-trodden pawnshop for a few dimes. It sported berets with gleaming insignias of the Celtic Cross, heavy black shirts, paunchy riding breeches held up by heavy belts that would have done pride to a fancy-dress rodeo show. And mellow burnished leggings leading the eye down to heavy military jackboots. And in the dim light the owners of this regalia seemed as fat as Goering, as sweatily obese as Mussolini.

And the crumbs had brought their banners with them. The center of the floor, where frightened couples had enjoyed a last fox-trot together before the *flics* pounced, was now beflagged like a parade ground, the banners gently flapping in the Gauloise-ridden breeze that emitted from Ritzi's intermittent electric fan. And one thing that hit you only after a few seconds: there was a real shortage of dames around the place. Steve's eyes did a rapid search round the smoky hall and were able to detect only eight or nine genuine broads. And most of those were whores, cheap pickups from the bazaar, rejects from the Medina, floozies who'd never make the grade with Madame Carpentier. And now in twos and threes they were staggering across the floor to where Bobbi was delivering a cool, lingering interpretation of "Smoke Gets in Your Eyes." That took him back. That certainly took him back. Bobbi gave them a lazy look and broke into a medley of recent hits by Hoagy Carmichael as a *chanson* started to erupt from the well-oiled throats of these followers of Jacques Doriot's fascist-inspired PPF (or Parti Populaire Français). A crude communal *chanson* with the refrain, *"Contre tous les salauds, adherez mes braves."*

And then a hand softly touched his shoulder, and Steve swung round, the safety catch already off the Walther, the squat muzzle whizzing round to engage the quiet menace from behind.

"Mister Steve, Mister Steve," came a deep melodious voice, still impregnated with all the sadness of an Austrian Jew. "Why you here?"

"Hi, Rubin," said Steve, eyeing Ritzi's faithful old dogsbody and waiter. "Yeah, it's me. Thought I'd just come around to see how they are minding the store."

"These are brutal people, Mister Steve. Not your kind of people, Mister Steve."

"Got any of that Jack Daniel's bourbon still stashed away in the cellar, Rubin? In the old days they didn't keep a customer waiting so long."

"Mister Steve, Monsieur Ritzi knows you are here."

"So what?"

Rubin's eyes rolled, and then he shrugged his shoulders. He meant there was that little matter of a hundred thousand francs.

"OK, I'll see him," Steve grinned. "Maybe I can squeeze you another raise."

As usual, Ritzi was wearing a pair of white and blue "co-respondents," shoes with extra leather on the heels to increase his height. And he was still a squat little Libyan with hair stuck down as though somebody had emptied a bottle of water on it, who didn't look you in the eyes even when you had taken him for one hundred thousand francs.

"I'm surprised to see you here, Monsieur Wagner."

Steve said, "That's right. I owe you one hundred thousand francs."

"Monsieur Steve," Ritzi lisped, "it was a crazy thing to do. And you, I thought such a practical man, such an *homme d'affaires*. And all for a woman who . . ."

"Yeah, I know," Steve said, trying to look casual, "flew out to Algiers en route for England or some damn place—to wait for another guy."

Ritzi fitted a Turkish cigarette into an onyx holder. "For myself I might understand, I am a romantic too, but there is also the police. I am afraid, Monsieur Steve, as far as they are concerned, you are Public Enemy No. 1."

Steve saw a hairy little hand fidget in the direction of the telephone.

He said, "Hang around for a week, Ritzi, and I could even pay you that one hundred thousand francs."

It wasn't so far off the truth. Claude Lupin had promised a substantial cash reward on the successful elimination of General Keller-man. And the balance could just about be made up with counterfeit Vichy notes. Besides, just now he didn't want to have to get the hell out of the place. Funny thing when you considered all the deeply sentimental reasons he had for hating it.

"You are kidding?" the little Libyan chiseler asked, trying to smile sophisticatedly but looking damned interested all the same. "I won-der what security you are offering, Monsieur Steve, for that under-taking."

"I guess you've got plenty of security right here in Ritzi's—sorry, I should say, 'Chez Maurice,' shouldn't I?" He glanced at a photo-graph of Maurice Chevalier, beaming backstage with a party of German officers. "I mean, if I don't deliver you've got a few bully-boys around here who would help me to disgorge. Why not give it a try, Ritzi? It's your best hope of seeing your money again. Well, don't tell me the police are going to refund you."

Ritzi poured himself a liqueur glass of benedictine. He said, "I do not know what brings you to Casablanca, Monsieur Steve, except that you are possibly mad. But it may be a pleasure to do business with you again."

"There's only one condition. You don't tell anyone I'm here. At least not till payday next week."

"To that extent Chez Maurice will respect your privacy, mon-sieur," Ritzi smiled greasily, lifting his minute liqueur glass.

Steve toasted him back with an invisible glass—the one Ritzi hadn't given him.

"I'm afraid I've got to say it. The clientèle hasn't exactly changed for the better since I went away. You know it, Ritzi. There were never that many nickels in the beer trade, however much they pour down. You've lost your class customers. The champagne-drinking mob with an itch for gambling. Be honest, Ritzi, how much do you turn over a week with this jackboot crowd?"

Ritzi shrugged. "We survive, Mr. Wagner, we survive. And we lay our cards down for better, more prosperous days."

"Whatever newfangled name you call your place, you'll never wash the place clean of this kind of crap," Steve told him. "You've fixed it so the place will stink forever, like crap up the nostrils, for all the class people I tried to bring in."

Ritzi (née Rissoli) reached up and placed a hand on Steve's shoulder. Was it supposed to be fatherly?

"Casablanca has changed more than you'd guess. Today you don't see anything, you don't hear anything. You survive. Tonight there will be another unfortunate incident. Tell me, Mr. Wagner, how would you deal with a scene like this?"

Ritzi had opened the door and together the owner and his ex-croupier peered across to the center of the bar. A gilded banner with the slogan "À Jeanne d'Arc, Libératrice du Territoire," had been suspended over Bobbi's grand piano. But Bobbi was no longer fingering those ivory keys with his cool wistful touch. His eyes were eerily focused on a minor atrocity.

His trousers removed, his long underpants garlanding the flabby comfortable contours of his wobbly bottom, the elderly waiter Rubin was being ceremonially flogged and kicked by well-polished jackboots.

Steve's emerging hand, grasping the Walther, was, once again that night, restrained, this time by Ritzi's clammy grip.

"One man against a mob of thugs. As I thought, you are crazy," he sighed.

"The sucker for all time," Steve agreed, replacing his Walther.

"Do not worry for Rubin," Ritzi told him. "He is a fine old ham. He screams before he is hurt. These *salauds* are too drunk to do him much harm. Besides, look at them. They are mostly middle-aged. Out of breath, out of condition. In a few minutes they will collapse on the floor and leave Rubin to clear up the mess. But I'm afraid that sooner or later he will have to go. Jews are not favored by the authorities these days."

The hall had quietened down as Steve slunk out. Ritzi had advised him to take the back entrance, but he'd wanted to see Rubin once more. Just to see him, give him a look, show him he still had a friend. He walked quickly round the darkened outside of the room, dodging the limelight and the groups of PPF members. And then something intuitively halted his pace, slowed him right down, as in a dare game, down to a slow tread, each footstep slowing the tempo of its predecessor. Until he stopped altogether, and leaning against a familiar pillar, did what he had done a thousand times before—pulled out a cigarette, clicked on his lighter, steadied up, and very deliberately lit it, like in a bit of slowed-up movie. Holding his stance by the pillar, he gradually drew in the smoke, deep into his lungs, then let it go. For a second or two the smoke screen of that first puff totally obscured his line of vision. Then it cleared.

And slowly, very slowly, the face came into focus, the face to end them all, with the slightly snub nose and cool, clear eyes that gave a strange effect of dreaminess, and of sadness. And then she turned and looked in his direction, at the dark obscure figure, now frozen still, that he must have presented to her gaze.

And now it was no longer a question of Steve defying panic, of his slow, disciplined, sustained game of "dare." He did not move because his body was suffering from a kind of hypershock, a shock that sent his pulse racing, his heart pounding, whilst a soft irresistible warmth began to undulate through his body.

And that was the first time Steve saw Helda on his return to Casablanca.

The U S Army Air Force Captain lit a Camel. The heat was such that it was sweat-soaked the moment he put it between his lips.

He said, "So you represent the Sodersheim Syndicate? You're still crazy if you think we can fly you to Casablanca."

Nad Klaf looked out of the window of the shack onto the blistering tarmac of the Pointe-Noire air base. There was a Liberator with US markings sitting idle on the tarmac. You might have thought a little more roasting out there and it would melt. You might have thought it would have been a helluva lot better employed in the air, flying north.

"I'd see you didn't lose by it, Captain." Klaf wiped his liquid brow. Was he still feverish or was it just this lousy heat? "I know a lot of people in a lot of places. Ever thought of a career in the movies, Captain?"

"Listen, buddy, nobody gets to fly to Casablanca from Pointe-Noire. You want to know why? Because we never heard of the place. We never heard of Dakar, Rabat, Tunis, or Algiers either, because that's Vichy country and that's a dirty word down here . . . you sick or something?" The Captain suddenly wanted to know.

"I'm fine," Nad Klaf lied, sinking onto the Captain's trestle table.

"Anyway, Uncle Sam acquired this dump courtesy of Charles de Gaulle and his Free Frenchmen. As far as we are concerned, they're the only Frenchmen we ever heard about. You know people in the movies?"

"I'm *in* the movies, Captain—that's why I gotta be in Casablanca."

"We don't fly to Casablanca. You ever met Ann Sheridan?"

"I know 'em all," Nad confided. His head had stopped spinning like a Liberator's prop. He wasn't feeling exactly like his old self, but he felt able to continue with confidence. "Rita Hayworth, Paul Henreid, Lana Turner, John Garfield, Ingrid Bergman, and Greer Garson are personal friends of mine. Shall we just say I met Humph Bogart—handed him the biggest break the bum ever got? I'm not calling that slob a pal."

"You met Ann Sheridan? I'd sure like to meet Ann Sheridan."

Nad Klaf was observant enough to notice a flush of desire on the Captain's heat-soaked face. Maybe he was recovering.

"Sure. She's a really cute girl with a lovely talent. And you know success hasn't spoiled her a darn. She's still a lot of fun to meet. Say, maybe . . ."

"I'd like that," the Captain said, "I'd sure like to meet Ann Sheridan."

Nad Klaf had a telephoto-lens memory bank. When Georgette blocked the exit marked "Smuggler beat," another thought came to Nad through the miasma of fever. He had got a six-hour start on Georgette. He'd hailed a taxi in the center of Brazzaville and told the driver to go like hell for Pointe-Noire. A two-hundred-mile drive along some of the least promising roads even this talent scout had traveled, but that could still be insufficient distance to have between himself and this adhesive whore. Georgette had a native sense of intuition which amounted almost to voodoo. Also vindictive cousins and relatives all over the shop. It was time, if it wasn't already too late, to pull out the hip flask and push it across to the Air Force Captain. Time to slide him over his card—the one that said, "Nad Klaf Motion Picture Consultant," and had an L.A. address on it. Time to scribble on the back of it a telephone number that could just have been Ann Sheridan's, although the chances were the subscribers were a Chinese laundry. Time to slap this honest officer on his humid shoulder and say, "You know, it's funny. Everyone's got to get someplace. For you it's Hollywood. For me it's Morocco. Why don't we drink to that?"

They had a drink to that. And then they had another—to Ann Sheridan. Then the Air Force Captain said, "OK, they're gonna bust me for it, but I'm gonna give you five minutes to get across that tarmac and get into the bomb bay of that Liberator. And if anybody asks you what the hell you're doing in there, don't tell them I sent you."

"I'm not going to forget this, Skipper," Nad promised as their perspiring hands squeezed. "I'm going to call up Ann Sheridan as soon as we make base and tell her about this Air Force hero who's on fever heat for her. By the way, when do we touch down in Casablanca?"

"You mean Norfolk, Virginia," the Air Force Captain muttered to himself as Klaf started to waddle across the toasting tarmac. "That's as close as you're getting to Casablanca!"

Claude Lupin was by nature a cautious man, but like his revolutionary mentors, Robespierre and Lenin, he favored audacity at times. That was why, pending the arrival of his two gunmen from Brazzaville, he had literally taken the bull by the horns and delivered something not more subtle than an ultimatum to a sympathetic waverer in General Nogues's Resident-General's office at Rabat (an air trip of two or three hours). That was also why he was now touching down at Casablanca in the Dewoitine passenger aircraft after twenty hours of delicate negotiation that showed every sign of being fruitful. Of course his name didn't feature on the passenger list. He was registered as a Señor Gomes, importer of textiles. It wasn't an elaborate cover, because although officially he was *persona non grata*, unofficially he was expected.

As a result of his discreet communications with the Resident-General's office in Rabat it had been arranged that he would be met by a Colonel Masson of General Nogues's staff, just in case the police or the SOL should look too closely at his papers. In fact General Nogues's office had been good enough to book a room for him at the opulent Hotel Lyautey in Casablanca's own Vendôme, the Place de France. There in a few hours he could expect an incognito visit from General Nogues in person.

One thing was certain with this shifty proconsul; he was ready to listen to overtures from practically any quarter. Lupin had a twofold plan designed to ensure he gained the General's maximum attention. A Pavlovian combination of the stick and the carrot. At their first meeting Lupin intended to dangle the carrot—if a common or garden vegetable could be said to describe the glittering prizes he was empowered to suspend before the pouchy eyes of the ambiguous Vichy commander.

The first prize was the suzerainty, in a Gaullist take-over, of the whole of French North Africa, a prize which Lupin calculated would seem even more attractive when he let slip the information, reliably authenticated by BCRAM agents in Washington and Vichy, that the Americans were hawking the job around between Weygand, Darlan, and even the naïve escaped POW General Henri Giraud.

The second prize was perhaps as tempting as the first. This was the offer, under a Gaullist restoration of a marshal's baton, a logical step up, Lupin would deferentially suggest, for a soldier of Nogues's caliber. It was indeed astonishing, he would add as an afterthought, that Vichy authorities had failed to recognize the fact, notwithstanding all the services he had rendered, including shipping back associates of Georges Martel on the *Massilia* for sentence at the notorious Roum treason trials.

Of course there was a booby prize, although it would not be paraded for the Resident-General's inspection. And this was a private promise Communist Lupin had made to himself, that on the liberation General Nogues would be brought to trial and guillotined as a fascist jackal and enemy of the people.

Sufficient unto the day. He would leave General Nogues to chew on his carrot. Then the stick would be applied, or rather an MAS 36 rifle. Result, the death of a highly placed Wehrmacht general enjoying the Resident-General's special protection. It needed no great understanding of politics to foresee the unfortunate repercussions this would have on General Nogues's career, nor any great knowledge of psychology to anticipate that the embrace of de Gaulle might seem extraordinarily comforting after the foulmouthed recriminations of the peasant Laval.

Claude Lupin didn't hurry out of the aircraft. He let the crowd of Portuguese and Spanish businessmen, rich refugees and obvious Axis spies, elbow one another down the landing steps. Then he stepped coolly onto the tarmac: a solitary and easily identifiable figure in his new panama hat and white summer lightweight.

It was a beautiful afternoon and everything was radiantly blue and white: a blue sky, a gleaming white terminus building. He didn't notice the black shadows it was casting. At the passport inspection gate Lupin, alias Gomes, received a tap on the shoulder.

Lupin looked at the stranger. The immaculately cut fawn-colored suit suggested an army officer in mufti. The rest of the man was not so military. There was a certain resemblance to the popular film actor Jean Marais; but although the hair was as blond, the physique was less muscular, and the blue eyes were more dreamily penetrating than Jean Cocteau's film star protégé. "It's a privilege to meet you," the blond stranger added. He didn't seem to be joking. He was looking at Lupin with the awed curiosity of a student meeting a well-known author in the flesh. Lupin realized too that he was in the presence of a local celebrity. In fact he had the feeling that an insect was crawling up his spine. "You will be kind enough to tell me your name," he said unnecessarily.

"I am Chief Inspector Roth, Monsieur Lupin." He was still looking like a respectful student, though in fact he was a police officer in his thirties.

"My name is Gomes, Señor Eusebio Gomes," Lupin hissed, thrusting out his fake Portuguese passport. He was no longer a professor who had strayed into espionage. He was an animal with his hair bristling.

Lucien Roth took the passport and examined it with the same respectful curiosity with which he had examined Lupin himself. Then he snapped it at the spine and tore it methodically in half. "You are one of France's foremost authorities on the Inca civilization," he said, and added, almost as an afterthought, "you are also BCRAM's number one agent in Casablanca."

Roth started to make a little bow. His face met Lupin's foot coming up with a kick that was meant for his groin. Roth staggered backwards, holding his face, making curiously high-pitched noises. Lupin reached for the automatic under his armpit, but he was frozen in the movement by two plainclothes policemen.

Everything about the ambiance suggested sunshine and holiday travel. At Lupin's back there was a series of Air France posters advertising holidays, perhaps to a nonexistent audience, in the Vichy Auvergne, the Vichy French Alps, and Vichy Provence. But what was about to happen underneath these dream pictures would be the worst possible advertisement for Vichy France.

One of the plainclothes cops handed Lupin's automatic to Roth.

"You have no right to take that," Lupin panted. "I have been promised free conduct to General Nogues."

Chief Inspector Roth's cheek was still crimson from Lupin's kick, but he had recovered his politeness. "I regret that General Nogues will be too busy to see you."

"That is for the General to decide, not you."

"Perhaps," Roth said, stroking the lapel of Lupin's new lightweight suit with the muzzle of the automatic. Then he smiled, like a student grateful to have had the opportunity to touch an author whose books he knew by heart, and smashed the butt of the automatic onto Lupin's aquiline nose, breaking it instantly. "Take him away," he ordered.

They dragged Lupin into a waiting Citroën, a man bowed with shame, as much as with pain, that he could have walked into such a simple trap.

Steve Wagner had been sitting up all night with a bottle of Madeleine Carpentier's overpriced hooch. The muezzin's calls were already floating up from the downtown prayer towers; but he was a long way away from Casablanca, and a good distance from the year 1942.

Her name was Helda, and he only had to give her his heel's flick-of-the-eyelid kind of come-on to realize that his whole approach was crude, like a thirteen-year-old trying on his first rubber. So finally, *faute de mieux*, he came mincing back and personally machinated a tight little maneuver (common as crap but still effective) where he halted by her table and rummaged in his pockets for cigarettes, then looked down with that shy look on his face like no one on earth could be for one moment out of a smoke, so could the lady kindly oblige?

What's the word they use? Kaleidoscopic? First in a hundred fragments that somehow exploded together to make a weekend at Étretat. That weekend, the weekend of 18 May 1940. There was that look, but this time close up, and again the heel in him took a pasting, like he wanted to climb out from under those flashy Parisian two-tone brogues of his and hide behind a sand castle. And then a clink of recognition, like she recollected his face, and a smile that wasn't trying to cover something. Just a smile. Her smile.

Fit the bits together, build up that kaleidoscope. The empty hole, the vast rooms of the Golf Hotel with the shuffling servants. A few kids playing on the sand. The click of the roulette wheel, and the usual early evening collection of born losers huddled round his table, where he had taken crude advantage of the fact that the regular croupiers had been called to the colors. Meanwhile, la belle France herself was going skint somewhere a hundred or so kilometers to the north.

They said the panzers had broken through. The news was scary. The names—Guderian and a flashy new guy called Rommel. Reynaud's face there in the papers, denying things, always with that conniving mistress, the Comtesse de Portes, by his side. Reynaud, the Prime Minister with the look of a man who needed a double scotch just about every quarter of an hour. Beside him also, Georges Martel. Solid, a rock of a man, the so-called Lion of Limoges. Impulsive, undeviating Nazi-hater. Maybe for good reasons, because he happened to be a Jew. Hang on tight, Georges Martel, because you're the balls of la belle France, the only politician there who seems to have a man-sized cock.

Cut the openers, shorten by about two and a half hours that classic little piece of slimy seduction he started pulling off in the Bar de Normandie. Whilst Bobbi ran through a lazy repertoire of the last great *chansons* of the Third Republic and no one listened to his cool piano, not him, not Helda, not Joe dozing behind his bar.

Cut straight on to the third floor. The finest suite the Golf Hotel could crudely boast. They say the bathroom's papered with bank notes. They say some of the *Louis-seize* could be *Louis-seize*. They say the view from the balcony is real sea and copper-bottomed waves. And that enough real dough has reclined on its voluminously sprung double bed to weigh down and sink the Banque de France.

They say . . . but now you know, Prize Heel. You're there. Except that it's just not that kind of scene. The lady's lying there and she's kicked off her snakeskin shoes, and her dove-gray Schiaparelli creation is shedding a few francs' worth of value every minute, because she's just lying in it, and smoking, and telling you things. And it's positively not a screwing scene. And the big joke is that what's killing everything is this lousy war, the same one that's speeding towards our backwater, Étretat, with all the power of the panzers' Mark III Mercedes engines. And again you're aced because everything she says makes you feel more like a Heel (the meanest variety of the species in the whole of crappy old France).

Because there's his picture in the silver-mounted frame by the bed, and he's smiling—which isn't that typical because he'd seen the same mug glaring at him in inky black spots from Paris *Soir* on drizzly winter evenings. Not a face he took to, with its huge jutting forehead, sunken eyes, thick nose, and sarcastic mouth. But now Georges Martel was needed, the whole terrific bulk of him, and she was telling him why. Dropping the names. . . . Reynaud, Daladier, Pétain and Gamelin, and this man whose obsessive willpower had almost single-handedly been driving the French war machine. The man whose weekend here at the Golf Hotel, Étretat, had been shot to bits by Guderian's panzers. The man whose Ministry (that of Affaires Intérieures) was strung out on the railroad at this moment somewhere between Paris and Tours; ultimate destination, Bordeaux.

And then he knew. She was the dame behind the guy behind the whole shooting match, the one who could keep it shooting. What was the song Bobbi had been playing down in the bar? At about three in the morning she started to hum it, and she clutched back and somehow remembered some of the punch lines:

You can't write a new song
When the old one's still there.

And he drew the curtains, and he just heard the sea out there where the moonlight was playing on the waves. And then he stumbled down to the cellar and cracked open a couple of bottles of Moët. And they held hands and sipped the booze, and he remembered more lines:

You can't write a new song
When the old song's still there,
You can't right an old wrong
When it won't disappear.

And then it was dawn, and the fishing boats were drawn up in a half circle all over Étretat. The dawn of nowhere.

Auguste Berthier was snoring in his single cot. Funny how he looked, asleep in bed without a woman. He looked like a forty-two-year-old baby in need of a mother. Auguste Berthier, you inveterate nigger-screwer! You were so goddamn corrupt. Whilst all the other Vichy *fonctionnaires* were licking Hitler's ass, you held your own tiny court in Casablanca's Medina. Taking bribes, screwing girls, slimily covering up your tracks. Auguste Berthier. A tiny dose of pure uncorrupted corruption is like an oasis shaded by pomegranates in the heat of the desert. It is humanity making its point.

Come to think of it, Auguste, you must be the last verifiable piece of humanity I know. Hey! That's a reflection on humanity, isn't it? It's time to empty this bottle of so-called Napoleon brandy and consider that maybe it wasn't only Pétain and Laval who betrayed France in June 1940, it was the whole human race who betrayed the whole human race. Big guys like General Weygand and Admiral Darlan. Little guys like Steve Wagner and Helda de Billancourt. There could never have been a month like it for betrayals, national and personal!

Guderian's panzers had twisted around and hit the coast at Abbeville, thus nicely severing the arteries of the entire British Expeditionary Force, along with assorted divisions of French and Belgians. And then they stopped to regroup on a line fifty or so kilometers north of the Golf Hotel, Étretat. Anyone with any savvy was heading south in whatever kind of transport might offer itself.

So that left about four of us. Bobbi, because he was tied to his piano by an unbreakable umbilical chord. Monsieur Blanchin, because the Golf Hotel was the only asset he had left. Me, because I'd run out of places, and maybe because I was curious to see for myself Hitler's nasty race. And Helda?

We talked about it in a haphazard kind of way, whilst Bobbi tinkled his sad old tune. Talked about it over Veuve Cliquot and Dom Pérignon, Mumm, Krug, and Pommery.

"Here's to you, honey," I'd say, and she'd give me that smile. Those deep blue eyes like she'd seen behind the whole crazy human condition and read it, which was crazy, because if there was ever a mixed-up *femme fatale*, it was Helda, Countess Billancourt.

You can't write a new song
When the old song's still there.

Sure, that was right, Bobbi had to be psychic. She couldn't get her mind off that old prize bullfrog, *soi-disant* Lion of Limoges. Trying to fend off Pétain and Laval and Weygand and Darlan and all life's clever opportunists with something crazy called patriotism.

You can't make a new start
When your heart's still mislaid . . .
You can't write a new song
When the old song still hurts.

The rich velour curtains of the Golf Hotel's plushest stateroom were drawn against the afternoon sun. And she held him, steadied him down, got him down from racing, down to a kind of movement that was imperceptible. And then still slower, and he screamed crazy things to her, because in that empty hotel there was no one to hear. And she held him tight and firm between her legs and between her eyes. And all she could say was "Stevie." Just that. "Stevie." As if that amounted to communication. And he knew he was sweet nowhere. OK, he occupied her body. But Georges Martel had taken out a lifetime's lease on her mind and her soul and her heart. And he knew he had a week, a day, or maybe not even till tomorrow left, and then the panzers hit Weygand with everything they had and the line just went up in smoke, and he was left trying to salvage anyone who could fit into a five-year-old Citroën. But mostly Helda.

He'd broken into an empty villa up the road to Fécamp and requisitioned it to meet his own special human emergency. As it happened, the owner had already hopped it down to Juan-les-Pins, leaving his second-best car, which was nonetheless earmarked for a place in history. The very private, very special history of Steve and Helda. So there he was, shivering outside the Golf Hotel at five in the morning. And he can see the flashes in the sky and hear Guderian's guns pounding closer.

And then a white-faced Bobbi comes down and tells him the Lady's Vanished. Clean disappeared off the face of the map. Which proves a point about life, proves at least that politicians are smarter than ordinary guys. And if they're that smarter I suppose it gives them a kind of right to louse up everyone's life.

It seems Georges Martel had sent a government car, with gasoline, chauffeur, upholstery, all paid for by the French taxpayer, to shuffle her out of Étretat by daring, cunning, exquisite timing and general, impossible *force majeure*. And he's still cranking the engine outside the Golf at five in the morning. Jerking his shoulder off, swinging the crank around like he was setting out to be prize strong man in some fair in Oklahoma. *You prize jerk.*

Oh yes, they had met again. That's the whole corny, cliché-ridden thing about love. You meet again. Strictly against the laws of chance, she had turned up one night at his wheel at Ritzi's place in Casablanca just murmuring "Stevie." Nothing else. In fact when he worked it out it was logical. Georges Martel had sailed into town in an old warship called the *Massilia*, hoping to raise the standard of resistance to Nazism in Africa. General Nogues's reaction had been to throw him into jail. Someone had said that sixty thousand francs was all it would take to buy his freedom. When you came to think of it, who was there better than Helda de Billancourt to try and push through a deal like that?

You met again, once, but not twice. That was the precise and platitudinous law regarding love affairs that didn't work out. And so it had to be a ghost, or at least a mirage, he had seen last night at Ritzi's. Besides, he knew for a fact that Helda had flown to England to await the release of lover-boy Martel. He knew. He had seen the Air France Dewoitine taxi away down the tarmac at Casablanca airport. For all time. The question remained, what was it he had seen at Ritzi's last night? A ghost? A vision? A projection of his own mind? A trick of light? Steve Wagner knew only one thing for certain. He had to go back and find out.

Still the whirr of life from the little narrow road that threaded through the Medina. Still the mosquito drone of chanting, parrot-squawking, Arab street cries, babies squealing, and two-stroke exhausts popping. Still that sweet sickly odor—half jasmine, half Gauloise, with a pungent additive of diarrhea to hot it up. Auguste Berthier was putting his head into the lion's den, or to put it another way, renewing his contacts with the Casablanca police force.

The Medina police station there had seen a bit of scene shifting (different people, different times). The full-length oil portrait of the aged Maréchal in horizon blue that Auguste himself had had hastily daubed by one Mustapha Ahmed, a procurer of young Arab girls from the Casbah (who also turned in a few *jolies vues* for the tourist market), was still there in the central hallway, covering the spot where in balmy prewar days the irresolute features of President Lebrun had peered down quizzically. But now the portrait had a new companion: a poster showing the meeting at Montoire, in late 1940, between Hitler and Pétain. While the two men's hands were clenched in a handshake of sculptured perpetuity, the Führer's eyes threatened to bore through and annihilate the Maréchal's limpid gaze. Another change. They had had to add two more benches to accommodate all the extra people, visa-seekers, informers and friends and relations of unlocated prisoners, who wanted a discreet chat with someone in authority.

Auguste approached the old sergeant at the inquiry desk (Sergeant Marchand, wasn't it?) and winked timidly.

"My appointment is with Inspector Launay," he whispered. He looked anxiously around him, noted the crowd of hunched figures and the stamped-out cigarettes at their feet.

"Of course if he is busy I am quite prepared to wait." He really was. In fact he was wondering if, after all, it might be more prudent to tiptoe off again.

"Yes, I have your name here, Monsieur Berthier," the old sergeant said (his face had given no sign of recognition). "However, there has been a change. Your appointment is with the Chief Inspector himself. He will see you now."

It was as if the decrepit old sergeant had reached up and slugged him under the heart. The Chief Inspector of Casablanca's Deuxième Bureau! He was taking enough risks in approaching his old friend Paul Launay as it was. Only the knowledge that Launay was a fellow realist and would understand the subtle nuances of what he wanted to say had kept him on course for the one building in Casablanca he least wanted to revisit.

But there was another surprise in store for Berthier, and this was the identity of the new Chief Inspector of the Casablanca police force. In the vast fourth-floor office, where a certain Chief Inspector Berthier had slept off his hangovers in a peeling leather chair, sat that frighteningly serious boy, Lucien Roth, at one time his embarrassingly vigilant assistant in the Department of Fraud.

"You are the Chief Inspector?" He tried to make it sound like a statement, not a disbelieving question, but the question won out.

"As you notice, there have been a number of changes since your departure," the boy said. There was a neat new desk, an upright new chair, and a new picture on the wall. Laval, Darnand, and Reichs Ambassador Abetz reviewing a parade of bereted crackpots somewhere in France. "Perhaps you will agree there was room for improvement. We had become lazy and in some areas ineffective. Middle-aged attitudes were slowing our efficiency. There was an unhealthy smell of the old Third Republic about the police force. All that we are changing." He looked up with a proud little gleam in his blue eyes, as when in the old days he had uncovered some minor racket Auguste might have preferred to have left covered. "We are beginning to move with the times," he said.

"Time is precious," Auguste said lamely. "I did not wish to take up yours, Inspector Roth." His hands waved emptily.

"Yes, Launay told me about your telephone call, and I was interested. I mean in your reasons for returning to Casablanca. Particularly"—he was examining Auguste with genuine interest, not malice—"since you face charges of illegal dealings, desertion, and criminal misuse of your authority."

"I have information that may be of value," Auguste blurted out.

"Although I have not yet myself made a detailed study of your file, it is possible that you could also be charged with treason to the state," Lucien Roth said, again without malice, just interest in the possibility. "As you know, that is a capital offense."

"I have information that may be of value to you, Chief Inspector." Auguste bowed, looking up at the same time to note the brief stab of pleasure it gave this overgrown schoolboy to hear himself recognized by his full title by his former boss.

It was, of course, not the kind of betrayal he had intended to make. With this earnest young Alsatian (was he really aged about thirty, or more like forty?) a betrayal could be spelled out only in terms of simple black and white. With his old friend Inspector Launay it would have been quite different, and altogether more acceptable to the conscience. With Launay there would have been meaningful nods, shrugs, and inclinations of the head. Nothing that any outsider, even God, would recognize as a frightened man turning informer on his chief. Perhaps over a small glass of cognac the dealing might have become more precise. A broadly dropped hint, for example, that if pardons were to be extended to himself and his American friend Steve, he might somewhere in his sieve of a brain be able to trace the name and address of BCRAM's principal agent in Casablanca.

The transaction would have been so tactful and delicate that even Auguste himself would hardly have realized that he had betrayed the Kellerman mission for the sake of his own skin. Here with the streamlined new Chief Inspector Lucien Roth he was forced to admit this was exactly what he was trying to do, and as a result, he had to find a new motive which could even have been true: he was doing it for his friend Steve's sake.

"A certain professor," he confessed, "an authority on Latin American antiquities, but quite possibly traveling under an alias. You will be able to judge better of my loyalty to the Marshal when I tell you he is BCRAM's principal agent, now at large in Casablanca."

"You were wise, quite wise, to come here," Roth said.

I am mad, quite mad, to come here, Auguste thought to himself, but what else was there to do? That maniac Lupin had clearly managed to persuade Steve they were on a mission of sacred importance, and not a lunatic's errand. There was no way to stop this suicidal charade other than putting a stop to its deranged architect.

"I am talking of a plot, monsieur," Auguste said, "a stupid plot, planned and executed by one fanatic, and one fanatic alone."

He faltered. He did not seem to have the Chief Inspector's undivided attention. Roth had four or five pieces in front of him on the desk like small wedges, six-inch-long pieces of burnished steel honed to a point at one edge. He played with them with the absorption of a small boy with a toy building set, letting them slide through his hands, massing them together, and then dispersing them.

Finally Roth said, "You refer, I suspect, to the Jewish Marxist lackey called Lupin."

"You mean?"

"Yes, he was taken into custody this morning. But perhaps you would identify him for us."

They went down a passage, but not towards the six diminutive cells, where in Auguste's time dope traffickers had been given a night or so to cool off. They went through a door into a different section of the police station. A place of desks and files and old carpets, a kind of storage depot. Except that now they knocked on the door and it was opened by an armed policeman in shirt sleeves, the sweat dripping off his brow.

There were one or two other Vichy policemen in this room, and the degree of sweat they were exuding was something that had never till this moment infiltrated Auguste's delicately hairy nostrils. One small sniff of it had the vomit starting to move deep within his throat, erupting up in a paroxysm of disgust.

The clue lay in a body stretched across the plain deal table in the center of the room: both legs splayed wide out and tied to opposite legs. A naked body, which was now still and lifeless, a mop of black hair, resting on the tabletop.

But it was what had happened lower down that was making Auguste break his normal rules of politesse and start to vomit in public. Thick steel wedges, like the ones Roth had been handling on his desk, had been driven bang into the anus of this corpse, and then others splayed in and hammered home on the sides. The effect had been to split Claude Lupin's backside wide open to reveal in anatomical detail the entire lower part of the human alimentary canal. The corpse had literally been driven apart all the way up to the start of the rib cage.

"As you see," Roth said, "we have made some improvements in our interrogation techniques in the past few months." He wasn't joking. He was looking at Auguste with the same little gleam of pride that had characterized his minor successes in the Department of Fraud. "However, we did not obtain one-hundred-percent-satisfactory results. We are still anxious to ascertain the identities of his two accomplices. Code names X and Y."

But Berthier had already lurched from the room back into the familiar corridor. His whole body was convulsed with spasms of vomit.

They knew they were going to land somewhere, "over there," and that it was going to be on enemy-held coast. Hadn't they spent the whole of September climbing in and out of landing craft in Chesapeake Bay? What PFC Joe Offenbach and his buddies still didn't know was where they were going, and who exactly they were going to fight. They guessed it must be the Germans—those were the guys Staff Sergeant Eklund kept telling them would shoot their asses off if they didn't keep them down under fire. At the same time there was a rumor going around that it might be the Italians. Apparently Italians didn't keep spaghetti houses or sell ice cream in Europe. They marched about in jackboots, trying to kill people for Hitler. In point of fact they couldn't be sure they weren't going to fight the Japs; although the flat silhouette of Hampton Roads, Virginia, was crawling away to stern and they seemed to be heading the wrong way for the Pacific.

One thing was certain this early morning on 24 October 1942; they were going to hit somebody with a hell of a lot of stuff. Standing on the transport, Joe Offenbach and his buddy, Lou Alverson, could count thirty-six other transports. (Each with the deck crowded with GIs in battle order.) Up ahead the battleships *Massachusetts*, *Texas*, and *New York* were carving creamy white wakes out of the steel-gray sea. The giant aircraft carrier USS *Ranger* and the escort carriers *Santee* and *Chenango* were coming in to line to port, and two more escort carriers were visible to starboard.

Farther out to sea were streaks of foam, marking the progress of seven cruisers, headed by USS *Augusta*, flagship of Rear Admiral Henry Hewitt and temporary CP of the expedition's commander, General George S. Patton, Jr.

Farther ahead still, only visible because the sun was starting to show over the horizon, were the gnat-sized specks of eighty-one escorting destroyers.

"Look at it—take a good look at it, you lousy landlubbers," the overfamiliar voice of Sergeant Eklund boomed behind them, "you're never going to see a thing like this again—even if it is the goddamn navy."

PFC Offenbach took a good look. "Hope it scares the Germans," he said.

"Yeah." Sergeant Eklund's face freckled into a dubious smile. "Or the French."

"The French, Sarge?"

"Sure. You've heard of the French, haven't you? Guys who eat frogs' legs and screw other guys' wives."

"But, Sarge . . ." Joe Offenbach looked as worried as if his high school teacher had asked him to explain Pythagoras's theorem. "But, Sarge, the French are on our side, aren't they?"

"Not anymore they aren't," Sergeant Eklund told him confidently. "Do you think we'd be hitting them with all this firepower if the bums were still on our side? OK, you want to know where we're heading. Now we're under way I can tell you official—we're going to Casablanca to lick hell out of the lousy French!"

"Casablanca!" A look of dawning comprehension suddenly spread over young Offenbach's strictly nonintellectual face. "Hey! We saw the movie in Norfolk—that special preview Warner Brothers laid on. That's where Humphrey Bogart meets all those dames, isn't it, Sarge?"

"Hey, Vincent," Nad Klaf bawled down the long-distance wire. . . . "Yeah, it's me—Nad. Hey, Vincent, you'll never guess where I am—back in Norfolk, Virginia, for Chrissake! . . . Listen, don't hang up, Vincent—the crazy thing is I couldn't be anywhere in the whole darned world more relevant. Listen—are you there Vincent? . . . this town is crawling with *soldaten, militaros, hommes de combats Américain*—do you *savez?* . . . Jesus no, I haven't been drinking— there are some things you don't spell out on a transcontinental call in wartime! But I'm telling you the waters hereabouts are stacked with *barcas, bateaux de guerres,* Anchors Away guys—do you read me? It's good-bye Broadway, hello *parlez-vous,* if you get my meaning. But it's better than France, Vincent. I got talking to some guys with brass on their shoulders last night and over a few high-balls the whole scenario spilled out—it's Webster's Dictionary, Vincent. It's the copy of Shakespeare you buy at the drugstore. . . . The hell I've been drinking. I'm telling you the whole goddamn *expeditionay* is Morocco bound! I've wired Sodersheim—they're fixing me a passage. Tell me a great moment in history that Nad Klaf missed. . . .

"OK, so it isn't breakfast time yet in California, but here's the news. I'm gonna do two great things for you, Vincent. I'm gonna introduce you to the original Casablanca property, and I'm gonna give you an exclusive option on the sequel. . . . Yeah, *Casablanca the Second!*

"And, Vincent, if you picked up the hints I've been dropping you'll appreciate that's a property that's gonna make *Gone With the Wind* look like a B movie! That's some package, eh? . . . Are you there, Vincent? . . . And it's just for you because you're a personal friend of mine and by and large you've always treated me right. I'm not kidding, Vincent, when you get the new scenario—and don't you dare lose *this one!*—I don't think we're gonna argue about a little thing like my rights in *Casablanca One.* Vincent, I got to go now but . . ."

Nad Klaf was right. Norfolk, Virginia, this October was crawling with US armed forces, about to embark on the biggest amphibious operation to date in the world's history. Right now a red-faced brig-adier general was peering meanly into Nad's hotel phone booth, wondering perhaps what this seedy-looking citizen was shouting his mouth off about!

"Listen, I'll phone you back, Vincent." Klaf reluctantly hung up.

He had chosen a convenient time to revisit Chez Maurice, alias Ritzi's. The place had just been raided. He stood in the shadows, watching the trench-coated plainclothesmen walking back into their Citroëns with that hangdog air policemen have the world over when they are coming away empty-handed. An outraged official of the Parti Populaire Français had followed them onto the pavement. He was telling them in frank language that they had no business disturbing the wholesome relaxation of patriots. He was suggesting, with a wave of a brawny fist, that if they were proper servants of the state they would be flushing Gaullist rats out of their sewers around the Avenue Pasteur and pulling in more Jews from the Porte Negve ghetto. He was asking how they dared to waste honest taxpayers' money harrying sober citizens of conspicuous loyalty to the Marshal.

All this was fine by Steve. He slipped in as soon as the last police Citroën had departed. Being essentially a modest individual, it didn't occur to him that the man they had been looking for was himself. Bobbi was playing "Je T'Attendrai." It wasn't *their* tune, but he had played it at the Golf Hotel that early summer in 1940 while they were waiting for the world to blow up. It wasn't *their* tune, but they'd danced to it, and the tinkling melody was enough to make his heart thump at least as hard as a Luger at his back. Almost shyly, he searched the hazy gloom for the table where last night he'd seen this ghost. Yes, that was the table, but no, Jesus, that wasn't her. That was the pink bulbous neck of a middle-aged PPF officer and that was no lady he was holding in a bear hug. He lowered his eyes in disgust at the spectacle of a fat officer of Jacques Doriot's army of patriots planting juicy kisses on a boy in khaki.

There was another place where she could be, or rather where the ghost could be. Funny not to think of it before, because after all this was the room where every night, until one particular night, he had dutifully called, "Faites vos jeux," for Ritzi. This was the night Auguste Berthier had asked him to fix the wheel, remember? He had this new dame, dusky little Tasmin from the Sahara, he wanted to show a good time. He reached for the wheel, to start it. To place two thousand Vichy francs in the soft lap of the fair Tasmin. Except he looked up, by some croupier's acquisitive, predatory sense. Because bigger buffalo were entering the shooting compound. He scooped up the chips and paid the winner. Tasmin gave him a sticky little kiss. But he wasn't looking at her. This lady coming through the door was showing up only twelve months late. She was meant to be waiting for him outside the Golf Hotel at Étretat in the summer of 1940. Maybe there had been a mistake about the venue, because here she was at Ritzi's place in Casablanca in June 1941.

Helda, Comtesse de Billancourt, opened her handbag and placed twenty thousand on the table. She was a loser all right. She hadn't even had a fair toss of the wheel. Your eyes caught in a long swoony slow-motion. And held. And held. And held.

He strolled round and told her, "Gaming's over tonight, sister."

She said, "Stevie."

He said, "Didn't I tell you? The game's over."

She said, "Stevie."

He said, "Crap."

She said, "Can't we talk?"

He said, "I'd prefer a screw."

She said, "All right. Where?"

He couldn't touch her. He gave her a light and lit one himself. He said, "I don't go for you anymore. It's just that I hate to see money flung into the craphouse."

She said, "Just because I've lost a bit . . ."

He said, "You've got to take your place after Inspector Berthier's latest whore."

She said, "Can you make me win? Please, please, Steve. Just make me win."

He said, "How much?"

She said, "Sixty thousand francs."

He said, "OK, and then get shot."

He didn't have to be Einstein to figure out the deal. He knew all about lover boy. The hero who just failed by a millimeter to prop up the tottering Third Republic of France. Lost against Pétain and Laval, just as Helda today was destined to win, just so long as she then slid out of your life. That was the bargain. Flush old memories into the sewage system and start another kind of life. He had a word with Auguste Berthier. He said, "I want a boat out of Fedala tonight." He explained what Helda had told him. Nogues had found his price. Sixty thousand francs to let Georges Martel slip from his prison, and then Georges Martel, in just a few hours, could be resting in the Governor's house in Gibraltar. A more magical man than de Gaulle by far to lead the Free French cause.

Berthier grasped it straight. One good deed deserved another, or maybe there was more in it than that. He had a friend called Karl Bidelle. He kept a two-master in Fedala harbor. He had the OK from Auguste to get clear of Moroccan waters with the most majestic patriot of France, out of Nogues's dungeons, to bind together the Free French and bring all Africa over to the Allies. The rest was formality.

He said, "Number 13."

She said, "Isn't that unlucky?"

He said, "You're right. But that's the number."

When it came up he put a hand on her arm. "Keep it there." He wasn't in the mood for gratitude. She scooped up a hundred thousand francs. And she gave him a kiss on the cheek. Her arm slid across his shoulder. He told her straight, "Clear out. You've got your money. What the hell else do you want?"

She cleared out. And he phoned Karl Bidelle. That was how you and she met again in Casablanca.

What do you know, they had turned the place into a billiard room. No wheels, no dames. Just fat little fascist bastards leaning over the green baise showing big sweat patches around the armpits of their khaki shirts.

It was time to find Rubin. He needed a drink. A heavy hand on his shoulder. That old persecuted feeling.

"Hey, Steve, you crazy bastard, what are you doing here?"

Hal Newport, a rising star in the U S State Department was pumping him by the hand, giving him his big boyish smile. They had met before in Spain when Steve was fighting on the side of the Loyalists and Hal was sitting on the fence, along with the U S Government and the rest of the Western democracies. "It's a small world, Steve. Or is it? Weren't you a prominent citizen around here once?"

"I never try to be prominent," Steve said.

"Tell you what you've got to do—you gotta help split a bottle of champagne with me and Tina. Tina's my wife, incidentally. She's over here for the trip."

He was propelled over to a table with an ice bucket and a gray-haired woman with a big cleavage and a faraway smile.

"You another cop?" Mrs. Newport asked, shading her eyes as if she were looking out to sea at an unidentified warship.

"I'm just American," Steve told her, grabbing the chair nearest the pillar so as to protect himself from the public gaze.

"I told you I got nothing to declare, *rien à declarer,*" Tina Newport said.

He wondered if she had had too much to drink or whether it was just a little difficult to talk clearly when you had a champagne glass stuck permanently between your teeth.

"This is my old pal, Steve Wagner, darling," her husband explained. Out of the side of his mouth he added, "Maybe you've missed it. We've just been raided."

"This place is lousy enough without having cops crawling all over you. Hell, take a look at the clientèle. I mean, for Chrissake!" Mrs. Newport said.

"Now, darling, this is Casablanca, remember. It's got to be different from New York."

"No, your wife's right," Steve said. "There's a lot of things wrong back home, but they wouldn't let this gang of fascist thugs and perverts even stand on the sidewalk in New York."

"Steve, I can see you haven't changed a bit," Hal chuckled, although he was looking searchingly into the hollows around his old friend's eyes. "Hey, but I heard a report you were with de Gaulle's gang in Brazzaville." Another genial Hal Newport chuckle. "Guess that couldn't be true or you wouldn't be exactly welcome in Casablanca, would you?"

"The trouble with this town is that it's crawling with Americans," Tina Newport muttered, "everywhere you go, lousy American diplomats like Hal here!"

"Maybe they don't know you're here," Hal persisted.

"I'm not advertising the fact," Steve said, lighting a cigarette.

"Thousands of lousy Midwestern diplomats and their goddamn wives. Everyplace you go. We might just as well have stayed in fucking Washington!"

Hal smiled placatingly at his wife and said, "You know, Steve, more and more you remind me of someone out of the movies—Cagney is it? Or am I thinking of Bogart? You've got this kind of hunted look. They're not hunting for you, are they, Steve?"

"Know something else?" Tina Newport said. "This town is crawling with German officers. I mean real, live German officers. Know something else? They've got bigger cocks than our guys have—a whole lot bigger. You oughta take a look at their pants!"

"Forgive me, Steve, but I just had a crazy idea. That police raid just now. They weren't looking for you, were they?"

Steve said, "You haven't told me about yourself, Hal. You used to be one of the State Department's blue-eyed boys. If Casablanca's a promotion on Madrid, things must be hotting up around here."

"I'll say things are hotting up, the whole town is crawling with lousy Americans and Germans with big cocks. Suddenly everybody's crawling all over the goddamned Vichy French. Want to know why? Hey, give me another glass of that soda pop."

Hal dropped his smile. "Maybe you'd like to try something softer, darling."

"I said soda pop, Daddy-o. What the hell was I talking about?"

"Darling, we're talking about Steve. We're trying to find out what he's doing with himself these days. You're not still working for de Gaulle, are you, Steve? That could be kind of dangerous here."

"You were talking about big cocks," Steve reminded Mrs. Newport.

"Why don't you go order me a double scotch?" Tina told her husband. She turned her misting-over blue eyes back to Steve. "That's right. Know something? They've got a real big cock coming here next week. A genuine German general, name of Kellerman or some goddamned thing. Know something? I'd like to meet a real, live German general. Know what I'd do? I'd walk straight up to the bastard and tell him what I thought of that louse Hitler. I'd give him hell, even if the bastard tried to rape me! Know what I mean?"

Suddenly they had company. Two large-fisted cretins in berets were leaning very hard on the table. They were shouting in French that they understood English and resented any imputations on the honor of Wehrmacht General Joachim Kellerman—a man who had commanded French heroes in battle—particularly from Jew-loving American pigs. They were, incidentally, drunker than Tina Newport.

Hal Newport was almost diplomat enough to rise to the occasion. He invoked the spirit of Lafayette. He recalled Lindbergh's fabulous flight to Paris, and he quoted an appropriate snatch from the "Marseillaise." His wife told the pair of them to go fuck themselves.

Meanwhile Steve pushed back his chair and stood up ramrod straight. His knuckles had turned a new shade of white. He hated aggressive drunks, particularly aggressive drunks with the smell of beer and aqua vitae on their breath. But there was more to this pair of colonial collaborators than the smell of bad liquor. There was the sour smell of disappointed manhood and frustrated hate that somehow seemed to go with underarm sweat patches on khaki paramilitary shirts. It was a smell that made him want to lash out blindly. Before Hal Newport could stop him, he had suggested to the first bruiser that he come outside. In fact three of them came outside, into the little alley where Ritzi stacked his empties and the neighbors threw out their dead cats.

Hal Newport followed Steve at a distance. He said, "Steve, you know I can't get involved in a brawl." So it was three to one. The burliest contender had a knife. He took it out of his boot and turned it around in the crescent moonlight, crooning to Steve about how he intended to use it. His buddy, the thug nearest to Steve, looked as if he were going to use his fists, only with an additive. He was fitting a strip of metal around his right paw. A piece of bicycle chain maybe. Who waited around to be hammered with hard metal? Steve dummied with his fists and kicked the patriot hard in the crotch.

"Leave it there, Steve, you'll only make trouble for yourself," Hal Newport called as the patriot rolled around among Ritzi's empties. This brought in number three. He got Steve around the neck and started biting off his right ear. He would have made a better job of it if he hadn't stopped to tell him what happened to Communist pigs who picked fights with decent Frenchmen.

The knife owner saw an opportunity for himself. He came forward, mumbling about life, death, and politics. His knife was pointed well below the belt.

"They'd throw the book at me if I got involved in this!" Hal Newport exclaimed.

The ear-eater is taking a trip through space. Then he's rolling up against his comrade with the naked blade, and Steve is reinforcing the impact with mean clouts to a vulnerable paunch and another in the face. Then they're all rolling about among Ritzi's empties and other garbage nobody would choose to be too specific about. And although he's outnumbered in terms of fists, teeth, and toe caps, Steve has the advantage that he hasn't been swilling Alsatian beer with aqua vitae chasers all evening.

And finally Hal's words are getting through to him. "Leave it there, Steve. For God's sake, leave it there or someone will send for the police!"

"OK, Hal, I'll leave it there."

He got up and lit a Chesterfield from a flattened pack. One of the patriots got up too. He had a lot more suggestions about what happened to Communist Jewish turds who insulted France's allies, but he wasn't any longer trying to practice what he preached.

Steve told Hal to give his regards to his wife and walked straight home to Madeleine's. He didn't look his best. You could say he looked as if he had seen a ghost. Only he hadn't seen a ghost, or a mirage, or anything that could once have been Helda Billancourt. So he would have to go back to Chez Maurice.

There was another reason why he would have to go back. The battling boys of the PPF had done a lot of talking for street fighters, and one piece of information they had let slip was this: General Joachim Kellerman of the Wehrmacht was due to be the gang's guest of honor at a slap-up reception at Chez Maurice on Saturday night.

Nad Klaf sat in the ballroom of the converted liner USS *Oregon Star* and ruminated dully upon his fate. Look at it any way around, it seemed to work out as even steven. Sure, he'd hitched himself a ride on the invasion armada (ultimate destination, Casablanca), but the Atlantic was working itself up into a sickening swell. Sure, Sodersheim Syndicate had pulled strings and got him recognized as Official War Correspondent, with officer's uniform and all, but he'd forgotten to check out the fact that the U S Navy was strictly dry, and if the frogs in Africa put up any resistance he'd need all the extra high-proof courage he could get. Even so he'd have settled for the chance to get back to Casa and stake his claim to a nice little bit of celluloid real estate. But Sodersheim had got through to him just before the *Oregon Star* churned off into the wild Atlantic with new instructions.

"Get us the lowdown on the political setup over there," was the order. "Carve your way through the political jungle and give us a rundown on what our boys are fighting for out there. And how this guy de Gaulle fits in."

Now what political flea was licking which political ass hole was a matter of nil concern to Nad Klaf. (His spectacles had an exclusive silver screen tint to them.) But if he didn't come up with the goodies they'd bust him when he reached port—and then Good-bye to Casablanca.

"What's it all about?" he asked a friendly-looking Captain.

"Relax, Nad," smiled the freckled-faced Andy Delsarto. "Look, it's easy; in fact it's even mind-bending. Lift up any stone in Vichy France or French North Africa and what do you find? Some small-time politician or general crawling out to stake his claim to be Emperor of all the French.

"Let's try and put it simply," the freckled-faced young lecturer in Applied Psychology told him, "because this is important. We are a citizen army and proud of it. We do not obey orders blindly, we do not put our dumb heads over the parapet and charge. As citizens of a democracy we ask questions about the war. Relate the military operations to the overall politico-strategic situation. Somehow connect military means to political ends."

A loud burp from Nad Klaf brought Captain Delsarto's eyes up momentarily from his notes in owlish puzzlement. "OK," he grinned, "everyone else is playing pinups, let's join in. But I have to warn you, some of these specimens aren't one half as cute as Betty Grable.

These guys may not be photogenic, but they all have one thing in common. Egos big as King Kong's. There are a number of characters in this little *drôle de drame*," he was saying. "Our task, along with General Eisenhower, President Roosevelt, Secretary Cordell Hull, and the State Department, is to give them a quick frisk-over. Separate the boys from the men, and finally cast one of them for lead role. But as I get into it you'll realize it ain't that easy. Right. The little guy on the spot is a piece of *trompe-d'oeil* called General Auguste Nogues. He looks like a general, but strictly he isn't. He's a deft little politician who happens to like military drag. As of now he's top dog in Morocco. He's played footsy with Daladier and Reynaud and Pétain and Laval. He's a friend to everyone and loyal to none. He's as shifty as a desert coyote, and the State Department has stamped him UNRELIABLE. All the same he's there, so we can't exactly ignore him. Maybe we might even make a deal with him, temporarily, of course. However, this guy Nogues has under him another character, another soldier, but there the resemblance ends. Now the good General Béthouart is the local hero of the piece. He hates Vichy, loves us. When we put down in Casablanca he'd give his right arm to roll out the red carpet for us. And that's great news because he happens to be commander of the Casablanca Division, the liveliest force around for miles. Only trouble is he's a bit of a flyweight. So thanks for the promises, Béthouart, but we're not exactly counting on you."

"Thanks," breathed Nad Klaf, "as the guy suggested. Nogues supposes his toes are roses. Why the hell is the U S Navy always dry?"

"Of course we have our pinups too," Andy Delsarto was confessing. "But they're strictly uncaricaturable. One's Bob Murphy, who's splitting his ass trying to make quart-size Nogues go with pint-size Béthouart. There are other stalwarts in the list. Bobby O'Brien, Jerry Daniels, Hal Newport, to name but one."

The *Oregon Star* began to kick and spin in a mid-Atlantic upsurge, as likewise did Nad Klaf's head.

Auguste sat on his bed back at Madeleine Carpentier's perusing a picture book, designed sometime in the early thirties to titillate lackluster men about Paris. He was looking at the photograph of a priest who'd got his dog collar in the wrong place. Instead of the neck it was hanging round a fully erect penis. Of course there was a choirboy on the opposite page, or rather a girl half dressed as a choirboy, exposing a naked bum. At any other time Auguste would have smiled. Now he had to get up and vomit into the washbasin. The picture of the naked bum had acted like a lighted fuse to the horror of what he had seen in the Medina police station that afternoon. He wondered if he would ever be able to look at a naked bum again.

Steve came into the room when he was washing out his mouth.

"How you doing, old pal?"

"Steve, you're looking terrible."

"You want to know what you look like? You look like death."

Auguste lit a cigarette and tried to seem nonchalant. He thought how vile a cigarette tasted when you had vomit on your breath.

He said, "On the whole my news is good. I hope you haven't been in a fight."

"Just an unimportant argument."

"As you suggested, Steve, I have been renewing my contacts with the Casablanca police force. They took Lupin off a plane at the airport. He won't be returning."

"What do you know?"

"Did he leave any message to say it was canceled?"

"How could he? He was . . ." No. He must be careful not to let his friend know where he had been or, precisely, what he had seen. "It's not easy to get messages out of the cells of the Medina police station. Believe me, I know."

"Look, Auguste, we had an arrangement," Steve drawled. "If there were any fresh instructions, any change of orders, there was going to be a message at the reception desk at the Hotel Majestic. I went to the Hotel Majestic this afternoon. There's no message."

Berthier blinked at his friend in amazement. He knew that Steve could be headstrong. But this was just sheer oafishness.

"My dear Steve, Lupin is dead . . . or at least under close arrest."

"Here's another item of inside information," Steve said. "General Joachim Kellerman is cordially invited to dine by the dregs of Casablanca at Ritzi's next Saturday night, November 8. Auguste, that kraut general is going to be just five hundred yards up the block, swilling back Ritzi's poison and just asking to be a dead kraut general."

Auguste wanted to tug in exasperation at his moustache, but he had shaved it off as part of his disguise.

"Steve, is it possible that you've gone quite insane? The climate perhaps in Brazzaville. Or perhaps the whiskey—it tasted like wood alcohol, and I shouldn't be surprised if it was. Perhaps also your remarkable abstinence with women is beginning to have its effect. Can't you see it's irrelevant where Kellerman is going to be next Saturday night? He can be tucked up in bed next door for all I care, because there is no longer any necessity to kill him, if, indeed, there ever was. No, don't interrupt—listen. You don't listen enough, my friend. In your eagerness to slaughter Aryans in uniform, did you ever pause to ask yourself what the purpose was of this completely suicidal mission?"

"You're talking like the old Auguste," Steve told him with a snarling grin. "I mean the old Inspector of the Casablanca police force, Auguste the affable appeaser, the genial exponent of 'live and let live,' the archapostle of the quiet life. Auguste, if the Congo turned me crazy, Casablanca is turning you soft. What do you want? To sit around here until they give you your pension back? You lousy old Pink Baboon!"

Auguste shifted on his brothel bed.

"Steve, we don't have to sit around anywhere. We have money—good counterfeit money—we can go where we like, as long as we travel discreetly. This evening we could hire a car and drive to Rabat—I could arrange the necessary papers. We could catch the Lisbon plane from there. No, don't worry about exit visas. I'm convinced Lisbon would suit us, Steve. I understand it's quite gay and dissolute. Like the old Casablanca we knew and loved. Please think about Lisbon, Steve."

Steve said, "Sorry, Auguste, but I got a date at Ritzi's next Saturday night. I don't know exactly who I'd be offending if I broke it. I just know I can't break it. It's a date." He picked up a bottle of Courvoisier from the windowsill. "Drink," he suggested grimly.

It was the morning after their evening at Ritzi's. For Tina Newport most mornings were the morning after. She was sitting on the patio of the luxurious Anfa villa in a single-piece bathing suit sipping at a highball. Through a murky headache she was watching her husband pacing up and down the Moroccan-style tiles (actually made in Limoges) and wondering why the hell he didn't sit down.

He said, "It's no good, Tina. I've got to call Jerry Daniels about Steve."

She said, "Why, for Chrissake, don't you just pour yourself a drink? So we all feel like shit this morning."

"He didn't come clean with me, Tina. He's hiding something."

"So what? Did you come clean with him?"

Hal Newport threw out his arms despairingly. He looked pretty piquant and handsome in the bright Moroccan morning, a tall, well-built, late-thirty-year-old, accessorized by an English-style blazer, a Brooks Brothers shirt, and a St. Paul's tie: a model diplomat in any climate.

"Look, Steve's a pal, but heck, you should have seen him lay into those guys at Chez Maurice. I think he's working for de Gaulle."

"De Gaulle, de Gaulle, de Gaulle," Tina intoned. "I wish the hell you'd tell me what you and the State Department have against that guy. Maybe he's got BO."

Hal Newport flashed a forbearing smile. "Listen, Tina. It's wonderful you were able to make this trip. I want it to be a real vacation for you, and that means leaving the politics to me."

Tina clapped her hands for the Moroccan houseboy. It was only ten-thirty, but already she was feeling like another drink. She said, "Personally, I don't see why the hell you have to go round ass-licking these French creeps when back home five million dough-boys are boarding their transports—every damned man of them Morocco bound."

Hal Newport paled at this casual leak of the top-secret Operation TORCH. "Are you crazy, Tina? In front of the houseboy?"

"The poor kid doesn't understand a word of English. Do you, Mustapha? 'Operation TORCH.' Mean anything to you, sonny? Look, he thinks it's an indecent suggestion."

The boy poured Tina Newport her second drink of the morning and shambled back into the cool shadows of the villa.

Hal whispered, "We need the goodwill of the French authorities here to make sure our boys are able to land unopposed. Can't you see how a guy like Steve, operating under orders from de Gaulle, could screw the whole thing up?"

"Tell you one thing," Tina burped. "I'm sure as hell he's a better screw than you."

That settled it. Hal Newport walked stiffly back into the villa and put through a call to a Mr. Jerry Daniels, ostensibly an agent for an American shipping firm, but in fact a senior OSS agent in French North Africa.

Jerry Daniels was a graduate of Notre Dame University. Hal Newport was a Princetonian. Jerry Daniels was a crew-cut redhead who tended to sweat profusely under the African sun. Hal Newport had the breeding and deodorants to keep his cool. Jerry Daniels was an expert in espionage and dirty tricks. Hal Newport was a career diplomat, conscious that as a representative of US power he mustn't know what the left hand was doing. They were as unalike as two men could be, but they were linked by the urgent demands of necessity and Operation TORCH.

"Jesus!" Jerry Daniels whistled as he put down the phone. "We need this Steve Wagner like a hole in the head."

Even before Hal Newport's call came through, Jerry's office had been thrown into a turmoil. Until this morning everything had been fine and dandy. America had discovered its own de Gaulle. His name was General Henri Giraud, a political ignoramus well content to govern French North Africa on behalf of the United States. "Kingpin," as Roosevelt liked to call him, was already en route for Gibraltar. Then suddenly this morning the whole beautiful plan had started to come apart. Admiral Darlan, Vichy's most prestigious commander, had flown into Algiers on a sickbed call to his son, Alain. So long as Darlan was in North Africa there was no chance that local Vichy governors and officers could be persuaded to switch loyalties to Giraud. A whole new ball game had to be set in motion. An approach would have to be made to Darlan, and a brand new set of bribes would have to be dangled. There would also have to be solemn undertakings that no Gaullists were going to get a chance to rock the boat.

And then suddenly here was Hal Newport on the line in Casablanca saying he happened to have a gunman friend who'd just flown in from Brazzaville with every appearance of making mayhem on behalf of the Cross of Lorraine. It was the last straw.

"Steve Wagner," Jerry sighed to himself as he leafed through the dossier they'd already put on his desk. "Participated in liberal demonstrations back home. Fought for the Communists in Spain. Shanghaied a French civil aircraft on the Dakar run, forced it to land in Free French territory. . . . It figures."

Jerry bit hard on his wad of spearmint. Then he decided. "Someone's going to have to do something about taking this guy out!"

Hi there, lovely. Hi, you there. Juz settle in. Grab yourself a place on the couch and mebbe we can split a bottle of boukah between us honey-o. And if you've got the pox, the Arab pox, the Casablanca flea market syphilitic, one-hundred-percent-guaranteed New Deal pox, who gives a heck?

Coco was beautiful—hell, hadn't he done a keyhole job on her on the landings, the solitary gem of Madame Carpentier's sexual sweatshop? Doe-eyed and feather-fingered, long free-flowing hair that cascaded like the fountains of the Tivoli gardens all over your nicotine-stained fingers. And there she was, with her Arab sari limp against young, strong, dark-tanned legs and brilliant red toenails and soft looks from those beautiful doe eyes and those long-pointed tits just hanging out of the fold of her sari, and her thick-lipped mouth insouciantly shaping itself into a kiss. And with Coco it just had to be magic. A sweet little dame, young enough to be your daughter, and all you do is slurp another boukah into your tooth mug and croon something boring, like "Down the hatch."

Heck, she's opened those big brown doe-shaped eyes and Steve boy, you're in AS FROM NOW. So in you go, man, prick nicely on target, and feel how her young thighs clasp themselves around you and her breath starts to come in short gasps and her eyeballs do a kind of loop-the-loop *à l'arabesque,* and then she's got the whole of you in there and she's rolling off the globe and shrieking, and all you think is poor kid, poor goddamned kid, and how long have I to roll about before I get my boukah refill? You're dead, Steve. She's going through a Vision by Dante and you're just wondering if you can somehow manage to reach that long green bottle under the bed.

OK, you prize runt, you've done enough. Draw away. Lie back quietly beside her, count the flies on the ceiling, turn around and give Coco a nice little smile, a nudge around the chin.

Of course it could have been different, another earlier Steve could have dug this dusky little Arab rose in a big, big way. She was quite a sweet kid, except her eyes had to be blue, not dusky brown, the kind of blue you get from a little mountain lake fringed with snow. And she had to have fair hair, which smelled of nothing so much as a Norwegian pine forest (not jasmine-scented incense). And the body bigger and stronger and somehow fuller, more like a high-powered convertible that purred and soared under you. Breasts that would have graced a statue from Greece, legs that were long and even slightly muscular, and a pussy that was like no pussy you'd ever got to in your life. So soft, so warm, so welcoming that it was like the first time you'd had it, and once there, everything slid away and you only rated that one thing. Helda, you beautiful spook! And those eyes, those big blue serious eyes that looked at you straight and took you for what you were and rated this one thing she called "Stevie" and nothing else.

And, you prize slob, he'd been there. He'd made love to the Snow Goddess to end the lot, a mind-bending mixture of heat and ice and always those deep blue eyes, searching him out, deep and serious like you were acting out some Greek drama. *Are you somewhere out there—Helda?*

So when she came to him that night at the tables at Ritzi's and said she'd got to have money to spring Georges Martel, she had him by the balls for good, and no twisting away.

OK, Étretat had been something else. Those little windy seaside cafés, the snatched cocktails, the held hands, the kisses, and Bobbi with that damned tune that was for real, but he still held himself back, or mebbe he didn't have the time or he sensed that there was something in the way, like a heroic crud called Martel. And then he would have whipped her out of Étretat with those headlines about the fifth column and the front line collapsed, that feeling of deep-down despair and hot June pessimism. Out and away from the war, and maybe give Switzerland a whirl and get some village house high up in the mountains where the cows had bells on them and the old village postmaster has positively no letters for you, and he settled down in a warm little bed someone's granny had been born in and heard the snowflakes scudding outside. *Hi, Helda!*

So when she wasn't waiting for him outside the Golf Hotel it was like everything that was strictly nonevent in the world, like having his balls cut off and who gave a heck cause he had no more use for them.

And then she had come to him that night in Casablanca and he'd told her to scram, even though she was the coolest, freshest thing that had ever happened in that sewage system they termed Casablanca. And of course he finally relented. And looking back now, eleven months later, it had been many things, but it had also been the biggest, most fantastic screw that had ever happened to a guy since they thought up the idea.

And though it was hot, fetid Casablanca, somehow he and Helda were rolling together in the snow, her kisses like ice, her whole body cool as a cucumber, so that though he'd come into her five or six times and somehow in the process shed himself of a whole lifetime's bitterness she still came out cool as Miss Frigidaire. And then the final time he'd hardly moved, and himself held by those eyes of hers and their deep serious stare that took all the Mickey Mouse out of sex, and he just stayed there, and Christ knows how many times he said or thought, "Here's to you, honey!" And then she'd just put her hands right down and squeezed him there with strong cool hands, and baby, he'd gone to kingdom come like it had never happened to anyone before.

And "Stevie," she'd called him, "Stevie"—the only person who'd ever called him that.

The aircraft carrier USS *Ranger* looked as if it were about to take one nose dive too many. The mighty cruiser USS *Augusta* tacking across their bows was like a toy boat in a bath a kid was splashing water all over.

"Hell, Lootenant"—PFC Offenbach grimaced, clutching the rail of the shuddering *Oregon Star*—"Casablanca has gotta be better than this."

"You're darned right it's gonna be better than this," Lieutenant Al Hutter shouted into the Atlantic gale. "Didn't you see the movie?"

"Sure, I saw the movie, sir."

"You saw all that dry land. All those classy people. All these beautiful dames who need rescuing on account of Hitler's grabbed their country. All those roulette wheels. All that sin. That's Casablanca, soldier!"

"But, sir, that was a movie."

"Based on historical fact, soldier." Hutter smiled. Under his soaked service cap his face was just about as young and innocent as the private's.

Offenbach nodded and decided he wasn't going to vomit, at least in the next thirty seconds. He yelled, "Still, we gotta fight our way ashore, haven't we, sir? Those frogs are gonna throw everything they've got against us, aren't they, sir?"

He was short, he was by no means muscular, and if Suzie had ever wanted to run her nimble little fingers through a thick-matted Tarzan undergrowth, she wouldn't have chosen Auguste Berthier's pink little chest. But he had a *soupçon* of charm, a twinkle in his eye, a streak of naughtiness that could make an impressionable sixteen-year-old giggle.

Not that he was that playful tonight. He sat on the edge of the bed, and torrents of cold sweat seemed to pour off his overpale face. He placed a hand on her leg more for comfort than lust, and uncharacteristically it signally failed to slide up the knee to titillate Suzie's youthful, muscular little vagina.

A mere child behind her heavily mascaraed eyelashes, Suzie tried the oldest trick in the game, she put out an exploratory hand towards her lover. But it didn't take long to discover that it was not Auguste's night. He remained obstinately and uncharacteristically passive beneath Suzie's impatient massage.

"Don't you feel well tonight, *chéri?*" she asked.

"I have other things on my mind," her lover told her. "The world has suddenly become very black and very stupid."

"One of my friends, he is a bit like you. He will sit on that bed and sulk like a child. So what do I do? I pull him around. I give him a little surprise . . . like this!" Suzie had unbuttoned her free-flowing emerald-green skirt. She now climbed onto the bed and put her delicate ass with a cheeky flourish straight down onto Auguste's face. The old reflexes began to work in him. His tongue, forgetting for a moment the perils of the time, began to seek and then maintain contact with those delicately fuzzy areas of Suzie that, as yet, so few men had known. As she leaned forward to unbutton his shoddy disguise trousers, Auguste's tongue, with Pavlovian lack of forethought, crept up to caress one of the snazziest pieces of property to appear in Casablanca that fall, whilst something of the old arrogant virility began to assert itself as Suzie's lips made contact.

But not for long. Suzie was a born tart, though yet barely sixteen. As Auguste's reluctant cock relaxed the girl drew back. Through ears blocked and buttressed by Suzie's sinewy thighs, Auguste heard the words.

"You remind me of him. You're both so serious. He's always so embarrassed, as if it's just his first time."

"Do I know him?" asked the compulsive cop, hidden deep in Auguste, as he withdrew his tongue from Suzie long enough to say it.

"Oh, everyone does. He is a terrible man, really. The whole world is frightened of him. But he makes me laugh."

"May we know his name?"

"They say he has done terrible things. They say he is a monster. But when he starts to come the heavy with me, I have my answer. I just sit on his face and fart at him. I've never seen a man go like that for a bad smell."

For two or three seconds Auguste's Pavlovian tongue continued to slide easily backward and forward within Suzie before it quivered to an uncertain halt, hesitated, then totally withdrew.

"Lucien Roth," he suggested.

She nodded.

The very thought of Roth gave him a sharp lethal dose of revulsion. The full capability of Roth, the sum potential of what Lucien Roth could and would do if Auguste was ever caught in this adolescent fool's game that Lupin had cooked up, and the impressionable romantic suicidal fool Steve seemed hell-bent on executing.

"Get off," he screamed to Suzie as she still playfully rubbed herself against the ridge of his nose, "get your stinking bottom off my face."

Auguste had decided. This was no time for niceties. Getting his false teeth into the ready position, he sank them deep and long into Suzie's left buttock.

It happened very fast. A screaming Suzie shot away, tears of pain forcing their way through the barrier of crude purple mascara that clotted her turtle-green eyes, and in exact cacophonic synchronization with that came a violent hammering, a hammering that shook the tawdry crimson curtains, fringed with Moroccan baubles, that bedecked the bedroom side of the door.

As he stepped into the familiar room behind two plainclothes *gendarmes* with Lebel revolvers at the alert, it was Lucien Roth who confronted his ex-chief. What he saw gave his tight, handsome, predatory face just a passing look of geniality. Auguste was literally transfixed at the end of that bed. He was naked; a fringe of blood coated his lips, although his love bite had been in a different area from Dracula's. His penis was limp and tiny, and a wan parchment yellow. But all this was as nothing to the expression in his eyes. In a second thirty years of cynical veneer gave way before naked terror. Lucien Roth slowly savored his triumph, but it was not complete. He gave a cold, courteous bow to the weeping Suzie, who was holding a handkerchief to her bottom. He then gave Berthier a formal clip across the face.

"You will come with us, Monsieur Berthier," he said, "but first you will tell me at once where is your American friend."

You could say he owed his freedom to Helda de Billancourt. It was thinking about her, and finding that Coco wasn't any kind of substitute, that had made him restless. Steve was lying awake with a Chesterfield in his mouth beside the sleeping prostitute when he heard a car draw up with the assertive squeal of brakes that only police cars or drunken drivers make at 4 AM. So he got up and dressed fast. Of course there was another police Citroën in the back street behind the brothel, and here, also, he could see foreshortened little men in raincoats spreading out on the sidewalk to cover all the exits.

He ran back down the corridor, to try and wake Auguste, but he was stopped by their voices on the stairs—Roth's people didn't waste any time. That left only the skylight on the roof and a scramble over the rooftops; not the most original way out, but in the circumstances the only way a man could take who wanted to stay free.

After that he just kept walking until he reached the sea.

"Look, Andy, you've really been helpful," a hard-smiling Nad Klaf told Delsarto over a glass of canned orange juice. "But my readers are a pretty simple lot, you know. They don't give a damn about extras. Let's start real casting. Who are the real stars of this lousy frog show?"

"I know the suspense is killing," joked Andy Delsarto, who, not for nothing, had attended a fortnight's public-speaking course in Atlantic City, "but don't worry, the dénouement is near. Or put it another way, we've almost run dry of candidates. Well, I'll blast off now with a bit of heavier caliber. Those droopy, ugly features, those hooded conspiratorial eyes, that jutting nose and chin and slightly protruding stomach (better watch your waistline, fella) awake instant echoes in the mind. It's our old friend the Connétable de France. Others call him General de Gaulle. And he's an object lesson to all of us. If you get up on a platform, put a whole suit of shining armor on yourself and carry a pennant with the Cross of Lorraine on it as if it's your personal crest, then thousands of naïve young men will stand up and follow you. Well, we as a democracy are not so easily taken in. You see, nobody exactly gave de Gaulle permission to call himself the Soul of France. He wasn't voted in, he kind of emerged into history. And that's why his power base in ultimate terms has got to be just a few hundred square yards around Carlton Gardens, London SW1, or so say my State Department mentors. So great act, General, and no denying you're great copy.

"Getting a bit rough," commented Captain Delsarto as his orange juice spilled, "but don't worry. We're almost through the identification parade. I'm in the position to declare a winner. But first a tip of the hat to a gallant trier. Name of Georges Martel. This guy's solid as a bull. Bull neck, bull chest, bull legs, bull determination. But when it comes to infighting he's no slough, or bull either. Minister of the Interior in Paul Reynaud's 1940 government, and the hardest anti-Nazi of them all. Also called the Lion of Limoges (to mix a few animal metaphors), also accredited as the biggest dame fancier in the homeland of First Steps in Seduction. Last heard of, taking flight into North Africa on the good ship *Massilia*, presumably to raise his standard in African climes. Rumored dead, or near dead. Maybe he's alive, maybe he's got the African crap. Maybe he's stomping his way to freedom right across the Sahara. Who knows? But I'll tell you one thing: if we could get our hands around this guy we'd put him up for Governor. He's got the energy, he's got the votes, and the charisma. But we can't back a dead duck."

"Oh, my God," groaned Klaf in agony.

"It seems a long, long trail," Delsarto was saying, "but at the end of the road, what do you know, you finally hit pay dirt. OK, we've flicked through a good many duds, but the more you look at this new guy, the better he measures up. He's not just a cardboard cut-out. Not just a fine figure of a general, not just a leader every decent man salutes. He's a legend in his own lifetime. This man is restless, you can't pin him down; neither, for that matter, can the Germans. They captured him in World War One and put him in a POW camp, and what do you know? He walks out on them. Twice bitten, twice shy, the Germans capture him again in World War Two. This time he's given the special treatment. The krauts say he shall not pass. Except that our man has different ideas. Strolls through the outer walls and arrives back at Vichy. And why does he keep on escaping? For one good reason, because he's a Man of Destiny. So says the President, so says Eisenhower, and so says the State Department. Yes, I'm delighted to announce your lead role, Nad. And his name is General Henri Giraud. He's the one you build, Klaf."

"Do not be too severe on me, Chief Inspector," Auguste Berthier pleaded from the back of the Citroën as the late night razzle-dazzle of the Boulevard des Quatrième Zouaves gave place to the murkier lighting of the Boulevard de Bordeaux.

"Suggest a reason why we should not be severe with you," Lucien Roth said as the car cornered fast into the inky black shadows of the Medina.

"We are Frenchmen," Auguste Berthier squealed. "When you come down to it, Chief Inspector, you and I and these good gentlemen here are all Frenchmen. It is only foreigners who try to divide us."

"Like your friend Winston Churchill and his puppet de Gaulle," Roth sneered in the front seat.

"Like Herr Hitler, like Benito Mussolini, like President Roosevelt," Berthier dared to add. "Because we were defeated in 1940 the whole world feels entitled to decide what a Frenchman should be. Only you and I, my dear Chief Inspector, know what we are, and that is Frenchmen. Nothing more, nothing less."

"Even Frenchmen can be traitors," Roth snapped.

"We can toy with foreign ideas, foreign politics—that, monsieur, is perhaps the last privilege we have left as a defeated nation. There is only one thing we cannot betray, and that is ourselves."

"What am I supposed to do?" Lucien Roth asked himself with a frigid little smile. "Am I supposed to burst into tears? Recite a passage from Victor Hugo? Sing a refrain from the "Marseillaise," which in any case is banned? I'm sorry, Monsieur Berthier; if you want our sympathy you will have to tell us more interesting things."

Auguste thought he had never spoken more eloquently or more truthfully in his life. Clearly it was not enough. It would be necessary, as the Chief Inspector had suggested, to do a great deal more talking. There was just one snag. His lips had turned as dry as a desert.

"I'm sorry, General Joachim Kellerman, but you've still got to die," Steve Wagner whispered to nobody in the creeping light of morning. "I don't know who you are, or where you are, but you're still booked for eternity. No hard feelings, I hope, General. It's just that I've got nowhere else to go except towards you. It's just that my Walther P38 here is the only piece of luggage I was able to bring away with me. Besides, they've taken away my cowardly pal Auguste—the only guy left who would have saved your life."

In the meantime he needed a new place to hide. He was looking for the dockside doss house where he seemed to remember his friend Bobbi lived (with a one-eyed sailor, for all he knew). Was it 8 or 18 rue Maritime? Or was it another number in another street? Try 18 for luck.

A heavily built half-caste with a Gauloise on his lip leaned out of the door. He didn't know any pianist with blue eyes and blond hair. Certainly not one who lived in this ash can, Numéro 18 rue Maritime. Steve didn't stay to argue. He couldn't afford to hang around now it was daylight.

He walked back down the street like a shifty door-to-door salesman on whom all the doors have been slammed, a street of kids sitting on the sidewalk with their bums naked and Arab dock workers lounging around, waiting for God knows what. Then he had a glimpse of magnificence: the superstructure of the battleship *Jean Bart*, towering over the warehouses at her berth alongside the Mol de Commerce.

She was going to be the pride of the French Navy, a marvel of marine engineering that could have proved more than a match for the *Scharnhorst* or the *Gneisenau*. Then just as she was nearing completion, the Germans had marched into Brest. She had put to sea as she was, a super battleship in the making, just able to make enough steam to reach Casablanca. She was still unready for naval duty, on whatever side Laval and Admiral Darlan finally made up their minds she belonged. However, she wasn't harmless. That quadruple 15-inch gun turret was operational, and it was pointing out to sea.

The girl was standing at the end of the street, where there was an even better view of the battleship. A chic figure for this part of town, wearing a beret and the kind of broad-shouldered coat that was ultrafashion in the autumn of 1942. She was the kind of dame for whom war, politics, and terror might never have existed. There was nothing utilitarian about the coat, and her stockings suggested one-hundred-percent silk. She looked like a well-heeled tourist, the kind for whom Steve might have touched his homburg if he'd seen her on the promenade of Étretat before the war. She even had a camera. In fact she was taking snapshots of the *Jean Bart*.

She said, "What do you know? Another American. Small world."

She was an ash blonde under her beret and she made the most of it. She wore her hair just a fraction shorter than Veronica Lake. The eyes were good too: a kind of smoky blue—romantic, but with a teasing smile at the edges.

He was aware he didn't look anything like as good as she did. He was unshaven and hollow-eyed from his night of love and near death, and his lightweight suit, made in Brazzaville, was awfully crumpled.

"How do you know I'm an American?" He thought it was the last thing he looked like.

She smiled. It was quite a nice smile. She said, "Am I supposed to think you're a Berber tribesman?"

He guessed she was right. There was something about being born in Trenton, New Jersey, you could never hide.

He said, "What are you doing here—apart from taking pictures of warships?"

"I'm a spy. For the U S Government, naturally. They pay me to take photographs of warships and the occasional gun emplacement. It doesn't keep me in champagne and caviar, but it pays the rent." She looked across at the naval dock, where two *matelots* were on guard with fixed bayonets, and gave them a wave.

She was crazy or she was lying, but he had to admit to himself he liked her nerve. He also liked the way the nose turned up ever so slightly.

He said, "You want to know something? They're wasting you on warships. A glamorous spy like you ought to be seducing generals."

"Oh, I do that sometimes too. You get a dress allowance for that."

"No kidding."

"And sometimes I just follow people around. You get a dress allowance for that too. It's tough on a girl's shoes. Incidentally, isn't it time you introduced yourself?"

His eyes did a flick around the port. He knew he was awfully

conspicuous standing out here in the open with a girl who was taking photographs of a battleship.

He said, "I don't have a name. I'm just a guy."

"In that case I better introduce myself. My name is Laura—
Laura Caulfield. Incidentally, you haven't seen a guy called Steve
Wagner around town, have you? I'm supposed to look him up, on
behalf of OSS of course."

He didn't smile at this joke. He said, "Look, baby, what's your
game?"

She said, "I know it's only ten-thirty, but you get kind of thirsty
photographing boats." She indicated a seedy seamen's café behind
her shoulder. "I could use a pernod."

As it happened, so could Steve. They took a table inside the café,
in the darkest corner Steve could find in the dark, sweat-scented
café. She took off her coat to reveal she was a sweater girl. In fact
she could fill a sweater as well as Lana Turner.

"You asked me what my game was. Well, as far as I can figure it,
I'm working for a guy called Jerry Daniels. He's about the biggest
noise in OSS in North Africa, if you can call a top undercover agent
a big noise. Incidentally, I don't believe a spy should be too secre-
tive . . ."

"I've noticed that."

"People tend to disbelieve you more if you tell them the truth.
Have you got a cigarette?"

It was a corny trick, but it worked. Like a perfect gentleman, he
produced his cigarette case. It was engraved with the name
"Steve," a present from a lady he'd known long ago and faraway.

"Well, Steve—can I call you Steve Wagner for short?—my boss,
Jerry Daniels, is worried about you. He's worried about where
you've been and what you're doing back here in Casablanca. Oh,
and he doesn't like your friends, particularly he doesn't like General
Charles de Gaulle. He's bad news for American-French relations,
which at this moment are delicately poised, as they say in the best
diplomatic circles." She blew a smoke ring from Steve's cigarette.
"If we let his agents run around here in Casablanca like the Marx
brothers in every delicate china shop, well, things could get broken."

Steve signaled for another round of pernod. He said, "You know,
it's a funny thing. No one seems to be pleased to see Steve Wagner

back in Casablanca. The Vichy thugs aren't pleased. Nor, it seems, are you."

"Oh, personally I'm delighted to make your acquaintance. You don't look too like a hired political killer. But I've got to admit not everybody loves you." She looked at him with an unexpected shaft of tenderness. "They're on you, aren't they? You're running like hell from Lucien Roth and his merry men."

"Maybe."

She touched his glass with her glass, as if they were celebrating. "So why don't you do everyone a favor and get out of town? I could help you, I've got some nifty connections."

"Like your pal, Jerry Daniels? Don't worry about me. I can live with my problems."

This time he found her hand was touching his. It was a nice hand, a lot softer than her line in dialogue. "At least why don't you hide up at my place? I've got a cute little villa out at Anfa. It's got hot and cold water. Incidentally, you could use a shave, couldn't you, and maybe a breakfast of pancakes and maple syrup. And if you want anything else . . ."

There was a police Citroën outside the café doing a series of inquisitive turns on the cobblestones of the Mol de Commerce. In the circumstances Steve decided he would accept the invitation. He didn't really have a choice.

She had an Oldsmobile parked just off the Boulevard de Chayla. She seemed to have a lot of things for a young girl who was just beginning to make her way in the espionage business. They turned into the Boulevard des Quatrième Zouaves, Casablanca's long shop window, and headed up town for the Place de France and the Anfa Road. A siren started to scream. Then more joined in. Steve Wagner tried to shrink into the front passenger seat. A pack of leather-helmeted *gardes mobiles* was buzzing all around the Oldsmobile. Steve didn't have an opportunity to notice there was also a squadron of Morane-Saulnier fighters doing acrobatics overhead. They were riding the sidewalk now, scattering pedestrians without respect for race, color, or creed. The motorcycle cops powered on up the boulevard. And then a police Citroën nearly tore off their running board, but it didn't stop either. There was a big sleek 1939 Delage on its tail flying a tricolor from its lengthy hood, instantly to be superseded by a Mercedes convertible flying a black and scarlet pennant of another country. After this it looked as if they were going to be hit by another swarm of cycle cops, but they kept going at full throttle.

"What the hell was all that?" Steve asked.

Laura Caulfield lit a cigarette and turned round to look at him with her big smoky-blue eyes. It seemed that God hadn't just put them there for decoration. They were big, intelligent eyes into the bargain.

She said, "Don't say you haven't got a hunch."

"You tell me."

"That was General Joachim Kellerman driving with General Auguste Nogues to a reception at the War Ministry. But maybe you're not interested. Are you interested, Mr. Wagner?"

"General Kellerman, some kraut, isn't he?" Steve said.

General Kellerman's good humor was expanding under the Moroccan sun. And here at the War Ministry in the rue Blaise Pascal there was more champagne to help spread the goodwill around.

"You French are sly dogs." He was joking with General Béthouart, who, as it happened, had come fresh from a secret meeting with Hal Newport of the U S State Department. "By the terms of the armistice you are limited to an army of 150,000 men. I think I have counted 200,000 here in Morocco alone—and every one of them is armed with a bottle of champagne. That is better than rifles, yes? Hah, hah, hah! Seriously, I am not alarmed by certain reports that you are hiding tanks that should have been handed over to our allies the Italians. If they are the same tin cans we came up against in the Battle of France, you have my permission to hide as many as you wish. No, what I am much more interested to know is where you are hiding your beautiful women!"

He turned to Admiral Michelier, the sour-faced commander of Casablanca's land-locked naval forces.

"I am asking the General here where you are hiding your *jolies femmes,*" he bellowed.

Under the inevitable portrait of Marshal Pétain a more discreet discussion was taking place between General Nogues and Chief Inspector Lucien Roth.

"This is very disturbing, Roth," Nogues was whispering. "You are sure of it? Your informants are reliable?"

"It was definitely part of this Lupin's plan. Presumably to cause maximum embarrassment with our German friends."

"And it would. It would," Nogues hissed.

"However, Excellency," Roth had to tell him, "we have disposed of the ringleader and the renegade Berthier has been satisfactorily interrogated."

"Then General Kellerman can complete his itinerary?"

"Of course," Roth murmured, but he was bound to add, "we obtained from Berthier the identity of another accomplice, an American criminal called Wagner. We have not made an arrest as of this moment. There is an advantage in waiting to see if he leads us to other contacts or associates." Even an honest fanatic like Lucien Roth could find it necessary to put a gloss on the performance of his department.

General Kellerman was shouting at Admiral Michelier, "Apparently I am to be the guest of honor of the Parti Populaire Français at the café Chez Maurice on Saturday night. Needless to say, I am flattered. I am told I am to decorate French patriots who fought under my command in Russia. An old comrades evening! Nothing better. Thank God that later I am promised more nubile company. I am to meet a young lady who is wholeheartedly recommended to me by the Minister of the Interior. Can I trust him? Yah?"

"Chez Maurice is not a suitable place," Nogues confessed, "for a general officer of the Wehrmacht. However, we must make concessions to popular feeling, and I am counting on the fact that your security arrangements will be a hundred-percent watertight."

"They will be, Excellency." Roth saluted. "Besides, General Kellerman will be among friends."

A little man who might have been mistaken for a clerk if it hadn't been for his impressive SS officer's cap now approached Lucien Roth.

"You will be interested to know we have a dossier on you in Berlin. No, do not look alarmed. It is an excellent dossier. I have the impression that, perhaps unlike others of your countrymen here"—the rodentlike little eyes did a quick tour of the room—"you are a true friend of the Reich, who will not be easily shaken from his loyalty."

"I believe ardently in a strong united Europe, therefore I look to Germany. I believe that in a strong Europe there can be no place for esoteric elements like Jews, Freemasons, and Communists, because these are termites that undermine healthy structures." Roth was an intellectual who'd read his Nietzsche and his Houston Stewart Chamberlain, not to mention the hysterical pro-Nazi pamphleteer, Charles Maurras. He wasn't the first intellectual capable of talking rubbish with conviction.

"In that connection I am gratified to learn how rigorously you are implementing National Socialism in this colony. Apart from the anti-Jewish legislation you have introduced, your policy of enlarged penal camps for criminals is quite in line with the Führer's thinking. Also I understand they are administered with the highest standards of . . ."

"Severity," Inspector Roth suggested blandly.

The little SS Colonel took a peck at his champagne glass.

"Chief Inspector Roth, I believe you are a Frenchman I can talk with frankly. We are about to witness a time of trial for Germany, and of course for Europe. We have reports of strong attacks by the English on General Rommel's positions in Egypt. Again we have intelligence information suggesting that the Anglo-Americans may be poised to strike elsewhere in Africa. Conceivably even here. In any case we shall have need of our friends, Chief Inspector Roth. You, I think, could be an important friend, an official with the authority to ensure we are kept informed. I am thinking, for example, of Radio

Casablanca, which has served us admirably up till now. We shall be counting on a continuing flow of information through such channels in the future. Particularly if Morocco is temporarily overrun by Anglo-American rabble."

"I am confident in the ultimate victory of Germany and Europe," Roth answered. "I am at your service."

"Good. Then we must talk again. Perhaps at your office tomorrow morning. Now I must be sociable." The little murderer bowed.

General Joachim Kellerman had polished off three more glasses of champagne and was poking stubby fingers at General Nogues's white tunic. "Seriously, I do not care about your Hotchkiss tanks, I do not care about antique 75s, I want to know where you are hiding your saucy French tarts. Confess, Nogues, where are you hiding your secret weapons?"

Auguste Berthier was heading south again, surprised, it must be said, that he was still alive. A convoy of twelve four-ton Laffley AR35 trucks (a highly utilitarian truck, specially designed for colonial use in French North Africa) was weaving its exhaust trail through the mountain passes of the Haut Atlas, which separates Marrakesh from the desert frontier shantytown of Zagora. And beyond that the vast monotonous expanse of the Hammada du Draa, with its vultures and its lizards and its lack of even a mirage.

Just thirty-six hours since he had been sampling the joys of the petite Suzie. But now Auguste was chained among a row of convicts, facing a similar row of men who already seemed to have shed a few layers of individuality.

But already they were adapting. Their bodies adjusted to the rough pitching and jolting of the ingenious Laffley, whose designer seemed to have thought of everything except suspension. It was also ten hours since Auguste had touched a drop of water. Immersed in something midway between a sleep and a faint, Auguste could only murmur continuously and monotonously a single phrase: "You are Auguste Berthier, ex-Inspector of Police (Department of Fraud). . . . You are Auguste Berthier, ex-Inspector of Police (Department of Fraud). You are Auguste Berthier, ex . . ." The little caravan still had some five hundred miles to go before they hit camp.

"You ask whether you can serve our state again," Roth had said. "Well, the answer is yes. I offer you a small role in one of the greatest enterprises of Vichy France. I refer to the trans-Sahara railway—over a thousand miles of road blasted through the inhospitable desert. It's no picnic, I promise you. Many will die of heat, of thirst, of physical disintegration. But the railway will be built. Would you like to assist in this enterprise?"

"You give me no alternative."

"Not any you would wish to take," Roth had said.

It was early evening Saturday, 8 November 1942. She was lying back in an easy chair when Steve came into the room. She had her legs up on a coffee table, which was nice because they were nice sun-tanned legs and all she was wearing was a short beach coat. She was enjoying a whiskey sour after a bath and betweentimes she was combing out her long ash-blonde hair, like a twentieth-century mermaid. He felt like a real heel to pass up a scene like this to go and kill a German.

"Hey, why the clean suit? You're supposed to be on vacation, remember?" With eyes like hers, and lips like hers, any fool would agree he was on vacation here at Laura Caulfield's villa out on the hill of Anfa. But he was mourning a friend called Auguste Berthier, and besides, he was going to walk away to his death, or a German general's.

Steve said, "I've got an appointment in town; maybe you could call me a taxi."

"Could it by any chance be a girl?" she wondered.

He shook his head. "I don't think so."

"No, I didn't think so. But at least that saves us any embarrassment because I've got to come too."

"Who said you've got to come too?"

"Jerry Daniels, who else? I've got confidential instructions not to let you out of my sight. You could get into trouble."

She drove him to Casablanca in her Oldsmobile as the sun was beginning to slip level with the palms and cork trees that fringed the corniche and a magnificent view of the Atlantic. On the way they overtook a column of Chasseurs d'Afrique slogging up on foot towards the fortified point of El Hank. But Steve didn't think much about that, except to be glad they were soldiers and not cops. Chiefly he was wondering how to get rid of Laura, nicely.

He said, "Look, honey, where I'm going tonight is no place for a lady. They don't serve your kind of drinks. They don't crack your kind of jokes. They wouldn't even appreciate your looks because this little *boîte* is strictly for nut cases and perverts. It won't do any good to your faith in humanity. So why don't you drop me in the Place de France, and I'll meet you later for a drink in the Hotel Majestic?"

He felt like a heel about her. Every night she had tucked him up in bed with a glass of bourbon and told him if he wanted anything else he only had to call. He hadn't called. The ghost of Helda de Billancourt again.

At the juncture of the Boulevard Camille Desmoulins and the rue de Tunis they stopped at a traffic light. He got out just as the light turned green and she was putting the car into gear, and did his best to get lost in the crowd. But he had chosen the wrong kind of crowd to get lost in. They had established a police block on the sidewalk, and no one was getting through without careful scrutiny.

It didn't make much sense to turn back either. A van was unloading a cargo of native cops farther down the street to pick up the people who didn't want to be scrutinized. As he hesitated a woman put her arm into his.

She whispered, "Don't you know that when you try to slip Mother's apron strings you get into trouble?" Of course it was Laura. She added, "I don't know if you've seen Marcel Carné's *Le Jour se Leve;* personally, I've seen it more times than *Gone With the Wind,* but I guess I'd like to see it again. So would you if you've got any brain."

He hadn't seen *Le Jour se Leve.* He didn't want to see it. In fact he didn't have much time for art movies. But he decided to make an exception if only because they were just a few yards from the foyer of this movie house and it looked more welcoming than the police block a few more yards up the street.

They came in at the end in time to see a caged animal called Jean Gabin, a character outside the law with a kind of brooding integrity that seemed to make midgets of the law's officers, shooting it out, fatally, with an army of *flics.*

She said, "This is where you came in, isn't it?"

He said, "What do you mean? I've never seen this movie."

She put her hand on his leg. "Why don't you see it around again? If you don't like it, we can always hold hands."

It was an invitation anyone in his right mind would have accepted, but he said, "You're awfully cute. I mean that, kid, but I've got a date."

"Seriously, honey," she whispered, "this movie could have a message for you. Like, don't do it."

A fat woman in a large hat sitting in front turned round and hissed, *"Taisez-vous!"* Movie houses were the same the whole world round.

Laura put an arm round his shoulder, and her hand, straying down towards his breast pocket, encountered the shape of his Walther P38. "Not for de Gaulle," her gorgeous lips mouthed in his ear. "You'd be crazy to get killed for de Gaulle. Even Churchill's through with him. That's official."

Now he wanted to kiss her, whatever the hell she was saying. Any man in his right mind would have wanted to kiss lips as generous as Laura's, as close as they were now—even a one-woman man like Steve Wagner. But just at this moment the sound track erupted into a lunatic march. The words "Actualités de France" exploded onto the screen. In fact it was the highly slanted news from Vichy. A French voice, speaking with the hectic enthusiasm normal for a commentator on the Tour de France, announced it had an exclusive on an historic event at Vichy. The screen filled with a crowd of schoolgirls with nicely tied bows on their hair. Apparently they had descended in the thousands on the provisional capital to pay their respects to the "Father of the Nation." The camera cut to the entrance of the Hotel du Parc. Old Marshal Pétain, accompanied by his physician and adviser, Dr. Ménétrel, staggered down the steps to accept this youthful homage. A bereted SOL official in the crowd singled out a particularly undersized child, whom the hero of Verdun then lifted up and kissed. The old gentleman's face broke into a smile, like a victorious weight lifter.

"You've got to admit he's cute, cuter than de Gaulle," Laura murmured.

"Hitler loves kids too," Steve muttered back.

Now they were looking at a shot of the Eiffel Tower. Paris, the announcer revealed with strident pride, was still the cultural center of Europe, in fact never more so. The announcer didn't go as far as to quote the collaborator Marcel Déat, who had decided that the place of Paris in the New Order was to be "the brothel of Europe," but this was the sense of the next piece of footage. Steve had never seen so many biddable women in the Champs Élysées, and every one of them had a *Feldwebel*, or *Luftwaffe* officer, or a *Kriegsmarine* on her arm. There were of course a few old people going by on bicycles or horse-drawn carts who didn't have anybody on their arms, but they were in the minority.

Still, as the announcer insisted, in Paris it was always spring, and Parisian music hall artists were playing a leading role as morale boosters to the crusade against Bolshevism. The camera cut to a straw boater and a grinning face that together added up to the world's favorite Frenchman, Maurice Chevalier. Another cut to Edith Piaf rendering "La Vie en Rose" from the bottom of her heart. And then another cut to a wildly applauding audience of officers and men in Wehrmacht uniform.

The next feature was a roundup of news from the narrow little world of Vichy France. A short clip of Monsieur Vallat, Minister of Jewish Affairs, cordially discussing his anti-Semitic measures with a jocular Himmler. (France, said the announcer, had won for herself a respected negotiating position in the highest councils of Europe.) This was followed by what the commentary described as "an informal visit to President Laval at his home in Châteaudun." The camera showed a hunched figure in a white shirt and formal suit looking suspiciously at a rosebush and smoking a cigarette. There was an arbitrary dissolve to a bicycle race in Nice. Physical fitness, insisted the commentary, is an essential plank of the National Revolution.

"What's the matter with you?" Laura whispered. "Did the natives swallow your balls down there in the Congo? You've got to be some icebox to prefer Pierre Laval to me."

"*Taisez-vous!*" the fat woman in the big hat hissed.

She was right. He had to be an iceberg to sit here watching all this crap when next to him was a girl who smelled like a million dollars and looked like them too, even if she wasn't Helda. Besides, it was a long, long time since he'd sat with a girl in the back seat of the movies. For the first time in years Steve began to feel genuinely at home. They were sitting in a movie house a few blocks from Chez Maurice and his appointment with General Kellerman. But suddenly all wars and all generals, including General de Gaulle, were a long way away. He turned to her and looked at her softly (he didn't know if she could see how softly he was looking at her) and murmured, "You're a nice kid."

The scene was all set for a dissolve, two children of the movie world staging their own fade-out in the back row of a Casablanca cinema. Steve was even thinking maybe if he took this gorgeous dame home to her villa at Anfa and screwed her till the dawn came up, he might even manage to lay the ghost of his snow goddess. But he paused to look at the final item of the news. The scene was the

Gare du Nord. Frenchmen were leaving to work in Germany as part of Le Relève, the system whereby the Germans undertook to release one French prisoner of war for every three French workers who reported to the factories of the Ruhr. The announcer was gleeful. This trainload of manpower was loaded exclusively with volunteers, men eager to assist the repatriation of France's one million prisoners and to assist the war effort against Bolshevism.

But there was one little guy in a beret looking out of the train window who clearly didn't want to go. He was the kind of little Frenchman you would see after a day's work taking a glass of wine in the village café, as much part of the landscape as the trees. He was the kind of Frenchman who was rooted in France, the kind who just couldn't be transplanted. He was waving to his wife and children, and even the grainy black and white film showed that his eyes were filled with tears. This was no volunteer. This was a free man who didn't want to go anywhere—least of all into slavery.

When Laura looked around for him she found that Steve wasn't there.

He'd got it all figured out. The game was to pull a sneak-and-run. Had to be. It mightn't win him the Congressional Medal of Honor, it mightn't be the way they did things in the BREETISH ARMY, what, what! But if you had to do a crazy thing like bump off a kraut brass hat you wouldn't exactly want to have to stand up in court later and confess. Frontal approach? Strictly no dice. Ritzi's bouncers would flatten you before you could get close enough to the General to say "Hello." So what did you do? You did what all rats did, sneak in the back way—that little piss-alley where Ritzi stacked his empties and the neighbors threw their dead cats.

As Steve suspected, the door from the alley was unlocked. Had to be. The way the carousing was going on, they'd soon have to throw out more empty flagons of flat beer.

And then he did a bit of real nifty. It might seem to be the action of a prize nut, but in fact it was a surefire bet, in fact he bet Churchill himself could have got away with it, crunching up the stairway in his boiler suit and pausing on the balcony to blow a cloud of rich Havana their way. And if you wanted to know why a mean slob like him would risk his neck by mounting a flight of stairs in full view of the Parti Populaire Français and SOL militants, take a look at what's happening over there in the center of the bar under that huge hanging bauble of a Moorish lamp some visiting culture-vulture from Harvard had once assured him was *art nouveau*, whatever that might mean.

Where once a peculiar collection of deadbeats, hicks, dope peddlers, and beautiful dames had congregated of an evening now caroused the *jeunesse doré* of the French extreme right wing. And the piano which had given out cool jazz on a hot night under Bobbi's wistful touch was now ramping a medley selection from *The Merry Widow* under the battering of a red-faced Sergeant, whilst a chorus of male Vilias (six of the youngest and prettiest recruits to a chivalrous organization that called itself the Knighthood of Modern Times) did a slow and awkward striptease on an upraised stage. Steve Wagner stood there, and he took in perhaps eighty bereted thugs who were giving the male chorus, now reduced to frilly petticoats, a standing ovation. Then he found the man he wanted. His face and shape fitted the image, memorized from newspaper cuttings. The bald dome, the protuberant stomach, the jolly Bavarian grin, except that—hold it—he wasn't really smiling.

Steve guessed that Kellerman thought about this charade the

same way he did. Behind the sweaty forehead and the loud guffaws this man, like him, only wished for one thing—to get shot of the whole scene.

He was a dope not to have shot him then. A bullet just two inches below where that Iron Cross dangled. A quick exit through the little patio and over the wall while his aide-de-camp hollered blue murder and the creeps climbed out of their petticoats.

He slipped up the stairway, took a cool look at the scene from the balcony; calculated that the bullet would just have to skim the pendant on the Moorish lamp with maybe then another twenty-five Gauloise-clouded feet to go before it entered Kellerman's heart. He was a sitting duck (a bored sitting duck, wondering where all the women were), the way no target should quite be.

The lights were dimmed, the all-male cabaret had gone, the cheering, jeering heroes of the Chevaliers du Temps Moderne had scattered into small groups around tables. There was the soft buzz of female voices against a lazy piano; a haphazard cool scattering of notes that added up somehow to "Smoke gets in your eyes" and a thousand good times, here and other places. And where the dumpy SOL sergeant had sat barely minutes before was the lonely figure of Bobbi with that faithful-dog look still about him. The dog you couldn't quite ever shake off, even though it bored the pants off you.

Steve leaned for a second on the simple railing that overlooked the place that had once been home. If Kellerman had been a sitting duck before, he was now a Thanksgiving Day turkey, all ready to be carved up and smothered with cranberry sauce.

The General and his aide had conveniently moved themselves to a table over the far side, which happened to be nice and handy for the exit Steve proposed to make. All he had to do was to pass quietly along the dimmed side of the room between the pillars and drill him as he passed out. He would be through the patio and over the wall before they realized they were wining and dining a dead-duck general.

So it was farewell, Bobbi, thanks a million for having played that song again—just one more time. Thanks, Ritzi, for teaching an old rat a new trick. A fond farewell to Chez Maurice, and God bless all the jerks who drink in here.

He moved quickly in the dim light. Another ten paces and he'd be past the final pillar and rubbing shoulders with a hero of the Wehrmacht. Another two seconds and he'd be delivering the most lethal handshake since Joe Louis floored Max Schmeling.

Just concentrate on that gleaming red dome, buttressed on either side by the epaulettes. Put your hand in your pocket. Just casual, like you were feeling for your cigarette case. Another Chesterfield. Just . . .

But the dome was rising and becoming a six-foot-two stout general. Rising and extending his hands outwards, away from Steve, towards the dark center of the room.

So what? Before he'd been content to split the bone structure in his cranium. Now he'd get him through the back, enter the heart from behind. The Walther was out, the finger pressing softly the trigger. Just a millionth of an inch more and one additional fat kraut would be en route for the morgue. Just . . .

The General's hand did a tiny gesticulation, like the birth of a wave. But another hand was shaking. Not the General's, but Steve's. Shaking, so that the Walther jostled and slipped in his grip.

She was still wearing that wide-brimmed hat. And her gaze was like the cleanest thing he'd ever seen. And so was that little, slightly snub nose. And she carried about her a kind of coolness, as if she were remote from this whole crazy scene. And her eyes, as blue as a sky over Narvik in midsummer, took him in as well as the General, with total openness.

And then he was running, his Walther still trailing in his hand. Running for her sake, running for his sake. Running because in this crazy world the whole thing had about as much chance as a pea of making sense.

"My aunt is in the garden," said the BBC overseas radio announcer in his impeccable Oxford French. "I have two tickets for the theater. Robert is arriving. Will you pass me the honey, please? My father's cousin is indisposed. Robert is arriving. Do you take sugar in your coffee? The weather over the Channel is changeable. My uncle's lawnmower is broken. Robert is arriving. . . ."

It was the usual gibberish put out regularly from London concealing particular messages for particular Resistance cells in the occupied countries.

But tonight the announcer did seem to be going on a bit about the arrival of Robert. Even the dozy *Feldwebel* at his wireless set in the Hotel Miramar, Fedala, where the German Armistice Commission was installed, couldn't help noticing it.

"Can you lend me an English dictionary? My brother is in bed with a cold. Robert is arriving. Our cat has caught a mouse. Can you tell me where I can buy an electric torch? Robert is arriving. . . ."

Who was this Robert? And where was he arriving? The *Feldwebel* wondered if he should alert his superior, Major Schonaud, who was upstairs with the rest of the officers cracking a few more bottles of 1934 champagne. After all, it was Saturday night.

Saturday night was the loneliest night of the week for some people, but never for Tina Newport if she could help it. She had phoned everyone at the U S Consulate and told them to leave their goddamned desks at the Place de la Fraternité and come down to Anfa and crack a few bottles.

Now it was ten-thirty and no one had shown up.

"Where the hell are these jerks?" she bawled at her husband from the patio, where she was standing in a fetching new "Southern belle" evening gown, scanning the driveway. She had already helped herself to a glass or two of the party spirit.

Hal Newport came out onto the patio wearing a nifty new yachting jacket complemented by a pair of white ducks. The evening air smelled fabulous: the scent of jasmine and tamarisk underlaid by the tang of the sea. He had the phonograph on automatic action back in the villa. It was playing a new hit from the States: "Would It Be Wrong?" The mood was right for a kiss. He said politely, "That's a nice dress you're wearing, darling."

"I asked you," his wife burped, "what the hell's keeping those bums? Will you kindly tell me? They're your lousy colleagues."

"I said we're pretty well at full stretch at the consulate right now, Tina. It wasn't easy for me to get away tonight."

"What do you guys find to do there, anyway—apart from making a grab at every secretary you see? You told me yourself it's the most overstaffed consulate you've served in. OK, half of you are spies, lousy spies if you ask me; that still leaves a lot of strictly diplomatic people who could have the courtesy to keep an invitation to cocktails."

She said that personally she was going to have another drink. Hal said she'd do better to wait. She was pouring herself one anyway when a car finally showed and burly Vice-Consul Bill Baxter came bounding onto the patio.

"Robert," he panted, "Robert is arriving!"

"Hey, so you finally made it! Wonderful to see you, Bill." Tina beamed, with her party smile back on again.

"Robert is arriving! Robert is arriving!"

"Who the hell's Robert? Did we ask him, Hal? Sure we'd like to meet him."

"Shut up, Tina!" Hal snapped at her, which was perhaps a little hard since Tina didn't know that 'Robert' was a code word, not a person. In simple English, *Robert arrive* meant that Operation TORCH was about to hit the shores of North Africa.

"Stafford Reid picked it up on the BBC overseas broadcast this evening." Bill Baxter was still panting. "Robert is arriving! Christ, why didn't they tell us earlier?"

"What's your poison, Bill?" Tina asked him silkily.

Baxter shook his head. "Can't stop. I've got to get the hell up to Rabat to make sure General Béthouart's got the message. Boy, we haven't given him much time to pull off his coup and stop the fighting."

He ran back towards his Buick in the tropical gloaming. At the door he shouted:

"Hal, you'd better report back to the Place de la Fraternité. It looks like it's going to be quite a night. Better take Tina too," he yelled as he shoved the car into a screeching reverse and disappeared in a cloud of pink dust.

"I'm not going anyplace, least of all to your crappy old consulate," Tina said. "*I'm* throwing a party—remember?"

"Darling—can't you see there's no question of a party now?"

"So those consul snobs can't come. Let's invite the neighbors. Hey! And the German Armistice people—those guys like a drink. And what about your pal, Steve Wagner?" She sank another highball effortlessly. "Call him up, for Chrissake. I don't care a fart about his politics. I thought he was real sexy!" she added with a hip wiggle.

Hal Newport was a diplomat. So he didn't lose his temper all that often. But now he did.

"Listen, get it into your fat head the party's off! A little thing called History has intervened. Get it into your stupid brain that in a couple of hours all hell could break loose around here, particularly if the French decide to fight. You talk about parties—boy, you must be stewed!" He pointed savagely towards the ocean. "Don't you understand the whole goddamned U S Navy is out there and it's headed this way?"

Tina Newport poured herself another drink and looked mistily towards the opaque Atlantic breakers.

"I don't see any U S Navy," she said.

"I don't see any Africa," PFC Offenbach said as he leaned on the port rail of the USS *Oregon Star*, just over the horizon.

He didn't knock. He just pushed open the door of her office and walked in.

"Don't tell me I shouldn't be here," Steve cut her short. "I want to know what the hell's going on in this town."

For Madeleine Carpentier the night of 8 November 1942, had turned out pretty well, at least so far. She was back in favor with the Casablanca police. Although she had been provisionally released the day after Auguste Berthier's arrest, the threat of further interrogation, and perhaps imprisonment, had disappeared only this morning with the arrival of a smiling emissary from Chief Inspector Roth bearing flowers and an envelope of cash. Madeleine's talents as a procuress were to be enlisted by the government. Her confidential appointment was to cater for the urgent physical needs of no less a VIP than Major General Joachim Kellerman.

This, it had been stressed, was not an assignment for any of Madeleine's regulars. Chief Inspector Roth had in mind one of the more exclusive free lances that Madeleine kept on her books, or somewhere in her strawberry-blonde head. An ideal solution would be the highly expensive and highly elusive prostitute known to only a very few powerful men in Casablanca, incidentally, as "la Princesse." In fact if Madeleine could obtain the services of "la Princesse," her fee would be doubled.

Madeleine had obtained the services of "la Princesse," and her fee had been doubled. That is why when Steve burst into her office she was sipping a brandy she kept for her richest clients with a sense of special satisfaction. A luxury? Perhaps, but then it was four in the morning, and it had been a long night.

"A woman," Steve was shouting, "a Norwegian with a French title—called Billancourt—passed through town about a year ago, a friend of Georges Martel, the missing patriot."

She had always been fond of Steve. But now she wondered if he had gone completely insane. He looked insane, with those wild eyes bulging out of his face, and he sounded crazy too. An added embarrassment was that he was wanted by the police. And upstairs, at this moment, Major General Joachim Kellerman was enjoying "la Princesse" in her luxury-priced "salon du Sultan," discreetly guarded by Lucien Roth's handpicked plainclothesmen.

"Steve, I am always happy to help you," she said soothingly, "but now I think the best way I can help you is to insist you leave at once. You must realize it is very dangerous for you here now. You know they took away your friend Auguste."

"I'll come to Auguste later. First I want to know about Helda de Billancourt, and why I keep seeing a ghost that's so real you could reach out and touch it."

"Why do you ask me? How should I know about ghosts?"

"Because you know everything that happens in Casablanca, Madeleine. You notice everyone that comes and goes—particularly well-dressed, beautiful women. That's part of your professionalism. You keep in touch with what the world is wearing and how it's looking. In fact you don't miss a trick. That's why if anyone's conjuring up ghosts in Casablanca, you'd be the first to know who and why."

She poured him a glass of Napoleon's best brandy and sighed. "My poor Steve, you are so troubled, and I don't know how I can help you."

She was suddenly beginning to feel terribly bored with this man who had once represented to her the ultimate in sophistication. She thought that he was no longer, perhaps never had been, an international man. He was basically another boring American who should have stayed at home. Another boring Yankee insisting on seeing the world and determined to sniff corruption under every stone. She knew them so well from Paris, the type who would elbow his way into the best bordellos then start crying for Mom and blueberry pie. Why couldn't they leave the old world to its troubles and its necessary compromises?

"Ghosts don't walk around Casablanca unnoticed," he was insisting, "it's too small a town and people talk too much. What are they saying, Madeleine? Was I dreaming when I saw Helda de Billancourt half an hour ago in Ritzi's?"

General Kellerman's booming voice could be heard clearly as he jovially descended the opulently carpeted first flight of stairs (the second and third were more threadbare) from the salon du Sultan.

Steve gasped, more out of shocked disbelief than fear.

"Hell, you've got a German in here!"

"Is that extraordinary? We are a brothel. Now you must go—fast!" She motioned to a door behind her. A girl in Madeleine's line of business could never have made do with one exit.

Steve obeyed her as far as the door handle. Kellerman's chuckling voice was getting closer.

"A kraut in your place!" he murmured, shaking his head.

"We do not choose," she reminded him. "We are a brothel."

"You could say that for the whole lousy French empire," he answered by way of an exit line.

The door opened into a kind of *petit salon,* with a Madame Récamier couch where Madeleine, if she was in the mood or the money was right, would personally entertain the occasional client. There was also a window with access onto the street, which Steve supposed he was meant to climb through. For the time being he didn't oblige. He went back to the keyhole, and there for the second time that evening he had a target any U S Ranger or British Commando would give his trigger finger for. This time he was looking at a row of medals on a *Feldgrau* chest. Major General Joachim Kellerman, by courtesy of Fate or God knew what, was presenting himself for execution for a second time that night. Hey, presto, and there'd be another scarlet ribbon on that martial chest.

He heard a bottle and glasses being deposited on Madeleine's desk, and he heard Kellerman saying in his terrible French:

"Madame, I come to drink your health in your finest champagne. You provided a weary traveler with refreshment and pleasure fit for a king. *Prosit!* She was not perhaps too demonstrative, but we Germans know how to take a haughty princess in her tower. If necessary we will dynamite it. Yes? Hah! Hah! Hah! Yes, we will use the high explosive. Hah, hah, hah! *Prosit!*"

More than ever Steve wanted to press the trigger. There was just one snag: if he killed Kellerman now, he would destroy Madeleine too. Roth's gang wouldn't be amused when they found a dead German general in her office.

But now Kellerman had stopped boasting about his sexual prowess. He was chuckling over the way he had succeeded in giving his ADC and his chauffeur the slip.

"There are certain times," he confided to Madeleine, "when a gentleman wishes to be free to go his own way. You know what I mean? It does not do to have your staff accompany you on all your missions. Particularly delicate missions such as I am undertaking tonight."

The General was obviously in an expansive mood. He confessed to Madeleine that he felt like a young cadet again. No, he would not be sending for his official Mercedes and his tedious, disapproving eunuch of an ADC. He would be grateful if Madeleine could ring for a cab. He wanted to savor his little escapade in private, like any young buck after a night of adventure. He would return to Fedala in an ordinary taxi.

Steve wondered if he just might be able to find him one.

The disturbing message that General Kellerman had left Madeleine's place in an ordinary taxi didn't reach Lucien Roth immediately. Extraordinary developments were taking place fifty miles up the coast at Rabat, which for the moment were distracting the Chief Inspector's attention.

A routine call to General Nogues's office in the Residency had not got through. Further investigation had revealed that the lines had been cut. A call to General Béthouart's headquarters had produced the curt explanation that General Nogues's residency had been surrounded by elements of the Casablanca Division. The General was being invited to throw in his lot with the Allies, who would shortly be landing in North Africa.

Chief Inspector Roth was a youngish man. But he felt a nasty stab in his chest on receipt of this information, and for seconds actually wondered if he was going to have a coronary. It had been one of his responsibilities to keep General Béthouart under surveillance.

A call to Admiral Michelier had produced more reassuring news. General Nogues had telephoned him by a private line, which the mutineers had neglected to cut. Loyal forces were already on their way to rescue the Resident-General and slap Béthouart under arrest. The Admiral blamed the whole incident on the local American rumormongers.

Now a call came through that, in one direction at least, put Roth's mind at rest.

It was from Colonel Piatte, General Nogues's ADC.

Yes, the General was perfectly safe. In fact he was even now enjoying a glass of champagne. No, he did not require a detachment of *gardes mobiles*. General Béthouart's idiotic black troops were already being marched back to their barracks. Was there anything he could do for the General? No, the General would much rather he continued to concern himself with the safety of General Kellerman.

General Kellerman! Where was General Kellerman? At last Roth picked up the message that he was riding in a private taxi to Fedala. And then for the second time in this long trying night he wondered if, young as he was, he was going to have a coronary.

His incompetent sleuths had at least taken the trouble to interrogate the woman Carpentier. She had just confessed that the American assassin Wagner had been in her establishment that night.

Taxis weren't that hard to find at 4 AM in Casablanca if you knew how. In fact if you happened to have a couple of thousand counterfeit francs on you, you could get the loan of one for the rest of the night. Even Casablanca taxi drivers had homes to go to.

Admittedly it wasn't his idea of a roadster. Steve liked his limousines light on steering and with plenty of oomph. He had a penchant for snub-nosed crates or crazy convertibles that did a striptease on you at the drop of a knob. But at least it sufficed to cruise past Madeleine's door like any stray taxi in search of a late night fare.

This classy Citroën 10A Torpedo (pride of the Paris Motor Show 1934) was custom-built for a general, if not for Steve. It was a heavy ceremonial limousine with all the trappings of the *haut bourgeois;* too much squeaky leather upholstery, too much bouncy suspension, so you couldn't feel the road surface hard against your ass. But it had something that might stand him in good stead: monumental surging power, and a deluxe extra was the special insulated partition that divided driver from passenger. Steve wanted to keep that partition shut.

The main thing was to play it straight. He was en route for the Hotel Miramar, Fedala, amiably purring down the Route de Rabat at some 25 mph. Too bad that a mile or so from the plush hotel the Torpedo was destined to do a rapid *volte-face* over a few rough lanes to land its honored guest on Fedala's well-known dump heap, where his plugged body would add to its garbage collection of old tin crates, rotten oranges, and crapped-out buzzards.

Yeah, that was best. Just take him there. Plug him. Bid fond adieus. No fuss, no funny stuff.

They were cruising through the suburb of Arab shanties that clutter up the track that leads out to the sea at Fedala when he made his first mistake. Kellerman was trying to say something, and he had twisted his face round to hear him. A glance round had shown him that the General had reached into his greatcoat pocket and taken out a bottle of brandy. But twisting round like that was the kind of reflex you'd expect from a kid. OK, the old boy was tucking into the booze, but exactly how plastered was he? He felt heavy pressure on his arm and swung around again, the car swerving towards a hovel by the road before he righted it. He felt as itchy as a tap dancer.

"Here, my friend." Kellerman's deep voice came through in lousy French. He had slipped open the glass panel, so that there was no longer any barrier between them. "I want the whole world to feel as happy as me."

Steve took the bottle from the General's purple hand and took a long slug. It had to be Rémy Martin, and it was old, very old. If the old boy wanted to splash out the cognac, all right, he'd go along with him. He was definitely jumpy tonight; he felt the twitch in his face dancing just above his mouth. He needed that brandy more than the General.

"That was good, yes?" the General asked him.

"Yes, you're right, General," Steve replied. "That was good."

"Want some more?"

"OK."

"It's like liquid fire, yes?"

"You could say."

"Liquid fire, after melted ice. Morocco is a remarkable place."

Steve grunted. He was hitting a quicker bit of track now, and he wanted to keep his eyes on the road and speed her up a little. One thing he didn't need was conversation. He wanted to keep his mind on the job in hand, because though the General didn't quite seem to be clued up yet, this was strictly no joyride.

"I once had the same kind of experience as a young officer at a New Year's Ball high up in the Schwarzwald. A young girl, she must have been seventeen, not a day more. And a virgin, my friend, if you can imagine that. And suddenly the dance hall was stuffy and there was too much Strauss. But out in the snow beneath the fir trees, the thick deep snow, she slipped up her party dress, just like that. Her bottom burrowed itself a nice little hole in the snow. And together we made love in the snow. It was like that tonight, my friend."

"Yeah," agreed Steve, taking the Torpedo much faster as they sped beside heaped-up sand dunes and the signs said just five more kilometers to Fedala. "That's once in a lifetime. That kind of thing."

It was a double assault. A blinding glare in his mirror, a wailing of klaxons and sirens. Steve had experienced it before. It felt like a punch in the guts. His foot punched down on the Citroën's heavy accelerator and suddenly they took off as the long-pampered engines were given a license to fly. Steve cursed the Torpedo's other racing innovation—a specially illuminated rear number plate. Someone up there must love the General. The odds had been evened.

They knew they must be approaching Africa because they were now paraded on A deck in full battle order with two days' rations, but there was nothing but the sea. The lights of Casablanca were still just over the horizon. Sergeant Eklund was stalking up and down in front of them, waiting for the officers to arrive.

They could just make out that he was wearing a steel helmet. In a way it seemed to take some of the terror out of him. He was somehow dwarfed by the elaborate new U S Army battle headgear.

"Are they gonna fight or aren't they, Sarge?" young Offenbach felt emboldened to ask. It was a question that had remained obstinately unanswered throughout the voyage, in spite of the efforts of Captain Delsarto. The truth was that not even Western Task Force Commander General George S. Patton knew whether the French were going to object to being invaded. Nor for that matter, did President Roosevelt.

"You've heard the orders," Sergeant Eklund snarled. "You gotta wait till they shoot at you before you shoot at those French bastards." Then his voice almost softened. "If I were you I wouldn't wait too long, or you could find you're dead."

"Why?" spluttered the General. "Why? In the name of Gott, why?"

It was difficult to make the mind work after such an Arabian night, difficult even to focus. And this taxi driver, he was a good man. A madman maybe, but he had shared a good bottle of brandy with him. And now that he could see him face to face, he decided it was a face you could trust. A face that had lived, no illusions, no deceit.

So why?

What this man had done was very rash, and for a few minutes very funny. He had left the road and that was good. This man knew his Fedala, he was taking a shortcut. *Jawohl.* General Kellerman knew about rough rides. He had lolloped over the Ardennes in an army scout car; he had crashed into Minsk in an armored car. But this driver beat them all. He hardly moved his arms, just twiddled the wheel between his fingers in a touch-feel kind of way. And that was good—till they ran out of track.

Then the Torpedo was coughing and spluttering, up to its neck in a sand dune. And that had the General choking with merriment. And when the driver turned round, and twitched around the eyes and said "Get out," it was enough to make Kellerman explode, until he was staring into the barrel of a Walther automatic just four inches from his chin.

So why?

"My money," chortled the General, "take it, my friend. These are gold Reichsmarks. Go and buy yourself a lovely girl. Those are the best. As an older man I can tell you, when you pay for it, it must be good."

"Get out of the car. Put your hands over your head. And start walking," came the voice.

"But why?" echoed Kellerman.

"Move over towards those dunes."

"What kind of man are you?"

"I am for de Gaulle."

"Who?"

"General Charles de Gaulle."

"I do not know him. What do you want?"

It was never easy. And it didn't make it any easier when you had drunk his brandy and he'd had more than enough of the commodity. Also it didn't simplify matters that he happened to be a nice guy and was looking as if he trusted you. But you couldn't slide away from it now. You had to keep going straight for what you were meant to do, otherwise everything got confused. You had to know how to recognize your enemy in this crazy mixed-up world, otherwise you were just another smoothie who didn't know where he was, like Ritzi or Marshal Pétain.

So Kellerman had to be plugged. Because he was on the wrong side at the wrong time in the wrong war. Or maybe because it simply wasn't his night.

The General came out of the car with the remains of the bottle of brandy in one hand and a packed wallet in the other. And he was saying something like, "Look here, my friend . . ." except he never quite got as far as that because a whipped-forehand punch choked the words as they were coming out of the General's mouth, whilst a beautifully synchronized boot into the solar plexus had him stretched out on a sand dune.

It was a second or so before Kellerman was able to react to the violence inflicted on the lining of his stomach. When he did, it was not vomit that bubbled out of his mouth, but globules of blood and a complete set of false teeth.

Steve drew back to widen the angle of fire. He flipped off the safety catch on the Walther.

"I've come a long way for this moment," Steve told him, "but I'd like to assure you it's nothing personal. Except I've lost a good friend en route, so you could say it was quits."

But Kellerman wasn't going to make it easy. He couldn't talk, he couldn't walk, but he could stumble down onto the sand in a semblance of kneeling. And he could put out two beefy red hands and his eyes could manage a tear or two, which dribbled down his cheeks and joined the beard of clotted blood below his mouth.

But there wasn't only the General to look at. There was something else: it was as if the sand dune they were in were bursting into life, like bacteria under a microscope, little spurts of sand whipping up around them like moon craters exploding. The General was already on the deck, in a new kneeling posture. It took one simple movement on Steve's part, a kind of instinctive plunging to earth, to put one protective arm round the General's back and carry the top half of his body wham into the sand. And there they remained like two lovers, the sand tickling Kellerman's nostrils and forcing its way into his mouth, with Steve's arm still insistently holding him down, whilst the pinging bullets hit the top of the dune and made the tiny brown particles fly.

For Lieutenant Maurice Pajol, the night of 8–9 November had started like any other. In fact he had been snoring in his police Renault when his driver picked up the voice of Chief Inspector Roth, coming sharp and incisive through the static of the car's radio.

"General Kellerman, believed kidnapped . . . a black Citroën Torpedo . . . the Fedala road. Pajol, if you fail me in this, you'll regret you ever joined the *gendarmerie*."

Pajol's *gardes mobiles* outriders had caught up with the Torpedo just six kilometers outside Casablanca. Then Pajol, leading the car convoy, saw it. In total synchronization the whole convoy, and the Torpedo too, suddenly screamed into brutal acceleration. A matter of minutes later they passed the deserted Torpedo on a track through the dunes and had their searchlights cartwheeling brilliant arcs across Fedala's pleasure beach.

The strong smell of the sea was in Pajol's nostrils, the shrilling of gulls in his ears, but his attention was on one thing only: a jumbled human silhouette just fifty yards away, on top of a sand dune, beside a fisherman's boat.

"Fire!" screamed Pajol.

He was taking a risk, the possibility that his crack marksmen might hit Kellerman. But what alternative had he? If the General was in the hands of the Resistance, they would shoot him rather than give him up. The hope was to rescue the General by sheer force of arms. Pajol had over twenty men concentrated round the dune. He decided on an attack across the sand. There would be casualties, but he himself would not be among them. And the prompt initiative he had shown would stand him well with Inspector Roth. He looked at his watch. It was 5:45 AM on the morning of 9 November 1942.

Still keeping the corpulent body of General Joachim Kellerman clamped down in the sand, Steve raised himself up. For several minutes now there had been no firing. He guessed the reason why: he just wanted to make sure.

He saw about fifteen or twenty figures on the horizon, and they were still fanning out. It would take them maybe forty-five seconds to reach him through the thick sand. In that time he would have six of them. That left the interesting odds of ten to one. Did he say six of them? In fact he could hope for only five. He had a pessimistic hunch that he'd never have been able to shoot Kellerman in cold blood, which was stupid when you thought of the kinds of things the SS and Gestapo were doing back in Germany. And then when the police had opened fire, he had actually pushed him down into the sand. If he hadn't done that, a Vichy bullet would have been bound to penetrate that vast kraut target. And he'd have been clear and clean.

But now the odds were even. He was bound to stop a bullet. So, heck, what was the worry? Kellerman could go too.

"Sorry, General." He sank the Walther into the General's fat veiny neck and quietly pulled the trigger.

Then he was out and over the dune and behind the fishing boat, trying to gauge the mass of men lumbering towards him, like pantomime figures in oversized boots, through the slinky sand.

"Get lost," he croaked at them, those threatening black silhouettes of men. "Get lost, damn you."

And then it hit him. At first he thought they were trying to blind him by throwing in every searchlight in Casablanca. The pillar of fire was so eye-splitting in that dark dawn. And then he knew the real intent was to burst his eardrums.

Finally he realized he'd been wrong both times. The real intent was to bury him alive, as the sheer force of it pushed him down into a chasm of suffocating sand. Right down to where Kellerman's body was still pulsing out black blood from a hole in the neck.

It could have been a minute or an hour or just five minutes when he finally managed to push his body up again to the top of the dune. Certainly the dark had softened, as the first vague rays of half-light began to encroach the undulating contours of Fedala's *jolie petite place.*

This kind of light should have made it easier for him to descry his persecutors, even to read human shapes and faces into those grim black silhouettes.

But it appeared that fate had listened to his final prayer. His pursuers had literally gone up in smoke.

It was a sight Captain Maxwell had been waiting for ever since the giant invasion convoy of Western Task Force had steamed out of Hampton Roads, Virginia, and started to ride 4,500 miles of unbroken Atlantic breakers.

But now it was uncurling before his eyes like a kid's movie show, like some great mogul of the silver screen had fixed it up just for you. (Thanks, Warner Brothers!)

The city was ablaze with light, floodlit for the occasion. You could pick out the wide boulevards, the huddle of the old Arab town round the Medina, the more glaring, harsher illumination round the port.

The nocturnal vision unfurled before the startled eyes of these greenest of pea-green GIs as if it were some tale of Sinbad and his mariners, straight from "The Thousand and One Nights."

"Casablanca, sir?" asked PFC Offenbach, still waiting on A deck, where the shadow of their landing craft dangled from the davits.

"Yeah, Casablanca," Captain Maxwell nodded, "in Technicolor."

"Just like the movie, only better," Lieutenant Al Hutter chipped in.

"Is this where we get off?" asked the private first class through chattering teeth.

"Keep your mouth shut," Sergeant Eklund shouted under his steel helmet.

The Captain's finger swept leftwards, past the gay lighting of Casablanca's promenade, past a ten-mile pocket of total pitch black to a glittering diamond tiara almost out of vision.

"Place called Fedala," he murmured. "It's got a harbor, and they reckon it's an easier lay."

If the genie in the lamp had given PFC Offenbach magic vision he'd have seen it all right.

The sharp outthrust of Cap de Fedala, with its little bay; the glowing presence of the Hotel Miramar. And over on the far side of the bay the ominous silhouette of Fort Cherqui with its 137.6-mm guns on the promontory of Pont Blondin.

PFC Offenbach and his greenhorn company were earmarked for Beach Yellow, an undulating little *plage* where a man called Steve Wagner had just killed a man called Kellerman with a pistol shot that stood no chance of being heard around the world.

"Come closer, my lovely," crooned Nad Klaf as he got his binoculars to work on Casablanca's billion-watt waterfront.

It was unfolding itself before him, but his memory eye could probe deeper than Captain Maxwell or PFC Offenbach. He knew the seamy dives, the crude set-build behind the boulevards and esplanades, the gutters hung with whores, the slimy bazaars with their salaaming proprietors and cheap carpets. Probed even behind where his binocular lenses encountered total blackness a little winking neon with RITZIS BAR DANCING on it.

Knew the whole scenario better than the stagehands who had designed that all too Araby Warner Bros. set. Knew the gut feel of the real place.

And knew too that within a matter of hours he would be sitting there with a glass of scotch in one hand and a nice piece of Moorish ass resting on the other.

Foresaw Ritzi's slimy greeting. And a hack pianist called Bobbi Lamont, whose skin had mysteriously changed color to ebony in the Warner Bros. version.

But no matter, this night would even all. Robert was arriving. Along with a buddy from Hollywood called Nad Klaf, and the TORCH that would be lit would even light up Sunset Boulevard.

"Check equipment and line up over there by the bow," came the clipped instructions of a nineteen-year-old Lieutenant. "We'll be hitting the beach in under thirty minutes."

The Atlantic breezes, the release from highballs and martinis and manhattans had done Nad Klaf all right. It had been like a health trip. He'd never felt fitter in his life, he reflected as he stepped down into the landing craft to make his date with destiny.

It was a fluke, just a range finder. A probing shot from the boys behind the illuminations of Casablanca towards the dark, blurred oncoming armada. But it connected.

The landing craft felt nothing much more substantial than a jolt. But it was a jolt, a piece of shell fragment that stove in her hull.

A minute later Klaf was aware that the deck line and the wave line were somehow equalizing themselves out. People were making a dive for it. The young Lieutenant threw him a life belt.

And then he too was in the sea, with enough knowledge of old movies, of past *Titanics* and *Lusitanias*, to know that guys like

Clark Gable and Wallace Beery made damn sure they'd cleared the sinking craft before it dragged them down with it.

The water was warm, and the soldiers around him splashed around in the dark as if midnight swimming had been the main idea, and not invasion.

He could still see the lights of Casablanca, but from his lower level he could not, as before, so easily probe into its bowels to pin-point a crude little dive called RITZIS.

In the distance the guns were flashing deep orange. The whole world seemed too busy to want to bother to pick them up. They were out of the scenario.

The pillar of fire that took hold of Steve's pursuers en masse and scattered their entrails hundreds of yards apart, like a child smashing a jigsaw puzzle, was no divine manifestation, or at least not directly. It was the direct result of an order code-named PLAY BALL, transmitted by Admiral Hewitt, Commander of Western Naval Task Force, to Commander Durgin on USS *Wilkes*.

The hope had always been there: the French would throw up their arms and welcome the US troops, by tradition their fraternal brothers in times of war, into Vichy Africa as liberators. But for some time now the dark coast had been pinpointed by evidence of hostility. Here a scavenging searchlight, picking out the invasion fleet, there a burst of machine gun fire directed at US scouts on shore. Or a whirlpool of water opening up beside a US sloop as an onshore battery of 75 mms started to find the range.

Now the guns of Fort Cherqui on Pont Blondin began to engage USS *Augusta*, flagship of the mission. The scale of conflict was crescendoing with every minute. And then with a flash that broke every window for hundreds of yards around, the mighty 15-inch guns of *Jean Bart*, France's newest, if incomplete, battleship, opened up from her moored position by the Mol de Commerce in Casablanca harbor and the heavy pieces from the western promontory of El Hank joined in support. Early in the game Admiral François Michelier, fresh from Vichy and ardently pro-German, had engaged his queen. Now the Americans moved in theirs. Miles out to sea, with a raucous hooting, the USS *Massachusetts*, one of the mightiest battleships in the US fleet, swung her guns astern and flashed forth her first broadside. In this battle of the Titans the 6-inch shell that flattened Pajol's party of *flics* was strictly peashooter stuff.

"Relax, baby," Laura told a perspiring boss, Jerry Daniels, as they sat out on her veranda in the jasmine-heavy night, which was just beginning to become gently tinged with the reek of cordite and the smell of burning.

"The stupid bums," Jerry expostulated, pounding one hairy fist into the other. "The crazy mixed-up creeps! What do they think they're doing? Didn't they know the whole thing was geared to a smooth take-over?"

"Have another highball, Jerry," Laura advised. "And don't let the thing eat into you like that. OK, we bummed out. So what?"

"The goddamn tin-pan Vichy fucking navy taking on the USA?

All they need is Fred Carno's army, with Charlie Chaplin or Buster Keaton to lead them."

A terrific explosion from the general direction of Casablanca harbor shook the fragile villa and demolished Laura's bedroom windows.

"Well, for my money, I think it's scenic. I love a big display," she declared.

"And what do you think they'll twist our guts into afterwards, when the stupid shooting match is over? Our job was to make the take-over peaceful."

"OK, we said the French would grovel on the floor and do a big salaam. So what? That's American optimism. We think that just because we're the Home of the Brave and the Free the whole world's lining up to shake us by the hand. Who knows? Maybe they think we stink."

"Jesus Christ!" expostulated Jerry Daniels as the whole sea shimmered for a second into broad blinding daylight. And atop of Laura's villa a few Moorish ornamental tiles did a gentle cascade onto the patio and broke up.

"Jerry," Laura admonished, "in my house, just nobody treats a highball like that. They're made to be gently sipped. Not downed in one!"

Then from the harbor the *Jean Bart* opened up again, and Laura's dainty chimney pot hit the still blue waters of her swimming pool.

"They don't build them to last here, do they," she commented wistfully. "Well, I'll give them one thing, your lovely OSS. When they rented this joint, they gave us a grandstand view."

This was the moment when the French destroyer flotilla steamed out to sea to engage the invasion craft, on Admiral Michelier's express orders. The moment when the USS *Massachusetts* swung its guns around again to win game, set, and match in its one-sided battle with the quai-bound *Jean Bart*. The moment when General George S. Patton's personal boat, while being lowered from the davits on USS *Augusta,* was totally demolished by the blast from the cruisers' guns and went down with all Patton's belongings on board.

"Don't worry," Laura consoled him as he gazed grimly at the flash-punctuated sea. "You'll get it all back, Jerry. But from now on you'll just have to crap on them twice as hard."

The corpse of General Joachim Kellerman was about to have company. The beach he was lying on was not just an anonymous strip of sand. Its features were engraved in the mind of every officer of the U S Army 3rd Division; so were its tides and the velocity of its breakers. This was the strand, known to everybody from General Marshall and his planners back in Washington to the greenest GI in the Attack Group Center, Western Task Force, as "Beach Yellow."

Some Americans would never forget it. And some would die with its fine blond sand on their lips.

Steve Wagner hadn't heard about "foxholes" (nor about the U S Army padre who'd said there were no atheists in them); in his time they had dug ordinary trenches. All the same, he had made himself a foxhole. It had seemed the natural thing to do on a beach that was attracting so much mayhem. In fact what alternative was there but to claw at the sand like a rabbit until somehow you'd got your head and body below ground? From here he had a worm's eye view (the way he was feeling he might have said a rat's eye view) of the greatest amphibious operation to date in the world's history— at least until the shell with his name on it arrived.

A secluded little cove? The place was now positively bathed by searchlights. A blazing disc of light raced across the sand towards him. He forced his face into the slimy depths of his hole, and like that U S Army padre had suggested, he tried to pray; but the beam was headed out to sea, where it fastened on a gray shape, momentarily thrusting a reluctant destroyer into the limelight. Whoever they were out there, they preferred to remain incognito. A brilliant display of tracer came hissing back from the ocean. The dust the Oerlikon shells kicked up around Steve's hole suggested they were meant for him, although of course the aim was to blind the searchlights.

Even hell can't last forever, at least in one place. In fact it was only a few minutes before the barrage rolled on towards the French antiaircraft guns. And then abruptly everything became very quiet. You could have heard a bird sing if there had been any living birds left on Beach Yellow.

They were walking out of the sea with their shoulders hunched and their rifles at the ready. They looked like soldiers from another planet—no, maybe worse. Maybe Germans. Steve had never seen the new American-style helmet.

He heard an American voice say, "I don't see any goddamn Frenchmen."

Then he heard an American gasp, "This isn't funny. I've been hit!"

And then he saw a soldier had fallen over on the sand, and that there was a big Stars and Stripes patch on his left sleeve which his superiors had hoped might persuade the French to welcome him to Africa with open arms.

The Senegalese infantrymen, who had just been rushed into the sandbagged emplacements overlooking the beach, had no idea whom they were shooting at, and some of them would never know. In any case white men's wars had always been something of a mystery to them, even though they were usually in the thick of them. The irony of Americans locked in wasteful combat with their oldest ally would be lost on the average Senegalese rifleman. All he knew was that he once had a great white master called President Lebrun and now he was called Marshal Pétain, and that he must shoot the hell out of his enemies. As of this moment he was making a pretty good job of it, if you could call the United States the enemy of France.

They pinned the first wave to a line running just about parallel with Steve's foxhole. Close enough for a frightened PFC Offenbach to call across, "Hey, buddy, what outfit are you from?"

It made Steve feel strangely good.

Sergeant Eklund didn't like the line they were pinned to. It was too exposed, and besides, their orders were to move rapidly inshore. He got up to wave his rookies forward, and then he sat down again. A Senegalese corporal working hard at a Chatellerault light machine gun had put two neat holes in his mouth and neck.

Steve never had the pleasure of meeting Sergeant Eklund. So he couldn't feel all that involved in his personal tragedy. But the sergeant left behind an heirloom which he appropriated with gratitude.

He had had occasion to use its predecessor, the original 1928 vintage Thompson submachine gun with its unmistakable drum magazine, but this baby was a sleek new killer with a simple box magazine and a nicely balanced feel. For the first time in many hours Steve Wagner smiled, or nearly smiled. He wasn't alone any longer. He was with an army now. And he was armed with the handiest piece of close-combat fighting equipment the American war industry could produce.

"What happened to Sarge?" PFC Offenbach called across to him. He was just lying on the beach, looking around him to see what was going to hit them next.

"Use that goddamned rifle of yours, sonny," Steve called back, "or what happened to the sergeant is going to happen to you."

And as if to underline the point, Offenbach's buddy, Lou Alverson, stood up with the pain of a Chatellerault machine gun bullet in the shoulder and was knocked down by two more.

The battalion was forgetting just about every lesson they had learned on exercise in Chesapeake Bay. They had allowed themselves to go to earth at the first crack of hostile fire, and having hit the sand, they weren't moving a muscle to help themselves, either by digging in or by trying to pick off the black faces which occasionally showed themselves up there behind the sandbags. It was true they were never meant to be the first wave. As Captain Maxwell put it: "They said the Rangers were going to take this lousy beach."

The U S Rangers in question were wandering around "Beach Red" asking where the hell was "Beach Yellow," which made PFC Offenbach's company the first wave, whether they liked it or not. By the harsh morality of infantry combat they ought to have been annihilated, but at this moment Heaven decided to intervene, or rather the U S Navy Air Service. A squadron of stubby-nosed FeF fighters from the aircraft carrier USS *Ranger* screamed in low over the beach and hit the Senegalese bunkers with all the 20-mm machine guns they'd got.

"Let's go!" Steve shouted with the lost and found enthusiasm of his college football days. "Let's go get those bastards while they've still got their heads down."

About twenty US infantrymen got up, including Lieutenant Al Hutter from Texas, who started shouting what Steve Wagner was shouting.

They ran towards the temporarily silenced entrenchment, but for the GI infantrymen it was heavy going. The War Department hadn't yet learned that it was best to let infantrymen fight light. It had saddled them with enough equipment for a three-week camping expedition. Fine if you were going camping, but not so easy if you were trying to cross a beach on the run.

"Move before they get their heads up again!" Steve hollered.

"Move before they get their heads up again!" Lieutenant Hutter parroted.

Steve himself reached a grassed-over knoll almost under the sandbag positions. Lieutenant Hutter and PFC Offenbach were a few yards behind him. The rest were still stumbling across the open beach when the Senegalese corporal rubbed the dust out of his eyes, respectfully pushed his dead European Lieutenant off his Chatellerault machine gun, and started knocking over GIs like crawling ducks in a rusty shooting gallery.

"Throw your grenade," Steve yelled at Offenbach.

The young GI just smiled back at him with a sheepish kind of smile. It was his first battle. He had forgotten he had a pineapple grenade dangling from his belt, along with a lot of ammunition pouches, a first aid kit, and practically everything else a soldier might need on an extended tour of the Sahara.

"Throw your grenade! Hell!"

Steve started to crawl back to where Offenbach was lying. But he had to turn round for a Senegalese who'd popped his head over the parapet with a Lebel rifle and blast him out of sight with Sergeant Eklund's MI submachine gun.

Then he found that PFC Offenbach had forgotten not to detach his grenade. So he had to tear the thing off. Then he ran back to the emplacement, lopped the grenade over, waited for the inevitable explosion, and jumped up on the parapet with his MI going like crazy.

"Fix bayonets!" Lieutenant Hutter shouted. "And charge!"

Only PFC Offenbach obeyed him, because he was the only GI within earshot.

Still, by the time he had got in the defenders there weren't too many of them to stick. The first Negro he bayoneted was still breathing, but the second was dead.

The Senegalese in the trench above Beach Yellow were good soldiers, and as such they knew when they were enfiladed. So all the way down the trench khaki figures in First World War French helmets started raising their arms, or producing grubby white handkerchiefs from their pockets, in spite of their fierce loyalty to

President Lebrun, or le Maréchal, as he was now called. The dead-interrupted line of overloaded GIs got up again and stumbled forward to accept the victory. The U S 3rd Division had captured Beach Yellow.

"Who are you, anyway?" Al Hutter asked as they stood on the parapet, looking down on the Senegalese infantrymen who had died, as they thought, for Marshal Pétain (although history would find it harder to decide what exactly they died for).

"I'm an American," Steve said. "An American who needs a cigarette."

Lieutenant Hutter held out a pack of Luckies. Boy, it tasted good. It was the first fresh American cigarette Steve had smoked in years.

General de Gaulle's broadcast from London:

"COMMANDERS, SOLDIERS, SEAMEN, AIRMEN, CIVIL SERVANTS, AND CITI-
ZENS OF FRENCH NORTH AFRICA—STIR YOURSELVES! AID OUR ALLIES, JOIN
WITH THEM WHOLEHEARTEDLY! FORGET ABOUT NAMES OR FORMULAS!
A GREAT MOMENT HAS ARRIVED. THIS IS A TIME FOR SENSE AND COUR-
AGE . . . FRENCHMEN OF NORTH AFRICA, WITH YOUR HELP WE CAN RE-
ENTER THE LINE ALONG THE WHOLE LENGTH OF THE MEDITERRANEAN
AND THE WAR WILL BE WON, THANKS TO FRANCE."

"Here in Rabat calm has been restored," General Nogues said, breathing down the telephone perhaps a little more heavily than usual. "General Béthouart and his officers are under arrest. I intend to have them all sentenced to death by court-martial. How is it going in Casablanca?"

It was an embarrassing moment to ask Admiral Michelier, first because even a telephone caller from Rabat could hear the shells from the USS *Massachusetts* creating gory carnage on the battleship *Jean Bart*, and second because earlier that morning the Admiral had reported he could see no sign of American ships, and even if there were any they would be no match for the French Navy.

But there was something of the Villeneuve spirit about this little fascist Frenchman.

"We shall fight to the last cartridge, *mon Général*," he shouted from his cellar under the Admiralty building, in the Boulevard sur Djedid. If necessary we shall go down with all our ships. *Vive la France!*"

They were dug in astride the Fedala-Casablanca railway. Behind them a battery of 37-mm guns were being readied for action in an abandoned goods yard. Ahead of them were a dead GI and a lot of noisy flies ("You had better move him soon or he's gonna stink like all hell," Steve had said), and beyond that, if you were foolish enough to lift your head and look along the glistening tracks, you could see the "molehills" that marked the forward positions of the Moroccan 3rd Spahis. Beyond these was the city of Casablanca.

"We're gonna blast our way into town with every damned thing we've got," Captain Calvin Maxwell had said, "and this time I'm not having any civilians in my outfit."

He was right on the first count. A swarm of P40 fighters was buzzing around in the blue morning air over a city that many travelers, including General Patton, had decided might have been dreamed up by Hollywood. Meanwhile out at sea Admiral Hewitt's warships were trimming their turrets in preparation for a full-scale bombardment. On the second count Captain Maxwell had been mistaken. Steve had just carried on polishing his MI sub, and said, "I've come a long way to liberate Casablanca, Captain. I can't quit now."

For his part PFC Joe Offenbach would have quit any time his Captain asked him. It might be true that these P40s backed by the Navy's guns were going to blast hell out of Casablanca, but there were a lot of people in and around Casablanca and there was no guarantee that the schedule of destruction included those "molehills" five hundred yards or so up the Fedala-Casablanca railway line. In a few minutes they were going to have to climb out of their foxholes and start running towards them. As the veteran of three days of war, Offenbach knew that could be a hell of a lonely feeling.

In war it's meant to be the attackers who do the shouting. Which was why Lieutenant Al Hutter looked puzzled when the shouting started over in the French positions.

"OK, you guys," Captain Maxwell bawled along the line of foxholes, "it looks like these bastards are gonna save us the trouble of digging 'em out. Stand by to repel a charge!"

In fact the charge consisted of a single French officer. "Fire!" shouted Lieutenant Al Hutter. "Hold your fire!" hollered Captain Maxwell. "Can't you see the guy's carrying a white flag?"

It was a timely order as far as the Lieutenant of spahis was concerned. Although the marksmanship of Captain Maxwell's men was nothing to write home about, he made slow progress towards the American positions. This was not only because he was handicapped by an enormous white flag, nor because for a front-line officer he was definitely a little overweight; he also happened to be reeling-drunk.

"Hello, Yanks! *Chers vieux amis!* It's over. *C'est terminé. Vive l'Amérique! Vive la paix!*"

He nearly fell into Steve's foxhole. But Steve saw he was carrying a bottle of Martell brandy and caught him.

"Yes, it is for you. It is for all of us to drink to the cease-fire! Yes, that *idiot*, that *salaud* Michelier, has surrendered. We do not any longer have to die for the French Navy!" He raised the Martell bottle to his lips for a long time before Steve finally relieved him of it.

"You're kidding," Captain Maxwell said. But he wasn't kidding. Up the railway line little khaki figures were showing themselves above their molehill entrenchments, and some of them were actually waving. Suddenly everybody felt free to stand up.

"You do not know," beamed the Lieutenant of spahis, "what a joy this is for us who love France."

"I'll take a slug of that brandy," Captain Maxwell said.

"We did not want to fight you. We wanted to welcome you with open arms. It was those *crapauds* Michelier and Nogues who compelled us to resist. But now, look, I welcome you with open arms."

"Hey, lay off!" shouted Lieutenant Al Hutter, wrestling himself out of a tender embrace which smelled of half a bottle of cognac.

"I do not care that my family live in Chartres and will be arrested if I am not, as you say, a 'good boy.' *A bas les Boches! Vive la France!* Let us march together to Berlin. But first, *mes amis*," said the drunken but starry-eyed Frenchman, "it will be my pleasure to watch you kick those Nazi *salauds* Michelier and Nogues into the sea."

"I tell you one thing we're going to do first," Steve grinned. "We're going to have a drink on me at Ritzi's place in Casablanca."

"Seeing as everyone seems to be drinking champagne around here, why don't we?" suggested U S Army Colonel Hiram Tanner.

He was sitting with Jerry Daniels in the lounge of the Hotel Miramar, Fedala, in an armchair which only three days before had sustained the ample ass of Major General Joachim Kellerman of the Wehrmacht.

He had just watched a champagne-loaded waiter close the door on the smoking room where US General Patton and USN Admiral Hewitt were talking peace terms with General Nogues and Admiral Michelier of Vichy, two gentlemen who only a few days before had been drinking champagne in the same smoking room with Major General Kellerman and his colleagues on the German Armistice Commission.

"Why not?" Daniels grinned. "I guess we've all got something to celebrate."

The Colonel inspected the bubbles another perspiring waiter had deposited into his glass. "Yeah," he mused, "I guess we've got something to celebrate, but I don't see what it's got to do with those French bastards. As I recall, it was only yesterday those bastards were trying to kill us."

"That's why we're buying them champagne," Daniels said. "They're not trying to kill us anymore."

"That's nice of them," the Colonel agreed. "Just the same, there are three thousand of our boys lying back there on the beaches, and I don't believe their last wish was to buy Dom Perignon for General Nogues."

Daniels ran a hand through his close-cropped ginger hair. "Colonel, you know as well as I do this isn't a strictly military operation; it also happens to be a highly complex exercise in politics."

"That bastard Nogues. He walked in here as if he was doing us a favor. Hell, we licked him, didn't we?"

"I'm telling you, Colonel. This isn't a strictly military operation. OK, maybe we licked General Nogues, but we still need him."

"Funny thing, politics," the Colonel said. "Who was it told me General Nogues was the biggest Hitler-lover in Morocco?"

The door of the smoking room opened as the waiter came out for another order of Dom Perignon. A burst of genial laughter came out with him.

"Boy"—Colonel Tanner shook his head—"that's some surrender ceremony!"

Daniels shot him an impatient look. A look that could be dangerous if you didn't happen to be protected by the uniform of the U S Army, and even then you couldn't be sure this was protection enough.

"What do you want, Colonel?" he asked. "Washington and Cornwallis at Yorktown? Lee and Grant at Appomattox? I told you this is a different kind of operation. Everything that's happening in there is strictly in accordance with the briefings we've given General Patton and Admiral Hewitt. We've got to convince Nogues we're here as friends, not conquerors, because, frankly, we need his pull."

"Nice friend that bastard Nogues turned out to be." Colonel Tanner poured himself another glass of champagne. "They told us we were gonna walk ashore. They told us there was this guy called General Émile Béthouart who'd got the whole thing fixed. What happens? Nogues slaps Béthouart in jail and gives us all hell. Are you sure Nogues is the kind of friend we need?"

"Forgive me, but you've made my point," Daniels grinned, twisting his champagne glass around in his freckled hand. "Your pal General Béthouart proved to be one big phony. He told us he could bring over the whole Casablanca Division. He said he could bring over the French Navy too. Maybe he was a liar, maybe it was wishful thinking. The fact is he just didn't deliver. Now Nogues *can* deliver."

"Have you heard they put Jews in concentration camps here in Morocco?" Colonel Hiram Tanner asked irrelevantly. "Just like in Nazi Germany."

The smoking room door opened, General Patton came out with an arm round General Nogues, followed by Admiral Hewitt, arms linked with the sour-looking would-be Axis naval hero, Admiral Michelier. They were followed by a bevy of French and American aides, one of whom winked at Daniels, as if to say, "It's in the bag."

"Mind if I give you a piece of disinterested advice, Colonel?" Daniels said when the procession had passed. "Don't listen to any more Gaullist propaganda than you can help. We've got a long way to go in Africa, and we don't want any trouble on our lines of communications. Nice and clean is how they've got to be. By the way," Daniels smiled, an overgrown Norman Rockwell kid whose smile had turned disturbingly adult, "there's a Frenchman over here I'd like you to meet. Chief Inspector Lucien Roth of the Casablanca police force."

It was official. Admiral Darlan in far-off Algiers had finally bowed to the combined nudgings of Eisenhower, roving Ambassador Robert Murphy, and the American and British forces, and ordered a cease-fire. In so doing he had at one stroke guaranteed peace in French North Africa and his own position as official heir apparent. In the mind of President Roosevelt it hardly counted that Admiral Darlan had been one of the two or three most desperate appeasers of Adolf Hitler. What mattered was that Darlan was now in the position to deliver the whole of French North Africa in a moving spirit of *entente cordiale* into the camp of the Allies. Thus a few hours' *volte-face* put him light-years ahead of minor visionaries like General Charles de Gaulle. But none of these politics on high affected Steve Wagner at the moment.

His bloodshot eyes took in the familiar landmarks as the odor-coated streets started to fill with the proscribed crush of cheering, liberated, downtrodden people.

"Where are we heading, Captain?" shouted Lieutenant Al Hutter.

"Give you one guess," shot back Maxwell as the Stuart tank they were riding on chewed up a strip of road and the tank did a rapid slurch to the right, following a sign with the promise Center Ville emblazoned on it in French and Arabic.

"Hey what about Rick's Place?" Hutter gave him back. "Let's go screw Ingrid Bergman. Smash Humphrey Bogart's fake jaw in, and grab ourselves a souvenir or two. So let's step on the gas, Captain, or we'll be fighting the whole Western Task Force for a slice of Ingrid Bergman's camiknickers. Not to mention a slap on the back for my old buddy, Sydney Greenstreet, coupled with the immortal name of one Peter Lorre, and a nudge up the butt for that prize sentimental jerk, Paul Henreid."

But the mission got snarled up in Casablanca's Place de la République. Middle-aged ladies of the French colonial classes whose balconies (with their delicate iron fretwork) fronted the thoroughfare had done what Admiral Michelier's better-armed cohorts had not succeeded in doing: bringing General Patton's offensive to a slurching halt.

"Help me, Steve," appealed Lieutenant Al Hutter as an elderly lady crowned him with a wreath of bougainvillaea.

"What are you talking about?" growled Steve as he permitted a charming sixteen-year-old to kiss his stubbly chin. "You're a hero, aren't you?"

"You know Casablanca, so come on. Where are they hiding Rick's Place?"

"There ain't no such place," Steve told him as his hungry, whiskey-soaked lips dipped inside the French girl's blouse.

"You know. Rick's Place? Warner Brothers? Humphrey Bogart, Claude Rains? The dump the entire free world is hell-bent on liberating. But maybe we got a flying start. We saw the preview."

"Used to work in a crap hole," Steve told him, still hugging the girl's fresh-smelling blouse. "Run by an evil-smelling Libyan called Ritzi. Never heard of Rick's Place, but I'll take you to Ritzi's."

"Jeez," groaned Lieutenant Hutter, "the guy's lived in Casablanca and he's never heard of Rick's Place. How dumb can you get?"

Finally the Stuart came to a stop outside a café that didn't have any name, at least temporarily. If you were sober, which Captain Maxwell and his party weren't, you perhaps could have read through the fresh coat of white paint on the fascia that it had once been called, "Chez Maurice." Now an Arab signwriter was hurrying out a new designation that spelled something beginning with R-I, but he was having a problem staying balanced on his ladder. It looked as if the whole American Army were trying to squeeze into the place, whatever it was called.

"Sorry. Ain't no Rick's Place," Hutter bawled as he started to slam his way through the uniformed throng like an All-Star.

"It is, you know, Loot," yelled a pimply-faced GI. "It's the prototype. That's official. Manager said so."

"The what?" Hutter yelled as his massive shoulders ripped openings in the swarm.

"You heard what the kid said," Steve Wagner yelled at him as he neatly followed the jungle path cut by Hutter. "Prototype, you mindless brute!"

Inside the bar Ritzi was collecting large packets of notes in envelopes and stuffing them in his pocket. They happened to be each soldier's entire issue of French francs. And they guaranteed at least one hour's entertainment at Rick's—Ritzi's, sorry—Place. The fact was that Ritzi had turned on a dime.

That morning the bar was still, just, tremulously Chez Maurice. Now it was, tactfully, about to revert to its original name of Ritzi's. However, the arrival of Western Task Force was about to force another change. "Rick's Place" were the words that Arab signwriter was finally going to write.

Flashback: There was a guy and his name was Nad Klaf, or something screwy like that, and all that I remember about him was that he didn't pay his liquor bills, and fought shy of all the local dames like a man who'd just learned to spell "clap."

He was in Ritzi's for a long weekend around about the fall of '41. He never ate, and he didn't gamble, and he didn't date. He just slugged back bourbon and flicked open his big gray eyes and waited his turn for the plane to fly him to Lisbon en route for the States. One day, just before I cleared town, he managed to top me up to the limit with scotch, and I gave him the whole darn thing. I mean our little *comédie humaine*, with Helda and Auguste Berthier and Bobbi and Georges Martel, not to mention a certain slob by name of Steve Wagner.

The next day I woke up with a hangover that threatened to live as long as me. Even so I went straight out into the glare of the Moroccan sun to the Hotel Cambon, where Nad spent his nonwaking hours. I wanted to settle with him; he'd made me say things I didn't want uncovered. Things I wanted to die finally, just as I would. So I was hell-bent on punching the memory out of his system. Except that the jerk had vacated his room. That was why he pumped me that last night. He knew there would be no comeback.

I know your kind, Nad Klaf, you goddamn slimy pimping Hollywood scout.

And you know mine. After all, you pumped me.

Hal and Tina Newport were at Ritzi's the night of November 11; Tina because it seemed the most likely place to get stewed, Hal because General Nogues's sudden capitulation had put the "Newport for Ambassador" bandwagon back on course. If he put down enough scotch he might even forget those six thousand-odd casualties that showed the diplomats had read it wrong and convince himself the whole thing was hunky-dory.

So this night would be an exception. If Tina wanted to hit the bottle, her husband would be right there beside her, knocking it back, glass for glass.

"Know what's cutest about tonight?" slurred Tina at him as the whole center of the joint seemed to take off in a boogie-woogie. "It's a relief to meet some plain, honest, virile American boys for a change. The national sample around here recently has been a disgrace to the Stars and Stripes."

"There's no hiding they're mighty welcome," agreed her husband. "And by all accounts they've acquitted themselves like real soldiers."

"They're all Tarzans to me," commented Tina as she lurched from their ringside table and lashed in among the boogie-woogiers.

"Hey, Tina," shouted Hal in his thin Harvard voice, "here's Steve. The prodigal has returned. And he's brought a friend."

Hal Newport's eyes angled on a tottering Steve Wagner, a US service cap somehow hanging on the back of his head, held up lovingly in the fraternal arms of Captain Maxwell.

"I'm taking over, Captain," said a quietly twangy voice in Captain Maxwell's ear. "You are officially relieved."

Laura Caulfield was at Ritzi's the night of November 11. She was there because she thought she might be able to shake off Jerry Daniels in the most jam-packed joint in Casablanca. She was there also because she figured she might just find Steve Wagner again.

"You look as if you could use some sleep, hero," she told him as they clung tightly together in the midst of a raging torrent of GIs. Steve's arms moved round her. His stubbled chin rested lightly on her chic Barbara-Stanwyck-style hairdo. Laura's arms pressed him tighter.

"That's right, hero," she crooned, cradling him. "The war's over. It's time to unwind."

"You gotta meet a friend," he told her. "His name's Captain Calvin Maxwell, and what he's personally done these last three days deserves a Congressional citation."

"I met him," she told him. "He must be a great guy, but he hasn't got your oomph."

"He's my buddy," muttered Steve.

"In that case he's great," conceded Laura.

She was trying to work out in her mind how she could move a 154-pound, drunken, beautiful lover boy through a snarled-up traffic jam of rip-roaring GIs, back to where he belonged. Clean sheets, a soft bed, a room with a sea view. A dish of homemade scrambled eggs, whipped up Maryland-style. Laura Caulfield was a girl of resource, but she hadn't quite figured it out yet.

Jerry Daniels was at Ritzi's that night of November 11. Like everyone else, he had a mind to celebrate, but in fact, at this moment, there were two flies in the ointment; hence a sulky pouting of the lips on his boyish face. For a start Laura Caulfield, whom he'd personally chauffeured to Ritzi's, had got lost in a maelstrom of sweaty greenhorns, a poor preliminary to what was destined to be her night of nights. Jerry Daniels had decided to throw discretion and professionalism to the wind and screw his sleek-contoured subordinate. Later that night, he would, in her villa, on her booze, on her couch, take her through some sexual master stops, terminating with position 46 (a Daniels speciality).

But if losing Laura Caulfield wasn't enough, he had bumped into that goddamn bureaucrat, masquerading as a cop, Lucien Roth, and his swarthy hatchet man, Lieutenant Pajol. Sure, he had an appointment with Roth at the Sûreté tomorrow. Sure, they'd lay a plan to make the Commies and Gaullists of Casablanca cringe as they'd never cringed before. Sure, Roth was shit-keen on the job, a pliant tool.

But tonight was the night. The night on which Jerry de Sousa Daniels was destined by sheer dialectical necessity to hold the lovely Laura Valentine Caulfield in his arms and screw the cunt off her so hard they'd both be sore for a week.

Roth was thrusting a departmental map of Casablanca under Jerry Daniels's gaze to show how he proposed to clamp down with the full ferocity of the law on the unsuspecting riffraff of Casablanca. Lieutenant Pajol, lucky to be alive after what had happened to his men at Beach Yellow, was nodding his fierce agreement. And Jerry was sure-suring him in an offhand kind of way, whilst his skilled eye tried to separate out the tangle of the dance floor. But try as he might, he just couldn't spot that cute little body in the tangerine dress.

"Monsieur, Monsieur Daniels," Roth's thin voice was insisting.

"Sure, sure," drawled Daniels. "Tell you what, Roth, we'll kick the plan around tomorrow. Check it out for wrinkles . . ."

"But, monsieur, he is here. We have positively identified him."

"Know one thing, Roth, the whole crummy world's here. The only guy I don't quite see as of now is General Patton. But he'll be checking in by and by."

"*L'assassin, monsieur, le salaud.* The murderer of General Kellerman."

"You mean the guy who took out a piece of top-notch kraut single-handed? He's no murderer, Roth. He's done us all a favor. You, too, as an ally of this morning." Daniels put an arm round Lucien Roth's taut neck in a fraternal kind of way, like one ally to another.

"*Ici, ici, regardez, monsieur,*" the swarthy Pajol was shouting, and faced with such insistence, Jerry Daniels did condescend to angle his face in the general direction intended.

They were not in the center of the floor. They had crept beside a pillar, a matter of a few yards away. And they were deep in a long horny smooch, like a couple of popcorn-cracking teen-agers in some backwoods movie house. The man was sunken-eyed and dirty and unshaven. He had a look of John Garfield about him. The lady sported a tangerine-colored dress and a gently angular body, and her hand was cozily positioned on his unshaven cheek—just lying there.

"Jeepers creepers," squeaked Jerry Daniels as his knobbly wooden chair became an ejector seat and snarlingly he propelled himself into hostility.

Al Hutter, we know, was at Ritzi's on the night of November 11. Except he still wasn't convinced this was where he was. All right, it didn't look exactly like the movie set, but there were enough similarities to nudge Al's booze-clouded consciousness into a sense of *déjà vu*.

"Is this Rick's Place, or isn't it?" he demanded as he set off on a one-man pursuit of a very recent piece of American folklore.

The pursuit led him to put his footballer's physique to full use as he shoved and clawed his way through a hundred homesick buddies up the stairway to where the punk half-caste manager he had already spotted must somewhere be hiding. Hutter put his full weight to the locked door and burst in. He surprised Ritzi in the act of stuffing notes into his iron safe.

"I come bearing greetings from your allies," said Hutter, holding a bottle of scotch aloft. "The message is, either you spill or we requisition the joint for the exclusive use of Western Task Force personnel."

"How can I help?" asked Ritzi, waving his pudgy little hands appealingly. "Are you short on drink?"

"The booze is OK. If you don't mind, we've helped ourselves. But you gotta tell me, is this Rick's Place, or isn't it?"

"Everybody today asked me that question. Of course this is Reek's Place. There is no other candidate in Casablanca."

"OK, then tell me this," purred Lieutenant Hutter grimly. "If this is Rick's Place, where the hell is Rick?"

"I don't understand, monsieur. Who is Rick?"

"Haven't you seen the movie? Just about the one guy whom every decent American male has wanted to personally be like these past months. A simple globe-trotting ugly bastard with a way with women, and cards, and krauts. A manly kind of guy who managed to keep his heart while the whole world was losing its head. Do you know a guy like that, or must I waste a good bottle of scotch, blasting it out of you, you crap-eating half-caste?"

There she was, holding me against the pillar. And I s'pose she was the best broad I'd ever turned up, best for me, that is. Fatal for her. But as the immortal Bobbi once wrote:

You can't write a new song
When the old one's still there.

Not that she was. The world and his dog and everything from Charlie Chaplin to Charlie Chan was there, but not her.

And somehow I had to tell the one who was holding me to scram. Clear clean out. Because all I could honestly do for her was crap on her.

And though she held me nice and easy, and though she promised clean lavendered sheets, cranberry sauce, and a sharp, kind wit, she simply wasn't riding in my roadster.

And so I shook her. Just shook her and said something like, "Look, babe . . ." And I was trying to get the words together when it hit me in the back of the neck. Like somebody has a go at Bob Hope when he's kissing Dorothy Lamour and he thinks her kiss has knocked him clean out.

And then I was down in the general region of her skirt. And I noticed there was blood on tangerine, my blood on her dress. And there was this sour-faced *gendarme* saying something about a charge of murder. And I said you're right, and something about the stupid slaughter of thousands in the past three days and confidentially it made me puke. But he said "No," it had nothing to do with that lot. It was a kraut called Kellerman, a general of recent fond recollection. I said I remember him well, and you're right, he has no right to be a cadaver either, but that's show biz, chum.

And Laura was screaming, and my pink-faced old pal, Hal Newport, was saying that the frogs would be hearing from the U S Consul about it. And another Yank with a shiny face and ginger hair was trying to tell him that would do no good because "Moider is moider," in the immortal words of William Bendix.

And I took a personal aversion to the guy just on the grounds of a drunkard's hunch and got up to hit him, and someone tripped me up and I was up there staring at the stars on Ritzi's ceiling and trying to separate them from the stars in my head and failing.

And this Lieutenant Hutter was shouting to me to get up and something about Humphrey Bogart.

Oh, Humphrey Bogart. Oh sure!

"Hey, Vincent, why aren't you here? Golly Moses, you oughta be here!" Nad Klaf mentally cabled. "You've got the whole hot property here, the whole new scenario."

Finally Klaf had shaken off those navy nurses; told them what the hell was a swim in the Atlantic a slug or two of bourbon couldn't cure; brushed aside the suggestion that if he stayed hospitalized for a couple of days longer he could collect a citation for the Purple Heart. Sure, it was a good story. The Sodersheim Syndicate would be thrilled to hear their special correspondent had been sunk by a Vichy French torpedo. Those few chilling moments in the black ocean would make four columns, syndicated nationwide. But the old professional was after bigger game. So he had hotfooted it out of the arms of the USN, hailed a beat-up Renault taxi, and told the driver, "Ritzi's, and fast!"

Like he said, it was everything he had promised Vincent. It was *Casablanca* set to bebop, it was Warner Bros. with all Metro's extras thrown in; it was West meets East, Mickey Rooney meets the thief of Baghdad, Hemingway teamed with Somerset Maugham, Jean Gabin in collaboration with Bud Schulberg. All it needed was this guy. He had to be here.

Of course he was playing a hunch, but that was big-game hunting. Nad believed if you were a game hunter and the guy you were hunting was good too, you got to know each other's instincts. Follow that shared instinct and you found yourself at his water hole.

That instinct hadn't been wrong. He could almost smell him—this man Steve and his unique life. He shoved his way through the crowd of GIs and their perspiring women. "Anyone here seen a guy called Steve Wagner?" he was shouting, confident that any moment someone would jerk a thumb and there in a dark corner would be this sallow face, creased by God knew how many original stories.

And then he saw this girl in a tangerine dress. Great eyes. Nice figure. Class written all over her, but blood on her tangerine dress. And his instinct made him cry, "Oh hell!" before she said anything.

She shouted at him, as if she was crazy or something, "And this slob wants to know if anyone's seen Steve Wagner!"

"Don't bother to tell me, sister. I missed him again, didn't I?" Nad Klaf said, feeling as if he could use a drink.

"Why did you let those louses get him?" Laura Caulfield wanted to know. "All he did was shoot a German general."

It was the morning after they had dragged Steve away from Ritzi's. Jerry Daniels was leaning back in an easy chair in his new suite in the Hotel de Maroc showing a lot of teeth. His way of looking sexy.

He said, "There happens to be a law against shooting people in this country, even German generals, and we're respecting the law. That's part of the deal with Nogues."

"Guess in any other country he'd have got a medal."

"Eh, eh, Laura." Jerry shook his head. "In any country that guy is gonna get jailed as a number-one jerk."

"You bastard!" she murmured softly.

The OSS man stretched his shirt-sleeved arms. Two sweat patches glistened at his armpits.

"Don't worry," he grinned, "I like your boyfriend too. I like him an awful lot. I like the fact that he's got a nice long record of liberal agitation back home. I like the fact that he fought in Spain with the Communists. I like the fact that he's now working for de Gaulle. It kinda ties things up nice and tidy in my mind. De Gaulle's setup is a Commie setup, just like the State Department always suspected."

"You wouldn't be letting a little thing like personal animosity get into this, would you, Jerry?"

The arms spread outwards. "Honey, I never even saw the bum until last night. All I know is he's trouble, like de Gaulle is trouble. We've got to keep our lines of communications clean of this kind of shit."

He got up and walked to his fifth-floor window and looked down at the Parc Lyautey, a patch of green that could have been the Luxembourg Gardens, except for the palms and the odd jellaba among them.

He said, "Shucks, let's look on the bright side of things, shall we? The mission's a success. We've got our boys ashore. We got the French eating out of our hands, and the lousy Gaullists never got a look in. You and I ought to be celebrating. I mean, just you and I this time."

Laura tore another cigarette from an emptying Chesterfield pack.

"Jerry," she said, "you've only got to lift that phone and they'll let Steve go. They've got to do what you tell them. They surrendered, didn't they?"

"Shhhh!" A finger tapped against the fulsome row of teeth. "Don't let anyone hear you say that word—especially the French. The French and us are buddies—that's official—just like we were in the First War. Maybe there was a little misunderstanding at first. A few hotheads on either side with itchy trigger fingers. But now it's the *entente très cordiale.* We're allies, cobelligerents, whatever the hell you like."

He walked back from the window and put a hand on Laura's knee.

"You better get in line, honey, or your work could suffer."

"Steve's an American citizen. Doesn't that give him some rights?"

"I'm telling you, get in line, honey."

"At school they taught me no goddamn foreigners could put an American citizen in jail—and get away with it. Didn't you go to school, Jerry?"

"Know what I think you're trying to do?" Daniels grinned (one of his sexier grins). "I think you're trying to stall me."

He took his hand from her knee and reached under her silk chemise for her breasts.

"You know that working for me means—well, working for me. Listen to your boss, Laura. I told you we've got something to celebrate."

"I haven't got anything to celebrate," Laura said, "until you lift that phone and tell those cute *gendarme* friends of yours to let Steve go."

"Keep talking, honey. You look real nice and mean when you're sore. I like a girl to be nice and mean-looking," he explained as he perspiringly separated her bodice from its mother-of-pearl buttons. "It gets my dander up too—nice, clean, and straight and all ready for action."

His other hand was now wrestling with his fly. A shock of red hair finally showed, and then everything else that he had promised.

The trouble was that the twin actions of trying to strip Laura and remove his own pants had put him off balance. She only needed to stand up to tumble Jerry onto the plush carpet of his private suite at the Hotel Lyautey.

He made a grab for her ankles—they were very nice ankles—but they were already at the door. And she was already looking as composed as ice.

"Come back here," he bawled, "that's an order."

"Maybe some other time, Jerry," she said, hardly moving her beautiful pouting lips, "when you're feeling more like a human being." She gave his rampant display of masculinity a withering look and added, "Enjoy your celebrations." It wasn't a very dignified position for a senior OSS official to find himself in, but he made the best of it.

"Don't get the idea you're gonna see much of your boyfriend if and when he gets out of jail!" he shouted. "Remember this is Morocco, baby. Down in Berber country they're still feeding guys to the lions. I'm not saying they'll necessarily eat the bum. But Lucien Roth and his outfit have learned a lot of lessons from the Germans. You understand what I'm saying, you fucking society bitch? They're gonna crucify that pink pukey-bastard lover boy of yours!"

SECTION III

WILDERNESS

This Laffley truck looked and smelled as if it had been used for bringing goats to market in the Casablanca Medina. It probably had. But now it had been requisitioned for another purpose, which was to transport human scapegoats to desert places to help counterbalance the manpower wastage on the new trans-Sahara railway.

They were comparatively gracious to Steve, these Berber cutthroats turned police auxiliaries. They simply handed him up into the truck and threw him onto the raw wood floor, forgetting, or perhaps remembering, that being handcuffed behind his back, he wouldn't be able to protect his face. A little bald-headed man was hauled in next, and he was given a kick in the small of the back just to make sure he broke his spectacles. Another man, plump, late-fortyish, landed on the floor beside Steve with his head cut open by a slash from the muzzle of a Lebel rifle.

They threw in about twenty-five prisoners, one way or another, before they belatedly decided the truck was full. The last was in no condition to travel, least of all in a truck packed with handcuffed humanity. He was suffering from acute dysentery.

The truck edged slowly out of the prison gate. It wasn't built for speed even when it was empty. Besides, there was a lot of traffic in the streets; also a lot of people cheering.

Steve twisted round to look at his neighbor, the one with his temple cut open by a slash from a Lebel rifle. He grunted, "You all right?"

The man didn't answer the question. He just spat on the floor and said, "Yankee filth!"

"Easy, I'm an American."

The man hissed, "We risked our lives for the Americans—these were de Gaulle's orders. We guided them ashore. We showed them the minefields. Yes, we even directed their fire on our own French guns. And what is our reward? We have been thrown to Nogues's jackals and we are going to die. Believe me, Yankee. We will all die in the desert!"

The truck had come to a halt on a crossroads. Although Steve couldn't see it, the driver was having a dispute with a colored American Army MP on traffic duty. However, by levering his head over his companion he could see what was coming down the street, and this was the most impressive display of American military might he had ever witnessed. First a line of Stuart tanks, big white stars painted on their hull tops and smiling crew commanders waving from their turrets. Then a column of half-tracks drawing M3 anti-tank guns. Behind these a mass of US infantry, eyes-righting and eyes-lefting, as the girls of Casablanca went wild. Americans enjoying the same rapturous welcome that had been extended to Steve and his outfit only yesterday.

When the infantry came level with the truck, Steve crawled over his companion and started to shout through the wooden bars, "Hey, you, soldier, get us out of here, will you?"

But they didn't seem to hear, either because there was so much cheering or it never occurred to these plain GI Joes that a cattle truck like this could contain human beings, let alone an American human being. They just kept on marching past, smiling happily on their chewing gum as if no one in the world could have a bone to pick with them.

"Hey, you bastards. Will you get us out of here, goddamn it? I'm American, for God's sake. Can you hear me, you bums?"

The truck started to move. The Negro MP finally let it through. Steve caught a glimpse of him as they slid past, a smiling friendly man, basically happy to be helping out as best he could. He even waved the truck good-bye. After all, he didn't know where it was going.

Later there was another holdup at another crossroads. There would be quite a few before they finally jerked clear of Casablanca. But this particular holdup at the junction of the Avenue des Regiments Coloniaux and the Boulevard Moulay Youssef was the one that stayed in Steve's mind. An American colonel—a little guy in glasses—was out walking with a lady in a white picture hat. They were arm in arm, but they didn't look like lovers, or even husband and wife. They looked like a man and a woman who had come to a mutually beneficial arrangement. It was true the Colonel seemed to be whispering tender things into her ear. But the lady wasn't paying any attention. She was looking around her with the beady eyes of a professional scouting the lay of the land for the next customer. He wasn't dreaming. My God, he wasn't dreaming! The woman in the white hat *was* Helda.

In fact not *quite* everyone had been at Ritzi's on the night of 11 November 1942.

One quiet exception was Colonel Blink Burnside, one of the key egghead G2 planners on General Eisenhower's staff for the TORCH operation, with special responsibilities for liaising Western Task Force into the overall Allied strategy.

Blink Burnside was a contemplative kind of guy with a habit of screwing up his eye muscles in tense concentration, a balding academic turned staff man, with a docile wife and two ebullient teenage daughters back in Minneapolis. Although the termination of hostilities did give him some excuse to celebrate, Blink was already hot on the second stage of Eisenhower's plan, drafted months before in London. Tomorrow evening he would climb on board a converted Liberator en route for Algiers and a top-brass conference. But now, on the recommendation of a fellow egghead, he had dropped into a modest haunt called le Club Moderne, on the Route de Bouskoura, where a mixture of Moroccan writers, artists, professors, and savants were congregated to meet their newfound American allies.

And that was where she found him, sitting pensively by himself beside a little wicker table with an undrunk pernod in his hand, his large head peacefully nodding off to the strains of Debussy's "Arabesque," rendered by one of the most brilliant of Morocco's younger pianists. He opened his eyes . . . and blinked.

He saw her face haloed in the subtle candlelight of the Club Moderne. She was an instant stab in the heart, a vision of his homely Irma, a time-and-space game, in which Minneapolis was joined with Casablanca. But this apparition didn't smell of new-made Minnesota cookies.

Her perfume was one which had never teased Blink Burnside's susceptible nostrils before, except that if it reeked of anything it was proven unassailable class. She said very little, and what there was was straight, simple, to the point. But Blink soon realized that it wasn't her mouth that did the talking. That was reserved for other activities.

Her eyes, of a curious blue that took you latitudes north of North Africa, her eyes said everything. Their argument was irresistible; they held you in thrall.

So it was neither Blink Burnside's fault nor was it his direct decision that an hour later they should be lying naked together in his single bed in the Hotel Atlantique.

And there, too, there was little conversation but plenty of communication. The kind that might coax a nonviolent nonphysical egghead into paroxysmic ejaculation five times in about three hours. The kind that drew from his lips a strange and foreign vernacular like "Baby, I feel you, some screw. . . . I wanna fuck you, kid." Words and sentence constructions that Blink Burnside had never put together before.

And then he was doing all the talking, and she was lying back and smoking and looking at him across the crude lighting. And he was telling her everything. His courtship of Irma, the night little Beryl had tonsillitis. And then his drafting to London, his tense passage across the U-boat-menaced Atlantic in an old P & O pleasure cruiser. Weeks, months, sitting at Victorian mahogany tables whilst the British and American staff men fought their own war games over surf measurements at Fedala or commando support at Oran. Lonely weeks, checking back to a flat in Westminster, reading Shakespeare in the Churchill Club, writing to Irma and then tearing the letters up, because a man in the know like him had nothing possible to communicate.

And every now and again a glimpse of the real high-ups, Eisenhower, Bedell Smith, Alanbrooke, and yes, once he had entered a room in which the rich Havana tobacco smoke made him want to choke and had swapped eye lines with Winston Churchill.

Blink Burnside told all this, and once he slipped out in the shower room to clean himself up.

And he hadn't even noticed on returning that one of the brass latches on his brown leather attaché case was up when it should be down.

It wasn't just the plain GIs who were greenhorns in this war.

The next morning he thought at one time he'd never make it out to the airport. Patton had put on a triumphal parade, Roman style: the streets were flanked by long lines of GIs, *gendarmes*, and General Nogues's Vichy-serving forces. Some key roads were simply cordoned off. Blink Burnside's driver squealed out in pure Bronx, whilst the lady of the night before, wearing a white picture hat from Paris, held his hand and lit him a cigarette between her lips.

In the traffic jam Burnside was pondering one natural phenomenon. On any razzle like this he'd have expected a mighty sore cock. But he'd never felt better down there in his life.

Once when the car had been held up for half an hour and there was no way round, the two got out and looked at the scene, like a couple of tourists who just happened to be lovers too. Except that the lady's affection was now buttressed by a wad of bank notes. It was at this moment that, if she'd looked hard enough between the slats of a passing French truck, she might have seen the screwed-up face of Steve Wagner.

His voice she could never have heard. The general hubbub was too deafening.

Colonel Gisson, Commandant of Foreign Labor Group No. 12, in the Sahara, had a personal reason for his fierce loyalty to Marshal Pétain. He had served under him in two campaigns. The first, Verdun in 1916, had cost him his left arm, amputated at the shoulder to check a spreading gangrene. The second, Pétain's counteroffensive against Abdul El Krim's Riffs here in Morocco in 1926, had put a small crater under his left cheekbone—a shooting accident involving, as it happened, one of his own men.

On both occasions the Marshal had noticed, and offered his personal condolences. Those wonderful majestic blue eyes of his had filled with compassion for the wretched, lowly thing that was him, Gisson. What a man!

The collapse of France had been a blow to the retired Gisson, but the establishment of the Vichy state had gone a long way to compensate. It meant that France had at last got its priorities right. The Marshal first, France second, and the rest of the world could go to hell.

Vichy had also found him work. Fellow called Darnand, a first-class ex-NCO, who like Gisson had distinguished himself on the Verdun front, had got together this legion of ex-servicemen and patriots called the SOL to man the front line against all the Bolsheviks, Jews, and other international riffraff that were trying to undermine the new France and its empire. Perhaps the command of a labor camp five hundred miles into the Sahara, beyond the shantytown of Lagora, wasn't exactly the front line, but at least he was in uniform again, and serving the Marshal.

Sometimes when the desert sun seemed to be clawing like a giant crab at his left arm's stump, he would ask himself, blasphemously, if Foreign Labor Group No. 12 was really doing the Marshal a service. "How dare you question the Marshal's wishes, you vile turd?" he would sternly reprimand himself. All the same, there were problems. For example, the track they were laying for the new trans-Sahara railway at such cost in prisoners was clearly leading nowhere. Yet nobody back in Rabat or Casablanca seemed to be interested. Another worry: these SOL militiamen who staffed the camp had no idea of military discipline or order. The prisoners stank, the camp stank, and the guards themselves looked as if they could do with a good wash and a haircut. He didn't so much object to them beating hell out of the prisoners; he had been assured these were sworn enemies of the Marshal. But the soldier in him was sometimes shocked at the insanitary turn the SOL's severity took: forbidding the prisoners to wash, forcing them to shit in the mess tins they would have to eat out of, making them drink their own piss water. It was inviting disease. But here again, higher authority didn't seem to care, or if pressed, would confirm that these measures had the approval of the Hero of Verdun.

To tell the truth, the Colonel was sometimes puzzled to know exactly what some of these prisoners had done to offend the Marshal. For instance, this Czech he was about to sentence to execution for trying to stagger away to die in the desert had been a sergeant in Gisson's old regiment, the 7th Foreign Legion, and had fought at Narvok before he became this shuffling skeleton. Apparently on the signature of the armistice it had been discovered that the Legion contained a number of undesirables from Eastern European countries who needed to be treated as enemies.

"Your sentence is death," he rasped at the ghost of a legionnaire who was swaying in front of his desk, making funny little croaking noises. "Consider yourself fortunate that it will be by firing squad. You have disgraced your regiment."

They led him away still making those weird croaking noises, the explanation being that the man was trying to find enough saliva to spit. "Sentence to be carried out immediately!" Gisson hollered at his back, and suddenly felt more confident, more aggressive, more like a decisive field commander.

And at this moment in his cramped little wooden hut in the Sahara, Colonel Gisson experienced a revelation. How foolish, insubordinate, yes, and treasonable he had been to question the Marshal's infinite wisdom. In exasperation he pummeled the side of his head with the only hand he had, because he now clearly understood the Marshal's higher purpose. France had fallen because France had gone soft, soft as a rotten apple. Soft-bellied intellectuals, Freemasons, and Jews had sapped the country of all its Napoleonic vigor and ruthlessness, and had made the country the laughingstock of the world.

One day France would strike again! The rumble of French artillery would be heard in every capital of Europe.

But not now. For the time being there was just one task for a French officer and patriot, and that was to show the world that a Frenchman could be as tough, ruthless, and unpitying as the victorious Germans—show the smirkers and doubting Thomases there were no queasy stomachs in French uniform. For this vital task there had, of course, to be victims. Who they were was unimportant, so long as they suffered severely at French hands. Why let the Master Race have a monopoly in brutality? Two could play at concentration camps!

What a pathetic lump of ordure he was not to have grasped the Marshal's inspired concept.

Colonel Gisson poured himself another cognac and raised it in profound humility to the fading portrait of Pétain. (Everything seemed to fade in this damned desert!) There and then, at the top of his voice, although there was nobody else in his office, he rededicated himself to blind obedience to the Marshal and those he put in authority. There would be no more questions, even unspoken questions. Only one-hundred-percent loyalty.

The sound of trucks laboring into the compound with the latest batch of undesirables from Casablanca came to him as a sound from Heaven, or rather the Marshal.

"Never. Never," Colonel Gisson swore at the fading portrait of an old man. He meant that these new undesirables would never leave Foreign Labor Camp No. 12, at least not as sane men.

For the Newports it was to be the night of nights.

They were dining Mr. Bobby O'Brien, special representative of President Roosevelt in French North Africa (with license to rove, pry, and generally suavely roughride all opposition) in their swank little villa in Sef.

Others present included General Nogues; General Patton; USAF General Sam Susskind and his attractive young companion, Helda Countess of Billancourt; and other sundry notables at that moment resident in Casablanca, until such time as the war (and the action) rolled northwards across the Med.

It should have been a wow of a night.

Tina Newport's *agneau marocain* should have brought a glow of pleasure to Bobby O'Brien's red face and a discreet compliment in Boston Irish to the chef.

Hal Newport's four cases of Veuve Cliquot, topped up by a remarkable find in old Napoleon cognac should have procured for him further treasures on earth in the shape of a vivid new diplomatic assignment.

Helda de Billancourt should have charmed them all, from Generals Patton and Susskind down. The night should have finished on the veranda, under the stars of Morocco, with a curious mélange of French and American in the shape of a new barbecue dish called *Bananes flambées New Orleans au cognac de Napoléon.*

That's what the textbook said should have happened.

But the fact is that there was rust tonight in the diplomatic clockwork.

Hal Newport had read the auguries like all good diplomats should. And the signs spelled trouble.

They erupted half an hour after the guests had assembled with the late arrival of the hostess, Tina Newport, who seemed to have spent the entire afternoon in the bathroom. Then her husband led her forward to meet Mr. Bobby O'Brien. To the smooth Bostonian bow of Roosevelt's chief North African satrap Tina's response was a shrill "If it ain't the conquering Hero in person!"

O'Brien permitted himself a sleek side look at some of the other guests, as if to say he'd read the file on the Newports and knew all about them, but even so, weren't they just great people to have around?

"Been bumping off any more Gaullists, Mr. O'Brien?" the lady of the house inquired. "Or have you run out of cadavers for the junkyard?"

"Hang on, darling," cut in Hal Newport, "we've got some pretty heavy people around tonight."

"Sure, they're heavy. But I don't underrate Marshal Pétain, Pierre Laval, Ambassador Otto Abetz, or that rave charmer they call Butcher Darnand. How come we missed them out?"

"They'd certainly be interesting to meet," O'Brien told her. "In our profession, Mrs. Newport, we pride ourselves on talking to everyone."

"OK, who gives a hell about a crappy pack of boy scout Gaullists and their nose-in-the-air leader? They bore the knickers off me too," shrilled out Tina as her guests began to move in the general direction of the blood-red Moorish lamp that hung over the Newports' front door. "But you're not just screwing up your best friends and allies among the French and hobnobbing with appeasers. You're sending genuine American boys, *bona fide* American citizens, to the electric chair."

"I'm afraid I'm not getting you, Mrs. Newport," said Bobby O'Brien as his hand fluttered in a farewell salute to his hosts and he dived towards that Moorish lamp. "But if you had any *prima facie* evidence of these statements, my office would always be pleased to examine it."

"Evidence!" shrieked Tina Newport. "Do you trust your own paid sleuths? Is the word of the OSS good enough for you?"

"Shushhh," said her husband as one of the unmentionables was well and truly mentioned.

"Yes, the OSS. Do you realize that whilst we glut ourselves here they tell me there's a good American boy—covered himself with glory on the landing beaches just a few kilometers away—who's being roasted alive in the middle of the goddamn Sahara!"

"What's he doing there?" asked the departing form of Bobby O'Brien.

"Doing there? He's building the trans-Sahara railroad. That's what he's doing there. And if you want to know more, just ask your bosom pal, General Nogues. Because it seems it's his own very private pet scheme."

"Madam, you could not be more wrong," the diminutive Nogues twinklingly assured her as he grabbed for his *képi*. "Only Frenchmen have the privilege of working on the railway. It is a matter of national resolve."

A lot of people were shouting at Steve Wagner. They were telling him he had to stand up even though his legs were useless after two days in that stinking truck, but he wasn't listening. He was still asking himself how a ghost could walk at midday through the streets of Casablanca on the arm of a US staff officer. And he was still coming back with the answer that ghosts didn't go out with US staff officers, and there weren't any mirages to be seen in uptown Casablanca. The woman in the white picture hat walking with this jerk in spectacles *was* Helda. No mistake. No shadow of doubt.

They noticed he wasn't even trying to get to his feet, unlike some of the others who were trying and getting nowhere. A middle-aged delinquent in a beret and carrying a big stick came over and started hitting him around the shoulders. As far as Steve was concerned, he needn't have bothered, because as far as Steve was concerned, he was already dead.

A woman he had known walking with a man like any bored prostitute was what had finally done the trick—almost. He was still alive enough to be able to smell her. Even in that goat truck packed tight with unwashed men and a dysentery case some of them in their desperation had tried to throw out, he had had her scent in his nostrils. The cool sweet smell of pine forests shimmering under the midnight sun. And the really sick thing was he'd have preferred the smell of all that shit to the exquisite smell of Helda, a very exceptional woman he had known, turned whore.

In the end they got them all to their feet, except for the dysentery case. He wasn't even moving an eyelid. Steve vaguely noticed they were drawn up outside a wooden hut and an elderly man with a red face and a missing arm was staring at them from the portico.

"Stand to attention for the Camp Commandant!" someone was shouting.

He asked himself why. Why? For the two thousandth time that day. All right, if you were somebody other than Helda de Billancourt, maybe. If you were an ordinary woman and you'd stuck your head out all the way for a man called Georges Martel who went and got lost at sea, it was possible you'd go to pieces. But not if you were a woman like Helda de Billancourt.

"Do not expect us to show any weakness here," the popeyed veteran without an arm was piping at them. "We are French patriots who will sell the pass of French discipline dearly!"

But even if you were just an ordinary woman who had flown

away to a cleaner place, what would bring you back to Casablanca? Didn't they have whores in London too? Even if you were Helda Countess of Billancourt, why fly back over one thousand miles to go whoring in Casablanca? Why not Lisbon? Algiers? Cairo, or any damned city where he didn't have to be in a position to see her out of the back of a covered goat truck?

"If you were foolish enough to suppose that French ferocity, French virility, French pugnacity were defeated at Sedan, you will be obliged to think again," the one-armed lunatic was shouting. "If you imagine that France has lost its balls, I warn you, you had better look to your balls! Because what you will witness here in this camp is the regeneration of the old France. Not a weak, shameful, soft-bellied France. But a merciless, *fighting* France that spares nobody!"

And Steve thought that was the difference between Helda and any ordinary woman, or whore. There always had to be a mystery about her, a final unanswered question that meant you had to go on thinking about her, puzzling about her, even when you knew she was all up for sale to any highly placed brass with the necessary funds.

A bereted NCO with a big sweat patch round the waist of his tropical shirt was shouting into his face. (Boy, hadn't anyone ever told him about his breath?) He claimed he was grinning insolently at the Camp Commander. Steve told him, if he wanted to know, he was grinning insolently at himself. He said, "You're looking at a worse mental case than your boss."

That did it, or at least he hoped it might do it. Except that his experience to date told him that the curtain never quite came down. Somehow you went on living, maybe a little nearer to the edge of the world in less and less agreeable company. But you went on living.

("You can't write a new tune . . .")

The NCO with the bad breath, who sulked under the name of Goupu, hit him hard enough to wrench his head off his neck. But he didn't die. A couple of them dragged him across the salt-fine sand of the parade ground to a hut they seemed to be using as a tool shed. Here there were some more neanderthals who grabbed him as if they had been waiting for him since the fall of France and laid him out on the worktable, not at all like a long-lost brother.

And one of these woodwork enthusiasts said something about how he would like to take a saw to him, and another one said not this time, but how about a hammer?

And Goupu, the NCO who didn't use Ipana toothpaste, said he was expecting this Yankee Bolshevik to put in a full twelve-hour stint on the railway tomorrow, and how this was meant to be just a preliminary working-over session. Then Steve managed to get an arm loose and to uppercut the zombie nearest to him, which brought the whole party down on the concrete floor and may have temporarily saved his life. Because now they held him down on the floor, instead of on that gadgety workbench, and invited the zombie with the sore chin to take his revenge with his bare fists. It wasn't pleasant being pounded above and below the belt by a Vichy thug, but this one was no Charles Atlas. Practically any free man in a free world could have safely kicked sand in his face. Perhaps a lot of people had, because there was still a lot of hate in his punches, and besides, he never seemed to have heard of the Queensberry rule about not kicking your opponent with army boots when he was down.

But even before he lost consciousness Steve was far away.

A place with rich velour curtains drawn against the sun. The Golf Hotel's plushest stateroom. And she holding him, steadying him down from racing. And he screaming crazy things to her, because in that empty hotel there was no one to hear.

They kicked some more, but he was listening to music. He was listening to Bobbi's tune. In particular the point where the clarinet came in, like a mourner at a funeral with subtle smile on his face that somehow says a lot more than the corny old lyrics the preacher is reciting.

You can't right an old wrong
When it won't disappear.

Bobbi was also an American transplant, but of a different genus from Steve Wagner. He was a lazy Alabaman, a poor white from the cotton mills who discovered a deep affinity with the Deep South blues. He had met Jelly Roll Morton, played piano duets with Fats Waller, plucked a twangy bass against Louis Armstrong's trumpet in funny stop-off clubs on the outskirts of New Orleans.

It was a tribute to his sensitive nature that the Depression had depressed him well above the norm; he also began to feel his fragile talent in danger of being blasted out of the US scene by the sheer exuberance and decibel blitzkrieg of the big band sound of Ellington, Count Basie, and suchlike.

So he moved on, at first to Barcelona, where he played the blues on old battered keyboards till the cows came home or the revolutionary audience dropped off to sleep. He also experienced there the deep love of his life, a swarthy young lad called Garcia, who lived with him in a sleazy apartment looking onto the port. It was also there that he met Steve Wagner.

"What the hell are you doing bumming around here?" had been Steve's first articulate recognition of Bobbi's existence after he had sat at a table close by the piano and pondered him sourly with deep bloodshot eyes, while he reached the bottom of two bottles of Fundador.

Later he came again and told him, "If you ever want a break, kid, knock on Uncle Steve's door. He's not exactly David O. Selznick, but he could knock a few heads together and force someone to give you a break." A week later he turned up, smiled over at Bobbi, and said, "That's nice piano, real nice."

Then the war took an evil course. Bobbi got lost in the maelstrom, and so did Steve Wagner. They met up early in '39 at a bum bistro in Toulouse. Bobbi had lost Garcia, but still had a nice touch on the ivories.

The rest was a bizarre variation on the general theme of Faithful Dog. Where Steve went, Bobbi ended up not far behind. So there was a job for him at the Golf Hotel, Étretat, and later at Ritzi's in Casablanca. In the odd hours he'd tried his hand at composition. There were a few bosh shots, a lot of derivatives in the early Noël Coward idiom (to mark his rerooting into Western European culture). Then something from the blue that sounded like a melody line and had the nagging power to stick with you and bore the ass off you whilst you were lying in bed on sleepless nights.

It was the tune that Steve and Helda took to be "Their Song" because it emerged from Bobbi's long nicotine-stained fingers just about the time that they ganged up together. What Bobbi didn't tell them was that it wasn't their song at all. It was his, and if anybody else could claim a slice of it, it would be the dead Garcia, whose body was rotting somewhere in Murcia.

One thing more, the end line:

You can't write a new song
When the old song still hurts

was literally and poignantly true. Bobbi hadn't. And didn't.

But now someone again was doing the cruel thing of taking his talents seriously. Monsieur Ritzi had never been one of Bobbi's most ardent *aficionados*.

He had cursed him, overworked him, underpaid him, and generally, whilst Steve's back was turned, given him about the rawest deal in the history of music.

But now there was a change.

Under the new name Ritzi's had soared on fame and profitability. Night after night whole divisions of fresh-faced GIs, their hip pockets bulging with bank notes fresh from Uncle Sam's coffers, invaded the place. And the clientèle wasn't just confined to simple doughboys weaned on a mixture of wet dreams and Ingrid Bergman. Ritzi was attracting the topnotchers too, and the kind of high-class freespending skirt that went with it. They came because the *boîte* had suddenly become IT.

One day Ritzi summoned him and gave him a handsome raise without being asked.

"We've made it, *mon brave*," he told the startled Bobbi. "Imagine Ritzi's up there with the stars. Yesterday we were just a club. Today . . ."

The little Libyan swindler had good cause for smiling. He had been given a handsome offer by no less an authority than Radio Casablanca, which was now beaming out on shortwave not just to its usual audience of Arabs and *colons*, but to a congregation of rhythm-happy GIs.

"We've got our own program at eight o'clock on Tuesdays and Fridays"—Ritzi smirked—"and you'll be the star. It's gonna be just like that movie all these crazy Yanks seen back home—Reek's Place in *Casablanca.*

"What movie?" Bobbi yawned.

"*Casablanca,* you *salaud.* You haven't seen it? Nor have I. But I tell you it's got this great pianist, name of Sam, plays this tune called 'Play It Again, Sam'—has 'em all eating out of his hand. You're gonna be Sam."

"I'm not Sam," said the Alabaman.

"Listen, if my customers say you're Sam, you're Sam. If they want you to play it again—you play it again."

But Bobbi felt blue, he felt like those days in New Orleans when he was perfecting his own deadbeat version of "Life Is Just a Bowl of Cherries."

He needed someone or something to jack him out. In the old days Steve would have bailed him out, would have taken Ritzi by the scruff of the neck and made the sweat dribble out from his thick neck. But Steve wasn't exactly on hand to help anyone.

"My dear Steve, you look terrible!"

Where had he heard that voice before?

"However, they seem to have left you more or less in one piece. You can't always rely on them not to take away the odd souvenir."

The old Third Republican sense of irony that seemed to have gone right out of fashion. Who else could it be but . . . ?

"I've brought you some cognac. I'm afraid it's very bad cognac. Colonel Gisson has no palate."

Auguste Berthier! How was he, the old bastard? Just at the moment Steve Wagner couldn't see.

"I'm afraid this hasn't turned out to be a very good war for you and me," Auguste was saying. But the cognac tasted wonderful. It was just fine by his palate.

"You and I are crooks, Steve, let's admit it—and crooks, if there's any justice in the world, should do well out of wars. Instead, for what reason I can't frankly understand, we've allowed ourselves to become the most pitiable victims. Look at us."

Steve had just managed to get an eye open. He could see that it was Auguste and he looked a lot thinner, also that he could have looked a lot worse.

He said, "Auguste, I've got to tell you something. Helda is a whore."

"You astonish me," Auguste said with his weary little smile.

"It's the truth, Auguste!"

"My poor Steve. Has it just occurred to you? You must remember she was a woman who always seemed to need an extravagant amount of money."

"You mean you always suspected?"

Auguste shrugged away the question. He said, "Tell me something new, Steve. Is it true the Americans have landed in Morocco? Is it true they've made a deal with Nogues and that clever little creep Darlan? It sounds an unlikely tale, but then I only hear propaganda on the Commandant's radio set."

"I'll tell you something." Steve's eyes gleamed through the dark bruises that had nearly closed them. "I carried through the mission —I killed General Kellerman, the poor bastard!"

This time Auguste's eyebrows went up in authentic astonishment.

"Incredible. You know Radio Casablanca reported he died leading his officers against the American beachheads. I thought, what a relief, at least that's him off our conscience. My dear Steve, you *are* a hero. At least you must be to the Americans. What on earth are you doing here?"

Steve's bloated lips tried to grin. "You heard right. They've made a deal with Nogues and Darlan."

He could see just about well enough by now to take in where he was. He was lying on one of three otherwise empty bunks in a little timber room. There was a white box with a red cross fixed to the wall and another picture of Marshal Pétain. In the corner there was a little oilstove burning (a flickering flame against the numbing cold of a November night in the Sahara), which he was too new to appreciate was a very rare privilege indeed.

"You are in the sickroom," Auguste explained with an undertone of pride. "Hardly anyone is ever admitted. Perhaps because there are too many people here in urgent need of medical attention. In your case the Commandant has made an exception. He is anxious that you should be fit for work tomorrow."

"That frog without a leg, or was it an arm?" Steve said hazily. "Guy who keeps shouting about French balls."

"He should never have been put in command of a Labor Camp," Auguste whispered, "but there you are; *c'est la guerre.* It's not that he's a bad man, but I think he was slightly unhinged by his experiences in the Riff war. He saw how Abdel Krim behaved to his prisoners—flaying them alive, burning off their skin with lighted torches, feeding them to the ants, that sort of thing. It's given him a slightly unbalanced attitude towards violence. Also, he has been deeply affected by the defeat of the army in 1940. In a way I think he might be happier with de Gaulle, but you see what I mean; it's not a very good situation here."

Steve took another painful look through his half-closed eyes. He said, "They don't seem to be treating you too badly, Auguste, considering I thought they'd rubbed you out."

Sometime Auguste knew he would have to explain to Steve that he wouldn't be accompanying him to work next crack of dawn; wouldn't be splitting boulders for the trans-Sahara railways bed through the heat of the day and half the night; wouldn't be reeling from the heat and the blows of the SOL misfits; wouldn't be staggering home to a bowl of hot water it pleased them to call soup. Sometime he would have to explain that he had wrangled himself the position of servant and chief cognac bottle washer to Colonel Gisson, with all the life-sustaining perks that went with the post. But for the moment he decided that Steve had enough to absorb.

"I survive," he said.

"I like it, Bobbi," she told him. "In fact I like it very much."

The sentiment came from Laura Caulfield and referred to Bobbi's new Big Night outfit, in particular the ocean-dark-blue sheeny double-breasted jacket he was sporting to celebrate the first broadcast of "Soirée chez Rick."

The bar was as full as usual, only this night the clientèle was definitely higher grade. Dinner jacket and cocktail dress were the order of the evening and the well-heeled audience of Vichyite *fonctionnaires*. As for the U S Army, you needed an officer's tunic to slide past Ritzi's bouncers.

It was the snazziest little fashion display that war-begirt Casablanca had been allowed to feast its eyes on since the Yacht Club dinner of that distant September of the Phony War.

Bobbi was there to one side of the central platform, and around him was grouped a small collection of Moroccan players, who went under the general title of Bobbi's Band.

There was also a dusky creole singer called Annette, who hopefully might take some of the limelight away from the original of Sam.

But now it was just another fifteen minutes before they went on the air. Dinner-jacketed engineers from Radio Casablanca wafted around, making the last few finishing adjustments to the placing of the mikes.

There was a buzz of expectancy in the air.

"Excuse me, Mademoiselle Caulfield," cut in the voice of Ritzi, "I must have the stage cleared. Until the broadcast is finished only artists are allowed here. But for you and Monsieur Daniels, I have reserved a ringside table, the finest in my club."

"Get lost," Laura told the proprietor. "I won't sit with that jerk, even to get a better view of Bobbi."

It was put out on shortwave bands 548 and 329. You could receive it loud and clear in Casablanca and Rabat and Fedala, whose transmitting tower had been reconstructed after having taken a recent hammering from the 15-inch guns of USS *Massachusetts*. If you had a good set you could also pick up the broadcast in Oran and Algiers.

With supersensitive receiving apparatus you could even get the general gist in faraway Tunisia, which was nice because the entertainment side since the war had been much too one-sided.

The Allies could thank their lucky stars that the general standard of home morale was regularly topped up by the massive firepower of the world's biggest box office.

So it was perhaps only just that the German Command should be able to listen to "Soirée chez Rick" in their headquarters in Tunis. They particularly appreciated the moment when Ritzi took one of the paper "lots" out of the large Moorish brass bowl, into which the audience had been invited to put their choice for Bobbi's extempore numbers. As it turned out, Hauptmann von Best was treated to one of his favorite pieces of music.

His little eyes popped with interest as the ghostly chords from Bobbi's piano began to suggest lazy variations on that all-time Chevalier favorite of 1939, "Boum."

In fact as he listened, Hauptmann von Best's heart did respond to the music for a second or two with its own little "Boum."

They drew up on the little patch of tarmac outside the huts; it was about four in the morning. The wind was the kind you might encounter in Nevada at the wrong time of year. It scythed mercilessly into your body; up in the firmament a twinkling panorama of stars was slowly dissolving into hazy blue as the desert dawn came up.

Steve tried to prop himself up to face the wind. That night in the camp sickroom had been not bad; that is, he had wafted off into about the deepest sleep he'd ever enjoyed, a sleep that lasted about an hour and a half. Then one of the prisoners had come in, given him a rough shake, gestured in broken Marseillaise towards the open door and a pan of breakfast that stood on the floor beside his bed.

It was a camp joke. The pan was crammed full of camels' turd. The broken cup he didn't bother to sample; the liquid inside it was a greeny-yellow color, and he hadn't quite yet got to the state of swallowing urine.

But now the railway fatigue group was drawn up to go.

"What did they clobber you for, mate?" came a cheery voice.

Steve wearily craned his neck round and saw only riffraff in sagging Bedouin blankets.

"Come on, you're not the usual frog they send down here. What did they do? Hoik you out of a nightclub?"

Steve looked again. The man behind him was swathed in an Arab burnous. He looked like a reject for Ali Baba with his grinning gnarled black face and cavernous tooth-free mouth.

"Speaking to me?" Steve asked.

"Well, look at you. All done up for a night on the town, except you've gone and lost your dickie. And I doubt whether a hock shop would give you more than a tanner for that sleeveless coat."

Was it six days or six weeks ago that he was dressing up for the night, preparatory to bumping off a kraut called Kellerman, preparatory to joining in the US landings in Fedala, preparatory to slogging his way with Maxwell and Hutter up the highway to Casablanca, preparatory to blitzing into Ritzi's and having a ball, preparatory to a ride over the Atlas Mountains in a holiday sightseeing bus on the Road to the Real Morocco? Preparatory to the bit that might be called the icing on the cake.

That bittersweet hallucination of a girl called Helda in the arms of a weedy officer slob with glasses, seen memorably through the slats of a prison truck.

"Hear that, lads," guffawed the hooded stranger in broad cockney. "Our Yankee mate's got a little tickle in his throat. Or is it that he doesn't fancy goat's piss?"

Tears started from Steve's eyes as an arm chopped into his raw battered left arm and he half swung round in the pale ghost of a right uppercut.

"Steady, mate," came that warmly deep growl. "Take a swig of this."

Steve saw that the hairy arm which had been brushing against his excruciated one was grasping a routine army drinking canteen. As he took it he saw that a mermaid in red and blue was tattooed all the way up.

They sat in the Laffley as it hiccuped through the desert.

"This is Fred, that's Ron, that's Arthur Askey, and the fat one over there we call Bud Flanagan, all ship's crew aboard the late-lamented SS *Pimlico*. Used to be sailors, but we've now joined the Railway Builders' Union. Life was a lark until we put into Dakar the day before Winnie decided to blow a hole in the frog fleet at Murky Kebabs, or whatever they call it!"

"But we've landed in Morocco. Your own limeys are here in force. The Vichy government has collapsed."

"Touch of sunstroke, don't you think, Bud?" suggested the chirpy little Bedouin they called Arthur Askey. "Haven't heard that on their wireless."

"They don't give a crap for me. I'm just a wandering Yank from Nowhere. But you're King George's subjects. Can't you understand? Vichy's lost the war."

"They all start like this," mused Wally cheerfully.

"This is Radio Casablanca. Here is the news.

"THE BRITISH EIGHTH ARMY'S ADVANCE HAS BEEN HALTED OUTSIDE BENGHAZI, AND THE AFRIKA KORPS IS MOUNTING STRONG COUNTER-ATTACKS. FIELD MARSHAL ROMMEL SAYS THAT THE BRITISH LINES OF COMMUNICATION ARE DANGEROUSLY OVEREXTENDED.

"MEANWHILE GENERAL ANDERSON'S BRITISH FIRST ARMY IS ENCOUN-TERING STIFFENING RESISTANCE EAST OF BÔNE, AS THE AXIS BUILDUP CON-TINUES IN TUNISIA. IN RABAT THIS AFTERNOON RESIDENT-GENERAL AU-GUSTE NOGUES DECORATED CAPTAIN ALBERT LEPÊTRE WITH THE CROIX DE GUERRE. THE CITATION PRAISED THE CAPTAIN'S GALLANTRY IN ELIMINAT-ING, SINGLE-HANDED, A NEST OF GAULLIST TRAITORS WHO HAD BEEN AS-SISTING THE AMERICAN LANDINGS.

"AT THE MILITARY CEMETERY IN CASABLANCA TOMORROW THE RE-MAINS OF WEHRMACHT GENERAL JOACHIM KELLERMAN WILL BE BURIED WITH FULL MILITARY HONORS. THIS IS AT THE EXPRESS WISH OF THE GERMAN AUTHORITIES AND THE GENERAL'S FAMILY. IN A MESSAGE FROM PARIS THIS AFTERNOON REICHS AMBASSADOR ABETZ SAID, 'THE GENERAL KELLERMAN WAS A TRUE FRIEND OF FRANCE, AND DIED DEFENDING FRENCH SOIL. IT IS FITTING THAT HIS FINAL RESTING PLACE SHOULD BE AMONG FRENCHMEN.'

"THERE IS A WARNING TONIGHT FROM THE MINISTRY OF INTER-NAL SECURITY. THE PUBLIC IS REMINDED THAT THERE HAS BEEN NO RELAXATION IN THE EMERGENCY LAWS GOVERNING SEDITIOUS POLITICAL DISCUSSIONS. POLITICAL CONVERSATIONS OF ANY KIND WITH AMERICAN SERVICE PERSONNEL ARE EXPRESSLY FORBIDDEN AND WILL BE SEVERELY PUNISHED. THE MINISTRY STATEMENT CARRIES A FURTHER REMINDER THAT THE AMERICAN FORCES ARE HERE AS GUESTS OF THE ETAT FRANÇAIS AND HAVE NO JURISDICTION WHATSOEVER OVER LOCAL AF-FAIRS."

"What the heck's that all about?" asked PFC Offenbach, twiddling the knob of the Marconi radio he had just picked up in the Medina for a carton of Chesterfields.

"How should I know?" said his buddy, Lou Alverson. "It's French, isn't it?"

The convoy of Laffleys drove about fifteen kilometers down a track in the desert and then stopped.

It was seven in the morning. The sun was beginning to come through with irresistible force. Steve's teeth ceased to chatter; instead he saw a surrealist nightmare of pink and purple spots in front of his eyes as he was bundled out onto the sand.

"See that one over there? Not a bad geyser, name of Weill; he's a banker, arrested just before you because someone shaved off his foreskin when he was about three days old. That hefty chap over there is a bloody hero. He tried to get the North African frogs to fight the Nazis. And that weedy chappie is a schoolmaster who kept tuning in to the BBC. The whole bloody lot needs a putty medal for refusing to see which side their bread was buttered."

When Steve could get his aching eyeballs together he saw that they were in a kind of ravine. Shiny strips of rail caught the Sahara sun like searchlight beams laid across the sand. Piles of heavy wooden sleepers lay around. Steve was given a pick and told to break up rock. The sergeant with bad breath came towards them.

"Watch him, he's a right bugger," whispered the little cockney Jew they called Arthur Askey. "They call him Goupu, and he's not a bit like Goofy."

He was right. When the guy with a hooked nose who looked like a lecturer from the Sorbonne collapsed on the job, Goupu stood over him, kicking him with his brilliantly polished boots.

When he had finished there was no sign of life from the man who had once educated his pupils in the principles of Liberté, Égalité, Fraternité.

"He knocks one off like that every day," Wally whispered. "When we get back next morning, the ruddy vultures are sitting on his head, pecking his eyes out."

At about six that afternoon the sun blinked apologetically and then started to slide down the sky, bleeding as it went. A chilly wind blew up, and Steve's teeth started to click together like a Maxim gun. Then Goupu fired a shot from his revolver. They formed lines outside their trucks.

"One of these days I'll take my kids for a ride on the railroad," said Steve Wagner.

"Haven't you savvied yet?" Wally asked him. "This ain't a blooming Brighton Belle, mate. It's more like a human breakup yard."

"A crazy thing to ask me to play," Bobbi told Laura later that evening. "Maurice Chevalier strictly isn't my style. I just don't play that kind of music."

"Correct," agreed Laura. "It was unfair to ask you, but say it was a great bit of extemporizing."

"What a gag," laughed Bobbi mirthlessly. "You thought I just picked it up and played it because Ritzi took a bit of paper out of the bowl."

"You mean you knew it was going to be 'Boum' tonight? It was all a fix?"

"Has Ritzi ever done anything that isn't?"

Laura had grown to like Bobbi; she went for his gentle fatalism. He was also one other thing, just about the last surviving buddy of that fall guy called Steve Wagner. Wherever that crumb was, doing a Gary Cooper rendering of Beau Geste somewhere in the Sahara, under the sadistic vigilance of some local Brian Aherne, there was one thing for sure. Of present company in Casablanca only Bobbi and herself would find time for a tear.

"He was OK," Bobbi was telling her. "He knew how to lean on Ritzi."

"That was his trouble, the bum," sighed Laura. "He had a creepy, sentimental old piece of cheese for a heart. The jerk never bothered to think things out. His brain was pure sog, but what a body. But who the hell is *that*?"

The lady had been late for the Radio Casablanca broadcast, but the empty table to which she was now being ushered by Ritzi proved she was among the more highly rated customers of Rick's Place. Behind her came a USAAF general with a mean, hard look in his eyes. They sat down, and Rubin whipped on a bottle of Moët.

The air force General was telling her something and putting his hand on her bare arm.

"Boy, what a dish!" exclaimed Laura in instant envy. "The hundred-carat gold broad. Didn't know Casablanca boasted that kind of real hard rock. Wonder who dreamed up that little creation for her."

But Bobbi wasn't listening. He wasn't even looking. His hands were sliding over the keyboard, and what was coming out of them was an old tune that Laura Caulfield had positively not heard before, but which immediately struck her as leagues higher than Bobbi's usual.

"What's that?" she asked.

"Their tune," he told her quietly.

"You see, my dear Steve, life here is very simple. There are no la-dies. There is nothing to steal, nothing to embezzle. It is really very crude and very boring. The only thing you can be concerned with is this putrid thing called survival. As if, in the vast number of cases, it was worth a *sou*."

"Pass me that brandy, you old Pink Baboon," Steve said.

"Ah, those were the days," smiled Auguste with his weary, kind eyes. "Steve, how do you think I procure this brandy? I lick Mon-sieur the Commandant's hairy little anus. I grovel at the boots of our friend Sergeant Goupu. And I give them little tidbits. About the prisoners, I mean. The ones they should concentrate on!"

"There was one today, some professor guy. Goupu kicked him to death."

"He was a Gaullist and a Jew. Besides, he was very clever, but not very bright. He spat at me."

"I'm not sure I follow you," Steve said. Perhaps he didn't want to.

"I can also help a little," smiled Auguste. "For instance, this sickroom; it isn't the Hotel Georges V, but compared to the pris-oners' compound, it has distinct advantages."

"Not the least, this," smiled Steve, swigging a little more of the cognac. "Auguste, you're an evil bastard, but you're a true friend."

"I wish I could help you even more. Alas, some things are be-yond the power of a simple camp follower like me. But it would have been nice to even the scores a little. It might have helped to ease those pains of the heart."

"You're not coming through, Auguste."

"You see that little hut over where the sentry's standing? Well, you know it's a bit of a joke. The other prisoners think the inmate is getting a special deal. But they forget, or maybe they don't know, that he's a special kind of man. Would it amuse you, my dear Steve, to know that just a few hundred meters from where you lie now is the man who's caused you more pain than any other living mortal? I refer to your excellent friend, Monsieur Georges Martel, the late, much respected Monsieur le Ministre de l'Intérieur."

"I thought he was dead. I thought he'd drowned in Karl Bidelle's yacht the night I helped bail him out of Casablanca."

"That was the story, it is true," Auguste remarked. "But then as this dreadful war drags on, one learns to give less and less credence to the things they choose to tell you. It isn't only Monsieur Goeb-bels who's made lying respectable. It suited Nogues to have fools like us believe that the Lion of Limoges was feeding the fishes. It tidied things up, and come to that, I doubt if de Gaulle shed too many tears either. One rival the less."

"Then why didn't Nogues just drop him back in the sea?"

The wrinkles shot up on Auguste's forehead as he gave his friend a mysterious smile.

"You know, Steve, that's also what I wonder sometimes."

"Maybe Nogues isn't the bastard you think."

"Or maybe someone up there loves Georges Martel."

"Don't joke, Auguste," snarled Steve in warning.

"And loves him still. That's why, my excellent Steve, I cannot do you the ultimate service and get the old buzzard decently garroted."

In the third week of November a new number started to creep into Bobbi's repertoire, or rather a horny old number called, "Le Fiacre," brought charmingly up-to-date by Bobbi's Eddie Duchin touch. The song's revival had little to do with popular demand—the new hits from America like, "Would It Be Wrong?", "Moonlight Becomes You," and "I'm Old-fashioned" were the rage in Casablanca that autumn—but somehow it kept getting reprised. At the same time "Boum" was inexplicably dropped from Bobbi's keyboard selections.

Incidentally, this was the week when the U S 2nd Armored Division stirred from its bivouacs in the cork trees north of Casablanca and started on a long journey to join the fighting in Tunisia.

"Oop-la, oop-la, oop-la, oh!" Bobbi crooned across the starlit desert wastes as the tanks and half-tracks began to roll and Hauptmann von Best in Tunis listened with beady-eyed pleasure.

Rubin was puzzled and also amused. He had worked for Ritzi for many years through various political regimes, and he had never known his boss to enforce his personal taste on the mood of the moment. Yet every night when the live broadcast was going out, he would stride proudly up to Bobbi's Beckstein and announce with glinting teeth that he had been showered with requests for that old French favorite, "Le Fiacre." He would pay no attention to the shouts from American officers and their French girls for the latest Frank Sinatra hit or Crosby melody; and certainly no attention to the boozy jokers who wanted to hear "Temptation." "Le Fiacre" got played no matter what else the customers wanted to hear.

"Monsieur Ritzi," Rubin grinned, passing his employer one Tuesday night with a tray of so-called Dom Pérignon, "why you keep asking Bobbi to play 'Le Fiacre?' You told me once you hated that tune." He didn't stop to notice that Monsieur Ritzi wasn't amused.

The trouble was he thought it was a kind of private joke between his master and himself. He kept going on about it. For instance, the next time the café went on the air he nudged the little Tunisian's white tuxedo. "It's 'Oop-la, oop-la, oop-la' again tonight, eh, boss? What they doing? Someone paying you to plug that song? Eh, boss? What's the deal?"

At 2 AM the next morning when Rubin had washed up the glasses and was leaving for home he was met by a police Citroën at the back door of the café.

"Hey, what this about?" he wondered when he had been helped into the back seat. "I done nothing wrong."

No less a person than Chief Inspector Lucien Roth looked round from the front passenger seat. "Don't pretend to be so innocent. You know what your crime is?"

It was the first thought that came into Rubin's head; it didn't seem to make any sense, but he blurted it out. "I was just joking about that song. That's the truth, I swear!"

Roth hit him very hard, and then, noticing there was a lot of cushioning flesh on his face, hit him again, harder.

"You're a Jew," he said, "and that's enough. Moreover, you failed to inform your employer you were a Jew, which is a major infraction of the law. As you are well aware, it is illegal for a Jew to work for a non-Semite. You will be severely punished."

It was hard to count time in a place like this, hard to reckon that one day might be Wednesday and another Sunday. Harder still because Steve Wagner no longer went off to earn his keep in the desert. His interest in the trans-Sahara railway was now more that of a voyeur. Auguste had got him a luxury ticket. If he was sick enough to spend his nights in the camp sickroom, didn't it make sense to spend his days there also, eating the crudely spiced couscous the camp guards cooked up for themselves and the privileged few, slapping it down with vinegary Moroccan wine? After all, wasn't he sick? Didn't his body ache every moment of the day? Didn't his head throb with nonstop hammerblows? Didn't he seriously feel as if his mind had come off its hinges? Yes, he deserved this lousy bed. Hell, why shouldn't he put up his legs and hear them go off in the morning and wonder who was today's candidate for Goupu's boot?

Not that he gave a cuss. Whether a few filthy human microbes were smudged out in the desert or allowed to sweat and shit for a few days longer wasn't something he could be bothered with. After years of futile globe-trotting and folksy philosophizing he, Steve Wagner, had come at last to know better. Hello again, "Pink Baboon"!

And when Auguste wasn't there, going about his duties, whatever those might be, he left his brandy flask behind. And then Steve would stare up at the tatty ceiling and ponder how in this global ass hole they could procreate something like Helda. And then he would see that had to be the crappiest joke of it all. Which led him on to thinking about that other dumb cluck they called the Lion of Limoges. The guy who had tried to fight the shit in 1940 and ended up in the sewage system himself.

They'd put the boot in him in 1940, they'd run him out of France and then slapped him in the jug right here in Morocco, and he'd stood there and seen his beloved France ground into the dust. But all the old bullfrog was really suffering from when it came down to it were the flies, the mosquitoes, the bedbugs, and the lousy food. He still had a soft spot for people.

One person in particular.

What he didn't know was that his beloved Helda was a high-class tart, douching out the semen of any little US colonel who happened to have a few dollar notes tucked away beside the photos of his wife and kids.

This Sahara dump was just a physical hell for Martel, not a real searing hell that made you want to thump your head against the walls of your cell. Until your brains spewed out.

And as the days passed by and he heard the work squads forming in the dawn and the Laffley exhausts choking out along that desert track that led to a railroad that led to nowhere, Steve Wagner knew that he had to take that last bit of peace away from Martel, had to eliminate those last final illusions of the man who once spoke for France. Had to stuff down his throat the irrefutable, unacceptable truth of the Lady Helda de Billancourt.

She wasn't the spitting image of Ingrid Bergman. The profile wasn't so finely chiseled; the nose wasn't so delicately *retroussé,* and the eyes weren't so deliciously trusting. On the other hand, her lips were fuller, her eyes were perhaps a little larger, and her complexion was nearly as radiant. Even if her features weren't quite so exquisite, there was no doubt she was worth almost as loud a wolf whistle as the fabulous movie star.

Besides, from Ritzi's point of view, she had one positive advantage over Ingrid Bergman: she happened to be here in Casablanca and, as it were, available.

Renaming the café "Rick's Café Américain" had been a great idea. The "Soirée chez Rick" broadcasts had been another. But now the customers wanted something more—the pigs always did—than just an ambiance they could associate with this amazing movie. Ideally they wanted Ingrid Bergman, not to mention Humphrey Bogart, Claude Rains, and "Cuddles" Sakall. However, Ritzi wasn't turning over that kind of money yet.

But at least there was Helda, Comtesse de Billancourt, also a Scandinavian and also beautiful. Besides, she had a past with teasing affinities to what he understood to be the love interest of the film.

Of course she had been instrumental in losing him some ten thousand francs, which he now seriously doubted Steve Wagner would ever be in a position to repay. But then perhaps this was her opportunity to help him to earn it back.

So Ritzi had gone out of his way to make Helda welcome at "Rick's Café Américain." Whenever she dropped in with a US officer, he would bow low and insist that the champagne was on the house. Once he even allowed her to win a thousand francs on the tables. Soon Helda became a regular nightly visitor, usually with two or three high-ranking Americans, and the champagne (at least the first bottle) was still on the house. By now Helda's clothes were quite something to look at too. Ritzi arranged it that she and her party always occupied a balcony table so that the customers on the ground floor could have an unimpeded gawp at the most glamorous woman in Casablanca.

You could say she became the uncrowned queen of Ritzi's, and as it happened, every night she was the object of a touching little ceremony of homage.

"And now a song you've been waiting to hear all the evening,"

Ritzi would announce, "a song inspired by a lovely lady from Norway who is here tonight in the café, in person."

Then a spotlight would pick out Helda's table. And Ritzi would blow a kiss "to our own beautiful Ingrids," and Bobbi would start to play that new smash hit, "As Time Goes By." In return Helda would raise her champagne glass and give the assembled company a dazzling smile. She was genuinely flattered by Ritzi's gallantry, although she didn't understand why he called her "Ingrids" or why Bobbi always played her that tune. It meant nothing to her. After all, she hadn't even seen the movie.

There was a good deal of champagne-consuming speculation as to what exactly had happened to her legendary lost lover. Most people agreed he was an American. Many insisted he really was Humphrey Bogart. Some people said he had shot a German officer on a foggy night at Casablanca airport and had walked off to Lake Chad. Others said he was drinking himself stupid in Ritzi's cellars on account of a broken heart. And others said he had taken a vow of celibacy and turned into a priest doing missionary work in the Sahara. A little bespectacled major in the Signals Corps whom nobody wanted to listen to said he'd met a guy called Nad Klaf back in Hollywood who knew the whole story and had sold the idea to Warner Brothers; only they had reworked it out of recognition. And then there was another rumor that this Rick, Brad, or Steve (opinions varied about the name too) had flown off to Hollywood to become a star.

Laura Caulfield knew different. She had actually seen what had happened to Steve. She also had a rough idea where he had gone, which certainly wasn't Hollywood.

It was a good knife to start with. It was long, it was sharp, and it had a rough wooden handle. It was the kind of knife a chef might use for cutting slices off a joint, peeling them off in tiny slithers. Since Auguste had given it to him that morning he had spent the best part of a day on it; oiling it, sanding it, scraping its blade against a flint. And now he sank it into the neck of the young lad of the SOL who had been slouching outside the entrance to Georges Martel's hut.

The boy uttered a wisp of a moan as he slithered to the ground. Steve withdrew the knife and wiped the black blood off on his trousers.

The knife had done the first of its tasks, but Steve's mind figured another.

Maybe he would just offer it to Martel, or maybe he would do it for him, like a man might shoot a wounded dog. Because there were things that even Georges Martel, the Lion of Limoges, could not face.

He was small and frail. He must have lost sixty pounds in weight, and his trousers didn't hang about his waist. He just held them up.

"I've come to free you," Steve told him. "Free you from yourself."

"But pardon . . ." Martel was gesticulating. "It is so long since I met . . ."

"We didn't," Steve snapped, "meet, I mean. But you may have felt my breath on your neck. A politician's canny!"

"Monsieur, I can assure you I never . . ."

"In things she left unsaid. Things she didn't do, or did differently, after she'd met me. Yes, I see it in your face. You know me. Not my face, not my name, but my presence."

"You are Steve Wagner," said Georges Martel, advancing upon him. "You saved me a year ago, at least tried to. I would like to shake your hand."

"Sure, sure. My hand," said Steve Wagner. "That's great. But watch the knife. It's bumped off one guy already tonight."

"Monsieur Wagner, permit me to say, you are not well," said Martel with concern in his deep gray eyes. "I am, as you see, less than my old self. But I am better than you. You are physically fitter than me, but when I look into your eyes I am worried for you."

"My eyes, yes, my eyes. What did some savant say? The eyes are the mirror to the soul. Well, only a crazy creep would say what I'm going to tell you now, Martel. But you must know, whilst you've been busy trying to save la Belle France and coming out with egg all over your face, I've been quietly slinking my cock into your fair Helda. Screwing the living daylights out of her. But so what? Who the heck hasn't? Her most recent protector is a scrawny little squealer of a U S Army colonel in bifocals. But the qualifications are a walkover. Just a nice fat wad of greasy bank notes, preferably dollars from Uncle Sam, and you can screw Venus till the cows come home."

"Have you seen the camp doctor?" asked Martel. "I would earnestly advise you . . ."

"Can't you get it into your great stupid cranium that the lady's a whore? She sucks cocks for a living. Got it? Mine, yours, John Doe's, Joe Stalin's."

The meager form of this once huge man strode over to where Steve was standing and a comforting arm was put around his shoulder.

"I always knew what she felt for you, Monsieur Wagner. But until this minute I had no means of knowing you loved her too!"

The knife fell from Steve's unclenched fist and rattled onto the floor of the little hut.

One night Laura Caulfield decided to probe the mystery of this woman whom Bobbi called Helda and Ritzi called Ingrids. She had been sitting at the bar having a drink (well, two or three) with Lieutenant Al Hutter, talking about Steve and what two ordinary people could try to do for him, when this performance in the balcony started.

They'd been playing "As Time Goes By." Spotlight. Applause. A regal smile from the Comtesse. It detonated something in Laura.

"Mind if we join you?" she snarled, approaching the glittering table with a reluctant Lieutenant Hutter some distance behind her. "I believe we have a mutual friend. Steve Wagner. Name mean anything to you?"

She looked at Laura with an empty kind of smile.

A brigadier general turned round with a randy grin to say Laura was interrupting an important conversation.

Laura said, "I'm talking to the lady."

Al Hutter didn't like the way the Brigadier General was looking at him, nor the air force Colonel sitting on Helda's other side. He said, "Come on, Laura, let's dance, or have another drink."

She said, "I'm asking the lady if she knows a guy called Steve Wagner. In which case maybe she can tell me what the hell they've done with him!" Her eyes fastened on a glinting diamond Helda was wearing at the cleavage of her white sequined dress. Steve had called her Snow Queen. Now she was consciously dressing the part.

"Hey, that's real nice," Laura purred. "Steve give that to you? No, I guess not. Guess where he is they're working with other kinds of rocks!"

Helda said, "Yes, I knew Stevie, a long time ago."

"Come on, you can do better than that, baby!"

"Once he saved the life of a dear friend of mine."

"You're making me cry."

"Who is this woman?" the Brigadier General growled.

"Don't push it, Laura," Al Hutter pleaded.

"You know something," Laura said. "Maybe you could just repay one good turn with another. You seem to have a lot of pull with the High Command. Why the hell don't you give these sugar daddies here an extraspecial kiss for Steve? And this time ask for Steve instead of diamonds. They're killing him out there in the Sahara!"

Helda's lips moved, but words didn't come out. Or if they did they were drowned by the Brigadier General and the air force

Colonel, who stated they weren't going to sit by and hear a lady insulted even if it was by another lady. And then before Laura could land another verbal hand grenade in among them, there was a roll on the drums and Ritzi was shouting for quiet because Rick's Café Américain was just about to go on the air, and then Bobbi was singing, "Oop-la, oop-la, oop-la, oh." So that far away in Tunis, Hauptmann von Best could trace the latest progress of the U S 2nd Armored Division.

"You goddamn sap, she loves you, baby. Sure she does, sure she does. Sure she does! I'll tell you something, Lion of Limoges, she loves me just about as much as she loves you. Except you were the big-city boss and I'm just a crumb she picked up and later spat out into the gutter. I'm not running for Governor, or President. In fact I'm not even running for Saviour of France. I'm just running."

Like now. Snatch up the knife and scram. A wave to Martel, stoop to pick up the knife because knives have a habit of incriminating.

Then out into the cold night festooned with stars and drag that body out and away from the hut. But watch it; that cadaver, dumb cluck, carries a trail of red stuff that will lead Sergeant Goupu's posse of sleuths straight back to Georges Martel, and all you wanted to do was to leave him clean with his bum ideals and his phony sanity.

So take off his cloak and wrap it around his neck and scuff fresh sand over the gore marks like a dog hiding its mess. And then over to that empty convoy of trucks and with one twist of the shoulders swing our young soldier into the back, with a ticket for Heaven in his knapsack. Lucky they're all snoring-drunk in the guardhouse.

Then back to cover your trail, because you owed it to Auguste to play it clean, and to Georges Martel. So that we can all hang around and wait for that final cracking point.

It's as surefire as Roosevelt for President. Sooner or later Georges Martel is gonna eat shit, and I'd like to be around when it happens.

Then crawl back to the sickroom to tell Auguste these tidings of great joy. Scrub the whole darn thing; forget the bitter things I told you, Berthier *mon ami*, rub the slate clean because despite appearances to the contrary, the lady loves me. She even told Big Boss, and all the dumb cluck wanted to do was shake my hand.

So it's happy ending, Auguste. All I've got to do is stagger out into the desert and go and bring her back. Smash my way into her whorehouse and beat the crumb that's screwing her into the wall and then take her up in a fond embrace and put my tattered old coat around her naked shoulders and say, "It's all right honey bunny. It's OK, I tell yer. OK . . . OK. . . ." Keep on crooning. Cradle her in your arms and wait for that heavenly choir by permission of Paramount Studios to bring the curtain down.

Where are you, Auguste? I'm lying on my bed and jerking down the brandy you kindly left under my pillow. Gulping it. And I wanna tell yer the lady loves me.

Because you're my buddy, Auguste. The sweetest, truthfulest, kindest guy I ever knew.

One of Jerry Daniels's covers, now he was no longer posing as somebody in the import-export business, was chief PRO for the United States presence in Morocco.

In the first weeks of Operation TORCH the job could have been described as a sinecure. There weren't all that many newspapermen around to be soft-sold on the Roosevelt-Nogues deal. But as Christmas approached, a growing number of budding war correspondents managed to talk their editors into agreeing that Casablanca was the front they ought to be covering.

One December afternoon, the nineteenth to be precise, Jerry found himself addressing a packed press conference of khaki-clad US newsmen and newswomen, many of them still puzzled to know why they weren't under daily bombardment from the Germans.

"So here in Casablanca we're fighting a new kind of war," Jerry wound up, "a war in which the olive branch is as effective as a Garand rifle. To paraphrase Julius Caesar, we came, we saw, and we conciliated. If the French authorities here ever had any doubts about the U S Government's good intentions, they've been well and truly put to rest by the way we've learned to *parlez-vous*. I guess we can all feel proud of what your ordinary John Doe is doing here in Casablanca. Sure, he represents one of the mightiest fighting combinations in the world today, but he's also a roving representative of the traditional 'put it there, pardner,' attitude of Uncle Sam. Are there any questions?"

"Yeah," said Lurleen Marx of *Time-Life*. "Can you tell me where they buried the US dead from the landing? My editor wants pictures and a story."

"The big story is that we buried the hatchet," Jerry told her with a glinting smile. He thought maybe he could find time for Lurleen Marx if Laura Caulfield continued not to find time for him.

"How many troops are we sending from here to the fighting in Tunisia?" a novice from the Los Angeles *Times* wanted to know.

"Hitler would like to know the answer to that question too," Daniels grinned radiantly. "That's why I've gotta say, 'No comment.'"

He got a little round of laughter.

"Back home," said a lady in steel-rimmed sunglasses, representing the Denver *Post*, "we've read a lot about General de Gaulle and how he warned the world about those German panzers, what he's doing for French freedom . . ."

"What's the question? I've gotta have a question before I can

come up with an answer." Daniels swooped in with a timely pre-
emptive strike. He wasn't going to have any cats letting that name
out of the bag.

Again he got a laugh. He was handling this press conference just
dandy.

"Mr. Daniels, I guess I haven't been in Casablanca long," said
another cub reporter from another Western paper, "but it don't
seem anything like the movie we've got back home. How come?"

"I haven't seen the movie. Any more questions?" Jerry effortlessly
crushed this inept interrogator.

"Is it true General Nogues is fascist?" Lurleen Marx pitched in
again.

"That's a typical liberal smear," Daniels answered, briefly turning
on his sincerely outraged look. "Trouble with you newspeople, you
don't read anything but your own papers."

He got a titter from a few women, and a genuine handclap from
the Chicago *Tribune*'s man.

Maybe he wasn't a bad PRO at that. "Any more questions?"

"What have you done with Steve Wagner?" A voice from the back
of the room.

Daniels's eyes narrowed. There was a lot of cigarette smoke, and
he was a little shortsighted. But he thought he could trace the question to a middle-aged guy, name of Nad Klaf, who had just flown
in for the Sodersheim Syndicate.

"No more questions?" he grinned. "Good, because I've done so
much talking I could use a drink. I guess you folks could too."

"I said, what the hell have you done with my hero, Steve Wagner?
The lovable, crazy guy who inspired Humphrey Bogart in his juici-
est role to date."

"Look, I'm only a PR officer," Jerry protested. "Maybe you need
the missing persons department."

Another little titter.

"Some of us pressmen would give a lot to meet the man whose
example helped put Casablanca on the map," Nad Klaf's voice
drifted back.

There was a murmur of annoyance from the thirsty press and
just a few of interest.

"Why haven't I heard of him?" Lurleen Marx turned round to
ask.

This was bad. The conference was slipping off its nicely prepared rails.

"I guess we've just about run out of time," Jerry said. "Course if you want to talk to me over a drink . . ."

"I'm asking what happened to Steve Wagner. We know he was one of the Gaullists who helped our boys to get ashore in Africa. But what happened after that? People like Steve don't exactly fit with the fascist regime they're running here in Morocco. Maybe that's why nobody's telling me where he is. Steve Wagner was a great guy. That is, for a chronic dipsomaniac."

"Is there any truth in these allegations?" Lurleen Marx switched round to face Jerry with a penetrating stare. He thought maybe after all he wouldn't be finding time for her.

"That's a question for the French police," he said. "As I explained, they're still running the civil administration here."

"Are they what happened to Steve Wagner? Have they garroted my greatest liquid asset?" Nad Klaf wanted to know.

"I think I answered that question."

"Can you tell us where we can get homogenized milk in this town?" the lady in the sunglasses suddenly decided to ask.

"We're sending a Liberator to collect Beulah the cow," Jerry cracked with a great smile of relief.

Everybody fell about laughing, except Nad Klaf. In the genial hubbub Jerry gestured towards the refreshments and slipped gracefully away.

He was looking at a hole in the wall from which emanated a blinding light, like a truth ray.

Then Steve's mind clicked and he realized this multiple fusion of bright light was nothing less than his little hospital window on the world in full glare of noon.

Another thing kept irritating his eyes. The red cross on the medicine chest, or rather two red crosses that seemed to dip and elevate and follow each other around like two randy coyotes.

To swing his head farther right would have been an effort, but this was precisely what his instincts told him he must do. Because a voice was rasping in his ear, "Get up, *salaud;* stand to attention."

And to help him achieve this turn of the head something crashed into his left leg, and the tears that started from his eyes somehow cleared them. Colonel Gisson had seen this man but once. He had seen him arrive. Now he was trying to work out how come he was lying in the camp hospital.

"What's wrong with you?" asked Colonel Gisson. "Why are you here? Who let you in?"

"Don't worry, I'm sick," Steve told him.

"Camp workers are never sick," cut in Sergeant Goupu with another blow from his whip onto Steve's feet, snuggling beneath the lice-ridden blanket. "They work. And then they drop."

"Yeah, I've seen a bit of that," smiled Steve sickly. "You must own the happiest vultures in all Africa."

"Get up, you swine," hissed Goupu, and for the second go-round Steve went senseless under a cascade of blows.

"You know, Sergeant, this kind of thing is against orders," said Gisson, his face and arm stump twitching with irritation. "Who has the keys? How did this fellow get in?"

Sergeant Goupu took up the limp, frail, senseless body of Steve Wagner, and carrying him slung across his shoulders, kicked open the sickroom door and flung him onto the crude piece of tarmac outside frizzling in the midday sun.

"There is only one possibility, *mon Colonel,*" he said. "Berthier."

"You know something, Al?" Laura said, brushing her ash-blonde hair out of her face and putting down another highball. "This place stinks. It stank a lot before our boys got here, and now it stinks even more."

Al Hutter thought she looked wonderful, even though she had had too many highballs and had shouted at a lady like no lady and had got her makeup in a mess. He said, "Hey, why don't you and I go take a taxi ride?"

Laura ignored the suggestion. "You know something else? There's something awfully funny about that Helda bitch. I mean, nobody minds a girl being a prostitute. Some of my best friends are prostitutes. But why can't she mix it up a little? I mean, have you ever seen her with an ordinary GI, or a humble *matelot* or simple little sultan or an unaffected little phosphates manufacturer? Why has it always got to be staff officers?" She thought about it for a while and then she added, "Why the hell?"

"Give her one thing. If she's a whore she's the best-looking whore I guess I've ever seen, except for you, honey; I mean . . ."

"Flattery will get you nowhere." Laura shrugged the awkward compliment aside. "But I tell you one thing I'm thinking. I'm thinking, goddamn it, I'm supposed to be a spy, and here I've been for two weeks sitting on my ass, feeling sorry for myself and Steve and spying on nobody. It's time I got back on the job. Started following somebody around in my usual inconspicuous way. I could lose a bit of weight. Guess I could make a start with the lady Helda. You never know, it might lead somewhere."

"Mind if I follow her with you?" Al Hutter asked.

"You're just a born lecher," Laura smiled. "But let's have one last drink to the noble art of counterespionage.

"Rubin! Let's have another couple of highballs. Rubin! Hey, what's happened to Rubin?"

"You are guilty. *Coupable, tout à fait. Coupable!*"

"Sure. Sure. *Coupable.*"

"Guilty of flouting the penal provisions of the Etat Français as laid down by our leader, Marshal Pétain."

"Pétain. He's a dead duck."

"You won't win this way, Gisson, you one-armed screwball. All the kicks in the world won't get the Americans backfooting it onto the beaches and into their landing craft and away across the Atlantic to Norfolk, Virginia. You may have faith in your Marshal Pétain, but he can't put out the TORCH which has been lit. Robert has arrived, *mon brave;* now he may or may not be the most welcome of visitors, but he's here to stay. And one day he might care to pry a little into his new kingdom. Nose around a bit. Even discover a nice little rest camp deep in the Sahara where they're still flaying the hide off the friends of the free world. Where buddies of Roosevelt and Churchill and de Gaulle are being thanked for their services to the Allied cause by having their balls singed off."

"So crawl up off the ground and say it again."

"Your grandpop Pétain is a dead-duck piece of ninety-year-old waxwork!

"He last chalked up a success for himself way back in 1916. Only this happens to be 1942, and that Verdun uniform isn't going to wrongfoot many people anymore. It's just an old, faded, moth-eaten prop, not a Santa Claus outfit from Macy's."

"You are guilty . . ."

"Sure, I'm guilty.

"Yeah. I clobbered a guard. Sliced a six-inch piece of steel into his vertebrae. Sure, I faked sick. Heck, I *am* sick. But I'd have faked it anyway. Sure, I played idle. Sure, I backed de Gaulle. Sure, I admire Churchill. Sure, I hate the guts of Pétain. Sure, I'd like to urinate on Laval. Sure, I think you stink. Sure, I can smell the six-day-old crap in Sergeant Goupu's pants. Sure, you guys make me vomit. And sure one thing more. I'd like to stay alive just long enough to see your face when the US marines arrive. Or is it the Seventh Cavalry? Christ, Custer, you've been one heckuva long time arriving. If you don't come soon, the redskins are going to collect my scalp."

Colonel Gisson sat at his desk and watched four of his soldiers pick up a piece of horseflesh called Steve Wagner off the floor and carry him out of his office.

On the face of it he had nothing specific against the American. He wasn't a Frenchman, and that was unfortunate. He'd shirked his work, but then decadents like Americans do that kind of thing. He'd killed a guard. Or had he? Wasn't it obvious that Wagner was suffering from the *cafard*, the Sahara sickness? He clearly had hallucinations. Why, there were times when Gisson had them himself. It needed a peasant like Goupu to stay immune from these crises of the imagination that might have affected stronger men than Wagner in this waterless hellhole. No, by the book there was only one thing against him. Defeatism. How could we win the war when people like Wagner kept on saying that we'd already lost it?

All this talk about American landings.

Of course something *had* happened back on the coast, but it made no difference, for the simple reason that the essential chain of command was still there for every officer to see. Darlan, Nogues, Michelier, Lacroux. All the best friends of Pétain and Vichy were still up there in supreme power, dealing out justice in the same old admirable way.

How did he know?

Simple. You might think the camp was in the back of beyond. Well, it was remote, but modern contrivances like radio enabled Colonel Gisson to check into the great outside world. And what did the radio say? It told him that the government of North Africa was pursuing the same aims as ever.

The only change was that Nogues, clever old rat that he was, had somehow tricked the Americans to change sides and help Vichy against the Russians and the British.

So they could still hope that Rommel's Afrika Korps, as optimistically forecast in the news bulletins, would hit back and beat the hell out of the advancing British Eighth Army.

And they could still get on with the really serious things in life, like eliminating the Jewish virus from the body of France.

So he could close his ears to the insane babble of this mad American, because now that Admiral Darlan had ruled in Algiers his own personal allegiance was reinforced. Darlan was the Old Marshal's dauphin, his aider and abettor, his skillful adviser. Darlan, deadly enemy of the British and their Bolshevik allies.

In those difficult days a simple soldier like Colonel Gisson in a faraway outpost couldn't count on that many things in life. But one thing he did know. Day after day, for the foreseeable future, clever old Admiral Darlan would be winding those gullible Americans round and round his elegant little finger.

So who was winning the war?

"What do we do about the American?" Sergeant Goupu was eagerly inquiring.

"Put him out to work," his Colonel told him. "He is suffering from *le cafard*. We can cure him. My remedy is severe physical effort to rid his mind of hallucinations."

"And Berthier?"

"He is a traitor. Lose him somewhere."

"This is Radio Casablanca. Here is the news.

"THE NEWLY FORMED LAFAYETTE SQUADRON OF THE FRENCH AIR FORCE HAS FLOWN ITS NEW AMERICAN P38 LIGHTNING FIGHTERS TO VICHY. THE SQUADRON COMMANDER SAID ON BEING WELCOMED TO THE PROVISIONAL FRENCH CAPITAL TONIGHT, 'WE ARE GRATEFUL TO THE AMERICANS FOR THEIR GENEROSITY, BUT OUR PLACE IS BESIDE THE MARSHAL.'

"REPORTS ARE COMING IN OF A SERIOUS DETERIORATION IN MORALE AMONG THE TROOPS OF GENERAL ANDERSON'S BRITISH FIRST ARMY, NOW RETREATING FROM BÔNE. THE MEN COMPLAIN THAT THEIR EQUIPMENT IS NO MATCH FOR THE PANZERS AND THAT THEY ARE EXISTING ON HALF RATIONS. OUR CORRESPONDENT, WHO HAS JUST RETURNED FROM THE FRONT, SAYS THAT BRITISH TROOPS ARE RESENTFUL THAT THEY ARE HAVING TO BEAR THE BRUNT OF THE FIGHTING WHILE THEIR AMERICAN ALLIES ARE ENJOYING THEMSELVES WITH THE YOUNG LADIES OF ALGIERS AND CASABLANCA.

"A STATEMENT FROM THE MINISTRY OF INTERNAL SECURITY TONIGHT REVEALS THAT THE CURRENT SHORTAGE OF MATCHES IS ANOTHER RESULT OF A LARGE-SCALE JEWISH CONSPIRACY TO HOARD VITAL COMMODITIES. IN THE SERIES OF RAIDS CARRIED OUT BY CHIEF INSPECTOR LUCIEN ROTH'S POLICE OFFICERS IN CASABLANCA THIS AFTERNOON, IMPORTANT STOCKS WERE DISCOVERED, AND A NUMBER OF HEBREW INDIVIDUALS WERE ARRESTED. THE MINISTRY STATEMENT GOES ON TO WARN THE PUBLIC THAT ALL COMMERCIAL CONTACTS WITH JEWS ARE STRICTLY PROHIBITED BY LAW."

"Hell," said PFC Offenbach, "why do these bastards have to talk so fast? I mean, I can make myself understood in French—specially with Lucille, but darned if I can understand it."

"Hold on, Joe," said PFC Lou Alverson. "We're going over to the 'Soirée chez Rick.' You can understand music, can't you?"

"I wouldn't give too many bobs for that bloke's chances in life," commented Wally, late of the SS *Pimlico*, to Steve as he held a ten-inch iron nail between his fingers and Steve whirled his mallet above it to drive it deep into the desert subsoil.

"Which one?" asked Steve as he brought the mallet crashing down and one more sleeper took its place in that noble enterprise called the trans-Sahara railway.

"Ouch," complained Wally, "you almost circumcised my thumb, mate. I'm not Goupu, you know."

There was a small group of frail workers over in the distance. Office workers, civil servants, savants, some of them weak and spindly in their convicts' overalls, others obese, with sagging bellies and inadequate chests. One thing they all had in common, a Star of David on their shoulder.

"I think the floppy one with the india-rubber grin is hot favorite to cop it first, though that gray-haired bugger with the wavy beard might turn out to be the dark horse. There they go. Uncle Sam's latest little present to the desert vultures."

Steve blinked hard into the sun. There were pools of color where the troop of workers were, riotous splotches of scarlet and black. But through the wish-wash of mind-bending Technicolor he could descry a group and one little silhouette who seemed to be the energetic center of the circle. A silhouette figure, all arms and legs, around whom the others seemed to flow and collapse. Steve knew that silhouette. It was a silhouette called shit, a principle of hate called Goupu.

And as his eyes got accustomed again to the sun's glare and the Paul Klee puzzle of black lines became people, he noticed something about the guy. Goupu was leaning on the one, Wally, who his buddies thought was next for the chop-chop.

It was twenty-five yards away, it was straight into the blinding sun, it was reflected into eyes that were bloodshot and weary and crazily confused, and through the eyes into a brain into which a colony of desert ants seemed to have channeled their way.

But still the same floppy shoulders, the floppy, curly light brown hair, the floppy smile, which even under Goupu's treatment still seemed to preserve something of its naïve good nature.

That wasn't a silhouette, it wasn't a greyhound, it wasn't a dog; it wasn't a betting ticket either.

It was a human being called Rubin, and the fact that he was now upended in the middle of the Sahara, three hundred and fifty kilometers from his trays and drinks and his tips, could prove only one thing.

The mind of Steve Wagner had finally gone spare.

"Clean forgotten the words," said General Oakland to Helda de Billancourt, raising a bottle of Bollinger Brut '34 to his mouth. "The ones they said in the movie? Humph to Ingrid. Know what I mean?"

"You're drunk, General," Helda laughed charmingly. "I don't know what you're trying to tell me." Then her eyes slid downwards to the bald-headed USN Commodore who was making a meal of her left foot. "Careful, sailor," she giggled. "Even for a girl like me silk stockings aren't so easy to come by."

It was party night at the Hotel Majestic, and Helda de Billancourt was entertaining a few friends.

"Whadya mean I'm drunk?" General Oakland thundered. "Wouldn't you be if some goddamn bellhop kept giving you this piss water? Here, *garçon*," he shouted at the "room service," a perspiring Franco-Moroccan knee-deep in sprawling senior officers of Western Task Force, "what did you do with this Bollinger—leave it out in the desert to fry?" The champagne bottle cartwheeled through the air inches over the room servant's head and splurged to earth on one of the Hotel Majestic's richest carpets.

"Goddamn it, don't you have refrigerators in this country? I asked for champagne on ice—ice; do you *savez*? And bring the lady some too."

"General, you are being very naughty," Helda chided. "And making everybody feel very nervous. Don't forget this is my party."

"Here's to you, lady," the General said, aiming to raise her thigh to his lips. "Tell you another thing. We'll always have Paris. No, don't get me wrong. I've heard the inside story. That dame wasn't Ingrid Bergman, it was you. It's your alluring life story, honey. Right? Here's looking at you, kid."

"General, do you treat your lady friends like this back home?"

"I'm worried about Tunisia," said a young G2 colonel sitting nibbling at a bowl of caviar at Helda's feet. "The British may be good friends, but they're so goddamn slow. They're looking awfully exposed, too, up on that Bône–Bizerta road. They could be in a lot of trouble if the krauts throw a southpaw punch!"

"Stop talking politics," the General ordered. He was busy pouring a new bottle of champagne onto Helda's knee.

"I'm talking military strategy, sir."

"You're talking crap," said General Oakland, pausing for a moment from licking champagne off the Countess's knee. "We're gonna plug that gap. Here's looking at you, kid."

"Hey, I'm getting wet," the naval Commodore said.

"Tad's made a point though, sir," said Colonel Blink Burnside, wandering into the discussion with two tumblers of Courvoisier. "It's beginning to look like the British haven't got the necessary oomph to get to Tunis on their own. Strictly off the record, I think we ought to have sent George Patton up there—he's an oldie, but he can certainly step on the gas. The British are the best troops in the world at holding ground, but not so hot at covering it! So why spearhead with the British?"

Jerry Daniels was standing on the fringe of this group with his hands in his pockets, eyeing Helda.

These old lushes have got nothing to offer you, honey, except blood, sweat, and tears. So how about letting me hop onto your branch? I've got a real bushy tail!

"Why spearhead with the British?" he chipped in. "I'll tell you why. Because Tunisia's the only place we can put those limey bastards. They can't stay in this territory because the French hate their guts, and no wonder after what they did at Mers-el-Kebir, Dakar, and Syria. We gotta spearhead with the British because we can't afford to have them hanging around here lousing up our contacts with Nogues and Darlan."

"Maybe we ought to be supporting them," the young G2 Colonel suggested, chewing on a spoonful of caviar. "They're short on armor."

"Stop talking politics!" General Oakland said. He was trying to pour champagne over Helda's breasts, but was having a problem with her tight-fitting sequined bodice.

"Anyhow," he confided, relapsing like a child with his bottle into her noncommittal arms, "didn't I tell you jerks we're gonna plug that gap? As of tonight we're mobilizing General Fredendall and II Corps. We're giving him the 2nd Armored Division, and we're putting the whole outfit into the line east of Tébessa. Don't let anyone here tell me we're not supporting the British."

"You men and your wars," Helda giggled, giving the General a delicate kick.

"What are those lines now?" General Oakland asked. "Something about love and glory."

"I'm starving for lobster," Helda told him. "Go and get me some of the cold lobster, and come back and tell me more about General Fredendall."

On a couch at the far end of Helda's palatial suite WAC Captain Sally McNair was trying to do a bacchanalian act. In other words, she had stripped off her khaki tie and was leaning back voluptuously, holding a bunch of grapes over her mouth.

"It doesn't work, does it?" she finally admitted to Colonel Hiram Tanner.

"No, I guess it doesn't," said the Colonel.

"You don't find me exotic, alluringly irresistible in an occidental kind of way?"

"You're a nice girl, Sally."

"But you're looking at her all the goddamn time. OK, she's not wearing uniform. She's dressed like Macy's on Christmas Eve. So what's the fatal attraction?"

Colonel Tanner leered across the room at Helda, who was playfully tipping a champagne glass over the heads of her drunken retinue. "Fatal attraction, I guess," he said.

"Who ordered couscous?" Jerry Daniels wanted to know.

"Yeah," shouted General Oakland. "Who sent for all this coon shit?"

Three waiters were somehow trying to cross the room with steaming platters of Morocco's choicest delicacy. Then there were two as the other waiter went down, felled by a direct hit by General Oakland's bottle of champagne.

"Hey, you dumb bastard, you dropped it on my feet!" shouted a purple-faced Brigadier General, stamping the glutinous mixture into the rich carpet.

"What do you know, chicken Maryland!" shouted a whooping air force Major, relieving another waiter of his tray and zigzagging across the room. "Have some chicken Maryland, honey," he suggested, stumbling over the divan where WAC Captain Sally McNair was lying with her bunch of grapes. A sheep's eye and a wad of steaming semolina landed with a plop on her unbuttoned army shirt.

The WAC Captain screamed. Colonel Hiram Tanner socked the air force Major. Couscous sprayed across the room like a white Christmas.

"I tell you what II Corps is gonna do to those krauts, kid," said

General Oakland to Helda. "It's gonna march up through Tébessa, nip through the Kasserine Pass, and zap right across those bastards' communications. Here, I'll show you what I mean. Waiter, pass me some of that coon shit." He staggered and grabbed the last intact platter of couscous from the last standing waiter. "Here's II Corps, see," he explained, weaving back to Helda. "And there"—he pointed at the window—"is goddamn General von Arnim. See what we're gonna do; we're gonna hit him like this." There was a raucous shattering of glass as the dish sailed off into the night.

"Hey," said General Oakland, "I've got this junk all over my hands. Screw it! Here's to you, lady," he murmured affectionately as he slowly wiped his hands on Helda's half-exposed breasts.

"My," said Laura Caulfield, who had just walked in uninvited through the door, "Princeton on football night was never like this!"

"You're in luck, buddy."

You lived through another day, and the fact that you're thinking proves something or other, like you've got to have some kind of savvy left or you wouldn't be thinking. Savvy?

"And you were lucky. You hitched a ride back in a friendly old crate called a Laffley. Idle runt."

That's luck because Goupu's turning the screws these days, like sometimes you get a ride back to base camp and sometimes you walk back with a few trigger-happy SOL kids behind you on motorbikes, just so you don't opt out by the wayside.

The newcomers come later. You're already in your cozy cot, trying to collect your thoughts on a bare board and a lice-ridden piece of stuff they call a blanket. And he's over there, and you're OK even if he isn't, because the phantom of the desert has become flesh and blood (though the flesh is tearing away a bit and the blood seems to be running out).

And the tears are running down his cheeks to keep pace with the blood pulsing out of his groin; in fact our old *garçon* friend called Rubin of the tribe of Reuben, late of Ritzi's, late of Chez Maurice or whatever creep name they've now decided to call it, is in danger of liquefying.

And he's saying something about Bobbi. Sure, how's Bobbi? How come he ain't here to make it a party? And Rubin's in a bad, bad way because he's singing little bits of a song like "Oop-la, Oop-la," and *"On y danse, on y danse,"* and "Stars Fell on Alabama" and "Boum, Why Does My Heart Go Boum?" And he's murmuring something about the tunes not just being tunes. Something fishy about Ritzi and a police creep called Roth. And that's why he's here. Because he digs music. Because he wanted "Boum" when Bobbi wanted to play "Stardust" and Ritzi wanted "Oop-la, Oop-la." That's crazy, Rubin, that's a real crazy scene, you poor bastard. So lie down and I'll cradle you, because there's not much flesh left on my arm, but it's better upholstered than a worm-eaten piece of hardboard. And when you've woken, we'll get to the bottom of this musical shit parade.

A GI was saying, "Excuse me, ma'am, but if you're not doing anything how about . . . ?" when the black Citroën swooped. Suddenly Helda de Billancourt wasn't getting accosted by every passing US serviceman on the Boulevard Camille Desmoulins. She was disappearing down the rue de Tunis in the back of a police car.

"You are becoming extremely popular with our American guests," said Lucien Roth, looking glumly at the windshield wipers, which had been activated by a soggy Atlantic mist. "That should be beneficial for us."

"Yes," Helda agreed without any pretty smile. "It has been beneficial for you."

She handed him an envelope which he took in the front passenger seat without turning round. He read the contents and said, "You realize we can verify this information. As you know, we have other sources."

She said, "They will show it is correct."

"In that case you are to be congratulated," Lucien Roth told the camouflage-green-colored traffic. "You will be glad to know that my latest information on the Jew, Georges Martel, is that he is in reasonable health. Of course you appreciate I am talking to you in the strictest confidence. It was never more essential for stability here that he remains officially dead."

"And the American?" Helda asked Roth's raincoated back. "Have you kept your promise with the American?"

"The man Stephen Wagner is alive," Roth assured a passing U S Army truck. Then he turned round to look at her with eyes that were always eager to learn.

He said, "Helda Svenson, can we for the moment forget your fraudulent title? You are a very interesting woman. I am beginning to believe you are in love with two men."

She said, "You promised you would not hurt him. You promised he would not be sent to one of those camps."

"To care so deeply for two men is a very rare thing in a woman. In a sense it is praiseworthy, but of course it makes you more vulnerable." Roth was looking intently, almost ardently, into her gorgeous eyes, although he didn't feel any special ardor for them. Roth's sexual interests lay elsewhere. In other circumstances he would have been delighted to roll over on the back seat and let her settle on his face with her, no doubt, delectable naked bum. But for the moment he was concentrating on her eyes for professional reasons, looking for the mechanism of a woman who could love two men.

She said, "You have never kept your promises. You promised me they would hold Steve at Port Lyautey, that he would never have to work on that railway. You never keep your promises."

"Perhaps that is because you are always increasing your demands," Roth countered, turning back to examine the hissing windshield wipers. They were cruising past the Monument aux Morts, an impressive piece of masonry depicting a mounted *poilu* clasping the hand of a Moroccan horseman; both were dripping from the sea mist. He said, "It is possible Georges Martel would be free today—after all, you donated the necessary funds—if you hadn't come back to us with this additional demand. You remember, don't you?"

She didn't say anything, so he reminded her.

"We went to considerable trouble not to hinder the escape of the dishonest croupier Stephen Wagner—at your specific request. We even provided him with a companion," Roth added with the ghost of a smile. "My corrupted superior, Auguste Berthier. It would be simpler for both of us if you loved only one man."

"You get good value from me," Helda told him.

General Oakland and Colonel Blink Burnside and a host of others would have been distressed to see the tears that were welling in her cute little eyes.

"If you could bring yourself to love just one of these men, you would get better value from us," Roth answered. "Let me give you another example. You flew back from England on the understanding that in return for certain services we would honor our pledge to release the Jew Martel. You kept your side of the bargain, we were on the point of keeping ours. But then you learned that this Wagner had returned to Casablanca, you became anxious for his safety, and came back to us with a new request for leniency. In fact you lied to us, Helda Svenson. You tried to persuade us that the American criminal had returned to Casablanca entirely out of affection for you when he was actually a member of a Gaullist assassination squad. As a result we lost precious days in making an arrest. You deliberately obstructed my officers in preventing the murder of a good friend of France. But then of course General Kellerman was a good friend of yours too, was he not?"

"What is one more murder to me?" Helda asked bleakly. "There are thirty thousand murders in the information I have just given you."

"Is it really possible," Lucien Roth wondered aloud, "for a woman to love two men? My experience of love is limited," he confessed. He could have added that pretty bums were easier on the heart than pretty faces. "However, in your case it is no problem. The number of men you take to bed appears to grow from day to day. Some might even call your appetite voracious!"

They were now making a tour of the docks. The battleship *Jean Bart* was monopolizing nearly all of the view, a gray monster spreading across a gray December afternoon. Men with acetylene torches working on its ravaged gun deck provided the only sparks of light.

"For instance," said Lucien Roth, "I find it hard to believe that you are able to love a man like the Jew Martel and the criminal Wagner in equal measures. One is elderly, a would-be statesman, a man who lives and breathes politics, however undesirable these politics. The other is younger, an international vagabond with no political sense. May I suggest that he is the lover you would prefer to have in your bed?"

"You ask enough of me," Helda said. "These questions I do not have to answer."

"Perhaps I could put it another way," Roth said, turning round to look at her again with his studious eyes. "Suppose, for argument's sake, these two men were put up against a wall in front of a firing squad. You have power to reprieve one of them. Whom would you reprieve?"

"That is not a reasonable question."

"In fact it is. Did you know they are both being detained in the same camp? Also that the Commandant is a madman? Now imagine them both there, blindfolded. You must make your choice."

She was looking at a crater in the Mol de Commerce made by a shell from the USS *Augusta*. Even now they had managed to fill in only half of it.

"Imagine you have to choose," Roth insisted, "you *have* to choose. Who goes free?"

"Georges," she blurted out, looking back over her shoulder at the crater. "Of course it would be Georges Martel."

"Of course you are lying," Roth said. He turned a wan eye on a heated argument between a U S Navy jeep driver and an Arab with a donkey cart. "Like any woman, you are lying to protect the man you love. So after all you have a preference—it is the American criminal Stephen Wagner."

He noted with interest that she was sobbing. He wondered if her no doubt delectable bum was also convulsed with sobbing. In other circumstances he would have liked to feel it trembling softly against his upturned face.

He said a little less harshly, "In any case we have kept you long enough. We must take you home. Besides, I have an appointment at Radio Casablanca. The letter you have given us will be music to their ears," he added, allowing himself to crack the ghost of a joke.

"It's the tune everyone's been asking for this week," Ritzi announced the next Tuesday night to the listening world.

Some of the audience at Rick's Café Américain were already humming it, at least humming the tune that was top of every GI's personal hit parade that week. It had to be Irving Berlin's latest smasheroo, "White Christmas." There was only one dissenting voice and this was the joker who always wanted to hear "Temptation."

"Please, please," Ritzi hissed, raising his hand from the microphone to hush the burble of two hundred or more amateur Crosbys. "No, this tune so many of you have asked to hear is very old and very French; but, boy, it's got rhythm! Ladies and gentlemen, you're gonna hear 'Sur le Pont d'Avignon,' by the inimitable Bobbi."

The frisky little tune had difficulty in getting airborne with the groans that Ritzi's announcement unleashed. For all of thirty seconds Bobbi sat mournfully at his piano, waiting for the noise to die down. Personally, he couldn't wait to produce his own variation on this new tune called, "White Christmas." But the contract said he played what he was told to play in the order he was told to play it.

"And they call this 'Rick's Place,'" a disgruntled GI patron snarled. "Why, this crappy pianist isn't even a nigger."

Over in Tunis, Hauptmann von Best didn't wait to hear any more, much as he admired Bobbi's playing. As far as he was concerned, it was sufficient that the tune had been announced and that it was the third number on the program. He scribbled something on a note pad and immediately left the monitor room.

General von Arnim himself would be wanting to know that the US II Corps was mobilizing, and would be concentrated in the Tébessa area.

Suddenly Admiral Darlan had discovered that nobody loved him. Roosevelt didn't love him because to his surprise he had found he'd got seventy-five percent of the American electorate on his back, wanting to know why he had made a deal with the old collaborator. Churchill had never loved him, and now he'd got the combined Conservative and Labour parties on his back wanting to know why he'd let Roosevelt talk him into a deal with the Admiral. Hitler had quite liked him, but now he was the Führer's public enemy No. 1 for allowing most of North Africa to fall into Allied hands. Pétain was disappointed in him for issuing proclamations in his name, and Laval was calling him a traitor. Even good old dependable General Nogues, a man who could be trusted to bend with every breeze, was worried at the way he was bending over backwards to accommodate General Eisenhower.

But this boy who was standing in the passageway leading to his suite in the Palais d'Été, Algiers, seemed to understand. His soft respectful eyes seemed to say, "I know how it is, Admiral; you are bearing the whole weight of France on your shoulders, and nobody appreciates the sacrifice you are making."

As Darlan, followed by his ADC, came level, the youth touched him on the shoulder—an involuntary gesture of sympathy, perhaps. The Admiral turned round to see that he had drawn a revolver. Before Darlan could ask for an explanation three shots scorched into his chest. A few hours later he was dead.

It was Christmas Eve, 1942, a date which Bonnet de la Chapelle, the boy with the gun, had hoped would live in the annals of patriotism.

"They will not shoot me," he announced in his prison cell. "I have liberated France."

All the same, on the morning of December 26 he was led out in front of a firing squad. "You will see, the bullets will be blanks," young Bonnet de la Chapelle said before he died.

General Nogues, who happened to be in Algiers, had insisted there could be no lesser penalty for the murderer of a grand admiral.

It seemed that young de la Chapelle had belonged to a right-wing clique, interested in restoring the Comte de Paris to the French throne. All the same, one of General Giraud's first actions on taking over from Darlan was to round up the usual Gaullists.

Sweat was pouring out from under Sergeant Goupu's armpits, tears were in his eyes, but peace was in his soul. He was lying on his bed enjoying a well-deserved siesta, having put back a bottle or two of Moroccan *rouge ordinaire*. But this was Christmas Eve. Even a man of Goupu's responsibilities was allowed a few hours of meditation on the meaning of this Christian ceremony, a few hours with that Babe wrapped in swaddling clothes, with his own wife and family celebrating the festival in Alsace.

The patterned curtains were drawn against the Sahara glare. The whole ambiance was conducive to sleep. In fact Sergeant Goupu had already closed his eyes. His whole body was peacefully slipping into stupor. His greedy eyes had blinked shut and then opened. They now set tight to let in sleep.

His mind was on a little village way up in the Vosges, just some twenty minutes' ride from Salestat, up from the Traminerbirt Route des Vins, up into the pine forests, where the little children gathered outside the half-timbered houses to sing carols and the nativity in the church was illuminated by a hundred spluttering candles, and the *éminence grise* of the Vosges rose steep behind the Romanesque basilica of St. Eustache, and above that the heavy black clouds, fecund with the promise of snow.

Mechanically his red butcher's hand, which had accounted for so many deaths, reached across to the radio and played with the switch.

He didn't find the solace of which his soul was at present in need. No Noëls, no Babe Christ, no tolling of the great bells of Avignon. He was getting the lazily velvet tones of one of the latest phenomena to cut a groove to fame and fortune on Victor records. Bing Crosby in his latest crooning masterpiece—"I'm Dreaming of a White Christmas."

"Just like the ones I used to know," sang Bing's almost ever relaxed delivery.

A slow exasperation was building up in the heart of the SOL sergeant. A desire to put the boot in, a twitching of his calf muscles, as on those occasions when he saw a Jew with the Star of David on his shirt slacking on the railway site.

The twitching became spasmodic, accompanied by the usual clenching tight of Goupu's jaw.

In another second or two the radio, Goupu's one and only personal link with the outside world and the family under Nazi domination in Alsace, would have ricocheted to the other side of the room, spraying valves and wiring from its busted wooden frame.

But Bing's "May all your Christmases be white" was cut off and the wireless clicked into a protective silence.

Then an announcer's voice came on: a voice in French.

It took Goupu a bit of time to realize what he was saying. To him Admiral Darlan was a shadowy, a spindly little admiral, without any of the hero potentialities of his near namesake, Darnand, leader of the SOL and the greatest single butcher in Vichy France.

One farty little admiral the less was hardly enough to make Goupu's eyes flick open. The muscles in his calf ceased their spasmodic twitching. He started to snore. So he didn't hear the door open.

Or the footsteps cross the stone floor to his bed. And he hardly felt the coverlet swept away from his body.

But the voice did the trick. The voice that had him up from the horizontal in two seconds flat, straining to attention, hand twitching at the salute.

"*Les assassins. La pourriture,*" Colonel Gisson was yelling, flapping his useless stump in the air. "They have slaughtered the Marshal's Own Anointed. Admiral Darlan, the one and only representative of our Leader here in Africa."

"*Ah, les salauds,*" agreed his shocked sergeant. "It could be only one group."

"You are right," shrieked Gisson, "and we still have some of those vipers lurking in our camp."

"We have been trying to lose them, sir," said Goupu.

"Precisely," the Colonel shrilled, slapping his sergeant on the side with his stump. "We all know how zealous you have been in the Marshal's cause. Even so there are some dogs still left. I want them rounded up and dealt with."

"The Jews, the Freemasons, the British, the Foreign Legionnaires?" inquired his sergeant.

"Idiot," thundered his Colonel, "I mean the Gaullists. They are the assassins of Darlan. They are the menace to the vitality of France. General Nogues has said so."

Hollywood had made one thing impossible, thought Steve Wagner as they tied his hands together behind the stump with leather thongs. Sergeant Goupu had slipped an old camel's thighbone into the leather and was busy using it as a pivot to make the thongs bite in. He was succeeding. The thongs were through the outposts of flesh and were engaging Steve's main arm bones.

Tears were starting from his eyes, but he didn't cry out. This was partly because he had come to doubt his own existence. Celluloid can't feel any pain. Sure there had been a time when a guy could be Davy Crockett, or Bowie, or Boone, or even John Brown's body.

But now what were you?

John Garfield, by kind permission of RKO. Errol Flynn on lease from Warner Brothers. Humphrey Bogart on a new contract. And now, thanks to Colonel Gisson, he was giving his usual poor performance as Gary Cooper's understudy in *Beau Geste*.

Because this kind of thing, like being staked up outside camp and left to the sun and the ants and the desert buzzards, was, he had thought, some hook to get popcorn-chewing teen-agers into the movies for a couple of hours.

It didn't happen, really. Nobody in life was as good as Cooper, or as evil as Brian Donlevy as his Foreign Legion sergeant major. Nobody had brothers as loyal as Robert Preston and Ray Milland.

Heck, he thought as Goupu left him and turned his attention to the next Gaullist strung up against the next pole, I haven't nicked any diamonds. I'm not as good-looking as Cooper. And I'm one hell of a lousy actor.

There must be some likelier guy lurking somewhere around the studio who could put in a better performance.

Then Goupu left them, and the sun gently winked its first Eastmancolor light at them from behind the mountains. The buzzards began to twitter, and along with his twenty-odd fellow *soi-disant* Gaullists, Steve Wagner raised his eyes to salute the last dawn of his life.

Then the sun peeped above the mountaintop in swirling majesty and said hello to his naked body with a gentle warm caress.

"Hi, sun," murmured a celluloid creation called Steve Wagner. "Glad to make your acquaintance, you old sun of a gun."

Half an hour later he was thinking, Hey, this ain't exactly friendly, sun. You're not a sun, you're a gas jet in some goddamn tenement oven. OK, you can boil me up, but what kind of jerk wants to eat roast celluloid?

Then he went to sleep against his pole; or more likely just lost consciousness.

His final thought was a song—a song in which Helda, Laura, Auguste, Gisson, Ritzi, Bobbi, and Jean Sablon were all joining. "Sur le Pont d'Avignon." All had a greater or smaller Hollywood starring role.

Why the hell did they make you play "Avignon," Bobbi? he wondered.

It's just not your kind of tune.

Al Hutter would never have got there if it hadn't been for Laura Caulfield. When she'd invited him back to her villa at Anfa, he thought, There you go, you son of a gun, it's clear as a gag from Bob Hope the Lady likes the Lootenant.

As for the Lootenant, it was no secret he fancied the Lady. In fact she added up to one great swell broad who, as it happened, had a nice line in making homesick U S Army officers feel at home.

So when he lounged in the swing chair on the veranda and sipped his whiskey sour, it seemed to Hutter only a matter of time before the lady in question would offer him the keys of her citadel.

Wrong-routed him at one stroke.

"Al," she said, "just you tell me. What can we do to bail Steve out?"

"Steve who?" responded Hutter, sensing at once The Other Man.

"Hell, hero, he's your buddy as well as mine. Haven't you been crooning over his exploits on Fedala beach?"

"Oh, you mean Steve Wagner, the crumb. Good question. What in hell did ever happen to the guy? Sure I'm worried. Well, they say he's Rick, but I tell you, man, Bogey would never have fallen for the sucker punch they dealt him out at Rick's Place."

"He may not be the brightest guy on top, but the movie isn't finished yet, Al. Or maybe it is. Maybe they've just murdered him somewhere in the Sahara."

Sure the Lady had wrongfooted him, but soon she had him as hot on the trail of bailing Steve Wagner out of his Sahara hell as he had been on the more immediate business of infiltrating the Lady's camiknickers.

The diplomatic route was closed. All her initiatives had foundered on the bland unhelpfulness of Hal Newport, and whenever they had seemed to be making some progress there was that freckled-faced whiz kid called Jerry Daniels to sneer them out of court.

That left the military, and here they finally hit a winner. Hutter's divisional commander, General Harrison, was distinguished by one thing. He loathed the guts of his commander, General George S. Patton. While Patton perversely put all his considerable military might behind the Vichyist policies of Nogues, Harrison fumed at the injustice of it all.

When Hutter, who was one of Harrison's favorite young officers, came to him with the news of Steve's arrest, Harrison resolved to right the injustice by a bit of classic blind-eye. He equipped a party of about twenty hefty GIs, put them in two Liberators, swathed a MI submachine gun round each sturdy shoulder, and put Lieutenant Hutter in charge.

A cooperative G2 staff man on Patton's CP came up with a map of "Foreign Labor Camps" and rested his finger on Numéro Douze." The operation was the most successful US military feat to date. The control tower officer of the lonely Sahara air station was opening a packet of *marrons glacés* that warm Christmas morning when he saw a couple of Liberators dip over the landing strip and, uninvited, touch down.

It was the one thousand, nine hundred and forty-second anniversary of the birthday of Christ, the season of goodwill. It didn't take Hutter's tough little posse long to weigh up the opposition and have it for breakfast, or rather Christmas dinner. Soon Lieutenant Hutter was leading his party of avengers down the rough track to Colonel Gisson's penal encampment No. 12.

Some crazy casting director had cast you to be THAT GUY, but somewhere the wires got crossed. It's Christmas morning, but Sergeant Goupu doesn't buy it. Instead the guy's insisting it's Good Friday. So he's fastened you to a pole and left you out in the desert to die.

Big Joke. The Wise Men in the East finally arrived, but they're gonna waste their frankincense on a cadaver.

Not that Steve wanted them around. But he wouldn't have minded taking a quick dip in an icy fjord and looking up and taking an instant refresher from those clear blue eyes. ("Stevie," she'd say—nothing more.) Just for old times' sake. Just once more, although the vision had been requisitioned for use of U S Army personnel only.

Not that he could have seen her too clearly anyway. The Sahara sun was exploding in multicolored fireworks deep inside Steve's eye sockets. Like all he could descry was a crescendo of glare. But he felt something there. A hand pushing something towards his face, a big black silhouette intervening between him and the sunspots.

Gratefully he took the proffered flask and in one gulp downed it. The liquid was already past his throat before his whole body started heaving in revulsion. One thing he knew now, he would die with this taste in his mouth.

Sergeant Goupu smiled at the wasted figure bound to the pole and reflected that they always bought it, so long as you left them out long enough. Only trouble was he was running out of urine.

Lieutenant Hutter's avenging posse were all alumni of Fort Benning and Southerners, almost to a man.

The caravan of appropriated French Air Force trucks halted in a cloud of dust under the observation turret and massive barbed wire of Foreign Labor Camp No. 12. A couple of drunken SOL sentries looked up drowsily from a game of cards. The stake was a wristwatch belonging to an internee. The owner was lying nearby, on the barbed wire, where a Chatellerault machine gun had ended his pathetic waddle to freedom.

One of the guards got up and lurched over to Hutter's truck. He thought he was welcoming a new consignment of convicts. Hutter took a look at the man on the barbed wire fence. He noted that the Chatellerault machine gun had shot away half of his head. It was a sight to make a Southern gentleman trigger-happy.

The SOL sentry was worried by the look of these new prison guards, and uneasy about the formidable amount of weaponry that they were toting. He was about to wish Hutter a cautious "compliments" of the season, but the words were blown clean out of his Adam's apple before they reached his lips.

A volley from Hutter's MI submachine gun had practically sliced his neck in half. His companion ran afoul of a grenade and disappeared in a burning bush.

Then with a heart-quaking rebel yell the entire detachment crashed through into the outer compound, rammed their trucks round in a full circle, like wagon trailers fighting it out with Red Injuns, and got down to the serious business of bagging a few *cagoulard* scalps.

Lieutenant Hutter's orders had been succinct and noncontroversial. "If it wears a beret, mow it into the ground. If it looks like a cadaver, it's gotta be a friend."

But something had gone wrong. Sure, there were a few shots coming their way from the makeshift huts to their right. Sure, some guy had tried to chuck a hand grenade in the general direction of their wagons, but it had fizzed on like a bad firework on the sand in front and gone off with a harmless "plop."

"All right," shouted Hutter, standing up. "Come and get 'em."

It was going to be a cliché of 1945, but this was Christmas Day, 1942, so you could say Lieutenant Hutter's collection of roughnecks was bursting in on virgin territory.

It was going to happen at Auschwitz, Ohrdruf, and any number of liberated Nazi concentration camps—the sight of stinking, fleshless, degraded, apathetic humanity would bring out the latent Al Capone in simple gum-chewing GIs.

A lad from Louisiana dodged round the back of the compound and crashed his way into one of the main convict-detention rooms. As it happened, this particular room was a haven for sick and elderly convicts who had been taken off the working site and put on a starvation ration, on the theory that work, and only work, fills the belly.

"My, oh my, oh my," crooned the Louisianan whilst his boyish voice yelped for his Lieutenant. "Feast your eyes on this, Lootenant," he counseled Hutter.

"Any of you guys know the whereabouts of Steve Wagner?" thundered Hutter whilst the young Louisianan, overcome by the spectacle, was quietly vomiting his innards out over against the wall.

The prisoners shuffled towards him, and one, a prewar professor of philosophy at the University of Montpellier, did the semblance of an apologetic shrug with two formerly well-covered arms, which were now antlike feelers.

"Christ, man!" roared Hutter, shaking him. "Steve Wagner. An ugly son of a gun who looks a bit like John Garfield. Can you identify him?"

"*Pardon, monsieur, mais . . .*" managed the professor before he collapsed back onto the floor.

Then Hutter was outside. His own stomach was beginning to experience some of the Louisianan's nausea.

They tracked them down finally. They were in the large room over the other side of the compound, a room used for boozing and eating, games-playing and general socializing.

There were about fifteen of them in the hall, well-fed, fully paid-up members of the SOL, Vichy's modern order of chivalry.

Some of them were still wearing paper hats, one had a cracker dangling from his shaking arm, another's heavy lips seemed permanently glued to a bottle of Algerian plonk.

Scattered over the trestle tables were the remains of what had once been a very substantial Christmas binge.

The GIs stood at the entrance to the room and gave them everything they had. They seemed intent on one thing only—to shoot the recently swallowed *poulet rôti* out of the stomachs of the revelers.

They succeeded.

Vichy's chivalry of modern times took a whole weight of MI ammo, and then a bit more for second helpings.

They died as they had lived, with an oath on their lips and a well-lined belly.

After that it became a game of fox and geese. Hutter's men took the whole place apart. Individual bands of furtive berets were smoked out and died at high noon.

"Blimey," said Wally from Brixton. "The Yanks are coming! A few years late, like they were last time, but welcome all the same."

Then the whole thing collapsed. Bands of liberated convicts wandered listlessly about the compound. Two doughboys from South Carolina broke into the Commandant's office and held Colonel

Gisson and his chief aider and abettor, Sergeant Goupu, up at carbine point.

"*Merde!*" cried Sergeant Goupu.

"*Vive la France!*" murmured Colonel Gisson.

The sergeant used a bowie knife to dispatch them. Meanwhile a lad from Alabama, whose downy chin had yet to encounter a razor, was about to make the killing of the year. He thought he had spotted a potentially dangerous frog pillbox outside the main encampment. His carbine ripped a neat circle of holes in its door.

"OK, you lousy bum," shrieked the freckled-faced lad from beneath his heavy helmet. "Put your hands above your head and come out, whoever you are."

In obedience to the shrill command the door swung open and a figure emerged blinking into the golden-hued daylight.

It was not Georges Martel's day, but then it hadn't been his year, either. Also he wasn't to know that a beret at the present moment was an unwise form of headdress to sport. In fact Georges Martel and his beret had been near well inseparable over many years (as much a target for political cartoonists as Churchill and his siren suit).

As the still massive weight of his body floundered on the ground outside his solitary thirteen-month jail and the Alabaman stood over him to remove his brainpan with a final volley, Martel's keen political mind clicked over once more and for the final time.

They are murdering me, he concluded, only because President Roosevelt has ordered it.

In a sense he was right.

The sun was in his head. It had entered his brain. It had melted his eyes. It was burning his crotch. It was scalding his heart. It was teasing his toes. It was singeing his balls.

But he knew it was coming again. Smelled the presence, felt the breath of menace. Waited for the silhouette, and knew the trap was well laid.

Again there was darkness over the face of the earth, and something was hanging over him, reaching for his mouth, waiting to pour another flask full of syphilitic piss water down the throat of the thing they didn't even have the courtesy to call Steve Wagner. But he was ready for it.

As the flask touched his lips and gently parted his teeth, and the liquid began to flow down into his bladder, Steve Wagner struck.

His knee shot up and caught the tempter in the crotch with the most God Almighty wham.

A spluttering of fine Martell cognac flew out of Lieutenant Hutter's grasp and scattered over the sand. With a deep moan Hutter sank to his knees, cradling his balls in both hands.

"I didn't deserve that, Steve," he finally choked. "I never screwed your goddamn Laura Caulfield."

SECTION IV

FADE-OUT

You cried out for water, and they brought it to you with an ice cube.

You gasped for a cigarette, and they brought you a carton of Chesterfields, fresh from the USA.

You called out in your delirium for a slug of bourbon, and although they murmured it was, strictly speaking, against regulations, they brought you a bottle.

It was more like a dream than a U S Army hospital, which someone had told you was what this fresh-linened paradise really was.

There was only one similarity between the heaven of U S Army Field Hospital No. 3 at Fort de la Joncquière, Casablanca, and the hell of Foreign Labor Camp No. 12 in the desert. They both seemed to produce hallucinations.

For example, one morning (or was it one afternoon?) Steve had the impression that Helda was sitting at the side of his bed. He had the impression he was saying, "Scram. Get the hell out of here. I don't take sympathy from whores!" He thought he could see the tears running down her cheeks. He thought he heard himself tell her, "If it's any comfort, Georges Martel is dead!" It had to be an hallucination because when he looked again she wasn't there. It was just a nurse with another glass of iced water.

Another time he thought Laura Caulfield was leaning on the end of the bed. Perhaps she was; perhaps she wasn't. In any case, he heard himself telling her, "The way you look ought to burn up these bedclothes, turn me into a human torch. You know something, those curves of yours ought to make me sprout like a beanstalk—right through the ceiling. But I tell you something else, honey. You don't do anything to me, because there's only one woman in the world who does anything to me and she's a whore, a cheap, shagged-silly whore who bums around with colonels in bifocals."

And then he heard her telling him, "Yes, I know about your great love story, Steve. I guess you have to go back to the Middle Ages to find a saga of similar devotion. You know, you'd look awfully cute in shining armor, particularly on a well-behaved charger—and maybe that's how you've always seen yourself. A New Jersey Yankee at the Court of King Arthur. You've even got yourself a Guinevere. Sure, didn't you know she slept around with colonels too? But didn't anyone tell you the Middle Ages are finished, and so are Charles Boyer and Greta Garbo and Leslie Howard and Norma Shearer.

They've ridden all over them with tanks, flattened them out with bulldozers!

"You can't ride around on a charger anymore, because there are just too many tanks and jeeps and half-tracks on the road for safety. I know, Steve, it's enough to make you sick, but there's one thing you can do with all this mechanization around, and that's to latch onto the nearest piece of honest flesh and blood you can find."

Another time Lieutenant Al Hutter seemed to be hovering around the bed, and what he was saying didn't make any sense at all.

"Boy," he said, "they really threw the book at us for shooting up that lousy concentration camp. One time it was gonna be court-martial, detention with hard labor. General Harrison had to use all his pull to get us off that one. Know what, though? They marched us around to the frogs to apologize. How's about that! We had to stand there, cap in hand, and apologize to some fucking lousy frog official for busting up his little death camp. Tell you something else. I'm posted. Yeah, I guess it's good news. Anyhow, if I'm not in Tunisia tomorrow night I'm to consider myself busted. Well, I've only fought frogs up to now, haven't I? And I guess they don't count. You got to be up against Germans before you can say you've seen real fighting, correct? I guess I'm going to miss Laura, though."

"This is Radio Casablanca. Here is the news.

"THE UNITED STATES CONSULATE IN CASABLANCA HAS APOLOGIZED TO THE MINISTER OF INTERIOR FOR CERTAIN INCIDENTS THAT TOOK PLACE OVER CHRISTMAS AT A GOVERNMENT CORRECTIVE INSTITUTION IN THE SAHARA. IN HIS STATEMENT THE AMERICAN VICE-CONSUL, HAROLD NEWPORT, STRESSED THAT THE AMERICAN SOLDIERS INVOLVED WERE ACTING WITHOUT ORDERS AND THAT THE RINGLEADERS WILL BE SEVERELY DEALT WITH BY MILITARY LAW.

"ALTHOUGH THERE WAS NO EXCUSING THE MEN'S BEHAVIOR, MONSIEUR NEWPORT PLEADED THAT THE TRADITIONAL AMERICAN CHRISTMAS FESTIVITIES MAY HAVE CONTRIBUTED TO THE SERIOUS BREAKDOWN IN DISCIPLINE. HE PROMISED THAT THE UNITED STATES GOVERNMENT WOULD MAKE GENEROUS COMPENSATION.

"IN A STATEMENT RELEASED THIS AFTERNOON THE MINISTER OF THE INTERIOR DEPLORED THE CONDUCT OF THE AMERICAN TROOPS, WHO, HE EMPHASIZED, WERE GUESTS OF THE MOROCCAN GOVERNMENT. HOWEVER, HE ACCEPTED THE VICE-CONSUL'S ASSURANCE THAT THERE WOULD BE NO REPETITION OF SUCH INCIDENTS.

"THE POPE HAS SENT A MESSAGE OF NEW YEAR'S GREETINGS TO MARSHAL PÉTAIN. THEY ARE AMONG THOUSANDS RECEIVED BY THE HEAD OF STATE FROM ALL OVER EUROPE AND THE FRENCH EMPIRE."

Three months ago the French antiaircraft batteries at El Hank and Fedala would have loosed off with everything they had at this incoming "Commando" transport, especially had it been observed there were RAF roundels on its wings. This January afternoon the machine was permitted to cruise in lazily from the Atlantic Ocean, perform a graceful arc round the gleaming white dome of the Cathedral of the Sacré Coeur, and settle with a gentle squeal of rubber onto the tarmac of Casablanca airport.

A detachment of white-helmeted US MPs came to attention as steps were wheeled up to the door of the aircraft. A rotund figure in RAF uniform finally emerged. It moved stiffly down the steps because the special heating equipment installed in the aircraft had failed, leaving Britain's supreme warlord to draw heavily on his hip flask of brandy. As the MPs presented arms the figure raised two fingers in a groggy salute. "Air Commodore F," code name for Winston S. Churchill, had arrived for the series of top-level discussions, later to enter history as the Casablanca Conference.

Accompanied by General "Pug" Ismay, Air Commodore F moved stiffly down the line of elite US troops, nodding scowling approval at their officer. Then he staggered on to greet the reception party, where he shook hands with General Patton, returned General Oakland's snazzy salute, and even flashed a weary victory sign at Colonel "Blink" Burnside.

But who was this five-star French General with shifty eyes and a mousy little moustache giving him this suave but unmistakably patronizing St. Cyr salute? His visit was supposed to be top-secret, at least as far as the French were concerned.

"This is General Nogues, sir," said Ismay, "the Resident-General."

"On behalf of the Sultan, Monsieur Churchill, may I cordially welcome you to Morocco?" General Nogues said, perhaps just a shade less warmly than he had welcomed General Joachim Kellerman of the Wehrmacht.

"I've heard of you," Churchill growled, and reminded himself that what he had heard he didn't like. This was the man responsible for the disappearance of his old friend Georges Martel, the man who, by removing the best hope of France, had been indirectly responsible for saddling him with de Gaulle.

"If there is anything you should require for your comfort or convenience during your stay . . ." Nogues gestured. He was going to ask if the Prime Minister would be requiring a woman—all these for-

eign dignitaries seemed to require a woman. Then he reminded himself that this visitor was British, and that the British were fastidious
about such things.

Churchill shook his head. He had heard another thing about
General Nogues, and this was that he was still in contact with Vichy.

"*General Nogues,*" he warned, "*j'espère que vous ne téléphonerez
pas à Vichy que nous sommes ici. Parce que maintenant clair
de lune*"—he waved at the blue sky—"*très bon pour bombarder; vous
comprenez?*"

"Monsieur, I do not understand."

"*Si vous bombardez nous, on bombardait aussi vous,*" threatened
the old bulldog, giving the French General one of his most virulent
two-fingered salutes.

One morning when he was beginning to feel better Steve Wagner had another visitor.

"How you doing, old pal?" Jerry Daniels wanted to know. Steve wondered if he was supposed to have met this ginger-haired, ferrety-looking character before. He reckoned maybe he had, in some inauspicious circumstances.

He said, "I'm doing OK. Who are you?"

"I'm a friend of Laura Caulfield," the visitor grinned, depositing a bunch of grapes on the bedside table. "She's told me a lot about you. Golly, some people wouldn't believe your bad luck!"

"What's my bad luck to you?" Steve asked.

"To begin with, I'm a fellow American . . ."

"You're kidding."

"Also I happen to have a little pull around this town; not much, but it could just wangle you a ticket to the States when you're fully recovered."

"I've seen the States," Steve said.

"Another thing," said his visitor. "If you've got any complaints about the treatment you've received, I'm the person to take them up with. It's one of the little chores the State Department has given me. Seeing that US citizens who've got into trouble with the French authorities over here get a fair hearing. I also control the purse strings on compensations. If you've got a good case I could help see you get compensation."

"You must be my fairy godmother," Steve said. "Incidentally, didn't you bring any liquor?"

"Of course," Jerry Daniels grinned. "Like I said, a lot of people just aren't going to believe your story. I mean, what you've been through just doesn't happen to an American citizen in 1943, even if this is Morocco. I guess even when you look back on it, the whole thing seems like some crazy dream, something you imagined."

"You ought to try it," Steve told him. "Try a spell at Foreign Labor Camp Numéro Douze and see if it's just your imagination."

"Don't get me wrong, Steve," Jerry Daniels said. "I believe you because I've heard the whole story from Laura. But a lot of our people over here wouldn't. Particularly people who reckon it's important to keep in with the French. Know what I mean? Even true stories can be unpopular. That's why I could be the one person who could get you compensation."

"Haven't I seen you before somewhere?" Steve asked.

"OK, you've been to the States. There's still got to be a lot of places in the world you haven't seen, even a globe-trotter like you. They tell me Rio can be really swell in January, and there's no war in Brazil."

"Would you believe I like it here?" Steve said.

Daniels took a walk to the window and took a peep through the blinds in the direction of the city basking under Allah's blue heaven. He put his hands in his pockets, which Steve reckoned was supposed to make him look casual. Steve didn't think he looked casual.

"Oh, you're fine and dandy here in the hospital—incidentally, who wangled you this bed? But I'm wondering what you're going to do when you leave the apron strings of the U S Army Nursing Corps," Jerry Daniels confessed. "You wouldn't want to hang around a dump like Casablanca, would you? It wouldn't suit your health."

"I've got a few things to settle up when I get out of here," Steve said. "For instance, there's a little French bastard, name of Lucien Roth." He stopped. Suddenly he didn't like anything about the way this ferret guy was looking at him, the way he seemed to be hanging on his words.

"Yeah." Jerry Daniels finally nodded. "I can see you've had a helluva time. Best thing you can do is rest up—and why not?—it's all at the expense of the poor old US taxpayer."

He almost tiptoed to the door, like someone in the presence of the very sick, even of the dying. "Yeah, you take care of yourself, old pal," he murmured. "No one's going to believe what you've been through. Nobody's going to want to believe it."

Laura came to visit him next morning. She brought a box of *pâté de foie gras* and a bottle of chilled chablis. This time he didn't tell her to scram.

He said, "Friend of yours called here yesterday. Ginger-haired little creep from the State Department. Didn't leave his name. Who the hell is he?"

She said, "It sounds like my boss, Jerry Daniels. What did he want?"

"I think he wants to kill me," Steve said.

Laura nodded. "That wouldn't surprise me. Maybe you'd be safer out at my place."

He'd almost forgotten what it was like to relax like this. The voluminous panama hat pulled down over his face, the muffled sigh from the striped canvas as it sagged to receive his weight, the sun beating down, like high summer in Provence. That creative nudge at his painter's elbow to splash it all onto canvas, the splutter of his half-smoked Havana as it loped from his widening mouth and perambulated downwards towards his shirt. This was Apollo in all his fiery splendor, as incandescent as in the days of old. But beside him were none of the habitual beachcombing celebrities of prewar days, none of that Côte d'Azur gallery of notables. Just a foot or two away "Admiral Q," code name for the President of the United States of America, took the African sun with a political smirk, like he might be welcoming a deputation from the Senate.

His wheelchair creaked as he sank down more deeply into his siesta.

Throughout the world in a huge arc from the Pacific to the shores of Africa the manhood of America was bracing itself for the showdown.

But this was vacation time.

The villas themselves were biased heavily to pleasure. Cool dappling pools, blazing white low-slung walls, and in the distance the delicate jingle of the cocktail trolley. This was therapeutic, a well-earned rest for the leaders who had on their backs the burden of the free world.

And it was catching.

"Have you had any reply?" mouthed the President from beneath heavy sunglasses. "Has he even deigned to answer?"

He was referring to the one positively annoying fly in this soothing vacational ointment—General Charles de Gaulle.

"Joan of Arc was stubborn too," the British Prime Minister reminded him. "It is not for nothing they call him the Constable of France. But if he proves a naughty boy we have our ways of chastising him."

"He represents nothing," replied the President. "He calls himself France, but nobody has ever voted him into any office. He has no credentials."

"He is better news than Pétain or Darlan or Laval or Nogues," replied Churchill.

"He is your responsibility," said the President.

"Don't worry, I will tame him."

There were urgent matters of state, besides de Gaulle, to discuss. There was the whole future of Africa, the demise of Hitler's Axis, the rout of Japan to plot. There were ambassadors and generals, and senior advisers and private secretaries to meet and to brief. But the Moroccan sun was beguiling and the two elder world statesmen unusually receptive. Lunch had been good, and soon they began to snore in their pleasure dome of villas while just a few yards away alert MPs mounted guard over Anfa's conference site, which heavy wreaths of barbed wire had turned into the world's most luxurious detention center. And the heavy breakers of the Atlantic drummed dully in Churchill's ears.

Laura looked up from her desk chair on her patio and said, "You're doing well. You can get up out of a chair, walk around on two feet, handle a whiskey sour like a high school kid. Looking at you now, I would say you were a hundred-percent OK in all your vital organs. But maybe that's just my incurable optimism."

The sun was going down over the Atlantic. Steve was looking out to sea, examining the same thundering breakers which as it happened were attracting Winston Churchill's attention half a mile up the hill of Anfa in the Casablanca Conference compound. Winston Churchill was marveling at the fact that Patton's landing craft had been able to put men ashore in these clouds of foam. Steve Wagner was thinking only how fresh and clean it all looked.

He said, "Jerry Daniels come here often?"

She said, "I wish you'd try and forget Jerry Daniels. I can forget him very successfully. And remember, he's my boss."

"You've got an invitation from him back in the house. He requests the pleasure of your company at the Casablanca premiere of a film called *Casablanca*. Is that some kind of joke? It says 'bring loverboy Steve' too. I don't like his tone. I don't like anything about him."

"It could be you're jealous," Laura said hopefully.

Steve turned round from the sunset and the ocean and smiled, even though he had almost forgotten how. He said, "It would be cozy, wouldn't it, if it was just that?"

"I tell you, forget Jerry. I'll bet he's forgotten you. The little runt has a lot on his plate, remember, now President Roosevelt and half the U S Government have hit town. One way or another our Jerry has some er . . . accounting to do."

"You said accounting . . ."

"Forget him. Do I have to remind you you're a convalescent case and I'm your self-appointed nurse? Why don't you have another drink, or even kiss me, or something? I'm tired of politics."

"Laura, you know more about Jerry Daniels's operation than you're letting on. You always have."

She lit a cigarette. The point glowed because the sun had all but gone. She said, "I know more than I want to know about too many people in this sad little town. And that includes me, you, and . . . well, who else is there?"

His eyes darkened. "You were going to say Helda, weren't you?"

"Look, Steve, why don't you rest up for a few more days? Then when you're feeling strong, I'll lift the lid off this whole goddamn rat cage for you."

"You found out Helda's a whore, didn't you?"

"Like I found out the thirteen colonies have just declared independence."

"You mean you know something else?"

"You know something?" Laura said, getting up and putting her arms round him. "If we're not going to bed, why don't we turn on the radio and dance to some music? I'm getting cold."

She led him into the villa and flicked on the radio. Then she slipped off her beach wrap and cuddled into his arms with just her bathing suit on. He didn't protest. Even Steve Wagner, the authentic one-woman man, wasn't going to stop himself from putting an arm round her suntanned back, resting his face on her cheek, and nosing into her ash-blonde hair, which was just a little shorter than Veronica Lake's.

The tune was "You Were Never Lovelier." The pianist was inspired. They weren't Fred Astaire and Rita Hayworth, but they knew they looked good together, knew they were moving well together. And besides, there was nothing like the magic of crafty old Jerome Kern to persuade a couple, anywhere in the world, they were dancing on the roof of the Waldorf.

"I can see you went to dancing class," Laura whispered.

"You learned a few steps, too," Steve said, holding her still more protectively because she had said she was cold, and anyway, it was nice having a dancing partner like Laura Caulfield, specially when she was wearing only a swimsuit.

It was too bad for Laura, and perhaps for Steve as well, that the tune changed so abruptly. Suddenly they were listening to the voice of Ritzi (née Rissoli) direct from Rick's Café Américain. He was delighted to announce he had been inundated with requests for that old French evergreen, "Le Fiacre." He said that Bobbi would be enchanted to play it as his next number because it was one of his favorites too.

"Oop-la, oop-la, oop-la, oop-la." It wasn't a tune anyone in a sentimental mood would choose to dance to, although, of course, if you were a tipsy vineyard worker celebrating a good year in the Beaujolais country, it might have been just the ticket. Or again if you happened to be Hauptmann von Best sitting with your earphones on at General von Arnim's headquarters in Tunis, it could well set your feet tapping, because you recognized "Le Fiacre" as the signature tune of the U S 2nd Armored Division and, from its place in the program, you deduced it was now moving up into the Fondouk area to support General Anderson's British First Army, leaving the American infantry looking awfully vulnerable down in the Tébessa-Kasserine region. "Oop-la, oop-la, oop-la."

"Rubin," Steve murmured. He wasn't dancing any longer.

"The name's Laura, in case you'd forgotten. I also happen to be a girl."

" 'Oop-la'; 'Boum'; 'Sur le Pont.' It didn't make sense."

"Maybe you'd like to sit this one out," Laura whispered in his ear, pressing her hips closer into his body. "Upstairs, for instance."

"All these crappy *chansons*."

"We could make our own music, honey."

"It wasn't his kind of music," Steve said.

He pictured the ex-waiter lying with his mouth open across a segment of track for the new trans-Sahara railway, waiting for a train that would never come. At least not for him. Rubin had died on Christmas Eve, 1942. Just twenty-four hours too early for Christmas and Al Hutter's merry rescue raid.

It wasn't his kind of music. It wasn't Bobbi's kind of music. It wasn't even Ritzi's taste in popular melody. Only trouble with Rubin was he had voiced his opinion; wanted to know why when the customers were all hollering for Cole Porter and Johnny Mercer they kept playing this old French *chanson* crap. Was that why he died on Christmas Eve on a piece of railway track that led nowhere?

"But Rubin talked," he said out loud. "They forgot to tear his tongue out."

Laura tightened her suntanned arms around Steve's neck. She said, "You're very cute—I mean that—but I don't know what the hell you're talking about."

"Rubin. You remember Rubin, at Ritzi's place?"

"Whatever happened to Rubin?" Laura asked dreamily.

"They killed him, on account of the fact he didn't like French corn. Funny, wasn't it?"

She was perhaps the most delectable example of undressed womanhood a man could hope to find in his arms, even in a country which could make most mirages possible; but he was looking straight over her nicely rounded shoulder at the unattractive memory of a labor camp in the Sahara, and a man lying with his mouth open across a line of track that wasn't leading anywhere.

She said, "Oh hell, it's happened again—it's always happening in this damned town. Politics is about to kill a budding relationship. It's tougher on love than the Germans—this goddamn politics!"

He said, "You're supposed to be a spy, aren't you? What does it mean?"

She kissed his ear and pleaded, "Tomorrow, Steve. Can't we wait until tomorrow, and I'll tell you what the whole of creation means."

"These tunes. They were supposed to be popular requests, drawn by chance out of a bowl by Ritzi. But according to Rubin, there was nothing chancy about it. These crappy *chansons* have to go on the air at a certain time, in a certain place."

"You're saying it's some kind of code?"

"I'm asking you."

Laura took herself out of Steve's arms with a sigh; put on her beach wrap and sat down and lit a cigarette.

"How should I know?" she finally asked. "All I know is there's a helluva big security leak in this town. We monitor Radio Casablanca news bulletins. We know they're crazily pro-Axis, but we haven't caught them giving away any confidential information. But, hey, we never thought of monitoring the 'Soirée chez Rick'!"

"'Oop-la, oop-la, oop-la'—what the hell's it saying to anybody?"

"Just possibly it's telling the world what some U S Army staff officer whispered in a lady's pretty ear last night. Now I come to think of it, even Bobbi couldn't figure out why he had to play that tune."

"Wait a minute. Whose pretty ears?"

Laura looked at him, and her eyes suddenly turned very tender. This was because Steve suddenly looked very vulnerable.

She said, "You really want to know? Helda de Billancourt has made a collection of just about every G2, G3, and G4 staff officer in Casablanca. They have a lot of parties. They put away a lot of drink. They talk a lot of careless talk. She's become quite an amateur strategist, your old flame. I understand she's fascinated by military logistics—sorry, but as you said, I'm supposed to be a spy. Most of Helda's friends are strictly American top brass, but there's one exception—a little pro-Nazi Frenchman called Inspector Lucien Roth. I don't know what they find to talk about. I'm sorry, Steve, but you asked."

"The inimitable Bobbi's gonna be playing another favorite from France later on in the program," Ritzi was announcing. "Meantime he's gonna play a song that was created here in the Café Reek and dedicated to a beautiful lady customer of mine with a sad love story. A song they put into the great movie called *Casablanca,* a movie based exclusively on my Café Reek. Listen to Bobbi play 'As Time Goes By.'"

Steve said, "I'm going to borrow your Oldsmobile and catch the end of the show."

"Well," beamed President Franklin D. Roosevelt in person, "what do you make of it?"

"It's got to be the best-kept secret of the war," the President's personal aide, Harry Hopkins, grinned.

"Guess you're rather surprised to see me here in Casablanca," the President insisted. "As far as the Axis and the free world know, I'm back home in my Oval Office in the White House."

"It's got to be the best-kept secret of the war, Nad," Harry Hopkins emphasized.

"Just for the record"—F.D.R. gestured from his wheelchair—"I'm the first President ever to leave the United States in wartime. What do you make of that?"

"This is your lucky day, Nad," Harry Hopkins prompted Klaf. "The President has just handed you a story Walter Winchell, Ed Murrow, or any other newsman you care to name would give his right hand for."

"And it's an exclusive," Roosevelt expanded. "In two days' time we're going to lift the security screen to reveal to the world's press that your President and a certain cigar-smoking 'Former Naval Person' have been in strenuous and significant deliberation here for some four days."

"You've got the President's authority to break your story back home tomorrow. Quite a head start, eh?" Harry Hopkins backslapped.

"What do you make of that?" the great Democratic President chuckled.

What did Nad Klaf make of it? He guessed they were right. This was a story any newsman would give his right ball for. He only wished they'd sent around this Cadillac to drive him out of Anfa any evening but this evening. Some other time when he could give the President of the United States his undivided attention. Life could be a nutty kind of dealer. It was like Life to deal him this one the same evening he had heard that Steve Wagner was alive and well, and back in Casablanca.

"I've always had a lot of respect for your Sodersheim boys." The all-powerful cripple flashed one of his irresistible smiles. "Of course, old Mort Karl is a personal friend of mine. He helped me a lot in '32, '36, and '40. You've got a very great President too, Mr. Klaf. So any favor I can do for Mort and his Sodersheim boys is just returning many favors Mort has done for me."

The President noted that Klaf had still to produce his notebook. "I guess you'll want to get your notebook out and start pitching in with those questions," he added with a little less of a smile.

There was another problem. The news about Steve had sent him hotfoot to the bar of the Hotel d'Afrique by way of quick celebration before he started to comb the town. And there'd been this WAC Captain sitting up there; a girl, name of Sally MacNair, sucking olives in what she had maybe figured was a sensual manner, who had asked who the hell is Steve Wagner, anyway? And it had needed four pernods before he had managed to get the answer into that dumb army whore's dumb head. So now even the part of his mind that was trying to concentrate on this Roosevelt exclusive wasn't functioning too well.

Ask him about General de Gaulle? Better not. Who was it said that was a taboo subject with the President? Ask him maybe if he knew where he could find Steve Wagner? He didn't look as if he knew. Ask him how's Eleanor? Maybe no.

"Are you going to win the '44 election, Mr. Roosevelt?" Klaf inquired. Hell, it was the only question he could think of.

He didn't expect Roosevelt to rap back at him, "Listen, my friend, if you imagine this Casablanca trip is some kind of an electioneering stunt, you've got the wrong idea of my mission."

"Ask the President how he's feeling," Harry Hopkins hissed. "Do you realize he's flown over four thousand miles, via the Dakar route, to get here?"

"How are you feeling, Mr. President?" Nad Klaf said.

"I'm feeling just fine," Roosevelt humphed.

"Ask him what he's been discussing with Mr. Churchill—off the record," Hopkins prompted.

"The future of the free world," the President revealed.

"Ask him what the new surrender policy for Germany and Japan is going to be."

"Unconditional," the President announced. "Our policy is Unconditional Surrender. We can have no truck with Tyranny!"

Don't go away, kid, Nad's mind murmured as his pencil dutifully zigzagged across the notebook page. Stay right where you are, down there in your old haunts in Casablanca. I'll be with you shortly, Steve Wagner!

No, this wasn't Ritzi's place by any chalk, long or short. It was pulsating in the foggy January back at him with alien confusing lights. There were great flashes of neon all over its outside. Things which shrieked, "Radio Casablanca," at you and, "Chez Rick avec Bobbi." And "Etonnant, la Musique de Notre Temps," and "Exclusive Casablanca Venue." And overpowering all else a gigantic pulsating RICK'S CAFE AMERICAIN.

But you couldn't stop to blink at all this glaring communication because there was another thing about the club. It was a fortress.

It was crawling with *flics*. Black shrouded figures on motorbikes, others leaning against the wall; one peeing. A police car parked bang next to the doorway, a police bus dozing empty at the end of that film-set little avenue of sin.

You put your head down, you pulled your hat down over one side of your head, like you'd seen it done on the movies. You somehow pushed your quivering, sick shoulders into a nonchalant stroll.

You cruised past the bastards because, what the heck, they didn't even know you. Monsieur Steve Wagner was no longer a recognized part of Ritzi's new floor show.

So you sauntered in like the Golliwog's Cake Walk.

Poor jerk.

"Hi there, we've been searching all over for you, you big beautiful lousy bum. We've combed the sewers of Casablanca. Visited every brothel in town, asked of every piece of Moroccan pox, 'Tell me, do, where is my boy in blue?' Combed the downtown bars. Given a quick jerk of the arm to just about every drunk sprawling in sawdust, just in case . . . We've put ads in the local rag sheets. Asked the whole goddamn world, 'You haven't by chance seen a Living Legend passing your way . . . ?' "

"Get lost!"

"Say, that ain't friendly," insisted Nad Klaf. "Take a drink; no, take a bottle. For old times' sake, coupled with the name of Nad Klaf, whoremaster extraordinary to the Court of King Tarbrush."

The face turned up to meet him with its ridiculously tilted hat. The face was still the cliché John Garfield symbol of defeat. The eyes still blinked, like they didn't quite get the drift of your spiel line.

"Know something, Steve?" insisted the soft fast patter of a voice. "In twelve small months you've grown authentic. You've put on one whole hell of verisimilitude. Right now you're craggier than Bogart, and a whole load sexier. Promise me one thing, don't change a single wrinkle on that careworn brow. You're bound for stardom, *mon brave*. You're gonna carve out one small slice of the great American history all on your little ownsome. *Capisco?*"

The eyes still blinked dead. But the mouth was opening, to reveal not one but three large gaps in front. The face was shabby and gray. Red lines zigzagged across the eyeballs.

"And if you're looking for any extra teeth perchance," crooned Nad Klaf, "they're yours, buddy, without backsheesh, gratis on demand account of Sodersheim Syndicate, who, as it happened, fixed up this Moroccan junket just so we could get together once more and do ourselves a power . . ."

And then he wasn't any longer looking into the dead eyeballs of the slowest-witted, most bathotic crumb on earth. He was looking into black. And over towards the center of the room they were swiveling searchlights as if somebody was about to do the marshaling yards at Ham for the hundred and eighty-fifth time. Or maybe it was just Twentieth Century-Fox putting in a counterbid against Warner Bros. for the whole lousy scenario.

It all happened overcranked, or as if some ace cameraman had turned on a pyrotechnic display of whip pans, frame-cutting, and crazy hand-held camera stuff.

Or at least that's how it seemed to PFC Lou Alverson as he sat with a nice piece of army nurse ass from Oklahoma and pondered how he could get inside her starchy undergarments.

The lights were glaring, and then the hideous crumb who ran the whole shooting match got up and somehow they were all applauding, and his wizened little eyes were racing up and the strands of his greased-down hair were quivering in the draught. And then he was cradling the mike, whilst upstage some radio guys made signals and somebody hoisted another mike on a great long ram of a pole that had to be all of ten feet long. And he was suggesting somebody ask the pianist to play something, and PFC Alverson knew just what he wanted, it was "Stars Shone on Alabama," like they might do for him tonight. But the lights were swiveling around and he just didn't seem to be able to catch up with them.

And then somebody had said something in French and the fat little owner was announcing it.

"And now in response to almost universal demand," Ritzi was

saying, "Bobbi will play his own inimitable version of that great Jean Sablon classic, "Je Tire Ma Révérence." And then the search-lights dimmed and turned on Bobbi, and a few notes came tumbling out and Alverson was finding the ear of the nurse from Oklahoma and breathing, "Who the heck is Jean Sablon, anyway?" But he didn't finish because there was a stir, over on the far side, like some drunk was shipping up a scene. And he was shouting out something about "Why not the 'Chattanooga Choo-choo'?" and Alverson was thinking, OK he's drunk, but she's gonna prefer Glenn Miller.

And then the figure was up on the stage shouting something like, "Stop playing, Bobbi. Do you hear me in Tunisia? Your plot's blown, you lousy kraut bums."

Except he was tripping up over himself and clamping down his hat on the side of his head and trying to seize the mike, bellowing something about the krauts and Vichy and how it wasn't his tune. What happened next clean took PFC Alverson's thoughts yards away from the nurse from Oklahoma's starchy knickers.

Either Chief Inspector Lucien Roth was acting on a hunch or he had had a tip-off. Chief Inspector Lucien Roth was not an overinstinctive man; he didn't have many hunches. On the other hand, he had established a good working relationship with Jerry Daniels, and it was a fact Jerry Daniels was keeping Laura Caulfield's villa under surveillance.

In any case Roth had flooded the place with *flics;* he had emptied the road outside. He was there himself to make sure that all hitches were eliminated.

And he was used to drunks. They'd been dragged off by his men, given a good going-over down at the *gendarmerie,* then he'd phone Major Douglas of the American Military Police, and together, over a glass of cognac, they'd sort the delinquent out. So when the stooping silhouette cut across the dipped searchlights and started towards the stage, he had made a sign to two right-hand men to move in and take him. And then something else had alerted him. Something about the luminously pale face of the man in the limelight. He had seen him before, he knew him from distant memory. From Paris, in peacetime, from the theater of around '38. Ah yes, he was Petrouchka, the stumbling clown with limbs of matchsticks. Petrouchka, with the white face and doom-ridden lurch. And then something else sent him leaping up from his ringside table up onto the platform to stop the man before he reached the microphone and Bobbi.

The words "kraut" and "Tunisia" had erupted on Roth's most exposed nerves.

And beside the man was a fake Petrouchka because the hat had slipped a little and Lucien Roth never forgot a face.

His Mauser was almost out of his pocket when it caught him. He went down on the stage with three bullets nosing around in his chest. That had been the one mistake of his life; he'd never rated Petrouchka as a marksman.

Nad Klaf was the fastest-moving current reporter on the payroll of the Sodersheim Syndicate. He also knew a good story, and his reactions were faster than those of the rapidly expiring Inspector of Police. Whilst Roth's blood pumped straight from his heart onto the legs of Bobbi's piano stool, Klaf had already guessed what would happen next.

There was only one exit, and there was no light. As Steve emerged through the vestibule, firing as he went with a ladylike little Beretta he had borrowed from Laura Caulfield, it must be recorded that Nad Klaf was close behind him. True, he was too late for a 1942 meritorious bonus from his grateful employers, but the sleuthhound was riding high for one in '43. If he survived the next few minutes, that is. As the car roared into life and shot off down the street, Klaf was somehow hanging onto the open door like a bit of farce from Abbott and Costello. For a second it looked as if he'd be thrown against a *pissoir* as the door swung crazily on its hinges and Klaf's fingers clamped tight upon it. Then they were in the straight and he'd climbed in beside the driver.

"Wowee," he breathed hoarsely, "you've proved it. You *are* Humphrey Bogart."

She sat tight on the sofa in her quiet little villa and turned the radio off and just let the sound of waves come at her through the opened windows.

She thought, He can come home as late as can be, home without him isn't anyplace to be. Then she got up, coolly put on some makeup, and grabbed a taxi outside.

She stopped just outside a club they called Rick's Café Américain and wandered through into the main bar. She was aware of a hell of a lot of flurry, but that figured. And the moaning of U S Army personnel figured too. Those colonels with bulging eyes, those ashen-faced air force majors. Poor crumbs, they wore uniforms but they couldn't ring the neck of a Thanksgiving Day bird.

And the mess on the platform figured too.

The body, even now being shuffled offstage on a stretcher, the blood everywhere, and Bobbi sobbing beside his piano.

Poor bastard, she thought as she wandered away. Poor crazy bastard, farewell.

Her favorite kind of guy had just become the hunted animal of Casablanca.

He was concentrating hard on it. Single aim: to lose this Hollywood rodent somewhere in the open sewage plant of Casablanca. Problem: the bum kept on clinging to the front door. He might swing far out on the turn but somehow he was still there to bounce back on the door hinge to deliver some new smart-ass punch line.

There were also minor complications around, like a couple of *flics* on motorbikes bringing up his rear, revving their engines as hard as he punched Laura's Oldsmobile; glint of black shiny helmets in his windshield and the scream of their sirens, messing up the reception of his passenger's, Mr. Hollywood's, best gags.

"Christ," he was screaming, "it's God's own scenario. It has a sweet inevitability, you crazy fool. Where are you going? Come on, come on, come on, where are you going?" ricocheted his voice as a juddery piece of cornering took him on a sweep of ninety degrees way out over the pavement, only to swing him heavily back against the car as Steve did a quick right-hander.

"Crazy fool," shrilled the man from the Sodersheim Syndicate, "you don't know where you're going, but I do. You're fulfilling destiny, you're edging towards Pulitzer status. You're sliding freely on grooves of solid gold. You've plugged the ugly, now you're gonna lay the chick. Did I say *lay* her? No, diddle her—sorry, Hayes Office! Romeo meets Juliette—it's a dead end. It's a cinch! Rick speeds home to Ilsa. If he can lose those frisky cops, that is. The wartime romance of '43."

"Get lost, you runt," screamed Steve as he took the Oldsmobile shuddering through the Medina.

"You can't forget me that easily," shrieked Nad, his face contorted with fear. "I'm not just the jerk you drank with. I'm fate, I'm golden opportunity. I'm Destiny with a capital *D*. And I can tell you where you're going."

"Going where?" Steve barked.

"To Helda, you prize mutt. To Ilsa the Ice Goddess. And your old pal the continuity man knows where. It's all scripted. Seventeen rue Sévérin, third floor. And the bed's a real rockaby baby."

"So that's where!" exploded Steve as he crunched his foot hard down on the gas.

"Yes, rue Sévérin," echoed something that turned into a yelp of pain. A simmering load he'd just managed to lose on the road. Bye-bye, Blackbird, thought Steve as he slammed the door shut. But not us, groaned the police sirens as they crashed into the scene again, bang on his tail.

Steve Wagner had a record of fast driving round the tight little *rues* of Casablanca that a dirt-track speedster might envy. That was why he stood a small chance of losing his faithful police escort some way before he sidled gently into rue Sévérin and paid an old flame a visit.

You know the area, it's the swanky side of downtown Casablanca, a street of old silversmiths and fancy little *bijouteries* and an old bookshop that specialized in rare copies of the Koran and upstairs little apartments, frequented by little broads with little kinks in their moral equipment, who in those funny old days of just a year or so back were draining financiers dry of their money and their semen.

It was vamps' corner with a touch of class, where the whores had hearts of marble and the sheets were always icily white. The whole thing just a muezzin's call from the Medina. So it was an OK abode for *soi-disant* Helda Svenson, *soi-disant* Countess de Billancourt to open those long slim legs and receive in her soft blonde pussy the organ of some top warrior in chief of the Republic in Arms.

He knew the layout. He twigged the venue. That classy little elevator with the mirrors and the inlaid panels of veneer that creeked you up to the Quatrième Étage, where your roving eye had ascertained the lady in question had established her abode and was eagerly awaiting the Tramp.

You push the bell, and it tinkles with a nice kind of genteel tact, and a little maid with a dark moorish face and a shining white frilly apron pulls open the door, and you murmur something about "the Comtesse expecting me . . ." as you push her aside and make down the passageway, noting the telltale U S Air Force braided cap, and the stiff service raincoat flung out over the ornamental fake antique *bergère* in the fake nineteenth-century little vestibule, announcing to Philo Vance, and all like-minded sleuths on the make, that gentlemen callers were abroad.

Put a nose in one room, a museum visualization of the old-world colon drawing room of the nicer nineties. A peep next door (it's your *bijou* kitchen). Then bullock your way into door number three, which by logical deduction just has got to be the High Temple of the Quick Fuck.

You stop at the door, you record sensations, like the night breeze flapping gently through the lace curtains and the big wooden headboard that framed the top half of her body. And though the sly side of you registers somehow that something's humming in the hall, like the lady's maid could just be phoning the cops, you've only got eyes for two fantastic tits that seem like half the Sahara desert and half a world war away from you. They urge you to go forward and bury your face in them, and above, the eyes firm and watchful and serious, as if we weren't acting out the crude farce of some bed-room comedy.

And you say, "Helda," and she says, "Stevie. Stevie," and then you're on the bed and you are burying your face in those breasts and she is leaning down and kissing your head, and something called tears seems to be flowing over those incredible nipples and you realize the wet must be coming from your eyes, and she's just stroking your head and somehow cradling you.

And then you look up and say something about her being a cheap whore. And was she going to deny she had even slept with Wehrmacht General Joachim Kellerman? And she says, "Lay me; go on, lay me. For you, Stevie, it's free."

You had pulled the sheet right back, you had given one long withering, lustful, bitter, desperate glance at that long body ar-ranged on the sheet, and you were also at the same time pulling off your pants like you wanted to take a slash. It must have been then that the little white door, which had been painted as part of the boudoir wall, opened and he came out swinging a towel under his arm.

He was King Kong. A whole fleece of coarse hair covered his chest and his arms and his legs, and the only other things that caught the eyes were a pair of piggy little red eyes glinting from beneath a heavy bald dome, and a tiny little pink uncircumcised cock that dangled somewhere into his Amazonian forest, a prick so minute it might have belonged to a kid of twelve, not a King Kong of forty-five.

But the farce won't stop; it's that guy Feydeau again, he of the itchy writer's finger. Basically two things are happening at once and both of them are broadly, even exclusively, physical.

The General of the USAAF is going through something that re-sembles the early convulsions of a stroke. That is, his brow is dark-ening, his body is trembling, and you've taken your eyes off his Pinocchio prick because you see a great heaving of forest hair in the general direction of his heart. But that's only half of the story. Because you're in, boy, you're right there in full possession of the lady, and somehow she's moist already and is receiving you loud and clear; in fact you're heading for Elysium in broad strokes to-gether, just as if the party was private. But the General's already in command again. He's smashed his great bulbous head out through

254

the window and is screaming blue murder, and the lady under you is shouting at him and calling him Sam and telling him to be quiet and to quit the place anyway because he was a lousy punk, or softer, subtler words to that effect. And just at that moment as it happens you get there and the whole thing explodes in your head and heart like the 16-inch guns of the USS *Augusta*.

And then you're running and doing up your fly and saying something to Helda about being back for more and ramming a forest of hair in its solar plexus as you make your exit.

Down the stairs at three a go and slap into another US general on the ground floor who's pressing the button for the escalator, only this one's army, and not air force; but like his comrade upstairs, he's got a real mean look in the eyes and a lot of spare beef around his body, and then you're out into a silent street.

It's three in the morning and you've nowhere to go, and your ears are just picking up the snarl of police klaxons like they're playing in another movie house down the road, or the sound's busted out and you're low on volume.

And you're moving on air, you've shanghaied a cranky old Renault, and it's got no answer to the rue Séverin's cobbled surface, but you're in an air balloon. You feel gloriously smooth and released. And you're smiling to yourself, and singing a happy tune. Something like Bobbi's "You Can't Write a New Song," but set to faster tempo, Fred Astaire-style. A kind of dream-sequence swirling waltz by courtesy of RKO.

And you thought how Bobbi would hate them for twisting his sad song and making it a riotous Broadway hit. And you were still thinking of Bobbi when the light caught you, and somebody tuned up the noise box and you heard those police klaxons now loud and clear. And then your rear window exploded as some marksmen hit it splat, and you were back in the game of cops and robbers.

"Bobbi, you old son of a gun," he panted, "so I finally got to find out where you lived. Nice place you got here, though I guess some of the neighbors aren't too friendly. Still, you've always been able to make yourself at home. I guess even in the middle of Shanghai you'd find yourself a serviceable apartment. Hell, will you let me in, Bobbi? The whole of Casablanca's on my back!"

Bobbi looked thin enough in a dinner jacket, but in his vest he looked as thin as an insect, a white, emaciated insect.

"You can't come in," he whispered. His face was as white as his spindly limbs. "It isn't safe."

"Where's safe in this town? Come on, Bobbi. I never asked you too many favors before, did I? I'm not asking for a bed. Under one will do. Just for the night."

"Who have you killed now, Steve?" There was a look of genuine resentment in the usually bland face which Steve didn't seem to notice.

"You saw it all, didn't you, Bobbi? You saw that French bastard pull a Mauser on me. You know what it was all about too. Those crappy tunes they had you play. They were strictly for German consumption."

"So who are you going to kill next?" Bobbi demanded with a waspishness that was altogether more stinging than his usual gay bitchery. "What about Ritzi? He chose those songs. Perhaps they were a code. Perhaps he just had a rather bad ear for music. But why not kill him just to be on the safe side? And while you're about it, Steve sweetie, why not put a bullet through me, too? After all, I played all that junk, didn't I, and even if I don't happen to be a spy, I haven't got a job any longer, so you could be doing me a favor by murdering me."

"Hey, hold on, we're pals, aren't we?"

"The trouble with you, Steve, is you don't know who or what you want to kill. You've been trying to find out ever since you got back to Casablanca—you and your itchy trigger finger. You've pumped a lot of lead into a lot of harmless people. But you still don't know what you want to kill, you poor bugger. Has it ever occurred to you it could be yourself?"

"Has it ever occurred to you I'm fighting a war," Steve snarled, "even if nobody else is?"

"Who against, honey?" Bobbi shrilled. "France, Germany, the United States? Or is it the whole stinking world? Well, for Christ's sake, if you must fight a war—go to fucking Tunisia. There's no war in Casablanca, haven't you noticed? It's about the only thing to recommend the sleazy old junk heap. That and the fact it's possible to scrape a living here. Or rather it was until you showed up again!"

A police siren howled in a nearby dockside street. Steve shoved

Bobbi back into the narrow hallway and closed the door. The place smelled of scent and sweat and yesterday's Gauloises. To his amazement, Steve saw that Bobbi was still trying to block his way.

"All right, you've got a sailor in the bedroom, or some prizefighter from Senegal. Don't worry. I'm broad-minded."

"Listen, do you act dumb, or are you really dumb?" the pianist hissed. "I told you it isn't safe."

"I understand, Bobbi. You've had an upsetting evening. You're worried about your future. But be a pal, I'm scared for my life."

"Do I hear a familiar voice?" someone asked from the bedroom.

"OK, beautiful, if you insist," Bobbi sighed.

He was sitting on the edge of Bobbi's bed, perhaps so as not to make creases in his new suit, looking at a photo montage on Bobbi's wall which had Josephine Baker, Sydney Bechet, Cole Porter, and Noël Coward in an international amalgam of grinning faces.

"Auguste! Jesus! Hell! How come you aren't dead?"

"Steve! My dear friend." Auguste Berthier rose from the dead (or was it just the bed?) as if he were going to embrace him. Instead he hugged the air, perhaps because he didn't want to make creases in his new blue suit.

"Auguste, you're looking great. Specially for a man who was supposed to be taken out and shot by Sergeant Goupu. Don't tell me he missed."

"Sergeant Goupu never missed," Auguste smiled. "He was of course a fanatic. Fortunately he also had a girl at Port Lyautey, at least a woman brave enough to submit to his amoral passions. Although I couldn't bribe him with money I was able to interest him in a small diamond one of the inmates had . . . er, mislaid. The *conchon* was a romantic at heart. It's important to carry trinkets when you're among savages. It got me a ride back to Ksar-es-Souk. From there the rest was comparatively easy."

"Auguste, it's great you didn't die. I mean that."

"I hope you're not being too sincere," Berthier said, lighting a cigarette.

"For a guy who's supposed to be dead, you're looking awfully well."

"You always say that, Steve, and it makes me feel guilty because I never seem to be able to say the same for you."

Steve searched his pocket for a Chesterfield and found he was right out. Auguste obliged with one of his Gauloises.

"There's been a spot of trouble," Steve said, sucking the smoke in hungrily. "Maybe Bobbi here's told you about it."

"Yes"—Auguste nodded, settling back carefully on the edge of Bobbi's bed—"and of course I'm sorry. We've obviously learned different lessons from our education at Foreign Labor Camp No. 12. I wonder if you remember a conversation we had back at that charming old desert academy. I think I said that two unscrupulous people like you and me really ought to have done better out of the war. And of course when you considered the cuisine, the company, and the little luxuries available at No. 12 that was understating it. I've taken the lesson to heart, Steve. I have decided that for the remainder of this global conflict Auguste Berthier is not going to be among the casualties." He turned to his old friend with a faraway smile. "You, I think, are determined not to use your natural talents for survival. I can't understand why."

Steve's eyes switched to Bobbi, who was pretending to be looking at old records by his 1935 one-speed phonograph. "He's saying the same thing you were saying; right, Bobbi?"

"I love you, Steve," the pianist confessed, "but I wish for Christ sake you'd get out of here."

"You want to know what makes me mad about wars?" Steve said. "It's all the crappy, lousy, stinking freeloading pimps, bums, and punks wars let out of the sewers. Wars themselves are clean, honest things; but not the people who crawl all over them. You don't have to go over to Tunisia to learn that lesson, Bobbi. The big, fat horseflies of war are swarming all over Casablanca. You're crazy, Auguste, to say I've got to be one of them."

"Yes," Auguste Berthier murmured, "I suppose our paths are diverging. But believe me, Steve, I will always look on you as a friend. Well who else would have done me the favor of eliminating that precocious young bore, Lucien Roth?" He saw the gleam of fellow feeling in Steve's eyes, noted the hand about to be stretched out in comradeship. He said, "I'm sorry, Steve, I'm talking from the career point of view. I should have told you, shouldn't I? I have been reappointed to the Casablanca police force. They have overlooked our past disagreements. There was a feeling that it was time to reintroduce a more liberal element, experienced officers who would be discreet enough not to shout 'Heil Hitler!' in the face of every visiting American Congressman. For that reason Lucien's regime was probably doomed in any case; but you certainly speeded up the process, and providing I can arrest his assassin, I am destined to replace him. You've helped me there too, haven't you, Steve?"

"Don't shoot any more people, Steve," Bobbi screamed. He needn't have bothered. Auguste Berthier had already pulled out a Lebel revolver from under the jacket of his new suit, so that the only thing Steve Wagner could do with his hands was to raise them.

"What do you do now, blow a whistle?" Steve asked.

Auguste squinted at the muzzle of his Lebel. "To be honest, I don't know what I do. I hadn't expected you to drop in like this, Steve. I was merely going my rounds, making routine inquiries among your friends."

"You mean you're alone?"

"I am sure if I asked him Bobbi would go and telephone for a squad car."

"No more blood," Bobbi screamed. "Not tonight, not here!"

Steve Wagner thought, My God, he believes Auguste is going to kill me. He's a sensitive character: he could know. He said, trying to make a joke of it, but in truth scared out of his mind, "Come on, Bobbi, Auguste isn't going to do a thing like that, not to an old friend, not on your carpet."

"It's important for me that you don't escape," Berthier said, looking over the mechanism of his Lebel. "I mean, for my career."

"Bang! Bang!" Bobbi shouted hysterically, picking up a mop and swiveling it round the room. "Let's all do it—it's the new rage. Look, I've got a bead on you, mister!"

Auguste looked just long enough to enable Steve to whip out his Beretta and suggest to Berthier that he put his Lebel on the floor and kick it over to him. The Lebel had wandered from the direction of Steve's chest. Auguste had to do as he was told.

"Don't touch it!" Bobbi yelled, swinging the mop handle round on his old *patron*. "Leave it right where it is, bud, or you're a goner!"

"Listen, Bobbi. This punk was going to kill me. You saw it in his face," Steve said, pocketing the Lebel all the same, but keeping the Beretta straight as a dye on Berthier's face.

"So it's tit for tat, RAT TAT TAT! You've got to kill him back. Why, you low-down, stinking coyote—walk straight out of that door and keep walking, brother, or this here shootin' iron's gonna blast you to hades!"

"Keep your hair on, Bobbi," Steve added for Auguste's benefit. "I'm talking to him, not you."

"I'm the one who's calling the tune. I'm the guy who's dealing the cards, cause I got this fucking big phallic symbol here called a Smith and Wesson repeating rifle."

Bobbi had turned his mop play into a series of obscene gestures. "I'm talking to you *mon brave, mein Herr*," he shouted, poking with the mop handle at Steve's face. "I've tumbled your little game, you *Schweinhund*, you rotter, you scheming oriental shit, and I'm telling you to scram, bug off, less you want a load of buckshot up your backside. Get out of here, for the love of God, you beautiful moron."

"OK, Bobbi, you win," Steve sighed. He looked across at Auguste with a sort of wistfulness, such as a man might turn on another man's wife, or a killer might direct at another killer's allotted victim. He said, "Be a pal and keep him covered, will you, till I get clear of here." Then he walked out into the night, where everyone wanted to find him.

It was a tribute to the memory of Lucien Roth, ex-Chief Inspector of Police in Casablanca, and his still living colleague-in-arms, Jerry Daniels of the OSS. It went like a bomb, just as Lucien and Jerry had hoped it might. It was the biggest manhunt in the town's history and it was laid on by a subtle interlocking of the US and French forces. There were moments that night when Jerry, sitting at police headquarters, felt himself so close to enmeshing the new Public Enemy No. 1, he could almost smell the sour odor of panic oozing out of Wagner's pores.

Secure behind Roth's desk with a street map of Casablanca in front of him and the phone bringing up-to-the-minute reports of the pursuit, Jerry Daniels had no fear that he would fail to catch his man.

He had been over at the Conference complex when the call came through that Roth had been assassinated by a hit-and-run Yankee gunman, with known Gaullist sympathies. Daniels had arrived at the prefecture in an opulent Cadillac limousine, loaned from the Conference. A quick look at the marble features of his old friend and associate, Lucien Roth, showed that he had been struck down by a viciousness worthy of an Al Capone. Not wasting too many thoughts on the dead man who had been laid out on an interrogation table, his arms folded across his chest, Jerry Daniels had proceeded to draw and then tighten his net. Wagner had been chased by motorcycle *flics* in the general direction of the Medina, who had then lost contact. Then a phone call from a lady's maid in the rue Séverin area about a man answering to Wagner's description pushed them right back there. This evidence was later substantiated by Generals Oakland and Susskind, who had been paying calls on the Comtesse de Billancourt at the time.

"Do they have an electric chair around here?" muttered General Sam Susskind menacingly. "Just slap him into a uniform and send him out on patrol," was General Oakland's solution to the Steve Wagner problem. "That way at least he'll die for his country."

Then came more news that had Jerry Daniels dashing over to Roth's old street map, moving drawing pins and strips of pink ribbon.

"Don't worry, gentlemen, we're gonna trap our rat. See what he's doing? Slinking off towards the port. There we can cut him off. Pin him down and then smoke him out. Right now he must be about the loneliest guy in Africa."

But this hope proved premature. Wagner, it seemed, had again shaken off the *flics*.

"Where's he bumming off to?" Daniels kept on asking himself. "He must have some funk hole."

There was another worry. Pinning the maniac down in the port area was all very well. But there was still a bolt-hole open, one that would lead him straight down the main arterial road to the coast and Anfa, and a little converted pleasure dome where two gentlemen called Admiral Q and Air Commodore F were looking down like gods on the sordid and pitiful affairs of ordinary men. And now the heavy arc lights in the Prefecture were picking out the sweat on Daniels's boyish features, with his weary deep-sunken green eyes surmounted by a carrot-colored crew cut.

If the punk drifted in the general direction of Anfa it wouldn't look good. Because on present form he might just be mad enough . . .

It was four-thirty in the morning, and Jerry Daniels declined to go much further down this avenue of thought. Punks like Steve Wagner didn't alter the course of history. They just tumbled into a gin trap.

It was officially the morning, but it might just as well still be night as far as PFC Joe Offenbach was concerned. The war for him was just about to flare into life again, but PFC Offenbach could look back with satisfaction on the successful outcome of one minor campaign in a theater of war into which future military historians were unlikely to probe too hard. After an arduous, ass-breaking ten-day siege, at the last moment when less obstinate campaigners might have thrown in the towel, Joe Offenbach had managed to get inside the salmon-pink camiknickers of Nurse Anderson from Idaho. And once there he had saluted her with three triumphal bursts that would have done credit to a 37-mm M3. He had finally come out of combat with his member dripping of blood and the shrieks of the ravished and hitherto virgin young nurse (whether of agony or ecstasy Offenbach couldn't quite figure).

But now, just forty-five minutes after he'd beaten a hasty retreat from Nurse Anderson's hospital annex, he was blowing his fingers in a jeep in the rue Gambetta, trying to decide whether it was etiquette to give an army captain a honk on the horn. Then the door opened and Captain Maxwell emerged, his eyes drooping with sleep.

"Step on the gas, Offenbach," he instructed tersely. "If we miss that troop train we might just miss the war."

"Casablanca was that bad," the doughboy grunted as he slid the jeep merrily round the corner, "a guy could bum around there and not do himself an injury."

"We've got something to finish, Joe," Captain Maxwell told him. "Up to now we've fought a load of *cagoulards* and Vichyites. This time we're gonna crunch up against the hardest soldiers in the world. Krauts, Offenbach. With all the experience, the equipment and the discipline to blow the entire Second Corps to kingdom come. Now you've got something real to compare bicep measurements against! We've got an appointment with a guy called Adolf Hitler and I'd hate to be late."

There was a hot, hard center of rising impatience beginning to come out in Maxwell's flat-ass pancake delivery. The reason was clear. The jeep had come to a halt. Offenbach slouched out of the jeep and strolled over to where a group of French police had barricaded the road.

"What the hell's happening?" Maxwell's voice bawled at him.

Finally Offenbach climbed back into the jeep.

"Looks like we'll have to do a detour, sir," he grunted. "Seems like some jerk's busted out. Killed the French police chief in Rick's Place, and now they've got him cornered in the dock area. They've got searchlights and a posse of *gendarmes* on every road leading through."

"OK, Offenbach," shouted the Captain. "Well, you'll just have to get us out of this crap hole and show us a piece of initiative. Somebody was saying you're a wise guy? Prove it!"

Throwing aside delightful visions of his member gleaming with Nurse Anderson's virginal blood, Offenbach got down to the serious business of driving. They said Captain Maxwell could be a hard man. Or a soft lay, if he happened to like you.

As he hurled the jeep round fog-ridden corners a little tune kept on encroaching into PFC Offenbach's mind.

Not Miller, not Crosby, not even the young phenomenon they called Sinatra. It was a frog *chanson* with a bumpety line that went, "Oop-la, oop-la, oop-la . . ."

So it seemed you went to Helda for only one thing these days. Your good, old-fashioned quick screw—the best admittedly this, or any side, of the Atlantic. You didn't go for consolation, or even sanctuary. Not with King Kong generals with peanut-sized phalluses hollering blue murder into the rue Sévérin. Helda was no longer any kind of haven, and her place was certainly no place to hide. The same went for Laura's place out at Anfa. They would have every window under observation, and this was a pity, because Laura was maybe the haven he should have been looking for all his life.

Come to think of it, there weren't many places left to go, or many people who would look pleased to see him. Hold on, there could be just one person.

He had seen him only on election posters; heard his voice only over the radio back home. "My friends—and I know you are my friends . . ." It could even be true. He had swept away Prohibition and enabled a lot of guys sitting on street corners to work up an honest thirst again. He was a cripple in a wheelchair, but he had given a lot of people hope, even the songwriters: "Yessiree, yessiree, he's Franklin D. Roosevelt Jones." And he was here at Anfa meeting with Winston Churchill to figure out what the heck to do with the world.

Yes, it was breaking rank, about as far as anyone could break rank, considering Steve was simply a man wanted by the police and he was President of the United States. But there was just a chance he would understand, maybe even say, "Well done," at least do something. After all, this wasn't any ordinary President, this was President Franklin Delano Roosevelt.

"Well, how about it?" Steve said to himself with chattering teeth in a sunrise that had once again been delayed by the Atlas Mountains. "How about it, Mr. President? How about a new deal for Stephen Wagner?"

He did the simplest thing a man could do who was wanted by everyone in authority. He got onto the Anfa bus and wedged himself into a window seat beside a fat Arab woman with a puke-stained veil and a baby tugging at her breast, opposite a fisherman and his wife with a crate of crayfish on their knees. It wasn't a comfortable ride, especially since police motorcyclists kept going past the window, but they were always traveling faster than the bus, which was one of the slowest, as well as one of the foulest-smelling, he had ever taken.

After about an hour of stopping and starting, the bus finally lumbered into the suburb of Anfa, only to be stopped by a US military policeman. It seemed the whole area around the Hotel d'Afrique had been cordoned off on account of this big military secret, which in fact everyone with a couple of good ears and eyes knew was the Big Two in Conference. This was where Steve Wagner got off.

He walked straight up to the barbed wire fortress which was the Casablanca Conference.

The sergeant on the gate was talking to a young British officer on Churchill's staff, a fact which was going to save Steve Wagner's life, perhaps for the last time.

"I must compliment you on your security arrangements, Sergeant," this British Lieutenant was saying, drumming his swagger stick on his ass. "At Chequers we have only a couple of policemen and some rather moth-eaten dogs."

The US sergeant, of course, didn't have any moth-eaten dogs. He was backed by three ferocious-looking MPs with MI submachine guns. Over to his left was a sand-bagged emplacement where two white-helmeted GIs were poking around with a Browning machine gun. Farther back behind this lot a squad of military policemen were familiarizing themselves with the mechanism of the new bazooka. The only civilians he could see were G-men with bulges in double-breasted jackets. The dogs came out at night, and they were definitely not moth-eaten.

"I want to see the President of the United States," Steve said.

"You what, buddy?"

"I want to see the President of the United States. It's important."

The sergeant looked at Steve's unshaven face, the collar that had got parted from its tie, and the suit that looked as if he had slept in it, which of course he had. He said with a sense of irony, which was as heavy as a Stuart tank, "And who shall I say is calling?"

"Tell him it's a guy who voted Democrat in 1932, name of Steve Wagner, who wants to see him make a fourth term. You could also tell him it's a matter of life and death for our guys in Tunisia."

"You have an appointment?" The sergeant grimaced as the British officer chortled merrily.

"He's the Commander in Chief, isn't he?" Steve answered. "I'm assuming he's interested in stopping every damn move his army makes from getting reported to the Germans."

"Oh sure, he'd be interested," the sergeant smiled, reaching for his field telephone. "The President of the United States is interested in meeting every bum and down-and-outer who shows up at this checkpoint. Incidentally, who told you he was here?"

"Intuition," Steve said.

"Hey, sir"—the sergeant said down his field telephone—"you'll never believe this, but I've a guy out here says he wants to see the President of the United States. Says he voted for him in 1932. Says his name is Steve Wagner. How do you like that, eh, sir?"

It seemed that "sir" didn't like it at all.

When the sergeant turned back to Steve his eyes were bulging and he had his Colt .45 out. He said, "You didn't tell me that every MP patrol in Casablanca is looking for you."

Steve started to back away. The MP sergeant took aim with his Colt. He shouted, "You stay right where you are, bud."

Steve started to run. What else could he do except, perhaps, ask if Mrs. Eleanor Roosevelt was at home? The sergeant fired, but he missed by a long way. The British officer had brought his swagger stick down on his sleeve. "For heaven's sake, Sergeant," he was shouting, "you can't shoot at an unarmed man!"

The MPs with the MI subs hadn't been educated at Sandhurst. They opened up with everything they'd got, tearing whole chunks off a concrete garden wall which Steve had jumped with a second to spare. Then the Browning machine gun joined in. They started to run towards him. The sergeant was bringing up the rear, dragging the protesting British officer along with him.

Steve let them have two rounds from Berthier's Lebel. He didn't mean to hit one of them on the collarbone, a young MP who started screaming as if he had shot away his face; but at least it had the desired effect. Like all well-trained soldiers coming under fire, they hit the deck and started ferreting around for cover. This gave him time to scram, over the walls, through palm trees, past the swimming pools, and round the cactus plants of this millionaire's paradise. For Steve Wagner, though, the pretty suburb of Anfa was very fast turning into another desert. What about that new deal?

The lights came up in the private cinema they had fixed up in the Hotel d'Atlantique.

"Congratulations, Mr. President," Winston Churchill said. "Once again your magnificent film industry has struck a powerful blow for our cause. Please convey my appreciation to the Brothers Warner and Mr. Humphrey Bogart, and indeed, to Miss Bergman. She is one of the most beautiful assets democracy can boast."

"I don't like that ending, Winston," Roosevelt said. "It's right out of line with the way we're thinking in Washington."

"And what inspired timing!" Churchill rumbled on. "To produce a film called *Casablanca* a matter of days after we launched Operation TORCH—your Warner Brothers must be psychic, as well as extremely talented film makers."

Roosevelt had turned to his indispensable aide, Harry Hopkins. "We shouldn't have let that ending through, Harry. It could create a lot of misunderstandings about US policy towards the French. Why don't you get on to Jack Warner and get them to reshoot it?"

"In all humility, Mr. President"—Churchill beamed ingratiatingly —"I personally liked the ending. I found it very moving. A symbol of America's determination to have done with Hitler and his henchmen."

"The trouble is, Winston, we've got Humph Bogart headed in the wrong direction," the President explained with a diamond-hard grin. "No American in his senses is going to walk off to Lake Chad to team up with that prima donna, de Gaulle. Tell you what I want to see Humph Bogart saying at the end of this movie, I want him and his French *gendarme* friend to make a declaration of one-hundred-percent support for our candidate, General Giraud, and I'd like to see a plug for General Nogues too. You don't get any tantrums from that fine French officer; he's intelligent enough to appreciate that the best friend France has is the United States."

"Mr. President"—Churchill salaamed—"it is now my privilege to show you a humble British offering from our own Pinewood Studios —Mr. Noël Coward's *In Which We Serve*."

"Promise me there's no Gaullist propaganda in it?"

"It's a straightforward sailors' yarn of gallant action on the high seas, Mr. President."

"You mean your studios do what you tell 'em." Roosevelt flashed his infectious crocodile smile. "I'll concede one thing, Winston, at least you never made the mistake of thinking up a lousy idea like the Four Freedoms. I envy you and Joe Stalin. You can shoot a film director any time you feel like it."

"What was that?" barked Winston Churchill.

The sound of automatic weapons being discharged at Steve Wagner had just managed to penetrate the walls of the two leaders' makeshift movie house.

"I can't hear anything," said President Roosevelt as the credits of Britain's costliest war movie came up.

"How the hell did he manage to sneak out there to Anfa?" Jerry Daniels was yelling.

"He has the advantage of being one man, a minuscule speck on the map," Auguste Berthier decided. "If we were looking for a gang, a number of conspirators, our task would be easier."

"You realize he's shot and wounded a US serviceman?"

"We are dealing of course with a madman."

"Hell, but you said you had him cornered down in the docks. How come he slipped through?"

"Alas, it is not always possible to anticipate the movements of a lunatic. Wagner has become a straw in the wind. The head of a Pavlov dog reacting to unpredictable stimuli."

"Maybe, Inspector Berthier, but how do you think it looks for me to have this trigger-happy nut running around free outside the Anfa conference compound? There are a lot of influential people out there who won't be impressed!"

"However, Wagner has returned to us," Berthier said, moving confidently towards the map. "I think we will find it profitable to intensify our efforts in the docks quarter."

"You've got a new lead?"

"We have an abandoned car, a Renault." Berthier elaborated on the principle that when you've only got a little good news it pays to drag it out. "The car was stolen from Anfa at 10:30 AM this morning. It was abandoned here in the rue de Toulon." He indicated a street near the Jetée des Phosphates. "Back in the docks. As you might say, Wagner's happy hunting ground."

"That's got to be him."

Jerry was beginning to warm to this new police officer. He had tact, brains, even a wry little sense of humor. The only question was did he have luck?

There was a telephone by the cash till in a dirty little bar called Le Mat'lot Noir. It wasn't very private, but at least it was safer than getting yourself shot in a kiosk.

Simply what he had to say was this: "Hal, Hal Newport. I guess you're the last person in this town I can talk to. I'm asking you to get me out of this place. No one's going to listen to me till somebody gets me out of this loony town. I want to be put on a Flying Fortress with a guard of US marines who know how to shoot in the right direction. I want to be landed in one piece in Algiers, Gibraltar, Washington, or anyplace where they're still trying to fight this war, where they're still sane enough to listen and do something. You can fix it for me, can't you, Hal? There's another thing I want you to do for me, Hal, and that's just to sit down quietly by yourself and try to figure out why the hell I would want to go and bust up that broadcast from Ritzi's place, assuming I was sane. Then I'd like you to ask yourself what was so important about that broadcast they had to ring the place with Vichy cops, why . . ."

"I'm sorry, sir," a coarse voice was saying, "Mr. and Mrs. Newport are in bed. They can't be disturbed."

The line crackled and went dead. He dialed again. No answer. It was the old phone, the one he'd used in the palmy, plush old days to set up a contact, make a sale. You took a swig at the glass of jungle juice pernod the *patron* cooked up in wood, stuff to send a man out through a little hole in his mind into a quiet country where tiny fishing smacks lolloped mechanically on a glass sea and huge cormorants swooped down and picked off your eyebrows, hair by hair. And someone tied a stone around your neck and your eyeballs popped out and rattled their way down towards the deep and you wondered why you could still see with empty eye sockets. It was a place just off the rue de Toulon, tucked in nicely into the labyrinthine sewage system of the *vieux port*. The *patron* was easy and you'd been here before, when you'd landed a consignment and phoned a contact, and no one asked any questions. There was a cellar where you could dump the stuff. And this was the stool that the old Steve Wagner had leaned on and looked inwards to the dark little bar. And you'd stared into the murk, into the empty eyeballs of the collection of human flotsam you might call the joint's regular clientèle.

And maybe if you closed your eyes you might see a crimson crab skidding by with your eyeball neatly held within his claws. And the blue iris of the eye of the guy they called Steve Wagner winked at you as it went by in the crab's claws.

And you'd said something like, "Look, this stuff is hot. But don't worry. I'll be collecting on Tuesday. And thanks."

But you didn't delude yourself. All right, the place was just another portside dump where they asked no questions and the clientèle slumped off their stools one by one, and there happened to be a good cellar where a consignment of firearms might find a temporary home from home.

But don't play games, you came here to swig back the *patron*'s own very special line of absinthe in the wood. And renew acquaintance with your old buddy Cancer the Crab, gliding past this human rock pool with your winking blue eyeballs in his clutch.

"Steve, I mean it. This time it's no go."

"Heck, Louis. We've been pals in the past. I'm not asking for a thing. Just four or five hours till these bastards climb off my back. Till they discover some new lousy bum to peck at."

Le patron looked at the piece of human wreckage that had floated or stumbled into his bar and tried to work the old shape and form of Steve Wagner around it. He used to wear a blazer and a pair of white yachting trousers. And two-toned shoes. He used to sidle into his bar with the odd friend. Particularly an American who owned a big yacht in the *petit port*.

Steve had a habit of winking at you as he threw back his absinthe in one. The Yankee friend was more evasive. He'd sniffed at his glass as if it contained explosive.

Steve had been a great one for tips. He was popular. He had a habit of slapping his clients across the shoulders as if they were his lifelong mates. He had a debonair look in his eyes. He was a welcome guest.

And this too was Steve Wagner. This human punch bag.

"Look, Louis, just give me a few hours. I'm dog-tired. Just wanna lie low. Just wanna crawl into the dust and settle there for a while. Just wanna sleep."

"Your friend, Steve. Can't he help?" he asked, looking at the phone hanging by its cord and clattering against the wall.

"I will find him, Louis. Don't worry."

In a sweaty bar the sweat of Steve Wagner was something yet again, something the twitching nose of the *patron* could not miss. He knew that smell. He knew, too, it meant bad business.

"You get in bad with the *gendarmes?*" he said. "All these police. You do something wrong, Monsieur Steve? They find you here, they close down the Mat'lot Noir. They slap me in jug."

But the thing that mocked the old image of Steve Wagner wouldn't be put out. He had put both arms round the *patron*'s throat. He was shaking him. He was saying, "You lousy bum, if you double-cross me now I'll write your filthy little bar right off the map, I'll plaster so much shit over you you'll be inside for the next ten years. I'll have your filthy booze poured by the barrel into the gutter."

The face within an inch of his was livid, the blue eyes bloodshot, and there was perhaps two days' stubble on the face. The diminutive *patron* cringed as Steve put his fist right up against his jaw, as if he were determined to propel him into kingdom come. But instead the face suddenly collapsed into what went for a smile and a twinkle wafted across those red-freckled blue eyes and the hands round his neck eased round behind his back and began to pat it. "Alternatively, you might carry on as usual, Louis," he croaked. "A very refuge and haven for mariners in distress. You will grow rich and prosperous and forget that time when the whole town was crying for Steve Wagner's blood and you took him in for old times' sake."

It was about eleven-thirty in the morning and nothing had changed—except for Steve, that is. Like in the old days, he moved inwards towards the bar, collecting another glass of home-brewed pernod en route. Moved inwards with a smile on his face to renew acquaintance with some boozing companions of old. There was a man who spent the day begging outside the Cathedral of the Sacré Coeur and the night sedulously rotting out his brain cells as the booze glowed down. There were a couple of fishermen, known as the Twins, who shared the same girl friend, who happened to be their stunted elder sister. There was a sergeant of the police who had been cashiered way back in the thirties and now had his hands deep in a dozen rackets. There was the *patron*'s younger brother, who had never been known to utter a word. A deaf-mute from birth. All these were faces Steve knew from way back.

But this morning Louis's homemade pernod had taken its toll. There was not a hint of recognition in their faces as Steve staggered back to swap a few yarns with some old drinking buddies.

"So what's new?" asked Jerry Daniels as he hurried into the Prefecture in the late afternoon with a smile that was superficially all bonhomie. Just the same, he was clearly a man in a hurry, a man, moreover, who was dressed to receive good news. Jerry was wearing a natty new white tuxedo in his capacity as organizer of the Casablanca premiere of the new Warner Bros. motion picture. He had a taxi waiting outside in the rue Clavenod to speed him to the Étoile picture house.

"We are intensifying our efforts in the dock area," a shirt-sleeved Auguste Berthier reported. "We have drawn a ring of steel around the district extending from the Grand Jetée to the Parcs de Charbon. There are no loopholes."

"Which means to say you haven't picked him up," Jerry said with a smile which wasn't so genial.

"We are expecting hourly to make an arrest," Berthier confided. "Knowing Wagner, I think he is obviously hiding out in a bar or brothel. We are methodically searching them all. Unfortunately the district proliferates with small bars and brothels. We cannot be everywhere at once."

"OK," Daniels suddenly shrilled, "I'll get you our naval police into the area. But let's get this straight, Berthier. You're gonna pick this guy up in the next sixty minutes or you're going to have to answer to President Roosevelt!"

"Le Mat'lot Noir," Berthier murmured to himself.

"What's that?"

"It can be done," Berthier smiled. "For your President Roosevelt it can be done." He asked himself was it possible he was getting absent-minded in his middle age? How could he have failed to remember that evil drink he had once had with Steve in that little disgusting cesspool called Le Mat'lot Noir?

He woke up. It was a trick. His watch still said a quarter past twelve. The light outside the bar was still semimurky, like dawn hadn't quite broken. Yet his head rocketed with the hammerblows of Louis's homemade pernod. A big session's boozing. What kind of a screwy trick . . . ?

He stirred. He shrugged off a body lying across him, arms round his waist. It was *le patron*'s no-speak brother. They had been cradling each other on the floor. Getting up, Steve kicked him aside and discovered that far from getting lighter, it was getting darker.

It was evening, not morning. Time hadn't maniacally stood still. It had moved on exactly eight hours.

He went past a few faces at the bar. He nodded to the *patron*'s wife, who stared back. He sat on the stool at the end by the phone and dialed a number.

He got the answer he expected.

"Yes, monsieur," said the servant at the Newports' villa. "I am sorry, they have just gone out. Just a few minutes ago."

It was a flick house called the Étoile. It seemed that the whole of Casablanca was hell-bent on cramming itself into its plush red seats. It seemed that the Newports weren't going to be left out. But that was okey-doke by Steve. There were worse places than movies for lying low. People went to movies for all kinds of reasons. You might go there to suck peanuts, doze off, or take a quick screw. You might also just conceivably use the place to talk an old friend and fellow countryman into bestirring himself to save your life.

Steve Wagner stood up from his stool, nodded back at the *patron*'s wife, opened the door, and stepped out into fresh air. There was an idle taxi nosing its way round the dockside roads, prowling for a cargo of tarts or pimps. Steve Wagner gave it a wave and slumped inside.

He asked for the Cinéma Étoile and noticed a billboard as the cab swung out. It announced the premiere of a movie called *Casablanca*.

A film called *Casablanca*—great joke.

Back in Le Mat'lot Noir the customers were at last beginning to show a flicker of animation. The place was methodically being torn apart by around two dozen *gendarmes*, supplemented by two jeeploads of U S Navy police.

There were so many men walking round in white tuxedos with cigarettes hanging from their lips anyone might have thought it was a meeting of the Humphrey Bogart Society. In a way it was. Practically the whole of the American diplomatic colony and their fur-wrapped wives had turned out for the premiere of the new Bogart film—just two months after the US premiere on 27 November 1942.

So many guys in white tuxedos, so many women with beaver stoles, which couple was Hal and Tina Newport? There were a lot of *gendarmes* on the sidewalk too. Fortunately most of them were busy holding back a crowd which had gathered on the incorrect rumor that Bogart, Bergman, and Rita Hayworth would be putting in a personal appearance. But they all had real Lebel revolvers with real 8-mm ammunition. These were genuine lethal Casablanca cops who had nothing to do with the entertainment industry. Hal, you've got to show.

That woman lurching out of that taxi with the big cleavage and the hair perm which was already fraying a little at the edges. Wasn't that Tina Newport? And this new arrival with the tuxedo that fitted him like a glove, who was digging around in his pocket so as to avoid having to tip the driver with a note. Yes, it had to be.

"Hal!"

The diplomat searched the sea of darkened faces that were pressing round the foyer. There was always the chance the greeting came from Bobby O'Brien or George Murphy, or even Harry Hopkins.

Steve stepped up to him before anyone could intervene and slipped his arm into the diplomat's white tuxedo arm just to show he didn't need his papers scrutinized.

He said, "Hal, I've been trying to reach you all day. You're the only guy left I can talk to."

"For Chrissake, Hal," Tina Newport said. "This is one movie I'm not gonna miss!"

". . . I'll answer anybody's questions, Hal. I'll submit to lie detector tests, anything, as long as you fly me out of this crazy town and get me a fair hearing."

"Who you talking to, anyway?" Tina wanted to know.

"You remember me, don't you, Mrs. Newport? Friend of your husband's from way back in Spain! We met in Ritzi's place. Steve Wagner's the name. I'm in a helluva lot of trouble, Mrs. Newport."

It was a hell of a long time ago as Tina Newport's life went, and besides, it was dark and she was drunk. She peered at him through a cloud of pre-premiere manhattans and said, "Remember the name, can't place the face. Hal, we're going to miss this fucking movie."

"I want a Flying Fortress, Hal, a goddamn armor-plated Flying Fortress. I'm a dead man if you can't fix that for me."

"Look," Hal suggested, "why don't we all meet up after the show? Have a drink, talk it out. Tina's never going to forgive me if we don't see this movie through."

He had managed to get his tuxedo sleeve out of Steve's grasp. Diplomat though he was, he couldn't avoid holding it up to the foyer lights to see if it had been soiled.

Steve grabbed it again and pressed it so hard Newport thought his arteries were being crushed. "Hal, I'm not going to be here when you come out. I'm not going to be anywhere when you come out!"

The diplomat struggled as diplomatically as he could, but his old pal wouldn't let go. That was how Steve Wagner got to see the movie *Casablanca*.

And this was also how he came to be spotted by Lieutenant Pajol. The police officer was at the door of the theater, worrying about the infringement of the blackout regulations the brilliantly lit foyer constituted and asking himself whether with so many highly placed American citizens present it would be tactful to press charges. He saw the Newports enter the theater with this shabbily dressed figure. There was no one better qualified to recognize Steve Wagner in a bad patch of blackout.

Up in the manager's office Jerry Daniels was wearing his other hat, that of PRO and general funmaker to the US press in Casablanca. This premiere had been his idea. "Hey," he had exclaimed one bright blue morning, "wouldn't it be kind of cute to premiere this movie *Casablanca* in Casablanca?"

Everyone had agreed it was a helluva cute idea. So here was Jerry Daniels at the center of the operations, resplendent in a tuxedo that was even whiter than Bogart's, although he personally hadn't seen the movie and didn't know how it turned out.

True to his new role as impresario, Jerry was puffing at a fat Havana cigar. He had another essential accessory to show business success. He had a beautiful girl kneeling at his feet. Her name was Laura Caulfield.

She was saying, "OK, Jerry, if you want it as corny as this, you can have it as corny as this. I'm pleading with you to save Steve. And I'm telling you if it's me who's the trouble, for God's sake, take me out and screw me. This time I'm not going to let a little thing like my honor stand in the way of Steve's safety."

"I like the proposition"—Jerry cigar-puffed—"I like the dress too; it doesn't hide much from where I'm sitting, but I'm not sure how sincere you're being."

"I'm being as sincere as all hell."

"Just to get this bum off the hook? No other strings?"

"No other strings. At least"—Laura's eyes smoldered—"I'm assuming I don't have to go to bed with you in order to get you to investigate the murder they're getting away with at Radio Casablanca. I'm assuming that's your plain duty as senior OSS officer over here."

"That crazy tune-code theory? It's a lot of crap, but, sure, I'm investigating it."

"Thoroughly, I hope, Jerry. You see, I'm also assuming you'd regard it as a disgrace to your department if I had to file an independent report. Incidentally, mind if I get off my knees? At least I'd like to try and preserve these stockings."

"You don't like me, do you?" Jerry wheezed. "You never did. I can't figure it out."

"Forget about that. Have we got a deal?"

Jerry Daniels waved his cigar. He had been thinking maybe when this phony war was over he could do worse than talk himself into a production job in Hollywood. He said, "Any time. But listen, honey, you've got to reconcile yourself to the fact that there are an awful lot of people in Casablanca who don't love Steve Wagner. I'm just one of a growing fraternity."

The telephone rang. When he put it down Jerry had a meaner look on his face. He said, "What do you know? The bum is in this theater."

"You're kidding. Well, tell your guys to get him out of here and put him on a plane. In the meantime I'll go home and cook your supper."

"Please, I'd like to see the movie first, honey," Daniels grinned with his hand on the door.

Steve Wagner said, "I don't know what this movie is about, but what I've got to tell you, Hal, is crazier than any movie; there's more action in it too. I don't want to spoil your entertainment, Hal, but it's happening right here in Casablanca—not Hollywood."

Someone behind him told him to quit talking, and a woman gave him a loud "Shhhh." Perhaps she was the same woman who had said "Shhh" when he and Laura had been watching that Vichy newsreel a few months back.

"Can't it wait till afterwards, Steve?" Hal Newport whispered.

So watch the movie. A world spinning round on a cloud of studio cotton wool. Into close-up on a dot on the world. The name "Casablanca" (as if God went around the world painting names on the towns). A long shot of a mosque he had never seen in Casablanca. A mock-up of the Medina. A lot of extras trying like hell to look like Moors. A *gendarme* blowing a whistle. A white-suited suspect asked to show his papers. The guy making a run for it, and getting gunned down under a poster of Marshal Pétain. Don't worry, it's just the movies; it's all acting, and those bullets are blanks. They pick up the body. They don't show what real bullets do to a person. They don't show how they can crack open a skull, disintegrate a nose, gouge out an eye or what have you. It's the movies. But wait a minute. They're opening the dead man's wallet, and they've produced a leaflet that has the Gaullist Cross of Lorraine printed on it. Is this where you came in? Don't worry, it's the movies. All the same a gentle dissolve to Jack Benny, Hope or Crosby, or Andy Hardy would be welcome. You're not in the mood to see a movie about guys getting gunned down on account of the fact they're working for Charles de Gaulle. Least of all do you want to see any more shooting, even though the bullets are blanks and it's just acting. You've lost your nerve about bullets, admit it. You saw what concentrated gunfire could do to walls, palm trees, and cactus plants out at Anfa, and you shuddered to think what it could do to fragile flesh. Admit it, you're still shuddering.

"Give you one thing, Inspector," said Jerry Daniels to Auguste Berthier in the police-crowded foyer, "when you French cops move, you certainly move."

"We aim to be of service to our allies and of course to President Roosevelt," Berthier answered with a bow which was somehow just a shade too cynical for Jerry's taste.

Jerry found himself asking with a savage little grin, "Even if that means pumping an old pal full of lead? I have got the record straight, haven't I? You were once teamed up with Stephen Wagner?"

Berthier's smile momentarily lost its complacency. It was going to be harder than he suspected to keep pace with the vagaries of these Anglo-Saxon *salauds*.

"I've always been anxious to establish the best possible contacts with our American allies. In this respect Monsieur Wagner proved a disappointment," he said.

If there is one thing a natural creep dislikes it's another natural creep. Perhaps this was the reason why Jerry Daniels was suddenly beginning to dislike this new man Berthier. He was cooperative enough, but he made him feel creepy. Lucien Roth had been different. He was a shit, but he wasn't a creep. You had to work at getting response from him, and when he gave you his nod of agreement you knew that you had earned it by the sweat of your brow. Roth was a pro-fascist bastard, looked it, and often acted it; but if you played ball with him, he played ball with you. That was the fun of the game. With a cynical creep like Berthier there was no game, no fun. In fact you could say no job. Jerry's prestige was built on his ability to get results from the hard-line Vichy French. For career reasons he needed his Frenchmen tough, surly, and seemingly uncooperative. He didn't need ass-lickers who any hillbilly from back home could push around.

It wasn't exactly rational, but he felt a sudden impulse to tell

Berthier to march his cops right back where they came from. Who was this bum Steve Wagner, anyway? Was he so significant he had to be hounded by half the Casablanca police force?

There was also Laura's offer. That was something he'd had to work for, something he had earned. OK, she might screw up her face with dislike when it came to the crunch, but then who looks at the face when you're stoking the fire?

And then Laura herself made the mistake of appearing on the staircase leading from the dress circle. She gave him a look as if to say, "Tell these guys to beat it and you can have me now." And he thought, Hell, who was some dame to tell him what to do, even if it was only with her beautiful smoky-blue eyes? Ultimately no dame respected a man who did what he was told. Ultimately they all wanted to be stepped on, trodden all over, by a real frisky fellow who knew how to play it mean.

"He's in there somewhere," he told Berthier. "Bring him out alive, and don't louse up the performance. A lot of good folk have paid a lot of good money to see this movie."

She's asking this colored pianist to play this song. He doesn't want to play it, but she insists. He's a nice singer; it's a nice song. But his boss comes in looking like thunder, tells him how he was never to play that song.

Then he looks up and sees her. And her eyes moisten, and he looks as if he's seen a ghost.

And then this *gendarme* comes up and says how it seems as if the two of them must have met before. Incidentally, he looks a little like Auguste Berthier with a full head of hair and a few more good meals under his belt. And Bogart nods and says, "Yes, we've met before," but his eyes are saying a lot more.

Who wrote this damned movie, anyway?

They are shining a torch along their row of seats. Could it be because Hal Newport didn't know about the French custom of tipping the usherette and she's trying to wreck the movie for him? No, little probing points of light are at work all over the theater. They're looking for someone. Guess who they're looking for. Careful, this beam is coming your way!

He was saved by Tina Newport. She swiveled round in her seat and, taking all the torchlight in her face, said, "Turn that fucking thing off, I'm trying to watch a movie!"

He's sitting in the dark now with a bottle of hard liquor (don't you know the feeling?) and he's telling his colored pianist to play that damned song again. And the pianist says how he should get out of town, forget the lady. And he says to play that song. And suddenly it's dissolve to Paris. The two of them driving in an open top down the Champs Élysées, cracking a bottle of champagne in a ritzy apartment, lounging about together on expensively upholstered furniture. And the only trouble is the Germans are coming. Where the hell did they get this story? Could Nad Klaf actually have been sober when he said he had sold your life story to Hollywood?

"Tell you something, Hal," he muttered. "They got it wrong. That was no lady, that was a whore."

"What the heck's going on?" Tina Newport hissed. "I came to see *Casablanca*, not some goddamn Marx brothers movie."

"I tell you something else, Hal. She didn't even write a letter to say she couldn't make it. Nothing. Not even a damn postcard. They've got the whole thing wrong."

Little inquisitive beads of light are approaching down the nearer aisle now. On the screen they've cut to the police Prefecture—this Berthier character again.

Meanwhile the house has been filling up with real policemen with real guns. They've got ten of them at least, at every exit. There's enough starshine coming off the screen to be able to pick out their *képis*. Perhaps Humphrey Bogart will tell you how you ever get out of a situation like this.

"This looks like our baby," Jerry Daniels said, peering through a little window next door to the projection room. "Yes, that's our boy, all right. He's coming quietly, too."

"Tell them they can't do this, Hal," Steve was shouting. "Tell them I'm a United States citizen. And I'm under your protection! Tell him the place they ought to be looking is Radio Casablanca!"

"Steve, I wish you'd talked to me before," Hal was murmuring. "If I'd known you were in this kind of trouble . . ."

"Will you guys cut it out?" Tina was screaming. "Humph Bogart has got more balls than the lot of you put together."

None of this could be heard in the projection room. From where Jerry Daniels was peering, the arrest of Steve Wagner looked like a nice, smooth, silent operation.

"Baby," he said, turning round to Laura, "you'd better start exciting the animal in me or God knows what they're going to do to this punk. Hey, why don't you take your clothes off now? Sure, don't be embarrassed. I don't mind my girl friends undressing in public."

Laura said laconically, "You know, Jerry, this is turning out to be a real night for the shattering cliché. First I go on my knees to beg you to spare the man I love, then you start playing cat and mouse with me like any old platitudinous psychopath. You know what I do next?" She slipped her hand into her bag and pointed it in his direction. "What else can I do? I tell you that this handbag packs a gun, and I remind you that you taught me how to use a gun."

The look of surprise didn't last long. A big grin was soon spreading across Jerry's freckled face. "I like it"—he gestured magnanimously, "I like it a lot; it's even better than the movie they're show-

284

ing out there. Laura baby, we're going to have a lot of fun together, a lot of games."

She shot a hole through her handbag and at the same time tore a chunk out of the ceiling just above Jerry's head.

"It may be corny," she said, "but I'm not fooling. You want to know what happens next?"

"You put that gun away or you're in trouble, sister."

"You don't say anything now, Jerry. You just walk in front of me down into that theater and tell your Hitler-loving *gendarmes* to let Steve go. And then you redirect them to Radio Casablanca. I'll be close behind you, Jerry, so close I couldn't miss, even if I *were* an amateur."

Like hell he was going to try and make a break for it. In the first place, they had sealed all the exits. In the second place, they had a lot of firepower. Imagine what even an 8-mm Lebel slug could do to a body at this range—imagine the damage twenty, thirty, and a hundred of them could do—more damage than an ax wielded by an insane lumberjack. Funny how it happened. He had spent half a lifetime getting into fights and wars. And suddenly he couldn't bear to think of the damage one 8-mm slug could do to his flesh. After all, Steve Wagner was coming quietly.

On the screen Bogart and Bergman moved into an explosive clinch. So intense they had to cut this clock tower or Warner Bros. might have been in trouble with the Hays Office. Then the camera cut back to Bogart standing at the window smoking a cigarette. In the afterglow of love they were planning to get away together from Casablanca. But would they ever make it?

A figure in a white tuxedo was coming slowly down the side aisle towards Steve and his police escort. It was dark; Steve observed only a white tuxedo until one of the cops beamed a torch in his face, and there was Jerry Daniels grinning at him. In fact it was the sheepish grin of a man with an automatic at his back. But Steve wasn't to know this. He didn't even see that Laura was following close behind him. He saw a gargoyle of a face, made positively malevolent by the effect of torchlight. And finally he recognized his enemy.

He had come a long way to find him. He had fought with a lot of phantoms and slaughtered not a few shadows, and somehow he hadn't begun to fight. He had even begun to doubt if there was an enemy, even to ask himself, as Bobbi had asked him, whether the enemy wasn't himself. All that had been changed in a torch flash. He had arrived at the center of his personal labyrinth, and now at last he had sighted the bull.

You could say it was the attitude Jerry Daniels represented, the political cynicism he embodied. You could put it another way and say it was all the gray slime he had poured on Steve's simple concept of black and white. You could advance a lot of reasons for the hatred that exploded in Steve Wagner's heart, but the fist that crashed into Jerry Daniels's face was powered mostly by pure instinct.

Instinctive blows are not necessarily meant to kill. By definition they have no preconceived purpose. What happened was in effect an accident. Mumbling something about how he was here to help him, Daniels had been sent hurtling backwards onto Laura's handbag and the jolt had triggered her gun.

That was why Daniels was now writhing on the carpet shouting, "Hey, Christ, go easy! The back of my head is all goo!" Whatever Steve Wagner's blow was intended to do, it had killed Jerry Daniels.

And this was the point where people started to scream and clamber over one another to get to the exits. The lights went up, but the film went on running. Either the projectionist had abandoned his projector or he couldn't bear to miss the end of the movie.

On the screen a faded Humphrey Bogart, Bergman, and Paul Henreid have just arrived at Casablanca airport. It looks foggy, and it's still uncertain who will fly away with Ingrid; but then in the auditorium no one is looking.

Steve Wagner has managed to slip his police escort in the chaos, but he has lost Laura and now he is trying to find her. You could say he had left it awfully late.

He has a glimpse of her, looking deadly-pale and more beautiful than he has ever seen her, and she is looking around for him. But a posse of panicking war correspondents hustle her out of sight. As he tries to climb over a seat to get to her he feels as if his left arm has been slugged by Joe Louis, and he knows he has taken a bullet from a Lebel revolver. He drops down to take cover somewhere behind the seats in row J. And the *gendarmes* start to clear the house so they can have a free field of fire.

Nad Klaf doesn't go without a struggle. "This is my boy. This is my scenario. I'm not going to have you louse up my ending," he yells in the face of an uncomprehending cop from Meknès.

Lurleen Marx screams she's an accredited correspondent of *Time-Life* and has official authorization to get to the bottom of this shoot-up. They have to carry her out, kicking.

And then suddenly it's very quiet in the auditorium. There's only Humphrey Bogart telling Ingrid Bergman how it's her duty to get on that plane with her husband, Paul Henreid; how they will always have Paris.

And then out of this comparative silence Steve hears Auguste shouting to him, "You're on two murder charges already, Steve. If I were you I wouldn't risk a third. If I were you I would raise my hands above my head and stand up."

A couple of goons reinforce the message with a full chamber of 8-mm slugs. One of them tears through the seat next to Steve. He winces to see what a small thing like a 8-mm bullet can do to a theater seat.

And then he cringes from another shot. He doesn't realize that this one is only acting. Humphrey Bogart has just pumped Conrad Veidt, playing Major Strasser of the German Armistice Commission.

"Auguste, will you listen to me?" he calls back. The blood from his arm is beginning to make a mess of his suit. It's fortunate he's not wearing a white tuxedo. "I'm not asking any favors," he calls to Berthier in English, "because I guess you're no longer a personal friend of mine. But I'm suggesting you've picked the wrong side again, Auguste. Roth is dead. Jerry Daniels is dead. Sooner or later they're going to make a clean sweep of all the fascist rats in this town. You'll have to switch sides again, and then it could be too late. Why not beat the rest of the crowd to it and do it now, Auguste? I'll put in a word for you with the right people. I promise."

No answer.

"I'll tell you another thing that could persuade you," he threatens or pleads—he isn't sure which. "You've always said you're a realist, Auguste. How about facing the fact that you've got to let me go?"

He is kidding, of course; he has this Lebel trained on a police uniform, but he can't see who's wearing it.

This time there is an answer, because although he has been talking in English for Auguste's ears only, he has given away his position. This time they knock a whole lot of splinters off the top of his theater seat. A stray bullet whacks into the screen and tears a hole in Ingrid Bergman's pretty nose, and another hits Steve Wagner in the mouth. He would scream with fear if he weren't half choking with the blood and the fragments of teeth running down his throat. Still, he manages to get in a shot at the police uniform. He hears a little sigh.

Sooner or later, of course, they are going to enfilade him and shoot straight down the row of seats where he's crouching. But two of Jerry Daniels's American gunmen who won't wait to avenge their ex-boss have a better idea. They lead a posse of French cops up onto the stage. They are dwarfed by Humphrey Bogart, who is looking heroically up into the sky, where Ingrid Bergman's plane is flying out of the picture, but they can see right down into the auditorium. They've got a perfect view of Steve Wagner's tousled head, neck, and shoulders.

They let go with everything they've got, which is quite a lot.

Enough to take the scalp off the man all Casablanca has been hunting for the last twenty-four hours.

The film is still running. Claude Rains, playing the devious French Prefect of Police, has just tossed a bottle of Vichy water meaningfully into a wastebin. He reminds Bogart there's a Free French garrison at Brazzaville. He could arrange a passage for them both. Bogart suggests, "Louis, this is the beginning of a beautiful friendship."

They walk off together into the fog. Two buddies going to fight Hitler with Charles de Gaulle.

It didn't look exactly like the arrival of the Conquering Hero. No President Roosevelt, no Winston Churchill, no General Marshall, no Macmillan, no Giraud, no Nogues. Just an obscure American general called Wilbur, representing President Roosevelt, and an English civil servant called Codrington, for Churchill. But there was a small band of the faithful out to welcome Charles de Gaulle as his plane touched down at Casablanca military airport.

Those that were present were lucky to be standing there to welcome their leader. They were the ones who had somehow managed to avoid being rounded up by the local French administration and put into a concentration camp.

But there was some kind of official reception too.

As de Gaulle strode down the thin line of welcomers, he soon arrived at the outstretched hand, clean shining *képi*, flashy uniform, and flickering smile of the new Chief Inspector of Police in Casablanca.

"What is your name?" asked de Gaulle.

"Berthier, *mon Général*," the Chief Inspector confidently replied.

"I have heard of you." The General nodded. "You have been with us from the beginning, have you not?"

"Well, almost," offered Auguste Berthier. "I joined the Free French in Brazzaville with the American, Steve Wagner, and later returned here to work with a Resistance cell."

"Ah yes," noted de Gaulle, "*un fou Américain*, but a man of honor. These are hard times, *mon ami*."

"Indeed," agreed Auguste Berthier. "I might have hoped that the Western leaders might have been here in person to honor you, but alas . . . they have a prior appointment with the Sultan."

"We will remember those who were here to welcome us," de Gaulle answered regally.

"Do not worry, *mon Général*," Auguste Berthier informed him. "It looks bleak now, but it will change. I feel it instinctively in my bones. What I fought for, what my comrade Steve Wagner died for, cannot be in vain."

De Gaulle put a reassuring hand round the new Chief Inspector's shoulders as they entered the official car.

Once again Auguste Berthier had taken Steve Wagner's advice. But this time he was going to come out on top.

FEBRUARY 14, 1943

On February 14, 1943, Captain Maxwell had finally settled into his CP at the tiny village of Sidi Bou Zid. It was in its way a kind of oasis. That is, besides the water there was a little bar where one could drink pernod, and a flea-bitten little brothel where Lieutenant Hutter mostly hung out, and a decrepit boardinghouse which Maxwell had made his home.

Maxwell was attached to Major General Manton S. Eddy's 9th Division, which in turn was part of General Fredendall's U S II Corps, which in turn belonged to General Anderson's First Army. The whole shoot being loosely strung out across the shallow uplands of southern Tunisia, a thing of dribs and drabs eked out in small green detachments over the tawny, flat, threatening lands of nothing and nowhere, a stony, rocky, desolate wilderness of a hole. It was a funny kind of war. Sometimes PFC Offenbach might vanish for a few hours and come back laden with a gazelle, which isn't that bad if you roast it over the grill. Sometimes Maxwell would spend a day trying to contact his battalion commander over at Kasserine and finally give up and take himself off to the bar. He had become a lone man in the loneliest spot on earth. So he began to get hot on discipline. Get sore if his men scrapped US equipment, scattered vital materials over the desert. He was known to tear a man apart for not wearing his necktie. For about a week he hadn't spoken to Al Hutter.

"I know he looked like a good guy to you and me," he'd told him, "but let's face it, he was a hoodlum. And he died a hoodlum's death. My, that guy was trigger-happy."

"Like when he helped us to rush those lines on the beaches," his friend commented. "Look, the man saved our lives and all they could do to him was to do a crap into his face."

"They don't shoot the ass off a guy without good reason. OK, Al, we liked him, but to the boys in the know he more strongly resembled Public Enemy No. 1. He got his just deserts."

"Jerk off, crap you," had been Lieutenant Hutter's rejoinder as he staggered back to his brothel.

And that was about the limit of the communication between Captain Maxwell and Lieutenant Al Hutter.

So all that was left for Maxwell was to follow a curious soldier's sixth sense and turn his lonely hell into a fortress: slap barbed wire round the perimeters of the Bedouin shantytown; get the Stuart tanks lined up, flat behind the mud houses; get every little vantage point over the tawny landscape positively bristling with machine guns and antitank weapons. Pile up the hand grenades, get the Garand rifles clean as a whistle; post lookouts on the mosque tower; kick a sense of omen and death and menace down the throats and into the guts of his slap-happy green compatriots.

And that wasn't enough.

The little fortress was a speck in the desert, but the krauts knew about it all right. They came at it in the early morning with Stukas and Henschel tank busters. Dropping the mosque tower and its attendant watchmen. Wiping out Maxwell's tank reserve in the little village square and brilliantly sighting and destroying one of his only two ammunition dumps.

But that was for starters.

When the dust of the air attack had dispersed, another bigger dust was discernible, rolling towards them at about twenty miles an hour across the undulating lion-hide landscape.

It was a compliment, really. Maxwell's greenhorns were to be amongst the first to savor the full impact of the new miracle weapon the Tiger tank, all sixty tons of it with its 88-mil guns and massive strength.

Captain Maxwell had counted about thirty of those raking Tiger muzzles whilst they were in the slow process of drawing a tight little bead on him and his small detachment. Then he lost count.

Instead he was vaguely conscious of himself and his shanty fortress and his company and himself going up in a blaze of bright smoke. He saw orange men with bright orange halos running past him, and some were dripping orange blood and one had lost his orange head and seemed to be groping somewhere down on the orange mud trying to locate it.

And he said or didn't say something like, "We'll hold on to the end, you guys." Because there was nobody much left to hear him, and besides, a fine four-inch piece of pure metal had entered his brain and rocketed him onto a tangerine-tinted Valhalla—later to be known as the Battle of the Kasserine Pass.

The sound of firing awakened Al Hutter in his brothel. He was deaf these days to most things, but he certainly heard those howl-ing Stukas.

He stirred up from his bed and stood full length beside the gilt mirror that adorned one end of the room and looked at himself, and toasted himself in a glass of pernod.

He was drinking a silent thanks to dead friends when an 88-mil shell shattered both the mirror and the man reflected in it. He died with a funny thing on his lips. A tune he had heard somewhere in another life.

And it had a bouncy kind of rhythm and went something like, "Oop-la, oop-la, oop-la."

And he hadn't been able to get it out of his brain because that jerk Offenbach had been whistling it all around town the last seven days.

"Oop-la . . . oop-la . . . oop-la . . . oop-la."

It was a screwy kind of frog *chanson* with which to die.

CREDITS

March 12, 1943

Dear Nad Klaf,

Sorry to take so long replying to your letter, but if the past two months of Warner Bros. going to war is anything to go by, give me peace.

Yeah, we shed Ingrid, and she's now teamed up with Gary Cooper on the Hemingway extravaganza *For Whom the Bell Tolls.* Shucks! However, to compensate we're about halfway through shooting an epic called *This Is the Army,* staring George Murphy, Joan Leslie, George Tobias, and a flash appearance from old Irving Berlin himself. And guess who's director? Our old friend Mike Curtiz. It's not as strategically prophetic as *Casablanca,* but it could persuade a few million greenhorns to offer their services to Uncle Sam. So the war rolls on, and Warner Bros. with it.

I showed your letter to our legal department, and they swear you haven't got a leg to stand on. OK, the two slobs you entertained in Casablanca might have had a semblance of similarity to the characters of Rick and Louis. Flukes will happen. But sorry, Nad, it also happens that *Casablanca* was based on a cute little play called *Everybody Goes to Rick's,* which appeared on Broadway some time, I think, before you submitted your rough scenario. Next time you see the movie look closely at the titles; you'll see something to the effect of "From a play by Murray Burnett and Joan Alison." Funny thing you hadn't noticed it before.

As for the follow-up material, to be frank, Nad, it seems plain lousy. I've seen something of the kind in those seamy French movies of the realist prewar school, and heck knows, they didn't move box office. Certainly at this crux moment in national morale it's no time to debase the proven idols of the silver screen.

Anyway, Nad, next time I see you around, remind me to buy you a highball, but regrettably there can be no up-front money.

Your good friend,

VINCENT
Vice-President
Warner Bros. Pictures, Inc.

APPENDIX

Their Song

You can't write a new song
When the old one's still there,
You can't right an old wrong
When it won't disappear.
You can't find words to fit
A new flirtation
When you're still
Smarting from that old elation.
You can't find a new theme
When the old dream won't fade,
You can't make a new start
When your heart's still mislaid.
You can do a lot of things
In life, my son,
But losing memories
Just isn't one!
You can't write a new song
When the old song still hurts.